PIGEONWINGS

HEIDE GOODY

IAIN GRANT

Paperback ISBN: 978-0-9571754-8-8

Ebook ISBN:978-0-9571754-9-5

Published by Pigeon Park Press

www.pigeonparkpress.com
info@pigeonparkpress.com

To the memory of Ade Hadley.

Ade came to the launch of Clovenhoof and told Heide that she should feel like a rock star. She thinks of him every time she demands M&Ms with all of the brown ones taken out.

ST CADFAN'S

There were five of them at the meeting in the chapter house, six if one counted Barry. Barry, a large sleek peacock with sharp eyes and an even sharper beak, sat in Abbot Ambrose's lap. All present knew it was unwise to discount the abbot's pet for although the bird tolerated the abbot's attentions, it had bitten chunks out of any unfortunate brother who strayed too near.

Brother Sebastian, the procurator, a middle-aged man whose slick manner and easy-going confidence suggested that, in a previous life he might have been landed gentry or, at least, a dodgy second hand car salesman, looked up at the high windows and the ceaselessly drumming rain.

"I think it's easing up a bit," he said.

From beneath his thick wig-like mop of grey hair, the abbot fixed Sebastian with a silencing glare. Barry gave him a beady stare for good measure as well.

"Are we here to assess the damage to the monastery or second guess the weather forecast?" said the abbot.

"Apologies, Father Abbot," said Sebastian with just the right balance of deference and sarcasm. "The storm brought down some tiles and stonework in the almonry. I must also say that the arches between the almonry and dormitory wing look quite unsafe now. Falling tiles also broke several panes of glass in the orangery."

"I hope your temporary repairs in the orangery are sufficient," said the abbot.

The novice monk taking the meeting minutes wrung a few more drops of water from the sleeve of his white habit and nodded damply.

"I used what plywood sheets we had, Father Abbot. I did the best job possible in that howling gale."

"The best job possible?" said the abbot sternly. "Novice Trevor, we are not interested in how difficult a job it was. You are not here to seek glory or praise but to record the decisions of this emergency meeting."

"Yes, Father Abbot," said the novice. "And it's Novice Stephen."

"Who is?"

"I am. Stephen, not Trevor."

"Are you sure?"

"Yes, Father Abbot. I get it a lot. Apparently, I have one of those faces."

"One of what faces?"

"A lot of people call me Trevor," said Novice Stephen. "I must just look like one."

The abbot's surly frown deepened.

"And what does a Trevor look like, Novice Stephen?"

"Like this, I suppose," said the novice and gestured to his own face.

"The point Novice Stephen was perhaps making," said Brother Sebastian, "is that we do not have the materials to hand to effect the proper repairs."

"This will not do," said the abbot. "We cannot allow the elements or sloppy workmanship to damage the integrity of the orangery."

"Father Abbot," said Sebastian smoothly, "surely there are more pressing matters. There is a hole in the almonry wall. Rain is pouring through the dormitory ceiling. We have twenty monks living on the island and some of them are getting soggy. The orangery is just a greenhouse which serves no-"

Abbot Ambrose slammed his fist on the oak table. Barry gave a hoot of alarm, his turquoise plumage standing on end.

"I do not care if the dormitory is under six feet of water! That orangery is home to unique plants of which we are custodians. And where will Brother Arthur spend his days of recuperation if the orangery is in disrepair?"

The assembled brothers looked at Brother Arthur. Arthur, the prior of St Cadfan's, had been wheeled into the meeting in his ancient wicker bath-chair and had spent the entire meeting gazing dumbly at nothing in particular. It would have been surprising if the prior had said anything at all. When Brother Sebastian had first arrived at St Cadfan's, the prior had been old, frail and clearly without either speech or wits. The situation had not improved since then. In fact, it had struck Sebastian more than once that the prior had taken on the characteristics of his bath-chair, becoming even more weathered, lined and creaky over time.

The idea that the prior was 'recuperating' was laughable.

"Tell the boatman to bring such wood and hardware supplies as you need when he next comes," said the abbot, forcibly smoothing down Barry's ruffled feathers and calming the bird.

"Because of the weather, there has been no boat from the mainland for seven weeks," said Sebastian. "General supplies are low."

"Ah," said the abbot. "No doubt that is why we've had such an unusual menu recently."

Brother Manfred, the refectorian, whose German accent, playful manner and bouncing grey curls, always put Sebastian in mind of some Eighties Eurovision pop star, shrugged amiably.

"The thing is," he said, his light, sibilant accent shaving the edges off words, "I try to be inventive but there is only so much you can do with a cellar full of cabbages, carrots and rhubarb, no?"

"Is that why we've had nothing but sauerkraut and rhubarb crumble for the past week?"

"Sadly, that isn't even sauerkraut. No, it is just very old coleslaw."

The abbot rumbled unhappily.

"I am not sure our collective guts can take much more of it."

"You must understand," said Brother Manfred, waving his pen to punctuate his speech, "a craftsman can only work with the materials to hand. I am many things. A cook, an embroiderer, a sometimes zither player and one-time unicyclist, but working miracles I cannot do, Father Abbot."

This last point was made with such force and passion that Manfred's pen slipped from his hands and skittered across the table. It rolled against the abbot's hand, leaving a tiny inky indent on his skin. Without a moment's thought, Manfred reached across to retrieve it. Barry pecked instantly and savagely at the back of his hand.

"Ow, that really did hurt," said the refectorian, cradling his wounded hand.

The abbot was unsympathetic.

"Oh, don't be such a sour..." He paused. "...puss. If we can put up with age old coleslaw, I think you can tolerate a little criticism. You know what happens to anyone who hurts me."

"It was an accident," said Manfred.

"Vengeance seven times over," said the abbot.

Brother Sebastian leaned in to speak.

"Whether the boat comes tomorrow or next month," he said, "I'm afraid we simply do not have the funds in our bank account to cover the kinds of repairs we are going to need to make."

"Surely, we have some money," said the abbot.

"Some, but not enough to pay for the kind of quality masonry and carpentry needed here. Unless you know of any other funds we can draw on, Father Abbot...?"

The abbot sat back and stroked his pet peacock thoughtfully. A tiny drop of blood glistened on the tip of Barry's beak.

"I can check," said the abbot.

"Thank you, Father Abbot. Perhaps in the meantime, we

need to do some serious thinking about how we can make ourselves some money."

"Fundraising schemes?"

"Commercial enterprises," said Sebastian.

Abbot Ambrose nodded in slow agreement.

"Why not?" he said. "What harm can it do?"

IN WHICH MOLLY SPEAKS FROM BEYOND THE GRAVE AND MICHAEL TRIES TO PUT OFF THE INEVITABLE

I f there was one advantage to being the devil it was that you were expected to be bad. It was part of the territory, it was in his contract. It was stamped throughout his metaphysical DNA like the name of the grimmest, shittiest seaside town in the grimmest, shittiest stick of rock ever.

Actually, Jeremy Clovenhoof decided, stopping outside the door of flat 1a, if there was one advantage to being the devil, it was the horns. From opening beer bottles to ruining perfectly decent hats to using them to store doughnuts, bagels and naan breads when your hands were otherwise busy, horns were the business.

But, horns aside, the key perk of being His Satanic Majesty was the expectation – no, the demand - that one should behave badly. All moral questions vanished from life. To kick a kitten or not kick a kitten? To recycle old newspapers or not recycle? To give visiting Jehovah's

Witnesses the time of day or not? All these issues were resolved without the need for introspection. Clovenhoof could recycle the kitten, kick the Jehovah's Witnesses and wallow in the gloomy disasters from last year's papers without feeling a single pang of conscience. The fact that no one on Earth (well, almost no one) seemed to see him as anything other than a ruggedly handsome, if slightly over-the-hill, bloke did not alter the fact, it merely added relish to every *essential* misdemeanour he carried out.

And so, on seeing that the door to flat 1a was open, Clovenhoof did not hesitate but walked straight in, already wondering what he might steal or defile.

The new tenant, Michael, was out somewhere. Clovenhoof had seen him go that morning. However, there were signs of activity: the glisten of fresh white paint on the living room walls, the sight of carpenter's tools in the kitchenette and the sound of mindless off-key whistling coming from the bathroom.

Clovenhoof went into the kitchen and investigated the contents of the new fridge freezer Michael had installed. He scoffed at the bottles of mineral water. Clearly, Michael hadn't yet discovered what taps were for. He turned his nose up at the rows of fresh fruit and salad. However, he was drawn to the foil-covered pots of Ambrosia Custard and so took two, one to eat now and the other to misuse later.

He moved on to the bedroom, eating the custard with his fingers. He rifled messily through Michael's suits in the built-in wardrobe and then poked around in the bedside cabinet, hoping to find something secretive and embarrassing that he could use to blackmail or humiliate Michael. There were none of the copies of Nuts magazine or the Catholic Herald that Clovenhoof had expected to find. However, there was a leather-bound notebook containing page after page of Michael's flowing script.

"Day ten of my mission among the people of Earth," Clovenhoof read aloud and rolled his eyes. It was like the opener to a bad sci-fi movie. How like Michael to treat his exile from heaven as something other than the punishment it was.

DAY *ten of my mission among the people of Earth.*

O Lord, I visited one of their super markets today. Its bright lights and well-ordered rows appeal to me. Moses may have led his people to a land flowing with milk and honey but this land flows with all manner of food and drink. The shelves are filled with a Babel of labels and logos.

CLOVENHOOF CLEARED his throat in irritation. Trust a bloody angel to take four sentences and two Biblical references to say, 'bugger me, isn't there a lot of choice at Tesco.' He read on.

I HAVE YET to establish what would be a suitable diet for a divine being such as myself. In the Celestial City, I had no need of any sustenance but your love. At the super market, I enquired after some heavenly manna but, sadly, they were out of stock. I bought such fruit and vegetables as I recognised and a quantity of a substance that purports to be ambrosia. It is yellow and viscous and flows in a manner quite obscene. Perhaps the food of the gods takes on these unseemly properties under Earth's crude physical laws.

My Earthly body has yet to adapt fully to life on this material plane. Not only does my body crave food but also it produces the most unpleasant secretions. I perspire from my pits and must wash several times a day to remove the stink of it. The inside of my nostrils are smeared with a disgusting mucous that replenishes itself constantly. There is also the matter of the waste water that gushes several times a day from... that _thing_.

My _thing_ bothers me greatly. It is the only significant change to my anatomy made during the transition. I look at it frequently. I'm sure there must be some mistake. It strikes me as quite wrong. I cannot imagine anything as wrinkled, misshapen and dangly belonging on a human body. O Lord, I cannot believe that you, in your infinite wisdom, would design mankind with such an odd appendage. I do not dare ask any of my neighbours to take a look and comment upon it in case this is construed as unusual behaviour.

CLOVENHOOF TOOK the pen from Michael's bedside drawer, drew a proud cock and balls in the margin of Michael's diary and labelled it, 'perfectly normal specimen.'

THERE HAS ALSO BEEN the problem of the disquieting rumblings from my gut. I had a fearful prescience that something truly foul and hellish wishes to escape my fundament. I fight it as I would *fight the very devil (who lives in the flat above) and so far I have managed to quell and contain my riotous innards.*

I distract myself from the inner turmoil and my anatomical worries by keeping myself busy. I have made myself quite at home and engaged several tradesmen to make my new residence more like my old home. As it is in Heaven, so shall it be on Earth.

I also intend to seek gainful employment. The stipend with which your invisible agents have provided me is quite generous but I feel that, if I am to live among these people, I must do my best to live like these people. I shall draw up a Curriculum Vitae and make myself available on the job market.

Ben Kitchen, the young man who lives in flat 2b, has, despite having few social graces and very poor taste in clothing, shown himself to be a friendly and generous sort and has promised to help me install my new Personal Computer once I have collected it from the shop. Ben is the closest thing I have to a friend in this world. I might perhaps show him my <u>thing</u> and ask him to comment on it.

CLOVENHOOF LAUGHED out loud at this delicious thought, spraying Michael's bed with flecks of custard. The atonal whistling in the bathroom stopped.

"Is that you, Mr Michaels?" called a voice.

Clovenhoof ignored it and read on.

I WISH I could say I felt a comradely fellowship with the rector of St Michael's Church. As shepherd of the local flock, Reverend Zack Purdey should be the one man I show my <u>thing</u> to but he is less the shepherd of my soul and more swineherd for every crone, *sluggard, waif and stray in the parish. On my first mortal visit to the church that bears my name, I tried to feel your presence and receive your love, but all I felt was a draught and all I got was a cup of tea and a Bourbon biscuit at the 'fellowship' after the service.*

I prayed so hard, O Lord. Did you hear me? Will you answer?

"Tosser," said Clovenhoof and threw the diary onto the bed.

"What?" said the young man in the doorway.

Clovenhoof frowned.

"Who are you?"

"I'm the plumber."

Clovenhoof looked at the man critically. He wasn't what Clovenhoof regarded as a *proper* plumber. This young man's jeans were secured with a belt above the bum-crack line, there wasn't a cigarette poking out of the corner of his mouth or tucked behind his ear and, when he spoke to Clovenhoof, he didn't address him as 'guv'nor'.

"I thought it might have been Mr Michaels," said the plumber. "You're a friend of his?"

"More of an arch-enemy," said Clovenhoof. "I live upstairs."

"I've just got an issue with the bathroom. I didn't know if you knew..."

He waved Clovenhoof through to the bathroom. Gone was the former tenant's bathroom suite, the avocado bath, basin and toilet. In their place was something far more severe and stylish: a narrow and steep-sided bath, a separate shower with a steel waterfall showerhead, a wash basin that seemed to be inspired by a brutalist Soviet monument and...

The plumber gestured at the exposed soil pipe where Mrs Astrakhan's toilet had once stood.

"Mr Michaels just asked me to get rid of it," he said.

"Get rid of it?" said Clovenhoof. "And replace it with what?"

"He didn't say," replied the plumber, scratching his forehead. "He said he didn't *need* one."

"Oh?"

"What he actually said was that he didn't need a foot spa. I'm not sure if he was confused. You wouldn't happen to know what he wanted?"

Clovenhoof looked at the jutting soil pipe.

I have managed to quell and contain my riotous innards, the diary had said.

But for how long? wondered Clovenhoof.

"Well, matey-boy," he said, "you know what they say: *the customer's always right.*"

Nerys Thomas woke from dreams of heaven.

There had been no angels or harps or drifting clouds in a perfect blue sky. Instead, there was a city of white stone and dazzling architecture, sort of how Venice might look if they had a tidy up and did something about the smell and the pickpockets. Nonetheless, it had definitely been heaven.

And in this dream of heaven, Nerys had been with her Aunt Molly, not Molly as the old woman she had become but the athletic young woman she had once been. But it wasn't just the pair of them in the dream. The woman vicar from St Michael's, the one who had been knocked down and killed some months back, was there too along with – and this was particularly odd – a feisty teenager in full plate armour. And, capering in the background, was a figure who sometimes appeared as a horned, goat-footed devil and sometimes appeared as Jeremy Clovenhoof, the lecherous weirdo from downstairs.

Nerys sat up in the armchair, shook the muzziness from her head and looked about her flat. She had had the dream several times in recent days. That she should dream of Molly, less than two months after her aunt's death, was unsurprising but the other elements were just plain odd. She had barely known the lady vicar, had no idea what the teenage warrior represented and as for Jeremy Clovenhoof as Satan, the idea was simply –

There was a knock at the door. Twinkle, the Yorkshire Terrier, barked underneath the pouffe.

"Crazy," she said to herself.

NERYS OPENED THE DOOR.

"I'm bored," said Clovenhoof.

"Ah, Old Nick himself," said Nerys.

"What?"

She shook her head.

"Just a dream. Come in. Cuppa?"

"Depends what it's a cup of."

"Coffee."

"Or?"

"Tea."

"No third option?" suggested Clovenhoof.

"Such as?"

"Whiskey. Brandy. Schnapps. Lambrini. Cider. Stout. Meths."

"No. Tea or coffee."

"Tea then," said Clovenhoof, shuffling into the room. "What's all this crap?" he said and kicked a stout cardboard box.

"I'm finally packing up Molly's things, the stuff I don't want to keep."

While Twinkle growled menacingly at his hooves, Clovenhoof poked around in a box, uncovering some ugly ceramics wrapped in newspaper.

"These are your Aunt Molly's Toby jugs," he said.

"Yes."

"I sold them on E-bay."

"I know. And I bought them back before she realised what you'd done."

"But now you're getting rid of them. Why did you buy them if you didn't want them?"

"To keep her happy, doofus," she said, going into the kitchen to put the kettle on. "I'm sure you do things just to keep people happy, to keep the peace."

"Absolutely not," said Clovenhoof. "Two sugars, remember."

"Tell you what," called Nerys. "You help me pack up the unwanted stuff and get it down to the charity shop and I'll stand you a glass of something girly and alcoholic at the pub on Sunday night."

"Sounds good," said Clovenhoof. He picked up the still-growling Twinkle, dumped him in a cardboard box and covered him with a layer of newspaper. The little dog scrabbled around angrily. Clovenhoof sealed the box and put another on top to muffle the sound.

"Hey, you're not throwing this out, are you?"

Nerys poked her head through the door. Clovenhoof had a chunky black mobile phone in his hands.

"Molly's pay-as-you-go phone," she said.

"It's cool," said Clovenhoof.

"That thing is a brick," said Nerys. "I think it's older than me."

"I've never had a mobile phone," he said.

"You want it?"

"I want it."

Nerys shrugged.

"I've no idea what credit's left on it. There's a charger in there somewhere. God knows if there's any instructions."

"I bet he does," said Clovenhoof.

Nerys had made a pile of documents and papers on the dining table. Aunt Molly had clearly left a lot of admin behind when she died.

He could see that Nerys had made a small start in sorting through the papers, redistributing some and creating small peripheral piles around the central one. Clovenhoof rooted through all the piles in search of some instructions for his new phone. He peered at some papers and cast them aside. Eventually, he found something that looked like instructions and, tired of having to read things, just stuffed them in his pocket.

Nerys emerged with two mugs of tea. She eyed him suspiciously.

"Don't go messing with my intricate filing system."

"Wouldn't dream of it," he said, taking a sip of hot sweet tea.

Nerys frowned.

"Is that box moving?" she said as Twinkle tried to escape from the cardboard box.

Clovenhoof looked over. "It'll stop eventually," he said.

THE ARCHANGEL MICHAEL watched as Ben Kitchen struggled with the cables under the desk. Ben huffed and groaned and then gave an 'a-ha' of victory.

"And that's your printer connected," he said, emerging from beneath the desk and wiping his hands on his jeans.

Michael concealed a little shudder. It wasn't just that Ben was the kind of man who would wipe his hands on his jeans or on one of his many ancient T-shirts. It wasn't just that Ben's jeans were threadbare and unshapely. No, it was also Ben's unspoken implication that something – anything – in Michael's flat was dirty enough to need brushing from his hands. Michael had seen Ben's second hand bookshop, *Books 'n' Bobs*. It was a place where the dust had gathered for so long that it probably contained mammoth DNA.

Ben stepped back from the large walnut desk and nodded approvingly at the computer set up.

"All done. I'm afraid I've got to shoot now. War-gaming night at the Jockey."

Michael understood that Ben did this war-gaming thing and that it involved tiny toy soldiers, gambling dice and other men with their own unique range of dubious habits. He chose not to enquire any further, fearing that the whole business was thoroughly sinful.

"Well, thank you, Ben," said Michael, opened his wallet and looked for a suitable tip for the fellow.

"Hey," said Ben, waving Michael away genially. "Just being a good neighbour. Buy me a pint sometime okay."

"If you say so," said Michael and showed him to the door.

Michael was inwardly pleased that Ben had to go. His computer was set up and ready to go and he wanted to put into practice all that he had learned that day.

Having seen that some foul miscreant had discovered his written diary, drawn lewd anatomical pictures in its margins and, strangest of all, spattered his bed sheets with specks of some yellow gloop, Michael had decided that a physical diary was both antiquated and unsecure.

Sitting at his PC, Michael opened Word, arranged his margins and indents and began to type, slowly at first but then with increasing speed.

DAY *eleven of my mission among the people of Earth.*

O Lord, I am making great progress in fitting in with the humans. Today, I attended a course entitled Computers for Beginners at the Paradise Street Adult Education Centre. I feel that if I can get to grips with the hi-tech core of modern human life, everything else will fall into place.

The tutor has deplorable taste in cardigans but seems to know his subject. Quite quickly he had we students (grey-haired ladies for the most part, many of them shameful divorcees) logged into the Windows and opening the Word and the Excel.

I must write a letter of congratulations to Mr Gates who is not only, I understand, a generous philanthropist but also the most amazing of inventors. Whilst the human world lacks order, grace, and subtlety, Mr Gates has created the most divine order in his operating system and applications. Though the world of documents and spreadsheets and databases may be small, its menus, its clipboards, its fields, style sheets and document version control represents the closest thing to perfection I have seen since my arrival.

Our tutor opened the door to learning, lifted the veil of mystery from my eyes and the whole workings of Mr Gates' wondrous tools became almost instantly known to me.

Half an hour after logging on, I asked my tutor whether a graph inserted from Excel into Word would update automatically even if the spreadsheet was not open and he gave me the most remarkable look and asked how long I had been using computers. I told him it was my first time and he professed disbelief (although the actual words he used were both colourful and quite unrepeatable). Before the end of the training session, many of the grey-haired divorcees were coming to me to ask how to format this or align that. I believe the tutor was pleased to have me helping him; there was certainly something that looked a bit like a smile fixed on his face.

On the way home, I visited the shops. Yet again, I searched the super market for suitably heavenly foodstuff. I bought an angel cake but am not convinced it will serve. However, I was able to call in at the electrical retailers and pick up the Personal Computer I had ordered. Also, on an unlikely whim, I purchased a stuffed toy bear with large button eyes from a greeting cards shop. I do not know why I did that. The stuffed animal has the name Forever Friends sewn to its foot but I have already christened him Little G.

MICHAEL RE-READ and reflected on what he had written, decided to delete the last three sentences and saved the document.

He spent several hours working on a Curriculum Vitae document. It was both exciting and a challenge, exciting to be able to use all manner of fonts, styles and formatting options, challenging in that he wanted his résumé to be impressive, truthful and yet reveal nothing of his angelic nature to the ignorant people of Earth. He tinkered with it, rewording this and rephrasing that, and idly wondered how one went about applying for the job of Prime Minister.

Afterwards, he went onto the internet and created a user login for his bank account. A bank account had been set up for him at the moment of his arrival on Earth and the appropriate debit cards were in his wallet the first time he looked. Heaven had been as thorough and as considerate as it had been detached and silent in the arrangements for his transition to life on Earth.

Michael looked at his bank balance in the browser window and noted the regular yet modest payments that Heaven's agents had paid into it. The Computers for

Beginners course at the adult education centre had opened his eyes to the powers and capabilities of Information Technology. He imagined there must be a way to trace those payments, find out where they had come from, perhaps even find Heaven's agents on Earth and then talk to them, reason with them, plead with them to take him back...

No. Michael silently chided himself. Heaven had sent him – The Almighty had sent him – to Earth for a reason and in His ineffable wisdom there must be a greater purpose to that relocation. Michael reminded himself to stay strong and to serve His mission with a glad heart.

He then discovered that he could use the internet to search for images and, on a curious whim, search for 'thing'. This, bizarrely, produced pictures of what appeared to be a wrestler with skin like a dried riverbed. A search for 'penis' produced unhelpful images that ran from the medical to the zoological. Michael attempted to recall some of the colourful synonyms he had heard Clovenhoof use and eventually hit on search for pictures of 'cock'.

Two hours later, Michael had gazed at hundreds of cocks, was none the wiser and suspected that he had been struck with cock-blindness from staring too long. And yet, he felt that his time had, inexplicably, been well spent.

It was growing dark outside already. Michael got to his feet and turned on all the lights in the flat. In his previous life as an archangel, he had visited Earth during the nighttime but had never been forced to endure it in its entirety, from dusk to dawn. There was no night in the Celestial City; there was always the glorious luminescence of His holy glory.

Night was the reminder that, on Earth, Michael was far, far away from the Almighty.

In his bedroom, he smoothed down the edges of his freshly changed sheets and repositioned his teddy bear, Little G, by the pillows. In the bathroom, he once again inspected the handiwork of the day, the new shower, the boxed in section where the toilet had once stood, and the thick white shag-pile carpet that had been fitted throughout in the afternoon. In the kitchen, he contemplated the contents of the fridge and, finding nothing that he wanted to eat, opened a bottle of water and drank it.

Back at the PC, further browsing revealed that the supermarkets all had their own websites and he could order his groceries on-line. He searched for some foodstuffs that might properly and appropriately sate his hunger. The pots of ambrosia in his fridge had turned out to be nothing but a slop of milk, sugar and unnatural colours. The angel cake was moist, sticky and unpleasantly sweet. Neither lived up to its promises. He tried all manner of key words in his search for something appropriate but none of the results seemed promising.

There was a sudden shifting and gurgling in his gut and, with an unholy raspberry, something gaseous parped from his fundament. Michael gave a little shriek and leapt to his feet.

"No!" he shouted. "Back! Get back!"

The vile emission might have been tiny but, oh, it stank. It was like the filthiest mire of Hell itself. But it wasn't the gas that he feared the most. He could feel something brewing inside him, something solid that yearned to break free.

"What devils are growing within?" he whispered in horror.

He knew he could not let them free. If he, an archangel, one of the most powerful beings in creation, could not hold back the forces of evil and debasement, then how could he be an example to mere humans? Michael clenched his buttocks and, straining internal muscles that he wasn't even sure existed, directed his entire will into *sucking* the foetid taint back up into his system. There was a tiny bugle pip of complaint and then all went silent.

"Not good," he said, shaking his head wearily.

He prepared for bed, carefully re-hanging his suit in the wardrobe and laying out a shirt and tie for the following morning. Dressed in his pressed pyjamas, he sat on the edge of his bed and carefully buffed and polished his shoes before kneeling at his bedside to pray.

"Lord, creator of all, guide me on this mission amongst the poor in faith. Reach out your hand and show me where I must go. I thank you for this opportunity to show my worth to you. I accept all the trials you place at my feet: the mysteries of human life, the Adversary in flat 2a, the flux in my belly, the frankly poor range of food items available for the angelic connoisseur. I accept them all. My faith in you is without measure."

Michael pressed his forehead against his clasped hands and tightened his grip until his knuckles were white. He stayed like that for a long time.

"Please take me back," he whispered. "I'm sorry."

He waited for a reply but God remained silent.

Michael cleared his throat.

"Amen."

With no response from the Big G, Michael had nothing else to do but climb under the bed sheets with the lights still on, cuddle Little G very tightly and cry himself to sleep for the eleventh night in a row.

ON SUNDAY, Michael woke from dreams of cock to see the sun's early rays peeping through the window.

He got up, turned off all the lights again, offered his daily devotional prayers, showered, dressed, ate a banana for breakfast, set up a web-based e-mail account for himself on both his PC and his phone and then went to church.

The subdivided pre-war house that Michael shared with the earthbound Satan and several unsuspecting humans stood in Boldmere, a leafy neighbour of Sutton Coldfield which was a benign suburban tumour growing on the side of the one-time industrial city of Birmingham. The closest thing to a compliment he had ever heard anyone pay Birmingham was that it was in the middle of the country so you could at least run away from it in any direction you wanted.

The sub-suburb of Boldmere had a long high street of pubs, curry houses, bakeries and charity shops. And halfway between the house and the high street was St Michael's Church. Michael had selected it as his own place of worship, not just because it bore his name (and had a huge tapestry of his greatest triumph hanging on the back wall), not just because it was five minutes' walk from his home but principally because he felt the rector, Reverend Zack Purdey, could do with all the help available.

In church, Michael found a pew next to an obese man in a hand-knitted jumper and a tiny old woman who fussed over him with such persistence she must have been his mother. Michael greeted the pair of them, dusted the wooden pew with his handkerchief and sat down.

Throughout the service that morning, Michael did his best to focus on praise, worship and Reverend Zack's sermon but involuntarily spent the entire time building up a mental checklist of things he would have sorted out if he were in charge of the church. For one, the floral displays in the transept were deplorably amateur and uncoordinated. The stained glass windows were clearly overdue a clean. The choice of hymnals seemed random and unstructured. Reverend Zack's sermon on the faith of early Christians erroneously interchanged the words 'apostle' and 'disciple' willy-nilly as though they meant the same thing. Also, the rector's stole, while the correct green for the post-Pentecost season was edged with an abstract design in red and yellow, which was, in Michael's incredibly humble opinion, wholly inappropriate. The standards of dress and personal presentation among the congregation were even worse. Very few people had made the effort to dress smartly for the most important day of the Christian week. A young girl over to the left wore an offensively short skirt. The large man's knitted jumper had a brown and pink crucifix motif across it. It might have been religious but Michael seriously doubted that woollen representations of the Lord were respectful, especially with the dangling stigmata tassels.

After Reverend Zack's final blessing, Michael stood and looked at the tapestry at the back of the church in which he, Michael, with a sunburst halo around his head and a golden lance in his hand, stood in victory over the defeated form of the Great Dragon, Satan. How could these people live with themselves in the presence of such divine excellence? Weren't the faithful supposed to aspire to perfection? To be flawed was to be human but to wallow in it, in bad knitwear and miniskirts was just wilful decadence.

Michael did not like the 'fellowship' coffee morning held in the church after the service – he found it poorly organised and spiritually dubious – but, intent on bettering his fellow Christian through example, stayed to help out. He found himself at the kitchen hatch, pouring teas from a battered tin pot and listening to the prattle of the old women either side of him. While they dished out cups and saucers and slopped milk into the teas he poured, they kept up a running conversation in which neither of them paid attention to the others. Between one going on about problems with her central heating and the other discussing 'dodgy plumbing' of a different sort, Michael swore he heard one of them say that she was going to have a hysterectomy in the spring and the other reply that she ought to get it replaced with a combi-boiler.

"What do you think?"

Michael looked up. It was the large man in the bad jumper.

"Sorry?" said Michael.

"When you pray," said the man. "I was watching you and

you had this look of concentration on your face. I just wondered..."

"You were watching me pray?" said Michael.

"I find it hard to concentrate some times. I'm Darren."

Michael passed him a cup of tea.

"I think of Heaven," he said.

"What?" said Darren.

"When I pray. I think of Heaven and how much I wish to be there, with God."

Darren nodded.

"It's beautiful, isn't it?"

"How would you know?"

"I've seen it."

"In a painting?"

The man shook his head.

"I was shown a vision. I know it exists."

Michael decided that the man was touched by madness.

"Humans are not granted proof of the afterlife," he said. "Or else what need is there for faith?"

The man was about to object but Reverend Zack appeared with a smile on his face and a kind hand on Darren's arm. Reverend Zack was probably quite young but seemed to be trying to reach middle age as quickly as possible. He had a predilection for sensible tank tops and a stolidly earnest manner.

"Now, Darren," he said, "we're not making a nuisance of ourselves, are we?"

"No, Rev," said Darren, "I was just talking to..."

"Michael," said Michael.

"We don't want to scare him away, do we?" said Reverend Zack. "Why don't you help Angela go set up?"

Darren reluctantly shuffled off. Reverend Zack smiled brightly at Michael.

"Darren Pottersmore's a character," he said. "A fervent believer but, well, it takes all sorts, doesn't it?"

"Does it?"

Reverend Zack nodded.

"Did you enjoy the service?"

Michael took longer than necessary to pour the next cup.

"Honestly?" he said.

"Honesty. Always the best policy."

"Yes," said Michael and proceeded to recount the failings, small and large, he had noted that morning, from the dusty pews to the overabundance of malted milks in the biscuit selection.

"I see," said Reverend Zack afterwards. "Refreshing comments, Michael. Thank you."

"You're welcome."

Reverend Zack grimaced.

"I assume you would like to help us address some of our shortcomings."

"Absolutely," said Michael.

"Mmmm. I think I might have a role for you next Sunday."

"Yes?"

"Angela's off on holiday this week. Perhaps a man of your learning could fill in for her next Sunday with the primary age Sunday School."

"Delighted to," said Michael graciously.

Reverend Zack gave him a final smile of a different sort and moved off to circulate amongst his flock.

"You're wrong," said the old woman to Michael's left.

"Wrong how?"

"There is proof of the afterlife."

"I don't think so."

The woman rummaged in her purse and produced a mobile phone.

"I got a call from my friend, Molly, last night."

"Yes?"

"Well, she's been dead seven weeks now. Listen."

She thumbed the answer phone button and pressed the phone to Michael's ear. Michael recognised the recorded voice instantly.

"It's me. Just thought I'd give you a bell, let you know that I'm having a smashing time, up here all by myself. Life's a party and you're invited."

Michael took his head away from the outheld phone.

"And, tell me, did your friend, Molly, sound like a drunk and gravel-voiced man when she was alive?"

"No," she admitted, "but everything's different in the hereafter, isn't it?"

"Not *that* different," said Michael.

BEN, reading *Model Militaria Monthly* at the counter, looked up when the door to *Books 'n' Bobs* chimed. It was Mr Michaels, the new tenant from flat 1a.

"Morning," he said.

"For six days, work is to be done," said Michael sternly, "but the seventh day shall be your holy day, a day of Sabbath rest to the Lord. Whoever does any work on it is to be put to death."

"Yeah? Well, my bank balance and Sunday trading laws say otherwise. Been and got your weekly dose of God, huh?"

"I wish," said Michael, downcast.

"What?"

"Nothing." Michael walked through the shop, running his finger along the spines of the hardbacks. "Do you have any books about health?"

"What kind of books? Fitness books?"

Michael had a troubled look on his face.

"I'm worried there's something... wrong."

"Wrong?" said Ben. Ben straightened up, his hands quivering slightly. If this was a prelude to a heart-to-heart about cancer or some other life-threatening illness then Ben, kind as he would want to be, didn't feel his constitution was up to it.

"I mean," said Michael, "there's the stomach complaint I'm having but that's not what's really bothering me. It's..." He floundered. "Human bodies are funny old things, aren't they?"

"I suppose so," said Ben. "I can make my ears wiggle. Look."

"Mmmm. Do you ever stop to think you might be physically... abnormal?"

Ben eyed him suspiciously.

"Have you been speaking to my mom?"

"Ben, I have a problem. I think. Downstairs."

Ben frowned. Michael gestured in the vague direction of his own crotch.

"Oh," said Ben, thinking that a heart-to-heart about cancer would be preferable to this. "You have a pain?"

"No."

"An itch? A rash?"

"No."

The words 'oozing' and 'weeping' sprang to Ben's mind but he was not going to go there. If he did, 'pustules' and 'sores' wouldn't be far behind.

"I mean does it all work properly?" he asked. "You know, you can write your name in the snow, like?"

"Is that what it's for?"

"I mean, can you urinate?"

"Oh, yes," said Michael. "I wish I could stop."

"Bladder problems, I see."

"No," said Michael. "I just wonder if my *thing* is normal."

Ben quailed.

"I could show it to you," said Michael.

"No!" shouted Ben, hands outstretched. "Please don't."

Michael looked disappointed, even mildly offended.

"It's not really my area of expertise," said Ben.

"I just thought, you being a man…"

"Well, I've seen mine, of course, but I don't tend to look at other men's."

"And you've never sought comment on yours?"

"No," said Ben, his mind flashing back to a mentally scarring game of Doctors and Nurses with Emma Kendall when they were six years old and to an even more brutally scarring date with a college girl twelve years later which ended with the girl pointing and laughing hysterically at exactly the wrong moment.

"Look," said Ben. "I'm not a man of the world. My experiences are limited. My... mine is pretty much used for only one thing. More's the pity. Guess I haven't met the right woman yet."

"Oh, I see. So you would show it to your girlfriend?"

"Yes. Not on the first date, though. That's more Jeremy's style," he said and then the answer struck him. "You need to talk to Jeremy Clovenhoof. He'd definitely take a look and offer an opinion."

"I see," said Michael.

"Actually, we're going to the pub tonight. You could join us. Talk man to man there."

"Perhaps."

"You do owe me a pint after all."

Michael took a book from the biographies shelf: *Bill Gates: King of Geeks*.

"How much for this?" he asked.

CLOVENHOOF RAPPED SHARPLY on the door to flat 1a and did a little hoofy tap dance while he waited.

Michael opened the door. Clovenhoof looked him up and down.

"You're wearing that to the pub?" he said.

"It's Desmond Merrion. Savile Row's finest."

"We're going out to quaff booze and talk bollocks. You're dressed like you're appearing in court."

"Frankly," the archangel said, "there's no appropriate dress code for supping with the devil. And what exactly are you wearing?"

"Bermuda shorts, velvet smoking jacket and silk cravat, Mickey-boy."

"Why?"

"Because it's cool, sophisticated and I'm as suave as buggery."

Michael peered along the hall.

"I thought Ben and Nerys were joining us."

"They're already down the road a way. I said we'd catch them up at the pub. Ben told me you had a problem you needed to discuss with me."

"Yes," said Michael, closing his flat door and locking up. "I suppose I do."

Summer was slipping into autumn and, though there was still a red dusky glow in the southern sky, the air was cool. Michael strode sedately and Clovenhoof trotted beside him.

"I remember when I first arrived everything was a bloody mystery to me," said Clovenhoof in his most avuncular manner. "Not even a year ago but it seems like a lifetime away. It's no surprise you're having trouble settling in."

"I think I've settled in remarkably well."

"I didn't even know what money was," he chuckled.

"I know what money is," said Michael.

"Even the paper ones?"

"Even the paper ones."

Clovenhoof was mildly put out, hoping to be able to teach him the difference between blue beer vouchers, brown curry vouchers and purple lap dance vouchers.

"Yeah, but then there's the other stuff. Like transport, yeah? You do know that you can tell a taxi driver to take you anywhere you want but not bus drivers?"

"I do."

"With buses if you want to go somewhere in particular, the trick is to be really, really threatening."

"I'm not sure that's the case, Jeremy."

"Trust an old hand, Michael. And TV."

"What about it?"

"You do know that it's not real?"

"I do."

"Because technology can be confusing."

"Frankly," said Michael looking up at the darkening sky, "it's one of the few things round here that makes sense."

"Really, cos I bet you haven't got one of these."

Clovenhoof whipped out his new mobile phone.

"Look at this bad boy, huh?" He waggled it boastfully in front of Michael's face. "I can use it to talk to people even if they're miles away. And I don't mean by shouting either, no."

Michael frowned at it.

"Did that happen to belong to Nerys's Aunt Molly by any chance?" he asked.

"It did," Clovenhoof admitted. "But it's not second hand, no. It's pre-loved."

"Uh-huh. And have you been phoning the contacts in the address book and leaving messages?"

"Just spreading myself about. Social maven, me. Centre of the bloody universe."

"Of course," said Michael tiredly.

"I can see you're jealous," said Clovenhoof. "You want a phone like this, don't you?"

"If I wanted a weapon with which to stun burglars, perhaps," said Michael. "I've actually got this."

From his jacket pocket, he slipped a flat, wide device which lit up at his touch. The whole thing was a screen.

"That's a tiny TV," said Clovenhoof.

"Smartphone," said Michael. "4G, sixteen megapixel camera, GPS, Wireless and Bluetooth."

Clovenhoof stared at the shiny wonder.

Yes," he managed to say eventually. "I mean that's all right, for doing phone things like calling people and sending telegrams but there's better. There are these things called computers. Now, they may appear to be witchcraft but actually –"

"I have one, Jeremy."

"Really?" said Clovenhoof, beginning to find the whole conversation intensely annoying. "But I bet you don't know how to use one. People talk about them being intelligent but you know you can't get them to do anything just by shouting at them."

"Mine uses voice recognition but, no, I don't have to shout."

"For fuck's sake," Clovenhoof muttered. "Isn't there anything you don't know?"

Michael took a deep breath.

"I tell you what I don't understand."

"Yes?" said Clovenhoof eagerly.

"I googled myself today."

"We've all done it."

"Searching for the Archangel Michael brought up three point seven million search results."

"Impressive."

"Satan, on the other hand, ninety-four million results."

"In your face, pigeon-wings," Clovenhoof cackled.

"Why would the human race devote more study, more content, more comment to you over me?"

"Cool, sophisticated and suave as buggery," said Clovenhoof. "Humans love me. Have you heard of Heavy Metal music?"

"I believe you subjected me to some at one point."

"I'm a god to those people. Oh, here we are."

The Boldmere Oak stood on the corner between Boldmere Road and Sheffield Road, its square, brick bulk looming over the junction.

"Home from home," said Clovenhoof.

"It's a pub. I'm not sure if I do pubs," said Michael.

"Think of it as an inn," suggested Clovenhoof. "I can recall someone dear to both our hearts who was born in an inn."

"Our Lord was born in the stable."

"Fair enough," shrugged Clovenhoof. "And if there's a Second Coming, he'll be born in a beer garden, somewhere between the parasols and the empty beer kegs."

He steered Michael through the door and to the bar. Clovenhoof threw a lazy salute to Lennox, the barman.

"A glass of your best Lambrini for me and...?"

He turned to Michael.

"Oh, just a mineral water for me," said the archangel.

Clovenhoof gagged.

"Belay that order, Lennox. Michael, you cannot come in here and ask for water. That's like going into a restaurant and asking for a bowl of cornflakes. You insult the fine institution of the public house with such profanity. You should apologise to Lennox."

Clovenhoof looked to the barman but Lennox was busy pouring Clovenhoof a wine glass of fizzy perry and apparently not listening.

"I'm not drinking alcohol," said Michael. "'Drinking too much makes you loud and foolish.' Proverbs."

"But who's to say what is too much? 'Do not drink only water, but take a little wine for your stomach's sake.' So sayeth St Paul."

"My stomach is not good I agree but 'wine and gambling are abominations devised by Satan.'"

"Thank you," said Clovenhoof with a modest bow. "But doesn't the Qur'an also say, 'from the fruits of the palm-date and grapes you will get wholesome drink and food'?"

"Does it?" said Michael, frowning. "I admit translation between Arabic and English and the tongues of Heaven are little murky..."

"Exactly," said Clovenhoof, slapping him on the back. "And look here!"

He tapped a condensation-smeared pump for Foster's lager.

"Yes?" said Michael.

"'The Amber Nectar,'" read Clovenhoof. "Can't get more heavenly than nectar. Lennox, a pint of lager piss for my friend."

Lennox poured and placed their drinks on the bar.

"Five forty," he said.

"Pay the man," Clovenhoof told Michael.

"You haven't got any money on you?" said Michael.

"Didn't say that," said Clovenhoof and sipped his Lambrini.

Michael took out a calfskin wallet and paid up.

"Cheers, mate," said Lennox. "Liking the halo."

Michael stared.

"He can see my halo?" he said in a horrified whisper.

"And my horns," said Clovenhoof. "Drink up."

"But how? Humans aren't supposed to be able to recognise us."

"It's a long story."

"Yes?" said Michael.

"Well, basically, Lennox can see us for what we are and... well, that's it."

"But why? How?"

Clovenhoof shrugged.

"What's life without a little mystery? Come on."

Even though there was no music playing, Clovenhoof sashayed and boogied his way across the bar to the table where Nerys and Ben were already halfway through their first drinks, a glass of Chardonnay and a pint of cider and black respectively.

Ben gave a little cheer.

"Flatmates, ho!" he declared.

"Come sit down," Nerys said to Michael, patting the seat next to her. "Let's toast your induction into a very special group."

"Special group?" said Michael, sliding in beside her.

"A tiny collective of sad and lonely sods who frequent this dive. Cheers."

"Cheers, I think," said Michael and took a first sip of his drink. Clovenhoof watched him closely.

"Is it nice?" he asked.

Michael peered into the depths of his drink and sipped thoughtfully again.

"What is this drink made from?"

"Hops," said Ben.

"Chemicals," said Nerys.

"Dead kittens," suggested Clovenhoof.

"It's..." Michael reached for a word. "Robust."

"Anyway," said Nerys, "I was just telling Ben I've had the strangest phone call from my sister, Jayne."

"Is that the one who shags sportsmen for a living?"

"No, that's Catherine. She's a WAG."

"A wag?" asked Michael.

"I have three sisters," said Nerys. "Jayne still lives at home. She called me to say she's had a text message from Aunt Molly."

"The dead one?" said Ben.

Nerys gave him a steely look.

"Yes. The dead one. Apparently the text said 'come up and see me sometime.'"

"How could something like that happen?" said Clovenhoof.

"Indeed," said Michael, fixing Clovenhoof with a meaningful look that he chose to ignore.

"Anyway, she's taken it as a sign," said Nerys.

"Of what?" said Ben.

"Of the need to visit. She's going to come up and stay for a while. So you boys need to be on your very best behaviour."

"Scout's honour," said Ben.

"As God is our witness," said Clovenhoof. "So, your sister Jayne, does she dress like a cheap Dutch tart and have all the charm of a great white shark?"

"No, Jeremy!" said Nerys, appalled.

"Nothing like you then?"

Ben snorted into the remains of his cider and black. Nerys drained her wine and placed it loudly on the table.

"I bloody hate you sometimes, Jeremy Clovenhoof."

"Makes the good times all the sweeter," he grinned. "Whose round is it?"

"I've barely started my drink," said Michael.

Clovenhoof rolled his eyes.

"You just need some practice. Tell you what would get the ball-rolling: drinking games."

By ten o'clock, Michael was feeling quite peculiar.

He hadn't understood Clovenhoof's drinking games. He had listened to all the rules, had tried to avoid pointing, saying any numbers, using anyone's name or any words with the letter 'J' in them and dutifully drank 'two fingers' each time he forgot. What he didn't understand was the purpose of the game. All it seemed to achieve was the increased consumption of alcohol and a rise in the volume of his neighbours' laughter. Having said that, the lager had inexplicably started to taste better the more of it he drank.

There was also the pressing and urgent sensation in his bladder.

He leaned over to Clovenhoof and whispered, "I've got to go."

"Go?" said Clovenhoof. "No, no, no. You cannot go."

"I'm going to burst, Jeremy."

"Oh," said Clovenhoof loudly. "You need a piss. Me too. This way."

Michael followed Clovenhoof across the bar. The floor seemed to have become uneven during the evening and Michael tripped more than once on the carpet. Clovenhoof put a comradely arm over Michael's shoulder and prodded him through a swing door.

The brightly lit, tiled room stank. It didn't just stink; it possessed a whole polychromatic stench that seemed to combine ammonia, marsh gas, harsh detergents and something else, a pungent anatomical whiff that Michael hoped he would never identify.

"Oh, Lord save me!" he gasped, putting the back of his hand to his mouth. "What is that?"

"It's the gents," said Clovenhoof, trotting over to one of the low ceramic bowls on the wall.

"Has something died in here?"

Clovenhoof opened his flies and boldly exposed himself to the bowl.

"Not recently," he said and began to empty his bladder.

"But why if the rest of the pub is so, well, so reasonable is this room so rank?"

"Because men piss on the floor," said Clovenhoof and, by way of an example, did just that.

Michael recoiled and yet the urge in his own bladder was insistent. Emboldening himself, he stood at the urination station next to Clovenhoof, took out his thing and, after a moment's shyness, released.

He could not quite comprehend how delightful a sensation it was, shameful though the act was. He looked down.

"Oh," he said.

"What?" said Clovenhoof.

Michael peered over at Clovenhoof and then back at himself.

"Yours is like mine," he said.

Clovenhoof made a big pretence at squinting hard to see Michael's thing.

"Yours is like a scale model of mine," he said. "Shetland pony to my stallion."

"And they all look like this?" asked Michael.

"Pretty much."

The toilet door swung open and a man walked in. He took one look at the two men comparing genitalia and, with a mumbled apology, walked straight out again.

"I just thought that... you know, it's not very attractive, is it?" said Michael.

"I think God was having an off day when he cobbled this monstrosity together."

"No, Jeremy," said Michael solemnly. "If this is what God intended then it is beautiful. The Almighty does not have off days."

"Yeah. Tell that to the duck-billed platypus. Or the naked mole rat."

Michael looked across at the cubicle at the back of the toilets and the squat round bowl on the ground.

"Why is there a foot spa in here?" said Michael.

"Um," said Clovenhoof. "Yeah, that's not a foot spa, diddy dick. It's a toilet."

"Also for urination?"

"Yeah and you shit in it too."

"Shit?"

"Shit."

"Sorry," said Michael, whose head was a bit woozy. "I don't understand."

"Shit. Crap. Poo. Defecate. Turdulise. Lay a brown egg. Evacuate your bowels. Back the brown Volvo out of the garage."

Comprehension slammed into Michael like the punchline of a sick joke.

"And that's normal?" he said.

"Not the ideal design but what goes in has to go out." Clovenhoof zipped up his flies and washed his hands at the sink. "But you know that, right?"

"I've resisted it. It's unconscionably foul."

Clovenhoof's expression was a mixture of admiration and disbelief.

"You've been on Earth for two weeks now."

"Twelve days."

"And you've never...?"

"No."

"That's one hell of a backlog, Michael."

"I'm not going to give in to it. There must be some other way."

"I think I can help sort you out," said Clovenhoof.

"You don't think I dress like a cheap tart, do you?" said Nerys.

"Cheap *Dutch* tart," Ben corrected her.

"Do I?"

Ben sighed drunkenly into his drink.

"As I've said once already today, I'm not a man of the world and my experiences are limited."

"Yes, but you must have opinions on women. Think about the women you've been out with."

"Um."

Nerys leaned in closer.

"You have been romantically involved with women, haven't you, Ben?"

"Sort of."

"Yes?"

"There was this Night Elf called Tsunali. We spent a magical weekend questing together."

"No, Ben, real women. No games avatars."

"I had a romantic dinner date with a latex love doll."

"*Real* women!"

"You dragged us out to that singles night once."

"That was a year ago. And you didn't pull. Has there been anyone else?"

"Before or since?"

"Either."

Ben took a long, long drink from his pint.

"No."

Nerys found such a notion incredible, almost obscene. Surely, it was unhealthy to go without for so long. Didn't people explode or something if they didn't get a roll in the hay every now and then?

"Fuck me," she exclaimed. "And that wasn't an invitation."

"It's okay. You're not my type."

"Ha!" declared Nerys exultantly. "You *do* have a type."

"I suppose there is such a thing as my ideal woman."

"Just what we were talking about," said Clovenhoof loudly as he and Michael returned to the table.

"Your ideal woman?" said Nerys.

"Men and women," said Clovenhoof. "Frankly, we think this whole human body thing could do with an overhaul. Human 2.0 if you like. I think Michael and I have identified the major issues."

"Have we?" slurred Michael in his now slightly crumpled suit.

"I think there are some perfect specimens about," said Nerys and gave the new neighbour a lingering pat on the leg.

"Nah," said Clovenhoof, digging out some paper and a pen from within his smoking jacket. He rifled through the papers, looking for a bit he hadn't scribbled on and set to work.

"Way I see it," he said. "We first need to jettison the useless stuff."

"Male nipples," giggled Ben.

"I'm talking about everything you've got too many of."

"Nipples," repeated Ben.

"Kidneys, nostrils, lungs. Let's keep everything central, everything symmetrical." He began sketching out his ideas. "You know starfish?"

"Not intimately," said Michael.

"Their mouths and their arseholes. Same thing. Everything in and out of one hole. That's efficiency."

"Well, we should call you starfish, the amount of crap comes out of your mouth," said Nerys. "So you reckon the perfect human would have only one of everything."

"Yes, *except* for the fun stuff. We should have more of them."

The sketching started to get a bit feverish and Clovenhoof's ideal woman was starting to look like someone being attacked by a swarm of flying boobs.

"Hang on!" Nerys said suddenly. "What's that you're writing on?"

"Paper," shrugged Clovenhoof. "I found it. Now-"

Nerys snatched the sheets of paper from him. There was printed type on both sides and, among the beer and ink stains and juvenile doodles, Nerys saw the words 'Last Will and Testament.'

"You took this from my flat."

"I thought it was the instructions for my new mobile."

"It's my Aunt Molly's will, you numpty! I've been looking for that for days."

"Oh, did she have much to her estate?" said Ben.

Nerys huffed.

"Only the flat and everything in it!"

She hurriedly scanned through the document, trying to guess what words lay behind the stains, trying to ignore the scrawl that Clovenhoof had committed to those pages. And then she found it, the bequest of the flat.

"Anything interesting?" asked Ben. "Nerys?"

"Shitting bollocks!" she said eventually and then, just to make the message clearer, added, "Bollocking fuck!" for extra emphasis.

ST CADFAN'S

Immediately following morning prayer, Abbot Ambrose crossed the cloisters to a door set deeply into the stone in one corner of the quadrangle. The door was short, heavily scored and darkened by centuries of exposure to the elements and the passing of human hands. Time had almost completely obscured the fan-shaped pokerwork engraving in the centre of the door. It was a peacock, carved at a time when the abbot, centuries before, had whimsically decided to bring the birds to the island.

As if in recognition, Barry hooted loudly.

Abbot Ambrose shooed his pet bird away, glanced around quickly to see if he was being observed, lifted the latch and went inside.

With the door closed behind him, Abbot Ambrose stood in utter darkness. He knew that two feet in front of him was a downward step and if he walked on he would fall down more than a hundred stone steps until he lay at the bottom, cold and broken and possibly undiscovered for weeks if not months. He found it a strangely attractive thought and savoured the darkness and possibility for a moment or two before taking the electric torch from the alcove to his left and proceeding downwards.

The abbot of St Cadfan's, in centuries before, had used a torch of wood and pitch to light his way and although a sturdy electric torch cast a harsher, less evocative light, it was certainly more practical and less likely to gutter and fail at the most unhelpful moment.

The first thirty-seven steps (the abbot had counted them and recounted them unconsciously hundreds of times) passed through one of the many crypts that existed inside and outside the monastery complex. The island was allegedly the final resting place of twenty thousand saints. There were certainly human remains to be found all over the place and there were over one hundred dusty, linen-wrapped skeletons down here, in tiered, bunk bed alcoves along both sides of the tunnel. Abbot Ambrose never inspected them closely and let them rest undisturbed except by the few questing tree roots that managed to reach down this far.

Beyond the crypts, the steps became steeper and less even and, as the space opened up into a larger cavern, the abbot was joined by the sound of trickling and dripping water. He always felt at this point that he was truly at the heart of the island and that the monastery, its stones and its history, weighed down on him in more ways than one.

The torch picked out the nearest of the chests before Abbot Ambrose reached the bottom step. There were twenty seven chests in all, of varying sizes, shapes and origins. The newest were Victorian trunk cases with perished leather straps and steel padlocks. The oldest dated back to beyond the Roman Empire, small and once beautiful works of filigreed brass and silver. Without looking, the abbot knew how much wealth in gold and silver was contained in each. He had read the manifest lists and made his own. He knew every doubloon, Frankish tremissis and Byzantine aureus.

Besides the chests of coins were the items of jewellery, the precious stones, the carvings in jade and ivory, and the assorted crowns and sceptres that had made their way here. And then, of course, there was the sword. Abbot Ambrose stood looking at the sword for a long time. It was by far the oldest item in the hoard.

Hoard.

This was, without a doubt, a hoard and it had accumulated to such size through many centuries of hoarding. Gathering and maintaining a hoard of this size required a certain mindset and it was one that the abbot shared.

He had come down here for a specific purpose and already knew he would be unable to fulfil it.

He opened a casket of Greek gold staters and watched his hand hover over them, unable to touch them. He considered a mass of necklaces, a Gordian knot of gold chains from a dozen cultures and would not remove a single necklace. He contemplated a small dish of rings and could not even take the smallest and plainest of them.

The abbot looked at a secret hoard worth ten times the contents of any palatial treasure house on earth, nodded to himself in understanding, and climbed back up the many steps to the surface.

He exited the ancient door and was pleased to find his return to the cloister quadrangle was witnessed only by Barry. The abbot went to the locutory to find Brother Sebastian, once again doing something inexplicable with one of the computers. Father Ambrose was not averse to progress but Sebastian's facility with computers struck him, at best, as suspicious and, at worst, devilry.

Sebastian looked up.

"Didn't see you there, Father Abbot. I was just tweeting some images from our garden webcam feed."

"Were you?" said the abbot who was not going to ask what any of that even meant.

"So," said Sebastian, "any luck?"

The abbot made a polite noise of enquiry.

"Finding funds?" said Sebastian. "To pay for repairs."

"Oh," said the abbot. "No. Sorry. I checked but there really are no reserves."

"Nothing?" said Sebastian, downcast.

The abbot put a kindly arm on the brother's shoulder.

"Sorry," he said. "Not a penny."

IN WHICH JAYNE ARRIVES IN BIRMINGHAM AND MOLLY MAKES HER LAST TRIP TO THE SUPERMARKET

L *ooking for God - My earthly body*

IN THIS BLOG, wrote Michael, *I hope I might help to ease the burden of fellow travellers. If anyone else should find, as I did, that they are suddenly bereft and Godless in an unfamiliar place then they might learn from, or at least take comfort from, this account of my own personal journey.*

THE ADVERSARY WAS DETERMINED *to see me flounder in my new life, so that he could gain some perverse pleasure from being the one to rescue me. I believe my swift adaptation to day-to-day life has caused him some frustration. He did have the upper hand in the matter of local customs however, so I allowed him to take the* lead on my first foray to the pub. In retrospect, this was a mistake...

My lack of experience with drinking games was key to some poor decision making later on. The consumption of a large doner kebab seems an unlikely local custom, but the Adversary was very insistent that it traditionally follows a night in the pub. The ceremonial manner of the cooking pleased me. The sedately rotating spindle, so like a Buddhist prayer wheel, and the reverential slicing of the outermost layers combined in my mind with the after-effects of the drinking games into a moment where I felt blissfully close to Our Lord. Even the smell, which made itself known to us while we were walking towards the place, some way down the road, seemed like a heavy incense, drawing me into a state of rapture. The offering was anointed with colourful sauce that could not, apparently be omitted. Eating this kebab was an experience that I cannot now recall without the utmost feeling of horror, but I have a very strong recollection that it seemed to be exactly the food I had been searching for since my arrival in this place. Was this 'donna' kebab so named because it was food worthy of Our Lady herself? Its sense of correctness was so overwhelming, that I immediately ordered a second one upon finishing the first, which seemed to please the Adversary greatly. For the first time, I experienced the feeling of a full stomach, and it was deeply satisfying.

It wasn't until much later in the night when I realised that something was very wrong. In an uncharacteristic moment of forgetfulness, perhaps caused by the drinking games, I had neglected to put on my pyjamas before going to bed. I woke a few hours later with the sure knowledge that some foul imp of hell had taken possession of my digestive tract. I had previously *experienced some disquiet, and small escapes of a noxious gas, but they were not accompanied with any painful experience. This new and urgent situation caused me to curl up in order to ease the crippling tension in my stomach. I realised, however, that a seismic shift would soon result from the movement of the demon, which was seeking an exit from my body, and moving swiftly downwards. I reached out for Little G, my bedtime companion. He has given me much comfort since my arrival. Fellow travellers might consider getting their own 'Little G', which can serve as a proxy for God's love, even when He chooses to remain silent. I clutched Little G to my chest as I ran from the bedroom. I now understood the purpose of a toilet, foul and barbaric as they are, but I had made the unfortunate decision to have mine removed. Indecision gripped me, and I doubled-up again as a strong spasm seized my insides. I remember calling out in my anguish, and using my free hand so try and stem the outpouring of the dreadful effluent. Except that my hand was not free...*

MICHAEL GOT up from his typing and put the washing machine on for a fourth time. He mulled over the last part of his blog entry as he watched the still soiled Little G begin another soggy cycle.

Michael had decided that his blog would be anonymous, and so should remain an honest account of his difficulties. Was he going too far with the details? No, he decided. Warts and all. Frankly, if Clovenhoof was the Luddite he had shown himself to be, his public blog would be a far securer outlet for his thoughts and feelings than the diary had been.

· · ·

THE CLEANUP IS UNDERWAY, *and has necessitated new carpets. I made sure that I kept a small sample of the terrible substance. I understand that humans must pass waste as part of the blessed cycle of life, but I had not imagined that it would smell so very dreadful. It matches nothing that I have eaten, with the possible exception of the kebab.*

MICHAEL GLANCED up at the jar that was on the edge of his desk.

I SHOWED *the sample to the Adversary and asked him if he thought it was abnormal. He gave me a long, penetrating look and said, "Holy crap, mate. You're showing me a jar of shit. Of course it's bloody abnormal."*

I may need to perform some further analysis.

NERYS PICKED out Jayne's distinctive silhouette as she walked out from the red brick train station. The word that was most often used to describe Jayne in the Thomas household was 'generous'. Depending on the context, and the person saying it, that could be a compliment or an insult. Mostly it was an insult. Interestingly (and Nerys decided it was nature's way of equipping a person to deal with life's difficulties) as much as Jayne was slightly plumper than the other women in the household, she was also decidedly less neurotic about her body image.

Jayne caught sight of Nerys waving and rushed forwards, her coat flapping open, her wheeled bag bouncing like an over-eager puppy.

"Nerys!" she shrieked and wrapped her arms around her sister. Nerys leaned back under the weight of the embrace. "I can't believe I'm here at last," said Jayne. "It took hours. The train took us all round the houses, down to Machynlleth, then Welshpool, Shrewsbury. Oh, and we had to change at Birmingham *International.*" Jayne sighed deeply and looked round at Sutton Coldfield's unlovely town centre. "It's so cosmopolitan!"

Nerys picked up the bag and placed it in the boot. It was not a small bag.

"Staying for long?"

Jayne twirled theatrically.

"In a city like this? I might never leave. It feels so good!"

"I bet it does," said Nerys, knowing exactly what she meant.

"Are Mom and Dad well?" asked Nerys as she started the engine.

"Yes, yes. They're fine," said Jayne distractedly. "Is the Bull Ring shopping centre close by?"

"No," said Nerys. "That's a few miles away, in the city centre. We're sort of on the fringes here. We can go there if you like though."

"Oh, I want to see everything! Aston Villa, Cadbury World, the Space Centre."

"Um, I think the Space Centre's in Leicester," said Nerys. "Let's start with Boldmere shall we?"

Nerys drove them through the streets, taking extra care

after Jayne leaned across in front of her to point out a billboard for a shop that was claiming to open twenty-four hours a day.

"That can't be right, surely!" she exclaimed.

"Oh, yes."

"No."

"Yes."

"It's like another world, isn't it?"

"Something like that," said Nerys, swung off the Boldmere high street, past the church and pulled up outside four hundred and something Chester Road.

Jayne got out of the car and looked round.

"Is this where you live?"

"Home sweet home."

"And it's all yours."

"No, only the top floor."

"My!" Jayne put her hand to her face. "What's that smell?"

"Nerys wrinkled her nose and looked at the open bin bags stacked by the gate.

"Rolls of carpet. They weren't there when I went out. Maybe someone's waiting for the council to take them away."

"What is that stuff on them?"

"I don't want to know. Come on."

Nerys hurriedly shepherded Jayne up to her flat.

"Penthouse living," said Jayne. "It must be wonderful to have your own space."

"I'll make us a brew," said Nerys and went into the kitchen.

"I'm surprised you haven't given the place a bit of a makeover," Jayne called. "It's a bit old-ladyish still, isn't it?"

Nerys held her temper and counted to ten as she filled the kettle.

"It's something I'll get round to," she said, "but I've been so busy at work, it's hard to find the time. I practically run that branch you know."

"Oh, the employment agency. Well they must let you have some time off. You're not a machine."

Nerys leant in the doorway with the weariness of the selfless martyr.

"I have a sense of responsibility for the others. It's up to me to keep it all going, and times are hard. I can't let them down."

"That's lovely, Nerys. Do you ever find time for yourself though?"

"I try."

"Do you have a man in your life at the moment?"

Nerys smiled boldly.

"My problem is that I have quite a few admirers. They all like to think they're the one for me, but I'm keeping my options open. I'm a bit young to commit, don't you think?"

"Oh. Well. How nice," said Jayne, turning away to inspect the ornaments on the window sill. Nerys wondered briefly if she'd gone too far by bringing up the question of age with the eldest Thomas sister. The comments about being left on the shelf kicked in at around the age of twenty three in a Thomas family gathering. Jayne suffered the double-whammy of still living at home to suffer the reminders daily and being a couple of years older than Nerys.

"Is this Aunt Molly's will?" Jayne asked, noticing the grubby document on the dining table.

As she had checked that the flat was tidy before going to fetch Jayne, Nerys had smoothed out the will on the table and shook her head at the stains. She had scraped it, sponged it and ironed it, but Clovenhoof's filthy mess remained. She had created a couple of her own stains in the margins to camouflage the lewd cartoons that he'd drawn, but parts of the text in the document remained obscured. She sighed and headed out.

"Yes. It's not all that legible. I had to rescue it."

"From where?" Jayne asked. "Inside a dog? Oh, where is...?"

Jayne looked around and spotted Twinkle curled up on the sofa, doing his best impression of a small hairy cushion.

"Oh, Twinkle, you beautiful pup!" said Jayne and snatched up the unsuspecting terrier. "It's been a long time since I saw you, Twinkle-winkle! Have you grown? Yes, I think you have!"

Twinkle bared his teeth as Jayne crushed him to her bosom.

"Oh, he's smiling at me! I think he remembers me!" Jayne cried.

Nerys made tea, listening to Twinkle growling and Jayne talking back to him in that awful childish voice.

"I think Twinkle's loved out," said Nerys returning to the room with two cups of tea. "Take a look at the will. You can make out most of the important stuff. I'm the executor, see that's on here. She wants some money to go to the Dog's

Trust, and once the probate stuff's all done, there's enough in her savings account to cover that."

"This bit about the flat's got some kind of ink stain on it," said Jayne, poring carefully over the wording.

"Yes," said Nerys, once more conjuring up the colourful images of painful torture she'd like to inflict on Clovenhoof. As always, she was confounded by the certainty that he would enjoy the attention.

"It talks about *my favourite niece*," said Jayne, "but then the part with the name is completely impossible to make out. Have you tried a magnifying glass?"

"I've tried everything."

"Yes, I can even see that you tried smearing grease on to dissolve the ink," said Jayne.

"Actually, that's just another stain, but it certainly hasn't touched the ink," said Nerys.

"Well that's interesting," said Jayne. "In theory it could be any one of us."

Nerys put her hands on her hips and glared at Jayne.

"Really?"

"I'm just saying."

"You want to say that?"

"In theory it could be one of four of us."

"In theory it could, yes," said Nerys frostily. "In practice though, who looked after her these last years?"

"Well –"

"Who cooked and cleaned for her?"

"I'm not denying you've been –"

"In fact when did you, Catherine or Lydia even see her last?"

"Oh Nerys," said Jayne. "You mustn't think that those of us who couldn't be with her cared any less."

"Is that so?"

"I used to send her knitting patterns in the post."

Nerys felt the rage explode from within her like a chest-bursting alien.

"You sent her one knitting pattern! One! She showed it to me. It was for a stupid hot water bottle cover with a rabbit on the front."

"I thought she might like it."

"No you didn't. You wanted her to knit one for you. That's the only reason you sent it. I can't believe you come up here and try to tell me that you might have been her favourite niece because you tried to get her to be your knitting slave."

Jayne made a *slow down* gesture with the palm of her hand, which made Nerys twitch with the urge to slap her.

"Now, Nerys. You need to calm down. This kind of outburst won't solve anything."

The twitching grew stronger.

"Right," said Nerys. "And you've got some brilliant idea, I suppose?"

"I think maybe you need a professional to take a look at this. Someone like a solicitor. Someone who knows how to execute this will properly."

"Right," said Nerys, "well we're already on shaky ground there."

"Why's that?" asked Jayne.

"This part here," said Nerys, pointing, "where it says that she wants her ashes scattered in the Dogpool Potters Field - wherever that is."

"What's wrong with that?" asked Jayne. "We should do whatever it says to fulfil her wishes."

"What's wrong with that? What's *wrong* with that?" Nerys walked towards Jayne, jabbing an accusing finger at her face. "I'll tell you what's wrong with that. If you'd been bothered to come to the funeral you'd know what's wrong with that. We didn't cremate Aunt Molly. We buried her."

MICHAEL SAT through Sunday's service, noting with approval that Reverend Zack had implemented some of his suggestions. The dust had been removed from the legs of the pews, and the windows were a little cleaner. The flowers still sat in hopeless lacklustre bunches. Michael wondered if he'd have to oversee that task himself, as clearly nobody here had any kind of an eye for floral aesthetics. Not today though. Today he had volunteered to help with Sunday School.

After the service, in the function at the back of the church, Darren (in a stunning piece of knitwear depicting the Last Supper that surely would not have been possible on a man with anything less than a sixty inch chest) led the twenty-odd children in adding further details to some complicated collage work that he pulled out from under the stage. The giant collage, composed primarily of sugar paper, pasta shells and glitter, appeared to be the backdrop for a Christmas performance. After thirty minutes of inefficient industry, the collage featured several new scenes, and Darren was smeared with more glue and scraps than any of the children.

"Story time now," called Darren, picking a sequin from his ear. "Take your places on the rug."

Michael walked to the front, sat on a chair and looked at the rows of expectant faces. The children gazed back. There were a couple of runny noses and persistent blinkers among them but they seemed a fairly docile bunch. Michael had met children en masse in his previous visits to earth. He could do this.

"Hello children," he said with a hesitant smile. "My name is Mr Michaels and I will be reading your Bible story today. Make sure you pay close attention and you will learn all about Adam and Eve."

He looked at the children's version of the stories, which had been handed to him in a loose-leaf binder. He suspected that the Reverend Zack had crafted much of the prose, as the language was rather bland, but peppered with unlikely elements, no doubt designed to be child-friendly. He snorted with derision at the suggestion that Adam was unsatisfied with the table manners of monkeys, causing God to take pity on him and make a woman. He closed the folder after glancing through the opening paragraphs and recounted the story in the only way he thought appropriate.

There were no interruptions until Michael came to the actual temptation of Adam and Eve by the serpent.

"'You will certainly not die,'" said Michael in his most hissingly evil voice. "'For God knows that when you eat from it your eyes will be opened and you will be like God, knowing good and evil.'"

Michael noticed from the corner of his eye that Darren,

sat cross-legged on the rug with the children, had his hand in the air.

"Yes, Darren?"

"How could it talk?"

"Sorry?"

"The snake. How could it talk without lips?"

"Because it's really Satan in disguise."

"Oh."

"And Satan is capable of subtlety and cunning." Michael thought for a moment. "Well cunning, certainly."

He continued with the story.

"When the woman, Eve, saw that the fruit of the tree was good for food and pleasing to the eye, and also desirable for gaining wisdom, she took some and ate it. She also gave some to her husband and he ate it."

Another hand went up. A small girl in the front row regarded him with a solemn expression.

"Why did God put the tree there if they weren't supposed to eat the fruit?" she asked.

Michael smiled.

"Let me ask you – Stephanie, isn't it? – why do you think God put the tree there and told them not to eat it."

"Because he wanted to keep it for himself," said a runny-nose in the back row. "Like my dad's lager."

"Did God want all the apples for himself?" asked another boy.

"Now, the Bible doesn't say it was apples," said Michael. "Common mistake. Well, let me tell you that God wanted to test them. They should have done what God asked them to do instead of allowing themselves to be tempted."

"That's not a test, that's entrapment," replied solemn Stephanie. "Everyone knows that."

"Let's move on," said Michael. "We're getting to my favourite bit."

"Which bit's that?" said the runny-nose with the lager-drinking dad.

"It's where God cast Adam and Eve out from the Garden of Eden. Do you know how he stopped them going back in?"

"Razor wire!"

"Piranhas!"

"Landmines!"

"No, Darren," said Michael. "He put cherubim in place to guard the gate."

A boy with glasses at the back put up a tentative hand.

"Are they the babies with wings that shoot people to make them fall in love?"

"No," said Michael with a gleam of passion in his eye. "They are warrior angels and God gave them flaming swords. They are dangerous, terrifying creatures, and God put them in place so that Adam and Eve would be afraid to enter through the gate."

A few of the boys leapt up and started brandishing imaginary flaming swords, light-sabre style.

Michael's smile faltered as he saw Darren's hand go up again.

"Did they have belly buttons?" he asked.

"What? The angels?"

Michael's hand went involuntarily to his own stomach.

"Adam and Eve," said Darren. "Did they have belly buttons?"

"Is that important? I think there are some more pressing questions -"

"They couldn't have had belly buttons," said the self-assured girl in the front row. "You have your belly button from when you're born and they weren't born. They were made by God."

"That picture up there has them with belly buttons," said the boy at the back. All heads turned to look at the badly-framed print on the back wall. The painting showed Adam and Eve covering their nakedness with leaves.

"Well that's most interesting," said Michael. "But I doubt the painter was there at the time. Remember Adam and Eve were the first humans. You are all descended from them."

Michael knew without looking that Darren's hand was in the air again.

"Yes?"

"How many children did Adam and Eve have?" asked Darren.

"Three," said Michael. "Cain, Abel and Seth."

"How did they make more people then?" asked Darren. "Who did they have sex with? If their mom was the only woman -"

"Enough!" snapped Michael. "I don't think it's appropriate to speculate, but I imagine God would have provided some suitable mates for them. That detail wasn't recorded. Significant events like Cain murdering Abel were on their minds perhaps."

"Mr Michaels, thank you so much!"

Michael span round to see Reverend Zack approaching. He wondered how long he'd been listening.

"Children, I can see that you've had a lovely time listening to the story of Adam and Eve. It's home time now, so you need to collect your coats and line up by the door. Darren?"

Darren got to his feet and Reverend Zack took a seat next to Michael.

"You did a good job there. I can see that you're a natural with them."

"Thanks,"

"I, er, wonder if we could impose upon your time for next week as well? Angela has run into a bit of trouble on her holiday."

"Trouble?"

"Local trouble. And we're not sure when she'll be back."

"Of course," said Michael. "I'd be happy to help."

"Angela is also the Akela of the cub pack that meets in here," said Zack. "I'm sure that they would be very grateful for any extra help they could get until she returns. Darren will tell you all about the cubs if you're interested. He's Baloo."

"He's clearly something."

"All the cub helpers are given names from the Jungle Book."

"Oh, I see. Let me think about that. I guess cubs is similar to Sunday School?"

Reverend Zack hesitated for the briefest of moments.

"I can't be sure it's quite the same group of children," he said carefully. "But I'm sure you'll cope magnificently."

.   .   .

BY THE TIME he got home, Michael realised he was quite exhausted by Sunday School.

Why were there so many questions, so much doubt? If these children were being brought up as Christians, surely they would accept the truths that were placed before them. Could it be that modern human life had so many distractions that God's message just wasn't getting through to people? Based on his experience so far, it seemed as though it was quite hard work to find evidence that God was around.

He turned to his computer and wondered if other people were having more luck. He tried some searches. Where were signs of God to be found? What did they look like, and did people believe them? A few minutes later he realised that signs of God were far more numerous than he had imagined. The silhouette of the Virgin Mary on a griddle. The face of Jesus on a leaf and in a puddle of sauce. For some reason the face of Mother Teresa was regularly seen on Danish pastries, and God liked to write his name in Arabic on the insides of fruit and vegetables across the globe.

Michael had been wrong. There were messages from God all across the world, he just had to find a way to see them and interpret them. He drummed his fingers on his desk for a few minutes then fetched his Bible.

"Lord, speak to me. Please," he said. "I need some guidance."

He opened it at a random page and stabbed his finger halfway down. He had landed on Chronicles 23:19. *"He also stationed gatekeepers at the gates of the Lord's temple so that no one who was in any way unclean might enter"*. His finger was against the word *gates*.

Michael bristled with excitement. Here was something he could work with! That simple word in that straightforward sentence made everything suddenly clear. He had work to do. God wanted him to take on the role of gatekeeper, to protect the church here on earth and make sure that people came to it in a pure and wholesome way. God had even hinted how he should fulfil his mission. He was to emulate Bill Gates. He would use the power of technology and put himself in a position of influence. Getting a job would be important. He needed to quickly become a captain of industry. Michael stared at the screen and wondered how he'd do that.

He searched the internet for "position of authority" but that simply brought up a number of news stories. "Captain of industry" was no better. "Seat of power" turned up nothing that would help with job-hunting, but the results included a bizarre Japanese toilet that played music, warmed the seat and provided a massage for the user. Michael was reminded that his bathroom still lacked a toilet. He read on, fascinated to find that there were some high tech options available. Was it possible that the whole process could be dealt with in a more pleasant way? Diverted momentarily from his need for a job, Michael began a separate quest for a solution to his more *fundamental* problem.

NERYS CHOSE to seize the bull by the horns and organised a curry night with the flatmates. Jayne would have to meet Ben, Michael and Jeremy eventually and Nerys preferred that to be on the neutral grounds of the Karma Lounge Indian restaurant. Besides, after her rant that afternoon, Nerys didn't want to spend too much time alone with Jayne right now, and introducing her to her friends and having an evening of mindless banter was easier to face than any competitive sisterliness.

Clovenhoof advised Michael on the most suitable meal for his unworldly constitution.

"Tindaloo, every time. You'll love it."

"It is a musical name," said Michael. "It sounds delicate and refreshing."

Nerys had an idea of what was going on, so she loudly told Jayne about the milder options on the menu, and warned her about the corrosive horrors of Tindaloo and Phaal.

Clovenhoof pouted.

"Nice top Nerys," he said. "Are Ann Summers having another closing down sale?"

Nerys ignored him and moved the poppadums swiftly out of his way before he could stab his finger through the pile as he often did.

"Actually, Jeremy," she said. "Jayne and I wanted to ask your advice on something."

Ben raised his eyebrows in surprise and Michael laughed softly.

"As you all know," Clovenhoof replied. "I am an authority on many subjects. Ask away."

"We thought you might know how to get a body disinterred, as you work for a funeral director," said Jayne.

"Why on earth would you want to know that?" asked Ben.

"According to the will that only just came to light," said Nerys, glaring at Clovenhoof, "Molly wanted to be cremated, and we buried her."

"Easy mistake to rectify," said Clovenhoof. "I wouldn't try and do it officially though, there's a load of paperwork that you'll never get through. We'll just dig her up in the night and burn her in the garden at the flats."

There was a chorus of 'no's, even one from the passing waiter.

Michael got up from his chair.

"Call of nature," he said. "Do excuse me."

Clovenhoof shrugged at the faces around the table. Jayne's mouth remained open in horror for longer than the others.

"Suit yourself. Why does it matter though? Molly's in no position to mind whether she was cremated or buried. Are the will police after you or something?"

"No," said Nerys. "It's just that we want to do the right thing, in honour of her memory. She wanted her ashes to be scattered in a place where she walked out with her first love."

"It's *so* romantic," breathed Jayne.

MICHAEL RETURNED FROM THE TOILET. He nudged Clovenhoof discreetly in the ribs.

"Can I show you something?"

Michael started to pull a jar from his jacket pocket, but Clovenhoof's hand pushed it firmly back in.

"No. Not now, not ever. I look at my own poo. I quite often

think I'd like to show other people when it's a good one, but I've learned that nobody's all that keen."

Michael looked downcast. He'd have to put the jar with the others, but he still didn't know if it was normal.

"Does it matter if it's really Molly's ashes?" asked Ben. "If you're doing it to honour Molly's memory, then maybe it's not important."

"Her soul's in Heaven anyway," said Nerys.

Michael noticed a look of surprise cross Nerys's face, as if she hadn't expected those words to pop out of her own mouth.

"You are dust, and to dust you shall return," he said. "You might say that all ashes are Molly's ashes. Earthly remains are unimportant."

"Are you suggesting," asked Jayne tentatively, "that we should get some other ashes and scatter them as if they're Molly?"

Nerys nodded slowly.

"It could work, I suppose."

"I'll get you some proper ashes from work if you like," said Clovenhoof, shovelling lime pickle into his mouth on a fragment of poppadum.

"I find it most perverse," said Michael, shaking his head.

"Oh really, Mickey? You think that's perverse?" said Clovenhoof. He leaned over and patted Michael's pocket. "Would you care to turn out your pockets and repeat that?"

ON THE MONDAY, when Nerys had gone out to work, Jayne decided to begin the search for the Dogpool Potter's Field where Molly had wanted her ashes scattered. The will had said it was where Molly had first 'walked out' with her love although that probably meant it was just the location of the bush where they'd had their first clumsy fumble or whatever it was kids did back in the fifties. Nonetheless, it would be nice to do one decent thing for Molly and, if she found it, maybe Nerys would be a little less scathing about Jayne's affection for her aunt.

A search of Nerys' A-Z revealed several roads called Dogpool and a Potter's Field retail park but no actual Dogpool Potter's Field. Eventually, Jayne chose to trust in fate, clipped the lead onto a playful Twinkle and set out into Sutton Coldfield with hope and good vibes to guide her.

Autumn leaves covered the pavement after a heavy frost from the night before. Jayne hadn't expected Birmingham to have so many trees, and she smiled at the sight of Twinkle scuffling through the drifts with his diminutive paws.

"Shall we go and look in the shops, Twink?"

She drifted in and out of the shops on the high street, carrying Twinkle in her arms in an effort to circumvent any no-dog policies.

She entered a second hand bookshop called *Books 'n' Bobs*. She browsed the shelves, murmuring to Twinkle about the interesting titles.

"Hello, Jayne."

She turned to the counter.

"Ben. I didn't realise you worked here."

"It's my shop," he said with a small, proud sweep of his hand.

"Really?" said Jayne. "A local businessman."

"I suppose I am."

"I love a good bookshop," she said and pulled a heavy history book off a shelf by way of demonstration. "I can lose myself for hours."

She blew the dust off the top of the book and placed it on a different shelf, where it quite clearly belonged.

"I have customers who've been lost for so long that I send sherpas after them," said Ben. "I issue balls of string to new people so that they can find their way back."

Jayne smiled and, putting Twinkle down to free her hands, continued to move books around to their *correct* positions.

"I'm sure I'll manage," she said, "I'm starting to get the hang of Boldmere now, I've walked all over the place today."

"Yes?"

"I'm looking for this park or field or whatever where Aunt Molly wanted her ashes scattered."

"Have you looked in the A-Z?"

Jayne pulled the street atlas from her pocket and gave Ben a look that she hoped said, 'I may be a woman but I'm not stupid.'

"Maybe we should try the internet," said Ben, gesturing to the computer on the counter.

Jayne gave an unconvinced shrug.

"So, do you like Boldmere?" said Ben, as he began his internet search.

"Oh yes," said Jayne. "I can see why Nerys chooses to live

here, even though I'm sure she could afford a huge place, what with her doing so well at work and everything."

"Really?" said Ben. "I had no idea, I thought she was just an administrator."

"Oh yes, she told me. That's why she's so busy and she doesn't have time to spend with the men who are always chasing her."

"Nerys? This was definitely Nerys?" Ben asked, coming closer.

"Yes, of course. Why?" asked Jayne.

"Nerys spends so much time trying to trap a man, I'm surprised she hasn't actually dug a pit outside the house."

"No!" said Jayne. "Surely not. That's more like my other sisters, Lydia and Catherine." She put down the book she was holding. "Actually it sounds like my mom too." She thought for another moment. "Actually... it does sound like Nerys a few years ago. I just assumed she had more luck since she moved to Birmingham."

Ben shook his head.

"Apparently not." He gave her a look. "You're not desperate to find a man yourself then?"

"No," said Jayne. "I don't go round looking as hard as the others do. I firmly believe that I'll cross paths with Mr Right when it's meant to be."

"Nerys believes the same thing," said Ben. "But she just makes sure she crosses a lot more paths than everyone else."

That made Jayne laugh.

"Here," said Ben and turned the screen around so Jayne could see. "I must admit that I can't find Dogpool Potter's

Field on most maps but there's a reference to it here and an old Ordnance Survey map I could print off."

"Could you?"

"I could," said Ben and did just that.

This was good news.

"Oh, Twinkle, we'll have some good news for your mistress, won't we?"

She looked behind her. No Twinkle. She looked behind and under the shelves.

"Twinkle?"

She turned on the spot and looked towards the open door of the shop.

"Oh no. Twinkle."

Ben scooted round the counter.

"Come on," he said, locking up the shop. "We'll soon find him, he can't have gone far."

"Nerys is going to kill me," said Jayne.

CLOVENHOOF HUMMED HAPPILY to himself as he tidied up a client at *Buford's Funeral Directors*. He had had the job for no more than five months and was continually surprised by two facts: one, that he still enjoyed it and, two, that he hadn't been fired yet. He worked for a few minutes on padding old Mr Waddington's mouth, wondering how much of the deranged gerbil look he could get away with. He sighed and adjusted his work. Manpreet, his supervisor, had strict ideas about this subject.

His mobile phone rang as he decided that he could get

away with giving Mr Waddington the 'gobstopper in each cheek' look. He answered the call to a cultured female voice.

"Hello, I have a dog here that belongs to you, I believe."

Clovenhoof thought for a moment. Did Twinkle have Molly's phone number on his collar?

"Little ratty looking thing? Bad attitude?"

"It's a miniature Yorkshire terrier, and he seems a fine fellow to me," said the voice.

"Well that can't be Twinkle then."

"Yes. Twinkle is what it says on his collar."

Clovenhoof sighed.

"Tell me where you are. I'll come and get him."

BEN AND JAYNE had strayed far from the high street.

"Twinkle!" called Jayne. "Nerys is going to kill me."

"I'm sure she won't," said Ben. "You were trying to do a nice thing, taking him for a walk."

"We've already argued about Molly's will. I'm sure she'll think I've done it on purpose."

"Jayne," said Ben, placing a hand on hers. "I can vouch for you. I know you were just distracted for a moment."

Jayne gave a small smile.

"We'll look for a few more minutes, but I think we might need to tell Nerys what's happened. I can't imagine that we'll find him now."

"Hang on," said Ben, looking at the sheet of printing paper in his hand. "We're near Dogpool Potter's Field."

"But Twinkle!" said Jane.

"It should be up the second turnoff on the left," he said, peering at his sheet. "There should be some allotments there."

They walked up the road that Ben indicated and then stopped as they saw what was ahead.

"Ben," said Jayne. "Is it possible that you've made a mistake?"

"No," he said after consulting his map on last time.

"That's not a field."

"No."

"That's a supermarket."

It was slightly more than just a supermarket. It was a huge supermarket, possibly the size of the entire field it had been built upon.

"I guess they redeveloped the area," said Ben. "What will we do?"

"Well, it's the place that she wanted."

"Well, you could just go ahead and do it."

"Scatter the ashes there?"

"Just, you know, really *quickly* while nobody's looking."

Looking for God - My search for employment

Today I sought some help with my search for employment. My upstairs neighbour, Nerys works at the Helping Hand Job Agency, so I went there to visit her.

She greeted me warmly upon my arrival. In fact, it appeared to me that she viciously elbowed some colleagues out of the way so that she might serve me herself, but I am inexperienced in office etiquette.

When she realised that I was looking for work she sat me down and gave me a number of forms to fill in. Details about my address and computer skills were easy enough to relate, but I hesitated when at the section which required details of my experience. If I reveal specific details of my working life prior to my arrival, I fear they will not be taken seriously. I left that part blank.

While I was writing, Nerys started to take some notes. I told her that I had seen someone on the television who had a job that I thought was very suitable. When I told her that it was the Commander of UK Armed Forces, she sat, with her pen poised over the pad and asked me what made me think I was suitable. I told her that I was a fearless warrior, but she kept pressing for details, so I said that I had military training but it was overseas, some time ago. Sometimes I wish I still had my flaming sword, so that I could more easily convey the magnificence of my military bearing (can't remember when I saw it last). I thought that might sate her curiosity, but then she started to talk about concentrating on my current skill set. She looked at the form and seemed pleased that I was proficient with computers. I asked if that would be sufficient for me to run one of the large pharmaceutical or petrochemical companies. They have a great deal that needs sorting out, in my opinion. She told me that they did not have that kind of vacancy.

She was also dismissive of my willingness to enter politics, as Prime Minister or Secretary General of the UN. She even suggested that the Adversary had persuaded me to come in and ask stupid questions (I believe he may have made a nuisance of himself *in the past). I was about to question the long-term viability of a job agency with such a narrow view of the world, when a commotion from the doorway disturbed us. Nerys's sister Jayne was there, with Ben.*

"Oh Nerys! Something awful has happened!" said Jayne.

Nerys stood up, clearly alarmed and asked what had happened, looking from one to the other of them. The door then crashed open and the Adversary entered, looking very pleased with himself. He held aloft the small dog known as Twinkle. The dog attempted to gnaw his horns, which I must admit made me smile.

Nerys was confused that the Adversary was walking the dog, and suggested that it was not a good idea to bring animals into a place of work. I pointed out that the Prophet would never enter a house in which there was a dog although that just seemed to cause confusion. Nerys then turned to her sister and asked her what the matter was. A curious look passed between Ben and Jayne and then Jayne started to talk about dusty books in Ben's shop, and the fact that some were mis-shelved. I can understand the frustration that this might cause a tidy person, but it did not seem like the kind of drama that should create such a scene and disturb my job hunting.

Nerys took the opportunity, while were all together, to make sure that we would all attend a small ceremony at the weekend to honour her Aunt Molly. I agreed on the understanding that she would seek out some suitable employment opportunities for me.

CLOVENHOOF SAW Michael emerge from the front door when the open-backed lorry pulled up. Michael stopped when he saw Clovenhoof.

"Are you smoking all three of those cigarettes?" Michael asked.

"Yup," grunted Clovenhoof, between puffs, and tapped the ash into the metal container on the ground before him.

"Are those supposed to be Molly's ashes?"

Clovenhoof nodded.

Michael peered inside.

"How many have you smoked?"

"Just topping it up," said Clovenhoof. I got the rest from the crematorium, but I spilt some while I was having lunch. Crunchy."

Michael left him and went over to the lorry. Clovenhoof craned his neck, but couldn't see anything apart from a plastic wrapped pallet that came down on the lift at the back of the lorry. Two men appeared and carried the heavy pallet into Michael's flat. Another man, dressed in overalls followed with a toolbox.

Ben appeared beside Clovenhoof.

"Did you see the label? It said *Soyuz Unit* on the side," said Ben. "You know what that means?"

"Something to do with vegetarian food?"

"That means it's something from the Russian Space programme."

"Michael's bought a spaceship."

"I doubt it."

Clovenhoof could bear it no longer. He knocked on Michael's door.

"What's your new toy, Michael?" he asked.

Michael stood in the doorway, while the sounds of banging and drilling could be heard from within.

"I really don't think I want to show it to you," he said.

"Yes, you do."

"It's to help me overcome a rather personal problem."

Clovenhoof wondered if Michael could possibly have said anything more tantalising. He trotted up the stairs, his interest level at Defcon One, formulating a plan.

CLOVENHOOF ANSWERED the door to Nerys on Saturday morning.

"We're going now," she said. "Molly's final wish, come on."

Clovenhoof groaned theatrically.

"Not sure I can. I've been up all night. Think I might have eaten a green crisp or something."

Nerys narrowed her eyes in suspicion.

"You have the stomach of a rhino. You never even get a hangover. Is it just that you can't be bothered?"

"Nerys, I had my best smoking jacket cleaned for this, but I just don't think I can do it. Five yards from a toilet and it'll be carnage."

"Hm. All right."

"Thanks for being so understanding."

"See you later," she said and added, "And no sneaking into my flat to steal food. Or toilet paper."

Clovenhoof nodded and closed the door. Nerys clearly

didn't believe a word, but he was free to check out Michael's flat while they were all out scattering Molly's ashes.

BEN, Jayne, Nerys and Michael assembled in the car park of the supermarket. Nerys had put Twinkle into a carrier bag. She was determined that he should not miss the ceremony, but knew that they would get thrown out if he was spotted.

Nerys turned and, once a trolley attendant had gone by with a train of rattling trolleys, addressed them all.

"We are gathered here today to perform the last wishes of Aunt Molly. Before we go in, I think we should each say a few words."

Jayne went red as Nerys pointed to her first.

"Molly loved this place," said Jayne, indicating the supermarket and its crowded car park with a sweep of her hand. "She stepped out here with her first love. It was a tranquil green area in amongst all the hustle and bustle."

Her last few words were drowned out by the reversing alarm of a large skip lorry that had come to empty the recycling units. They waited a few moments, and Michael spoke up.

"There is a time for everything, and a season for everything under Heaven," he said. "A time to be born and a time to die, a time to plant, a time to reap that which is planted. A time to kill, and a time to heal. A time to break down, and a time to build up. A time to weep, and a time to laugh. A time to mourn, and a time to –"

"Er, Michael, right now it might be a good time to move

out of the way," interrupted Ben as the skip lorry drove straight towards them.

"A time to dance," continued Michael once the lorry was gone. "A time to cast away stones, and a time to gather stones together."

"Was Molly a Byrds fan?" Ben asked Nerys.

Nerys merely nudged him to say something.

"Oh. Right. Well Molly was lovely, and I'll always think of her when we look at Twinkle. They look a bit similar. I know it's not really her that we're scattering today, but I hope she approves."

"Thank you all," said Nerys. "Well my main regret is that I only knew Molly when she was old. I've had these vivid dreams during the last few weeks of Molly as a young woman, and they make me happy, in a slightly sad way. I miss her a lot and I think of her every day."

She cast her eyes to the ground in a moment's reflection. Then she looked up and indicated the urn of ashes in the crook of her arm.

"Let's do this," she said. "Now everybody. It's *very* important that we act naturally."

CLOVENHOOF WAS inside Michael's flat, puzzling over the shiny new contraption in the bathroom. He had no idea what it was however he had watched a film called *2001: A Space Odyssey* a few months back and there was something of the robotic space pods and killer computer to this large, wall-mounted object.

"Hello?" he said, keeping a careful distance in case it lunged for him or declared that he must die 'for the sake of the mission.'

The device did nothing, apart from continuing to wink an amber light at him. The surface of the white box was studded with lights and handles and tubes. It all looked very important. There were no instructions to hand, just a few puzzling labels in Cyrillic script and, even though the Prince of Lies was a cunning linguist, none of it made any sense to him.

He approached cautiously and picked up a tube that appeared to be connected up for suction.

A smile spread across his face as he realised what the machine's purpose was. He was fairly certain he'd seen an advert for something similar in the back of a magazine. Michael's personal problem was clearly his tiny manhood, which must have been bothering him since he'd realised how much larger Clovenhoof's was in the Boldmere Oak. He'd been and bought one of those machines for penis enlargement.

"You tiny-dicked numpty," he laughed.

Clovenhoof decided that he needed to try it out for himself. He compared the tubes that he held in his hands, and saw that the larger of the two said, in Russian, *solids only*.

"Well, that's me! Solid as a rock," he bellowed as he rammed his penis into the end of the tube and flicked the most obvious switch on the device.

The suction created a secure and powerful vacuum around his genitals. The tube contracted savagely and bucked in his hand, dragging him to the floor. Clovenhoof howled with pain.

Through the translucent plastic tubing, he could just about make out his poor penis. The machine and the force of the suction would surely sever it clean off. He could not reach the switch from his position on the floor. He grappled for purchase, but he was securely wedged at the side of the hideous machine and it showed no sign of releasing him.

For a moment he genuinely considered praying for help and then, with desperate quick-thinking, reached for his mobile phone in his pocket. He thumbed at the keys blindly.

NERYS LED the group as they walked slowly through the fruit and veg section. They were very conspicuous, she realised. Perhaps trying to look like a regular shopper, Ben picked up a pineapple, but put it back down again when she glared at him. It was too busy in this section, so Nerys made her way to the back of the store. The others followed. A man in a brown acrylic suit, who could only have been a store detective fell in behind them. Were they that obvious?

"Do we do it now?" said Jayne.

An elderly lady nearby reached into her shopping bag to take out a ringing mobile phone.

"Too many people," Nerys said to Jayne.

Nerys saw the woman's puzzlement at the caller ID. She put the phone to her ear.

"Molly?"

Nerys stopped at that and watched the woman. She could

plainly hear screaming coming from the earpiece and, as the woman listened, her face froze with horror.

"Molly?"

She listened for a few more moments, and let out a piercing wail of anguish.

"Help me!" she sobbed to the passing shoppers. "Somebody help me, please!"

"What is it, love?" asked a man with a French loaf under his arm.

"My friend's being tormented by the demons of Hell! She shouldn't suffer like this, somebody help me!"

The store detective rushed forward to assist the lady and Nerys nudged Jayne in the ribs. She upended the urn onto the floor.

A large dusty plume of ash drifted towards the fresh meat counter. As one, the mourners backed away quickly yet solemnly, Ben making the sign of the cross as they went.

The last thing Nerys heard was the old lady shouting into her phone.

"Molly, you haven't even got a cock, so how can it be caught in a – oh my *God*, Molly, what have they *done* to you?"

ST CADFAN'S

Brother Manfred entered the orangery and a humid warmth that did not match the grey autumnal skies outside. The orangery, though an unusual feature of an island monastery, was a work of wonder. Whoever had built it had positioned it to make the very most of the sunlight and created a space that was home to luscious flowers, intense greenery and, of course, the apple tree.

Older than perhaps anyone at St Cadfan's and planted directly into a cleared patch of soil in the orangery floor, the Bardsey apple tree twisted its way up to the ceiling. Its topmost branches pressed against the sloping panes of the steepled roof. Its bottommost branches hung heavy with fruit.

"Brother Manfred," said the abbot.

Father Ambrose sat near the base of the tree beside the prior, Brother Arthur, and the procurator, Brother Sebastian. The abbot had a bowl of fruit puree in his hand and was trying to feed the prior although, given the dollops of brown puree that dotted the prior's bath-chair and the floor, without much great success.

"Father Abbot," said Manfred, approaching. "You wished to see me?"

"Yes. I hope have not dragged you away from something important."

"The vol au vents and salmon mousse can wait."

"If you say so. I wanted to talk to you about tapestries."

"Yes, Father Abbot?"

"We have a number of fine tapestries, in the library, the almonry and the prior's house."

"We do," agreed Manfred. "Sadly, they are all seriously faded. And, I think you will agree, the little moths have been going 'munch munch munch' on some of them."

"Exactly," said the abbot, pushing a spoonful of puree into the prior's mouth. "It would be a shame for them to fall into total disrepair."

Manfred nodded.

"Things of beauty. Naughty moths."

"Quite. Now, Brother Sebastian here had an idea about how we might make a little money from them."

"Not sell them, surely?" said Manfred in quiet horror.

"That would be profitable," said Sebastian, "but short-sighted. I was thinking we could sell photographic prints of the tapestries."

"Like postcards?"

"More like a limited range of fine art prints. Numbered, framed and sold on our website for a hundred quid a pop. They are valuable works of medieval art and worth millions."

"Millions?" said Manfred doubtfully.

"Well, that's the price I've convinced the insurers to put on them."

"However, worth millions or not," said the abbot, "they are in a poor state. I wondered if you would consider turning your embroiderer's eyes and skills to some simple repairs."

Manfred put a splayed hand on his chest in surprise.

"You would trust me and my little sewing kit with those treasures."

"I hear you're something of a marvel with needle and thread."

Manfred shrugged modestly.

"It would mean a lot to us," said the abbot. "The prior, who has been here longer than any of us, has often expressed his fondness for them."

The prior, who Manfred had not once heard utter a single word, gazed blankly into space, a dribble of fruit mush at the corner of his mouth.

"While we cannot yet afford to effect major repairs to the masonry and brickwork damaged by the summer storm," continued the abbot, "we can afford to kit you out with what you need."

Manfred nodded eagerly.

"I must say I know the most exquisite haberdashers in Caernarvon."

"There you go. Order what you need."

"I shall, Father Abbot," said Manfred and bobbed his head in excited gratitude. "Thank you, Father Abbot."

The abbot waved a gracious and magnanimous hand at

Manfred, a gesture slightly ruined by the fruit-gunked spoon he was holding.

"There is one thing, Father Abbot," said Manfred.

"Yes, brother?"

"Some of the tapestries are extremely faded. The pictures and scenes are, to be frank, unclear. Do we have any reference images for what was in them?"

"Perhaps there may be some pictures in the library collection. Or at least some references to the picture contents in chapter house meeting minutes. Brother Sebastian can help you."

Manfred smiled and nodded but he was sceptical.

"I trust your judgement regardless," said the abbot and returned to feeding the prior.

3

IN WHICH MICHAEL SEARCHES FOR TRUTH AND NERYS AND JAYNE SEARCH FOR REAL MEN

"Let there be light," said Michael, slamming the door behind him with more force than he intended. And there was light.

"Handel," he said and the opening notes of an oratorio filled the flat.

The concealed microphones and computer voice-recognition system were working a treat. So far, Michael had hooked it up to the lights, the central heating, the multi-room sound system and the five wall-mounted computer/entertainment screens placed around the flat. A man was coming in at the weekend to fit motorised blinds and Michael had seen on the internet an intelligent fridge freezer that, linked to his computer, would automatically know when his milk and run out and order some more.

Michael walked into the kitchen and, in that initial instant of seeing Clovenhoof standing before the freezer with his flies undone, crazily wondered what an intelligent fridge would make of the Adversary sticking his genitals in the freezer. Would it declare them out of date and try to order new ones?

"Is it your mission to stick your thing in every single household appliance?" said Michael.

"It's not at all normal," said Clovenhoof, peering down.

"Oh, I know it's not normal."

Clovenhoof turned. He had a large pack of frozen sweetcorn stuffed inside his trousers.

"I think your evil robot might have killed it. It's still all pink and swollen."

Michael nodded.

"The Soyuz toilet was designed to remove faecal matter in zero gravity without the need for cosmonauts to get their hands dirty. It wasn't designed for your unholy manhood. Do you not have any ice or frozen goods in your own flat?"

"Used all the ice," said Clovenhoof, forcibly doing up his trousers over the pack of frozen vegetables. "And the crispy pancakes kept leaving crumbs under my-"

"I don't want to know," said Michael, reaching past Clovenhoof to get a bottle of water from the fridge. "I've had a tough enough evening."

"Oh?"

"Cubs was *not* like Sunday School. Clearly, Sunday School is for Christian children with too many questions and the cub scouts is for ravening animals. They're like a tribe of evil pygmies. Their leader is a little villain called Spartacus Wilson."

"I've met him. Did he make disparaging comments about your mother?"

"That's the one."

"I got on quite well with him."

"Oh, then you can come and help us next time."

"I didn't say-"

"Offer your expert wisdom. I got quite agitated. And then, when Reverend Zack and I spoke about dealing with them and resolving conflict, he said, 'Blessed are the cheesemakers.'"

Clovenhoof smiled which deepened Michael's frown.

"Doesn't he know the Sermon on the Mount?" said Michael. "It's 'peacemakers.'"

"He's quoting a movie. *Life of Brian*."

"Was he?"

"It's a religious film."

"Oh," said Michael, feeling he was starting to understand. "Is it about the teachings of Our Lord?"

"Sort of," shrugged Clovenhoof. "I've got it on video somewhere if you'd like to watch it."

"I'm sure I could download it."

"I won't be a minute," said Clovenhoof and waddled out of the flat with a bulging crotch.

Michael went to his computer. His cute teddy bear lolled casually beside the desktop screen.

"Little G, find *Life of Brian*."

"Yes, Michael," replied the computer in a reassuring male voice. A red trail of lights bounced from side to side on the screen when the computer spoke.

"*Monty Python's Life of Brian* is a 1979 film written by and starring the comedy group, Monty Python, about a young

Jewish man in first century Judea," said the computer. "Would you like to watch it?"

"Yes, please," said Michael who believed that good manners should also extend to artificial intelligence and sat down on the sofa with his water.

Handel's *Messiah* vanished, replaced by the opening choral music of the film and the sight of three men on camels following a star across the desert skies. Religious indeed, thought Michael.

The flat door burst open and Clovenhoof and Ben piled in, an ancient VHS cassette clutched in Clovenhoof's hand.

"Found it," said Clovenhoof. "Ben had it but he thinks he might have taped over it with *Ben Hur*."

"I'm watching it already," said Michael.

"Cool," said Ben, plonked himself on the sofa next to Michael and screeched, "'He's not the Messiah, he's a very naughty boy.'"

"What?" said Michael.

"We haven't got to that bit yet?"

Clovenhoof was in the kitchen.

"What are you doing in there?" asked Michael suspiciously.

"Looking for booze," said Clovenhoof. "And changing my vegetables."

AN HOUR AND HALF LATER, as the jaunty closing number played over the credits, Michael sat almost entirely dumbfounded.

"Sacrilege," he whispered.

"It's funny," said Ben.

"It pokes fun at Our Lord."

"It treats Jesus himself with great respect."

"Too bloody much," muttered Clovenhoof, extracting a defrosted oven chip from his underpants.

"But it makes crucifixion out to be a... a nothing. The suffering of Our Lord is trivialised."

"It mocks *organised* religion," said Ben. "Petty people twisting the true spiritual meaning of life."

Michael shook his head.

"And Reverend Zack has watched this. He even quoted it to me."

"The man's got taste," said Ben.

Michael, his mind an unpleasant and confused whirl of contrary thoughts, got up and paced the room.

"It's getting late," said Ben, standing up and dragging Clovenhoof to his feet.

Clovenhoof popped the chip in his mouth and rummaged around in his crotch for another.

"Yes," said Michael absently and saw the two of them to the door.

He stood at the door for a long time and then went and closed the curtains against the night.

"A new blog entry, Little G," he said to the computer.

"Yes, Michael."

"*Monty Python's Life of Brian* is a horrible and blasphemous work," he began. His words rolled onto the screen as he spoke. "Our Lord was whipped, impaled and left to suffocate to death under the weight of his body in a hot, unforgiving sun. I should know. I was there. *Life of Brian* makes his supreme sacrifice seems as trivial as the pagan bunnies and Easter eggs that have replaced the true Easter celebrations. And yet..."

He stopped to gather his thoughts.

"And yet, *Life of Brian* pokes fun at the accidental misunderstanding of religious truth, at the ease with which false prophets can gain credence, at the almost impenetrable socio-political situation in which Our Lord lived. Perhaps this work of blasphemy is as close to the truth as the concept of Christianity grasped by the misguided flock at St Michael's church. In the absence of God's voice, is the church just an empty shell where half-truths are perpetuated. Is it a relic? A fossil?"

Michael wondered if his cynical mood was exacerbated by his weariness, his wretched evening with the cubs, and the nagging thoughts of what Clovenhoof had done with his frozen food compartment.

"Where is modern spirituality?" he said. "If we cannot access God through the church, how do we find him in this new age? Little G."

"Yes, Michael."

"Do a search with keywords 'spirituality,' 'God,' 'truth,' and 'new age.'"

"Yes Michael."

A flood of text and images filled the screens. Evidently, Michael realised, he was not the first to have these same doubts, these same questions.

∿

NERYS SLID a coaster along the coffee table and placed a steaming hot mug on it.

"A nice hot chocolate for you," she said to Jayne and then sat down in Molly's chair with her own drink and put her slippered feet up on the pouffe.

"So," said Jayne, stroking Twinkle as he sat in her lap, "would you describe this as an average Saturday evening?"

Nerys did a quick mental checklist. Big bag of cookies. A tub of ice-cream waiting in the fridge. Hot malty drinks. A dating game show on the telly.

"Pretty much," she said.

"Hmmm."

"What?"

Jayne sipped her drink and winced at its heat.

"I suppose you gave me the impression that your life was a non-stop high power rollercoaster of work, social engagements and so many eager men that you had to beat them off with a stick."

"Well, not non-stop," said Nerys slowly.

"And one of your friends suggested to me that perhaps you're not so much beating them off with a stick as trying to trap them with nets and harpoons."

"Did Ben tell you that?"

"I'm not saying who it was."

"It was Ben, wasn't it?"

"It doesn't matter what-"

"Well, you can tell Ben to keep his thoughts to himself. Just because he got down on his knee to me right there" – she pointed at a spot on the rug – "and I had to spurn his advances doesn't mean he can start spreading rumours."

"So, you really have men queuing up around the block?"

"Not round the block as such but there have been plenty of them."

"List them."

"All of them?"

"All of them in the last year."

"It has been a slow year," said Nerys. "Let's see. There was Mark and Graham. That was some night. There was Stephen." She paused. "Or was it Trevor?"

"Clearly a memorable relationship."

"It didn't last. He didn't like empowered women."

"Really?"

"And..."

Nerys stopped.

"Three men," said Jayne. "Two in one night and one whose name you can't remember."

"Definitely either Stephen or Trevor." Nerys shuffled uncomfortably. "Look, Jayne. I'm not necessarily the woman I used to be. Molly's death has given me a lot of perspective. I take things easier now. I've matured. I'm waiting for the right man."

"You mean you're too knackered to keep chasing them."

"Hey, I'm not the one left on the shelf here!"

Jayne slammed her mug down on the coaster and leaned forward, spilling a once sleeping and now surprised Twinkle onto the floor.

"I will have you know that Glyn Pettigrew gave me quite the snog at last year's Young Farmers dance."

"Right, sis. Listen. One, Glyn Pettigrew is not a *young* farmer. He's forty-five if he's a day. Two, with two whiskeys inside him, he'd snog one of his own cows. Three, that's one snog in twelve months."

"Ah!" snapped Jayne. "But you haven't taken population density into account."

"What?"

"If you consider the number of eligible men per square mile, my one Welsh snog is worth ten times your metropolitan fumbles."

"You think the men of Birmingham will flock to you over me?"

"Given the chance!"

"Ha!"

"Ha!"

Silently fuming, Nerys sat back in her chair.

"Next Saturday we hit the pubs and clubs."

"Bring it on," growled Jayne, grabbed Twinkle more roughly than was necessary and stuffed him back in her lap.

They sat there for a good minute while, on the screen, women far younger, blonder and thinner than them cooed over the muscle-bound hunk they were competing for.

"Ice cream?" said Nerys.

"Yes, please," said Jayne.

ON WEDNESDAY EVENING, Clovenhoof strode unannounced into Michael's flat and did several deep lunges to show off his knee-length hiking shorts. Michael, in the middle of a phone conversation, frantically waved for him to get out, a gesture that Clovenhoof chose to ignore.

"So, Friday morning," said Michael. "Ten o'clock." He nodded and uh-huhhed. "Thank you, Mistress Verthandi. I will see you then."

Michael hung up.

"You shall not suffer a witch to live," said Clovenhoof.

"What?" said Michael.

"You. Consorting with fortune-tellers."

"I have no idea what you're on about."

"Mistress Verthandi. Does tarot readings out of a shop off Birmingham Road."

Michael scowled at Clovenhoof.

"What are you wearing?" he said.

"My best scouting gear," said Clovenhoof, striking a pose. "Khaki shorts and a bright orange cagoule. I'd be wearing hiking boots and woolly socks if, you know, if I had any actual feet."

"It's hideous."

"So, you don't want me and Ben to come help tame the little scamps?"

"I didn't say that," said Michael quickly.

CLOVENHOOF IMAGINED that he would have the cubs under his sway within moments but realised the error in his assumption the instant they entered the church hall. Clovenhoof was good with adults. Adults stayed still. They listened to reason. They were predictable. They were easy to mess with and manipulate.

What he saw as he walked in was a mass of tiny green-clad people, running pell-mell around the room with such furious abandoned that they were innumerable and infinite. At the centre of the screaming maelstrom was a fat man in a cub leader shirt that did not fit him.

"I know him," said Clovenhoof.

"Pitspawn," said Ben. "He used to be into war gaming. And Satanism. Before he found God."

"Pitspawn found God?" said Clovenhoof.

"Apparently, he had a traumatic encounter with the divine."

Clovenhoof stared intently at his hooves, said nothing and hoped Pitspawn didn't recognise him.

"His name's Darren," said Michael. "Although at cubs we call him Baloo."

"Why?"

"Because cub leaders all take a name from Kipling's *Jungle Book*."

Something small and grubby kicked Clovenhoof in the shin.

"Hello, Spartacus," said Clovenhoof.

The boy narrowed his eyes.

"How do you know my name? Are you a paedo?"

"I was a teaching assistant at your school."

"Oh, yeah. I heard you had to leave because you got the head teacher pregnant."

"That's not true. And she was like ninety years old."

"I know. You're a dirty old man."

Michael strode to the heart of the chaos and held out his arms for attention.

"Pack! Pack! Pack!" he yelled.

The whirlwind slowed but did not stop.

"Oi! You horrible maggots!" bellowed Clovenhoof. "Listen to the man!"

That stopped them.

The cubs, who had transformed from an amorphous whoosh of noise into twenty small boys in green tops, neckerchiefs and woggles, stopped and then sat on the floor.

"Thank you," said Michael. "As you can see, boys, tonight we have new helpers. In the form of..."

"Baghera," said Ben with the haste of someone who had clearly been thinking about his *Jungle Book* name and didn't want anyone else to steal it.

"Kaa," said Clovenhoof with a grin.

"Baghera and Kaa," said Michael.

"Akela Michael?" said Spartacus Wilson.

"Yes?"

"Have they been CRB checked?"

"What?" said Michael.

"How do we know they're not perverts?"

"I'll have you know I'm the very finest of perverts," said Clovenhoof.

Michael put his hand over his eyes. Darren gave Clovenhoof a strange and penetrating look.

Falling back on the tactic of divide and conquer, Michael split the cubs into three groups to do some badge work. Michael's group worked on their hobbies badge, which mostly seemed to consist of fleecing each other with three card monte. Ben gleefully helped a bunch of boys with their camping badge and rapidly taught them a series of useful rudimentary knots. Clovenhoof teamed up with Darren to help the boys working on their emergency first aid badge.

· · ·

"Yes," said Michael to PJ, "but I don't think Rock, Paper, Scissors counts as a hobby."

Michael had made the mistake upon first meeting PJ of asking him what PJ stood for. The little lad had scratched his impetigo and said, 'Pyjamas,' as if Michael was mentally deficient.

"But I'm dead good at it," said PJ.

"Fine," sighed Michael and shook fists against the scabby boy.

PJ's rock beat Michael's scissors. They shook again and PJ's rock was bested by Michael's paper. PJ's scissors was beaten by Michael's rock and then both produced paper. And from that moment on, Michael beat PJ eight times in a row.

"Not fair, Akela," said PJ.

"I didn't cheat," said Michael. "I could see how you played."

"What?"

"Your strategy."

"I was just being random."

"No." Michael was lost in thought for a moment. "Nothing is random. Hey, Kenzie. Come over here."

"Now, you want a slipknot for your basic snare-style animal trap," said Ben, checking each of the boys' knots. "Of course, if you were forced to fend for yourself in the wilderness, you would need to fashion yourself a weapon. Blades can be made from sharp stones, especially flint. But if you need weapons for hunting, you could fashion spears out of straight branches."

A couple of the boys, taken by the notion, looked around the hall for any suitable materials.

"I suppose at your height, you'd need a spear thrower. I could show you how to make an atlatl which Palaeolithic man used to hunt Irish Elk."

"You do chat a load of guff," said Spartacus, who had until that moment been busy selling bags of sweets in exchange for other cubs' badges.

"If you're not interested in this," began Ben, "you can-"

"Do you live at home with your mom?"

"What?"

"I bet you do. Your mom's a great fat heffalump."

A couple of the cubs giggled.

"You don't know my mom," said Ben who felt control of his little group sliding out from under him.

"Yeah, your mom's so fat even light can't escape her."

The laughter grew in strength and confidence.

Ben panicked and he felt something he not felt in decades, the fear and embarrassment and impotent rage of being picked on by the biggest kid in the playground. He had almost forgotten what it felt like. He had pushed it down to the darkest depths of his mind but now it came bubbling back to the surface: the fear and the embarrassment but, more than that, the rage.

"Yeah?" he said in a quiet but furious tone. "And your dad's so tiny he has to wear a life jacket in the bath."

"Hey!" snapped Spartacus.

"Your dad's so tiny he gets bullied by Borrowers."

"That's not funny," said Spartacus but the other cubs disagreed. Several of them were sniggering.

"Your dad's so tiny he was mistaken for the Higgs Boson."

"You're not allowed to talk like that to me."

"You're dad's so tiny, he gets hand-me-downs from Barbie."

All the other cubs were laughing now.

"That's not fair," whined Spartacus.

"Do you want me to stop?" said Ben.

"Yes."

"Yes what?"

"Yes, please?"

Ben smiled.

"Good. Now, who wants to know how to dig a bear trap?"

Hands shot up and Spartacus's sticky mitt, whilst not the fastest, was among them.

DARREN WALKED from Clovenhoof (who was playing the role of the injured party in their first aid scenario) to Clovenhoof's phone (which was playing the role of a phone on a plastic chair) and pretended to dial.

"Nine nine nine," said Darren loudly. "I would like an ambulance please. My dad has cut himself. We live at thirty-two Windermere Crescent. Thank you."

Darren put the phone down.

"Like that."

"Well, that's not very true to life," said Clovenhoof.

"Isn't it?"

"For a start I'm clearly too young and good looking to be your dad."

"We're just roleplaying here," said Darren.

"But it's meant to be realistic. I spend a lot of time around injury and death."

"Do you?" said a cub called Jefri.

"I work in an undertakers," said Clovenhoof, "and I've seen the results of more accidents and mishaps that you could shake a stick at."

"Could you bring a body in for us to see?" asked Jefri.

Clovenhoof was immediately tempted but decided he liked his job too much to risk it.

"I don't think so."

"Could you take us to see one?"

"Maybe. Now, who can tell me what was unrealistic about that situation?"

"That phone," said Jefri.

"That's a real phone."

"It's a breeze block."

"What's unrealistic," said Clovenhoof, who was starting to take jibes about his phone personally, "is the lack of blood. I've just cut my arm whilst chopping potatoes. I'm likely to have hit an artery. Now, what we need is..."

He cast around and saw exactly what was needed.

"THAT ONE," said Michael, tapping a card.

Kenzie flipped it over. It was, once again, the queen of hearts.

Michael took Kenzie's money yet again, mentally adding

it to the total that would need to be reimbursed to Kenzie's earlier victims.

"How do you do it, Akela Michael?" asked Kenzie.

"It's patterns," said Michael. "There's an order to things. You think you are shuffling the cards randomly but you're human and you are drawn into behaving in certain ways. I'm sure I could come up with an algorithm to explain it."

Michael was excited by his discovery that ordinary human behaviour was apparently quite predictable. He was sure there was a link between human behaviour, the world at large and those signs of God he had been reading about on the internet.

He would have so many questions for Mistress Verthandi.

"Make sure you arrange the spikes evenly around the base of the pit if you want to properly impale the animal," said Ben from across the hall.

Michael looked up.

"Er, Baghera?"

He would have gone over to check that Ben was sticking to the proper activity but was diverted by Clovenhoof's first aid group.

"So, here I am, casually chopping vegetables," said Clovenhoof, "and, distracted by a passing zebra..."

Clovenhoof slipped with his imaginary knife, punctured the straw hole of a box of blackcurrant squash and fell to the floor screaming and writhing while purple juice squirted everywhere.

"Quick!" he screeched. "Call an ambulance!"

The first aid cubs, at once on their feet, dashed for where the phone had been.

"Where is it?" yelled Jefri.

"A phone is never where it's meant to be," said Clovenhoof, continuing to direct a spray of blackcurrant up into the air. "Where did you have it last? Is it down the back of the sofa?"

"We haven't got a sofa!"

"Don't argue with me! I'm dying here."

"I think we're making quite a mess," said Darren, taking in the range of cubs now spattered with fruit juice.

"I'm bleeding to death and you're moaning about how tidy the place is," spat Clovenhoof. "Typical. You want me to die, don't you?"

"Got it!" yelled a drenched cub, waving the phone.

"Too late," croaked Clovenhoof and went limp and lifeless.

CLOVENHOOF THOUGHT that the arrival of an actual ambulance (summoned by a cub who had dialled 999 on Clovenhoof's phone but couldn't make it stop) was simply the crowning moment of what had been a very entertaining evening. Michael was less convinced about the success of the evening although admitted it had gone better than the cubs of the previous week.

Back at home, Clovenhoof cooked himself three Findus crispy pancakes. They were the same pancakes that he had previously used to cool his machine-mangled manhood and the occasional pubic hair in his tea added a novel texture to the meal.

Settling down with a very self-congratulatory glass of

Lambrini, he phoned the *Skin Deep* shop off the Birmingham Road and, as he hoped, went straight through to an answering machine.

"Mistress Verthandi. I believe a friend of mine is coming to see you on Friday morning. Now I know you don't need my help to see beyond the veil, but I thought I'd share some details with you so you could give your reading some added realism. First up, Michael's toilet is an evil space machine that tried to eat my knob..."

MICHAEL ENTERED the *Skin Deep* shop and briefly wondered if he had come into the wrong place. This seemed to be a tattoo parlour rather than any gateway to spiritual truth, the walls hung almost exclusively with tattoo samples: arrow-pierced hearts, oriental ideograms, Disney characters and screaming skulls. But then he spied a revolving bookcase with titles such as *Healthier Bowels with Crystal Healing* and *A Guide to Identifying your Guardian Angel* and, behind that, a shelf of joss sticks, gemstones, CDs of whale song and a basket of what appeared to be Guatemalan worry dolls.

"Anything take your fancy?" said the woman, standing up from her table counter at the side of the shop. "Is it your first tattoo?"

Michael looked at the woman. She was thin, perhaps too old for the T-shirt and jeans outfit she wore, had a lined face that spoke of a tough life and a black patch over one eye that simply shouted it.

"Do not cut your bodies for the dead or put tattoos on yourself. I am the Lord," said Michael.

"Leviticus 19:28," said the woman with a smile.

"You know your Bible."

"I've tattooed it on more than one person," she replied. "Irony, I guess. You'd be Mr Michaels."

"Mistress Verthandi?"

She nodded and gestured for him to sit at the table.

"I had a phone call from a neighbour of yours earlier this week. I think he wanted to give me some insider information or maybe just twist any reading I did for you. Do you want to know what he said or do you want to know what I learned?"

Michael thought on it.

"What did you learn?"

Mistress Verthandi opened a pack of tarot cards and shuffled.

"You have fallen from a great height recently and your neighbour is delighted by this. However, he is frightened."

"Frightened?"

"Because you are picking yourself up again and climbing once more. He doesn't want you to succeed."

"Of course, he doesn't."

"But it's not because he hates you. In truth, your neighbour doesn't hate anyone. He's too self-centred to put that kind of effort in. He wants you to fail because he's jealous."

"Oh, I don't believe that's true."

"Your neighbour is also fallen but he wallows in his failure. He can't let go of the past. He wants you to wallow in failure too."

"I didn't fail."

"Sure you did, Michael," she smiled. "Oh, and you have some anal retention issues that even a tarot reading isn't going to sort out. Now, do you know anything about tarot?"

Michael shook his head.

"This is a Rider-Waite deck with major and minor arcane. I'm going to deal them out in the Celtic cross pattern."

"Why?"

"I find it's ideal for first readings and specific questions of which I guess you have a lot."

"No," said Michael, "I suppose I meant why deal them out in a certain way at all?"

"Because that's how it works."

Michael pursed his lips.

"No. You see, I do have questions."

"Good."

"But they're not questions about me. I'm a little lost at the moment, spiritually speaking. I know God is out there."

"I'm glad *you* know that."

"Okay, I know there is *truth* out there. Real truth. You say you can access it through these cards."

"I make no claims. People say it works. I'm an intermediary."

"Fine, but it works, yes? From the random order of the cards, from the pattern you lay out, truth emerges."

"Yes."

"I got the bus here today."

"Well done."

"But I waited for half an hour for a bus to come along and then three came along at once."

"We've all experienced that."

"Right! It's a cliché because it's true. What should I divine from that?"

"I don't think there's been much research into 'busomancy'."

"But people read signs in clouds and flights of birds and the movements of the heavens."

"And you want to know how it works. All of it."

"Yes, please," said Michael.

Mistress Verthandi began to collect the cards up.

"Some people think the whole fortune-telling thing is a scam, a confidence trick. It isn't. But if I even pretended to be able to answer your question, I would be lying to you."

"Please," said Michael. "Tell me what you know. Only that."

Her one eye met his two. It flitted across his face, reading him.

"What I know," she said. "Fair enough."

SATURDAY CAME AND, although the totally unofficial and yet mutually recognised man-pulling contest wasn't until that evening, Jayne's preparations began the moment she awoke. She ate a light breakfast, put on a face mask and watched six episodes of the informative show *Snog Marry Avoid* on internet TV. If a make-under TV show could transform snoggable slappers into milder marriage material, Jayne reasoned that she could reverse the show's messages to sex up her general frumpiness.

She took her lessons in snoggability to the *Boldmere Beauty* salon on the high street and, despite the gentle protests of the woman there, had her hair coloured a brilliant blonde, her whole body coated with fake tan and had the woman fit her with bright pink nail extensions. Feeling more snoggable already, Jayne browsed the high street, hoping to see some little extras to add to the outfit she had bought for herself earlier that week.

She nipped into *Books 'n' Bobs* to ask Ben which shade of body glitter he preferred. Ben's suave but dull neighbour, Michael, was chatting to him at the counter.

Ben stared at her.

"I'm sorry, madam, I think you've come to the-" He blinked and did a double take. "Jayne? Is that you?"

"Of course it's me," she grinned.

"I didn't recognise you," he said in an oddly stilted voice. "You look... different."

"Good different?"

He nodded thoughtfully for a very long time.

"Of course it's good. I'm sure it is."

"I'm dolling myself up for a night on the town with Nerys.

"Ah!" said Ben.

Michael nodded in understanding.

"That's why Nerys had the..." He mimed a pair of high breasts, massive eyelashes and then tottered around on some pretend high heels. "But I don't think we needed to see her sequinned underpants, did we?"

"Sequinned underpants," said Jayne thoughtfully. "I think I'd better up my game."

"Really?"

"If I'm going to bag myself a man."

"I think," said Ben with the hesitance of someone treading into unknown territory, "if you want to get yourself a man then you should really go for the natural look."

"Natural look?"

"You know, dress casual. Not too much, er, flesh. And men don't like women who wear a lot of make-up."

Jayne laughed.

"Oh, you! You're men. What do you know?"

And she left the shop reinvigorated in her search for an extra push-up bra, fake eyelashes, and something sequinned to go with her skimpy pink dress. She wondered if a feather boa might also be required.

"Right," said Ben, shaking his head as though dispelling a most unpleasant dream, "where was I?"

"Cruelly comparing my spiritual theories with the ideology of the Church of the Flying Spaghetti Monster," said Michael.

"Exactly. Just because your notions about self-ordering systems, pattern recognition and chaos theory have the air of science about them, it doesn't make them any more credible than Pastafarianism."

"You accuse me of pseudoscience?"

"You did start going on about bibliomancy and Bible codes."

"Kabbalah has been the subject of serious academic study for centuries."

"It's mysticism."

"As is all science until rigorously tested. I've had Little G crunch terabytes of data as background information."

"Little G?"

"It's what I call my computer."

"Why?"

Michael coughed and went a little pink.

"I named it after my teddy bear."

"That makes more sense than your theories."

"Ben, all I'm asking you is to help me with my study."

"Why would I want to do that?"

"It involves camping out on the street, counting buses, noting down their registrations, recording them on a tablet app and watching the instant analysis. I thought we could take some flasks of hot chocolate and some biscuits. I just thought it was very... you."

Ben, to his own annoyance, found a certain excitement stirring within him.

"You had me at buses," he said.

BIRMINGHAM WAS A BIG CITY. One of its few boasts was that it had more canals than Venice (although considerably fewer gondoliers). The city was home to a million people, over four hundred pubs and bars and more lap dancing clubs per capita than any other British city and, like African waterholes, the places where the canals converged were where the city's nightlife came to drink and hunt.

Nerys and Jayne started early, in a cocktail bar above Broad Street. By the time she had downed her third mojito, Nerys was convinced that any contest between her and her ingénue sister was already over. Jayne was starstruck by the city's scale and variety and constantly gawped at the people. Nerys could also see that Jayne had made some fundamental errors of judgement in her choice of clothing.

Jayne's pink latex dress with the choker collar and heart-shaped peephole frankly looked like bondage gear whereas Nerys herself had gone for a far more classy hot pants and tube top combo. Nerys had used two bras to promote and elevate her natural assets but Jayne had used so much scaffolding she couldn't get her drink to her mouth without the aid of a straw. Yes, they had both gone for the same high heels and false eyelashes but Jayne was already too tall for six inch heels and her eyes weren't big enough to carry off the lashes, no matter how much black eyeliner she used. And there was a clear difference between going for a bronzed skin tone and slapping it on like creosote. The extras, the costume jewellery, the glitter, the boa were all good in principle but Jayne really hadn't co-ordinated them in the way Nerys had.

Emboldened by her superior looks, Nerys linked arms with Jayne and hauled her over to a bunch of young men in open collar shirts.

"Evening gents."

Her presence stunned them. She could see that.

One of the lads had his mouth open in a huge grin.

"Boys, you shouldn't have," he said.

"We didn't," said his friend.

"Shouldn't have what?" said Nerys.

"I know you're only twenty-one once but getting me two..."

"Two what?" said Nerys and then realised. "No, we're not... You think we're strippers?"

The grinning birthday boy's grin froze and then collapsed.

"Strippers? No. Sorry. Did I say strippers?"

"Why would you think we're strippers?" said Jayne.

"I don't know," said a loud and lairy bloke next to the birthday boy. "I'm sure in that get up you were just on your way to visit your grandma."

"Hey," said the birthday boy reproachfully. "I'm sure these, er, lovely ladies have just got separated from their hen party."

"We're not on a hen do," said Jayne.

"Or their tarts and vicars party," said the lairy one.

"Are you calling me a tart?" said Nerys.

"Nah," he replied sarcastically. "You're the epitome of class, darling."

"Leave it, Karl," said his mate.

"Leave it?" he said. "I wouldn't touch *that* with a ten-foot barge pole."

"Hey!" said Nerys.

"Listen, love. Lots of men like a camel toe but I don't want to spend the night lip-reading."

"That's gross," said Jayne.

"I should say. *Your* skirt's so short your STD's showing."

The birthday boy put a restraining hand on his friend's chest but, in Nerys's incensed opinion, he was about ten seconds too late. Nerys opened her mouth to give him a tirade of abuse but was cut off before she started when Jayne's Bacardi Breezer bottle slammed into the lout's face with considerable force.

A rainbow of rum, fruit juice, snot and blood spattered the group. A shout of disgust and alarm went up. Nerys grabbed Jayne's arm to drag her quickly away but the bar's bouncers were already on them.

Things were not going to plan.

CLOVENHOOF, who had been enlivening the quiz night at the Boldmere Oak by shouting out random wrong answers before he was kicked out by Lennox the barman, staggered home, turning each merry stumble of his hooves into a tap dance worthy of Gene Kelly. He tottered up the high street, not yet decided if he was going to indulge in a goodnight kebab, curry or pizza, and saw two shady looking figures outside *Books 'n' Bobs*.

"There's nothing worth stealing in there," he called out.

"It's us," said Ben.

And it was. Ben and Michael were sitting on folding garden chairs, wrapped in winter coats and blankets, Michael with a clipboard in his hands, Ben with a computer tablet in his.

"We're doing a scientific study," said Michael, a phrase that Clovenhoof typically understood to mean 'spying on naked neighbours with a telescope'. As there were no neighbours, naked or otherwise, in sight, Clovenhoof was nonplussed.

"We're recording local bus traffic," said Ben, "and comparing it to relevant astrological data."

"What?"

"We log the bus and use its registration number to find its place and date of manufacture and draw up the corresponding horoscope."

"You're calculating the horoscopes of *buses*?" said Clovenhoof, who was quite sure he hadn't drunk enough to be making this up himself.

"Yes, Jeremy," said Michael. "We are studying the influence of the stars on the public transport system."

"It's bold thinking, I know," said Ben.

"It's insane," said Jeremy.

"Not at all," said Michael. "We are already starting to see some fascinating patterns. The evening's data points towards some kind of singularity, a critical event occurring within the next two hours."

"One hour and fifty-seven minutes," said Ben, consulting his tablet.

Clovenhoof shook his head.

"I don't know whether to call the men in white coats or just point and laugh."

"People laughed at Einstein's theories," said Michael.

"And his stupid hair," agreed Clovenhoof.

"We'll see who's laughing in one hour and... fifty-six minutes time."

Clovenhoof reckoned he could spin out a curry to last

that long.

"You're on," he said and walked away, pointing and laughing at them for good measure.

THE BOUNCER who saw them to the door was the clichéd embodiment of bouncers everywhere: broader than he was tall with a shaved head and a face that only a mother could love. He was also, Nerys decided, a lovely man.

"I totally understand," he said as he ushered them to the pavement and hailed them a cab. "Some people can be really cruel."

"They were," said Jayne, who in her heels towered over the man.

"And I'm guessing you two haven't come out like this for a while."

Nerys nodded.

"We just wanted to have a good night out and meet some men."

"Course you do. And you want to meet the *right* kind of men."

"That's exactly what we want to do," said Jayne.

"After you've made all this effort with your..." He gestured to them, head to toe. "I bet it's quite a transformation from your regular look."

"It is," Nerys agreed. The bouncer's words were so kind and the confrontation with the men so shocking that Nerys felt like having a little cry.

"I know the right bar for two *ladies* such as yourselves," said the bouncer.

The bouncer spoke to the taxi driver as Nerys and Jayne climbed into the back of the black cab. Five minutes later, the taxi pulled up outside a neon-festooned building on Hurst Street. Nerys paid the fare and led the way inside.

She instantly saw that this was much more her kind of place. There was old school dance music playing, there were actually people dancing, unselfconsciously and flamboyantly, and, best of all, there was a two for one cocktail offer on.

They grabbed stools at the bar and ordered a pair of margaritas.

"Right," she said with some determination. "Round two."

Jayne nodded in emphatic agreement.

"The manhunt is on."

They scanned the bar's patrons. There was a good mixture of age ranges, Nerys noted. It had perhaps been a mistake to go for younger men first off.

"Some handsome fellers," she said.

"Smartly dressed," Jayne agreed.

"I do like a man who takes pride in his appearance."

"Oh, I'm more of a rough and ready type. Although I wouldn't say no to a man with a few muscles."

"A few of them in here."

"Mmmm." Jayne sipped her margarita. "And the women here have really gone to town with their outfits."

"Very elegant," said Nerys.

"And tall."

"Aren't they just?" Nerys looked closer. "And with

surprisingly large hands..."

Jayne was silent for a while.

"Nerys?" she said, in a quiet voice, as though she was trying not to spook the local wildlife.

"Yes?" said Nerys equally quietly.

"Did that bouncer think we were transsexual men?"

"I think he did."

"What do we do?"

"I don't know."

MICHAEL PEERED over Ben's shoulder at the flow of graph data on the tablet screen.

"I didn't expect to see such positive results in such a short time span," he said.

"I'm sure there's an explanation," said Ben. "I can't believe that last bus was three minutes late because it was a Capricorn."

"I wonder if the results would be confirmed further if we considered the numerological significance of it being a number 66A bus."

"Next you're going to suggest we read its palm by studying its tyre treads."

"Ooh, good idea," said Michael. "Whatever the case, the confluence of patterns still indicates that we will reach a critical juncture just before midnight."

"One hour and twenty minutes," noted Ben.

NERYS CAME STAGGERING up to the bar and lunged for the cocktail Jane had ordered her. They had worked through the two for one cocktail list and were now on pina coladas.

"That's five for me," gasped Nerys.

"Five?" said Jayne.

"I just danced with Honey over there." She waved a hand in the general direction of the dance floor. "He works in recruitment too. We have a lot in common."

"Dress size for one thing," said Jayne squinting.

"What's your score then?" said Nerys.

"Seven."

"Seven?"

"I just met up with..." She closed her eyes to remember. "Donna and Lotta. Two at once."

"You slut."

"I know!" she laughed.

"There you are!" chorused a pair of voices.

Jayne spun round on her stool.

"Donna, Lotta, this is Nerys."

Nerys accepted an air kiss from Donna and waved at Lotta.

"I like your shoes," she said to Donna.

"Thank you," gushed Donna. "Loving the boobs," she added, giving Nerys's breasts an admiring squeeze.

"Are we dancing or what?" said Lotta.

"Dancing!" said Nerys.

"You do know," said Jayne, "that if we drink every cocktail on the menu, we get free Carmen Miranda hats?"

"Brilliant!" said Nerys with the kind of enthusiasm that only the drunk or truly happy could muster.

CLOVENHOOF STEPPED out of the Karma Lounge and loosened his belt.

A burning hot curry was a triple pleasure, particularly if the chef could be convinced to add a few more chillies to the Tindaloo. It was food and food was always good but, on top of that, the spicy heat was a faint and nostalgic reminder of the Old Place. It was true that no amount of curry could transform his stomach into a Lake of Fire but it was enough to bring a tear of remembrance to his eye. The third pleasure would come at some point the following day when he would be feeling the heat in a completely separate part of his anatomy and he would transform his toilet into a Pit of Unholy Stench.

Absently whistling the tune *Ring of Fire*, Clovenhoof consulted his watch and headed off down the high street. However, his journey and his Johnny Cash rendition were interrupted by sounds from an alley between two shops.

"You've got to make it bigger," said a small voice.

"I don't think wolves eat pepperoni," said a second.

The voices were somewhat familiar and Clovenhoof stepped into the alley.

Three small boys with what appeared to be spears in their hands were squabbling over a large rope snare they had laid on the ground.

"Spartacus Wilson, is that you?" he said.

"Move along, mate, or I'll be forced to stick you one," said Spartacus, waving his bamboo cane spear.

"It's Kaa," said Jefri.

"You know," said Clovenhoof. "I don't think you're going to catch a wolf in Boldmere."

"Not with pepperoni," said Kenzie with the tone of the wearily righteous.

"I'm all for juvenile delinquency," said Clovenhoof, "but don't you have beds to be in right now?"

"It's not a school night," said Spartacus.

"It's nearly midnight."

"Wolf catching time. There should be a full moon."

"You want to catch a werewolf?"

Spartacus punched Kenzie in the arm.

"You see! Mr Kaa thinks we can catch a werewolf."

"Hey," said Jefri. "Are you going to show us that dead body or what?"

"What?"

"You said you would. Cub leaders aren't allowed to lie."

"I didn't say I would."

Spartacus angled his wickedly sharp bamboo at Clovenhoof.

"My pointy friend says you will."

NERYS, on an upward crest in the rolling seas of her drunkenness, peered out of the bus window.

"I think we're in Erdington. Nearly there."

She adjusted her huge fruit-laden hat.

"We've had a lot of fun tonight," she said.

"We have!" said Jayne. "That was the most magical night ever."

"And the girls were so lovely."

"They were!"

They sat in silence for time, during which Nerys mostly thought about not throwing up. There was a strange haze over her right eye and, for a time, she feared she had finally made herself blind with alcohol. She then realised that one of her false eyelashes had come lose. She pulled it off and, for want of a better place to put it, stuck it on her cheek.

Jayne, without preamble or warning, burst into tears. It was perhaps a good thing that the upper deck of the 66A bus was empty or else she might have startled the passengers.

"Oh love!" said Nerys, patting her sister's back. "What is it?"

Jayne blubbed something lengthy and incoherent. She waved at her back.

"My bra's killing me," she said.

"Is that all?" said Nerys and slipped her hands under Jayne's dress to unhook the bra.

Jayne shook her head.

"I don't want to leave Birmingham."

"Who's making you leave?" said Nerys.

"I'm going to have to go home eventually, aren't I?"

Nerys shrugged.

Jayne sniffed and wiped her eyes and nose with her fingertips, spreading smeary clumps of glittery make up all over her face.

"I'm a fool. Do you know what I thought?"

"What?"

"I thought I'd meet a man tonight and that'd be it."

"It?"

"He'd sweep me off my feet, or I'd sweep him off his, and we'd be together. And he would be my excuse to leave home."

"You don't need a man to leave home."

"It'd help," sniffed Jayne.

"There are lots of men out there."

"Really?"

"I'm sure," said Nerys doubtfully.

"I just want one."

"You'll find one."

"Says who?"

Jayne shook her head again, dislodging a bunch of grapes from her hat so that they dangled over her forehead like unsightly growths.

"I'm going to find a man tonight."

"Tonight is over."

"The first man I see when I get off this bus," said Jayne emphatically.

Nerys looked at Jayne's smeared make-up and collapsing hat.

"If the first man you meet turns out to be Jeremy Clovenhoof I am *not* coming to the wedding," she said.

EVERY TIME CLOVENHOOF SLOWED, one of the cubs jabbed him in the back with a spear.

"Ow. That hurts."

"The sooner you show us a body the sooner we stop," said Jefri.

"Do you treat all your cub leaders like this?"

"That's why Akela Angela had to take a holiday."

They were halfway down the high street, a five minute walk from Buford's Funeral Directors. Clovenhoof had no idea what the savage little cubs expected him to do once they got there. The place was locked up for the night and he didn't have any keys.

"You're going to get in a lot of trouble for this," he told them.

"Shut up and keep walking," said Spartacus.

"I could take those spears off you right now," he said, which was a lie because he had already tried and failed.

Kenzie poked him in the bum to remind him of that fact.

"Ow. I should put you over my knee," he growled.

"That's child abuse."

"We'll tell the police that you tried to touch us."

He sighed heavily and turned round to face them.

"Listen, lads. You don't want to see a dead body. They're a grisly mess of flesh and bones."

"Cool," said Jefri.

"Most people can't bear to look at them."

"Not us though," said Kenzie, although there was an edge of false bravado in his voice.

"Some of them are an absolute state. You know, the car crash victims, the freak accidents. Some of them we have to stitch back together, bit by bit, like Frankenstein's monster."

"Bring it on," said Jefri.

"And they say some of the dead come to life in the middle of the night, to feast on the living. Fancy a bit of that, do you?"

"They don't, do they?" said Jefri, a little nervously.

"Look, mate," said Spartacus, "I've seen *The Human Centipede*. There's nothing you can show me that'll frighten me."

"Oh, I think we'll have a few surprises lined up for you in the Old Place then," muttered Clovenhoof and continued unhappily down the high street.

"What's this?" called Ben's voice from ahead.

Clovenhoof looked up. They were nearing the second hand bookshop and the pathetic bus-watching camp. Of course, thought Clovenhoof, these two would be able to reason with the young hooligans.

He saw that Ben's comments weren't directed at him but in the opposite direction, towards an oncoming bus. Clovenhoof looked at his watch. Nearly midnight.

"Right," he said, pressing onward. "See pathetic bus experiment. Point and laugh. Get rid of cubs. Bed."

"This is definitely it," said Michael, eyes on the computer tablet data.

"What are they doing?" said Kenzie.

"Perv alert," Spartacus warned his friends.

They followed closely behind Clovenhoof as the 66A bus drew up to the bus stop.

"It's a Sagittarius bus, just as predicted," said Ben and then saw Clovenhoof and his unwanted entourage. "Hello, boys. Out a little late, aren't we?"

"Shut it, Baghera," said Spartacus. "Kaa is taking us to see a dead body."

"Is he now?" said Michael.

"He says the dead come to life at night," said Jefri, almost pleading with someone, anyone, to tell him it wasn't true.

"I don't want anyone to eat me," said Kenzie and then jumped as the bus doors hissed open.

Two tall shambling figures lurched from the bus. The foremost one looked like the Joker, that was if the Joker had just head-butted a bowl of fruit.

"There's one," it slurred and lurched at Ben. It wrapped its arms around him, its red-smeared mouth open wide.

"Zombies!" screamed Jefri as the creature (which was wearing an overly revealing pink dress) thrust its lips against Ben's.

There was a clatter of bamboo spears falling to the ground and a cry of "Don't eat me!" from the rapidly departing Kenzie.

Michael caught the tablet computer as it fell from Ben's hands.

The second shambler, which Clovenhoof hesitantly recognised as Nerys, gave him a penetrating and drunken stare.

"What are you lot doing here?"

"Incredible data," said Michael, staring at the tablet screen, "but what does it mean?"

Ben grunted in a bid to come up for air but Jayne had a snogging death-grip on him.

"Right," said Nerys to Clovenhoof, "do I look a man in drag?"

Clovenhoof's gave her an appraising look.

"Most men in drag look better than that," he said, "even the ones with beards."

ST CADFAN'S

Abbot Ambrose picked up Barry the peacock and positioned him in his lap, thus signifying that the meeting had begun.

Novice Stephen kept minutes, writing the date and underlining it with a little ruler. Barry's ball-bearing eyes watched every movement of his hands. Stephen knew that all animals were part of God's glorious creation but Stephen reckoned there was more than a soupçon of the devil's handiwork in that particular bird.

"I have inspected the damaged masonry in the corridor between the dormitory and the almonry," said the abbot. "The temporary repairs are holding but proper reconstruction must begin soon."

Stephen noted down the abbot's words verbatim, only added silently in his own head that the temporary repairs were not only shoddy but also downright dangerous. Half a dozen battens of two-by-four currently supported several tonnes of stonework in that section of the monastery. Most of the battens had bowed like bananas under the weight and there was still a gaping hole in the wall that let in the bitter winds and occasional peacock. The two dozen brothers who slept in the dormitory avoided the corridor whenever they could and, when they couldn't, they dashed through it as though their very lives were under threat.

"Your assessment, Brother Sebastian?" said the abbot.

The procurator, who Stephen was given to understand had come to the monastic life after a career as something big, important and possibly immoral in the world of finance, drew his chair closer to the table and cleared his throat.

"A brick and mortar repair would run to thousands of pounds," he said. "To replace the damaged stonework like-for-like would involve the employment of specialist craftsmen and cost tens of thousands of pounds. Our budget pays for general upkeep and for our sustenance. We do not have access to the kind of funds required. In short, we need to make some money, and quickly."

"A cake sale?" suggested Brother Manfred. "Or a jumble sale? People always enjoy looking through the bric and the brac."

"Tens of thousands of pounds," repeated Sebastian pointedly.

"Perhaps you have some better ideas?" said Manfred.

"Indeed I do." He reached down to his side and brought up a presentation board and placed it on the table while he stood up to do his pitch to the other monks. The presentation board had an image of a food tin on it.

"Bardsey Pilchards?" read Novice Stephen.

Brother Sebastian nodded.

"You will recall that we were able to net some sardines in the rowboat last year."

"I recall getting soaked and chased about the boat by a very angry lobster," muttered Stephen.

"Your trivial travails are not relevant here, Novice Trevor," said the abbot.

"Novice Stephen, Father Abbot," Stephen meekly corrected him.

"What did I say?"

"Trevor."

"And you are?"

"Stephen."

"I'm sure I said Stephen."

"If I may interject," said Brother Manfred, "I also recall our pilchard harvest well. If memory serves me as it should, our entire catch provided only enough to do a round of pilchards on toast for every brother at St Cadfan's."

"And what delicious pilchards they were," agreed Sebastian enthusiastically.

"But that same catch would fill maybe eight tins, maybe nine. How much money would nine tins of pilchards bring in?"

"Ah," said Sebastian, rubbing his hands together gleefully. "Here's the clever bit. I was reminded of the example of holy water."

"Holy water?" said the abbot.

"It is a well-established principle that if I were to add a drop of holy water to a barrel of unsanctified water it would become a barrel of holy water."

"Yes?"

"Now I happen to know a Portuguese trawlerman who can deliver pilchards in bulk to the island. Surely, if we take our own Bardsey pilchards and add them to his haul then all of the pilchards have become 'Bardsey' pilchards."

The assembled monks thought on this for a while. Although, what exactly the prior was thinking about was anyone's guess.

"I think there are philosophical and theological flaws in your argument," said the abbot.

"Not to mention moral and legal ones," added Manfred not unkindly.

"Fair enough," said Sebastian, who seemed at very much at home with both immoral business concepts and having them shot down by the more scrupulous. "Idea two. Clothes. We already make our own habits. Brother Manfred has a loom. We go into business selling designer clothing items."

"*Brother Manfred*," cut in the refectorian, "is already busy enough, thank you very much. I am not a complainer but I am not only the cook, the tailor and the maker of fine embroidery but Father Abbot has also given me the job of making the restorative repairs to the tapestries."

"I am not doubting the vital work you already do," said Sebastian, "but surely you could train up some of the brothers to-"

"No, brother. I am deep to the knees in the restoration of a much faded and moth-munched tapestries of St Veracius and St Seneca and I simply cannot find the right shade of white for the clouds."

"Er, surely there's only one shade of white," said Novice Stephen. "It's white, isn't it?"

"You see?" said Manfred in a slightly strangled voice. "How can I make a clothier out of men who spout such nonsense?"

"Okay!" said Sebastian, hands raised in defeat. "Idea three."

He brought onto the table an item wrapped in a velvet cloth. Barry leant in close and swivelled an eyeball toward it.

"We have few abundant resources on the island," he said. "We need to make use of what we have."

Sebastian unwrapped the velvet cloth to reveal a cracked, weathered and mostly toothless human jawbone. Novice Stephen put a hand to his mouth and drew his chair back a distance from the table.

"Is it real?" he asked.

"Dug it up yesterday," nodded Sebastian.

Brother Manfred frowned.

"Please forgive me when you prove me wrong, but is there a large demand for bits of skeletons?"

Sebastian gave him a superior look.

"There is an enormous demand for the skeletal remains of saints. The informal trade of relics is worth several million pounds worldwide."

The abbot made a contemplative noise and leaned forward, using Barry as an elbow rest. The peacock chirped unhappily but did not resist.

"Two questions, brother," he said with beatific calmness. "First, how do we know that is the jaw of saint?"

"This is the island of twenty thousand saints, Father

Abbot. The odds of it being one of the twenty thousand are good. We can put that in the small print."

"Ah," nodded the abbot, "and, secondly, by 'informal trade' you mean.,,?"

"The black market?" suggested Stephen.

"The protocols for the sale of such items are vague," said Sebastian.

"Oh?" said the abbot in mock surprise. "Not clearly outlined by the papacy then?"

"There might be certain documents –"

"Which you need to read carefully before you draw the wrong kind of attention to our small community."

"It seems such a shame," said Sebastian, rewrapping and removing the jawbone before flopping dejectedly into his seat. "We have few natural resources of value on the island that we can turn a profit from."

"What about the fruit?" said Novice Stephen.

"What about it?" said Sebastian.

"The Bardsey apple tree is unique. So said that Royal Horticultural fellow –"

"Who I did not invite to inspect it," said the abbot gruffly.

"But if it's unique... Rarity has its own value. Think of Beluga caviar."

"Matsutake mushrooms," said Manfred.

"White truffles," said Sebastian, a smile returning to his face.

"No," said the abbot, a warning note in his voice. "I don't think our apple pies are going to make the same kind of money."

"I don't know," said Sebastian. "Think how much Prince Charles charges for his duchy biscuits."

"It's not just apple pies," said Stephen. "We could make sauces, jams, dried fruit mix."

"I don't think so," said the abbot.

"Or drink," suggested Sebastian. "How about Bardsey cider? Now that has a nice ring to it."

"We shouldn't sell the fruit," said the abbot.

"Or schnapps!" exclaimed Manfred with a sudden delight. "My grandfather showed me how to build a still."

"I said, no!" shouted the abbot, rising to his feet and spilling Barry to the floor in an undignified mass of iridescent feathers. "I forbid it!"

Three pairs of eyes stared silently and fearfully at the furious abbot. The prior's eyes seemed to be focussed on a patch of unremarkable brickwork and his emotional state was unreadable.

Abbot Ambrose looked at each of the younger monks in turn, his chest heaving with anger.

"I forbid it," he said in a quieter, shaking voice. "Vengeance seven times over for anyone who defies me on this matter. The apples are for private consumption by the brothers only."

Novice Stephen couldn't actually recall the last time that their home-grown apples had featured in the refectory menu but said nothing.

"We apologise," said Brother Manfred, bowing his head. "We did not mean to offend or upset you."

"Of course, you didn't," said the abbot with a wave of his

hand as he sat down. "My passions got the better of me. Continue."

"I have no more moneymaking ideas," said Sebastian.

"I have one more," said Stephen.

The abbot's stony expression spoke volumes. It quite clearly said, "I'm listening, Novice Stephen, but if this is a stupid or infuriating idea it will be your bones that are sold on the black market." The expression was so clearly readable that it had punctuation and everything.

"The monastery, Father Abbot," said Stephen.

"What about it?"

"It's a beautiful old building. People love beautiful old buildings."

"We already have daytrippers visit us," said Sebastian.

"But what if they stayed over?"

"You mean turn St Cadfan's into a guesthouse?"

Stephen twirled his pen.

"I was thinking a bit more upmarket. We could host functions, conferences, weddings even."

"Weddings," said Manfred. "I like weddings."

"We'd be doing the Lord's work," agreed Sebastian.

"And people would come here to get married?" said the abbot doubtfully. "We're a bit remote, aren't we?"

"Not remote," said Sebastian shrewdly. "Exclusive."

The abbot nodded slowly.

"It's not a terrible idea, Novice Trevor."

"Thank you, Father Abbot," said Stephen and didn't bother to correct him.

4

IN WHICH MICHAEL'S WORLD GETS COMPLICATED

Michael added *Can cats cure cancer?* to the pile of books that provided him with no helpful data and wandered into the kitchen.

"Little G, what's the progress of the tests you're running against the re-modelled algorithm?" he called as he rummaged through the fridge for a snack.

"Testing is complete, Michael," the computer replied, its red light swaying from side to side as it spoke. "Results indicate that the changes result in improved accuracy."

"What's the estimated accuracy now?" Michael asked, taking a fig and nibbling at it thoughtfully.

"Accuracy of predictions is now estimated at ninety eight point seven percent," said Little G. "Michael, you will need more figs in the next two days, would you like me to order some more?"

"Yes please. Now, what is the progress on uploading of the source material?"

"All identified source texts are catalogued. Input from trending topics on social media is scheduled to update twice a day, and all known prediction methodologies are analysed and programmed."

Michael checked off a selection on his fingers.

"You've catalogued key messages from the Bible, the Qur'an, the Torah, the I-Ching, Dear Deirdre and Lolcats?"

"Yes Michael. The application is now ready for compilation. Would you like to make it available for sharing?"

"I think that would be the Christian thing to do, yes."

"What name and icon you would like for your application?"

"Oh," said Michael, thinking for a moment. "I suppose it does need a name. Call it 'G-sez', Little G. The icon should be a small grey teddy bear, of course. Capture this image from the webcam and show it to me as a vector image."

The phone rang and Michael answered it on hands-free.

"Mr Michaels? It's Superuser Appliances here."

"Hello, Superuser Appliances," said Michael.

"I'm afraid there's been a problem with your fridge."

Michael, bear in hand, peered at the fridge through the open kitchen door.

"No problem," he said. "It's been a delight. It knew I was running out of figs."

"A problem with the payment," said Superuser Appliances.

"Oh," said Michael. "I authorised the debit instruction from my bank over a week ago, it should have gone through by now."

Superuser Appliances made a reproachful noise.

"It seems there were insufficient funds to complete the transaction."

"Oh, dear."

"You will need to make the payment to us in the next seven days or we'll have to take the fridge back."

Michael felt a sudden and surprising constriction in his chest. The intelligent fridge was the crowning touch to his flat. He had spent all of last night asking it questions about its contents hoping to catch it out. It even knew when his cheese was out of date.

"I understand," he said, sadly, and ended the call.

"You do have insufficient funds in your bank account, Michael," offered Little G.

"And no more money until next month?"

"I could trace the source of your monthly payments, Michael."

"No," said the archangel. "No, let me sort this out myself."

There was a text message on his phone. It was from Darren.

Cub trip to Birmingham Museum tomorrow. Can I drive?

Michael groaned at the prospect of taking the cubs into the wider world. He had his perfect oasis of automated control and calm purity in his flat. The rest of the world was so messy and brutal.

"Little G, I need some guidance for the coming week. Can you please issue me with a G-sez message?"

"Yes Michael. The frequency of your regular updates is currently set to daily, but you can make an ad-hoc request at any time. The text will be sent to your phone for later reference." Little G adopted a more formal and patrician tone. "*G-sez: When I was a child, I spoke like a child, I thought like a child, I reasoned like a child. When I became a man, I gave up childish ways.*"

Michael pondered the quotation for a moment. It seemed unhelpful, as the cubs clearly *were* children, and would remain so for the duration of the museum visit. Perhaps there was a more abstract meaning that eluded him for the moment. He decided to go and make sure that Ben and Clovenhoof would be on hand to assist with the cubs.

"Assume power-saving mode, Little G. I need to go out."

JAYNE ENTERED *Books n Bobs* and gave Ben a small wave. She saw him redden as he looked up.

Ben made a strangled noise that might have been "Hello."

"Hi," she said.

"Haven't seen you since - er, a couple of days," he stammered. Ben had been standing behind the counter when she entered. Strange how it seemed as though he was even *more* behind the counter now, as a barrier between them.

"I'm meeting Nerys at the solicitors at half past. We want to see if they can make head or tail of this will of Molly's."

"Ah," he said. "Time for a cup of tea?"

She nodded gratefully and Ben all but fled into the back room.

"Actually, I came to apologise," she called out to him.

"Yes?" came the reply.

"I was very drunk."

There was no reply.

Jayne tried not to let the silence weigh down on her. She busied herself reshuffling some hardback travel books on a shelf, bringing a luscious photographic guide to Cambodia to the front. Ben reappeared with two mugs.

"A beautiful country," said Jayne, indicating the guide book.

"You've been."

"Not yet." Jayne approached the counter. "Look, I was very badly behaved the other night."

Ben gave her an unconvincing look of confusion.

"Really? I don't remember…"

"The, um, kiss. Well, snog."

Ben waved an overly dismissive hand.

"Oh, that? Don't worry about it. I mean, it wasn't horrible or anything."

"No?"

Ben clearly didn't realise he was going to be asked for a follow up comment.

"It was sort of nice," he said.

"Sort of nice?" Jayne asked, head on one side.

Ben mouthed wordlessly, and looked down at his tea.

"Very nice," he mumbled, almost to himself. He coughed and Jayne thought he gathered himself a little. "Of course it was inappropriate and unexpected, but I do feel that I should tell you that it was most enjoyable. Or would have been, if the circumstances were different, I mean."

"Yes," said Jayne. "I know exactly what you mean. If the

circumstances were different I might find you..." Jayne's mind went into freefall. She had plunged into a sentence and couldn't see any way out of it. "Find you quite attractive and snog you when I was sober."

They both stared into their cups of tea for a few minutes, concentrating hard on blowing them cool. Jayne shifted in her seat, keen to dispel the fog of unintended intimacy that had descended. Ben was such a sweet man, in a rumpled, un-ironed sort of way.

"So, by way of an apology, I wanted to do something."

"Yes?"

"A drink or a meal or something," she said. "Is that too much like a date?"

"Is it?"

"I don't want to make things any more awkward, or end up accidentally snogging you again."

"No, God. Definitely no more accidental snogging. Any snogging should be... deliberate and purposeful?"

Ben's phone beeped and he turned away to look at it, evidently relieved to be excused from the conversation for a moment.

Indeed, the conversation wasn't exactly going how Jayne had envisaged. She had pictured a swift apology, an invitation out to dinner, the resumption of a possible friendship. But, here, she seemed to have upset and disturbed Ben more thoroughly than ever before. However, he had said the snog was 'very nice' and a little Jayne deep down inside her was doing a celebration dance.

How about the museum?" said Ben.

"Museum?"

"And art gallery in the city centre," Ben said. "Tomorrow. I'm going there anyway, apparently."

"Oh," she said and then thought on it. "Yes, that'd be lovely. I'd really like to see the city centre. The more cultured and less alcoholic part anyway."

"Excellent. Then it's a date."

"A date?"

"On the calendar."

"Absolutely."

MICHAEL WALKED DOWN to Buford's Funeral Directors and found Clovenhoof sitting on a low wall enjoying a huge sauce-spattered burger.

"Glad I've caught you at lunch," Michael said. "There's a cubs trip tomorrow to the museum and art gallery."

"I'll be ready for them this time."

"Oh, yes?"

"Bought myself a stab vest and a can of pepper spray on-line."

"Good. Well, you'll need to make sure you're up early without a hangover."

"Oh, I never get a hangover," said Clovenhoof. "I just like to lie in bed watching porn at the weekend, like anyone else."

He took a bite from his burger and chomped noisily on it.

"What is that thing?" Michael asked, wrinkling his nose. "It smells horrible."

"It's a multi-burger."

"Which is?"

"My own invention," said Clovenhoof proudly. "If you ask for it, you can have one of everything on the menu in a single burger."

"Disgusting."

Clovenhoof shrugged.

"Handy for when you can't remember what's lunch and what's part of a client. Down the hatch!"

Michael recoiled, to Clovenhoof's obvious delight.

"How can you treat your body that way?" he asked.

Clovenhoof made a show of pulling out one of the more questionable pieces of meat and holding it up to the light to examine it with a puzzled look on his face. He shrugged and popped it into his mouth.

"What way?" he said. "The thing is with this body, it just keeps on going. I threw myself off a building once and that couldn't hurt it."

"I remember."

"I've been in a house fire."

"Two."

"Two. I've been run over by a lorry, put fireworks down my pants and been beaten savagely with a zimmer frame."

"That was a busy day."

"So I reckon burgers don't stand much of a chance."

He smacked his lips with pleasure. Then he eyed Michael critically and leaned over to poke his stomach with a finger covered in grease.

"Whereas you, Michael, are getting a pot belly," he said.

"What?" said Michael looking down at the ugly smear on his shirt.

"Too much angel cake, my feathered friend," Clovenhoof

stood up. "Right back to work. Oh, and I'm driving the minibus on Saturday, right?"

"No, I've promised Darren he can do it."

"What?"

"He does at least know how to drive."

"Hang on, you've seen me on Grand Theft Auto. I'm a driving genius."

Michael shook his head.

"We're taking the cubs to the museum, Jeremy. If I ever need anyone to cruise round, picking up prostitutes and getting into car chases with the police, I'll ask you."

"I will hold you to that," Clovenhoof pouted and dragged himself back into the funeral parlour, grumbling as he went.

Michael rolled his eyes. He turned and made his way back up the high street, pulling in his stomach as he walked. Much as he wanted to ignore Clovenhoof's taunts, he suspected that there might be a grain of truth in what he said. If his body was a temple and God's spirit dwelled in him, was he failing to honour and maintain it as he should? Or was he becoming like St Michael's church, a sagging, flabby biscuit-filled temple that the Almighty would be ashamed to call home?

He stopped outside the health and fitness centre on the high street.

"I'm here to help you reach your goals, whatever they are," said the speech bubble above the smiling, athletic man on the poster in the window.

"Really?" said Michael, as much to himself and the Almighty as to the toothsome athlete.

AN HOUR LATER, he was signed up for a free trial in the gym. Getting into his shorts and vest in the changing rooms also gave Michael an opportunity to do a bit of covert genitalia comparison with the other men in there. He was sure Clovenhoof would have decried such behaviour as perverse but Michael felt that a spot of surreptitious cock-watching only furthered his understanding of his own body.

In the gym, he was given a beginners plan for the exercise apparatus. The cycling machines were a dream, sleek works of grey and steel with more displays and computer processing power than the flight deck of a jumbo jet.

"The technology is truly amazing," said Michael to the cyclist next to him.

The fresh-face young man with close cropped hair leaned over.

"You're not using all of the features," he said, pointing at some buttons in front of Michael. "You can use these function buttons to simulate different gradients."

"Ooh. That's nice."

"I'm currently cycling up Mount Kilimanjaro."

"Are you?"

Michael looked at the man's screen and the cartoon representation of a mountain bike riding up a dirt trail.

"I thought about getting a bicycle once," said Michael. "I mean, a real one. For the exercise. Good for the environment and all that too."

"But you didn't?"

"They're just so... messy looking."

"And dangerous," the young man chipped in. "Don't forget dangerous."

"But this, this is the perfect solution. It's like real cycling only more organised."

"And safer."

"Safer, indeed."

The young man stopped pedalling and mopped his brow with a small towel.

"Have you got to the top already?" asked Michael.

The young man jumped down. He was more than a few inches shorter than Michael. A little squat, compact. A gymnast's build.

"Nah," he said. "Can only do so much cardiovascular. I'm more of an anaerobic man."

Michael looked at the young man's upper arm muscles, straining at the seams of his lycra top.

"I can see that," said Michael. "Lovely muscle tone."

"Thanks, mate. All compliments gratefully received. You do much weight training?"

Michael looked across at the weights machines.

"I've not done that part of the induction."

"You mean you've never..?" The short man looked him up and down. "You've already got the build for it. It would be criminal to waste that body on just bikes and treadmills. I can give you the guided tour."

Michael let himself be sat down at a leg press machine and the young man stood over him, explaining the principal muscles the machine worked on, the various settings and the method for safe operation. The man's stomach muscles, a clearly defined six-pack of toned flesh, were right in Michael's eye line.

If the body was God's temple then this young specimen was a far holier shrine than Michael's neglected frame. Michael found himself thinking of a small Corsican chapel he had manifested in back in, oh, it must have been the seventh century if not earlier. Staring at those beautiful, smooth muscles put Michael in mind of the bevelled edges of the chapel altar, the perfect curves with a deliciously heavenly sheen on them.

"I said, 'What's yours?'"

Michael tore his gaze from the beautiful torso.

"I'm sorry?"

"I'm Andy," said the man.

"Michael," said Michael. "I just drifted off somewhere for a moment."

"Somewhere nice, I hope," said Andy.

NERYS SMILED as Jayne gave a twirl in a modest dress.

"Do I look demure and apologetic?" she asked Nerys.

"I'm not sure what that would look like," said Nerys.

"Sort of the opposite of '*Take me now, big boy*.'"

"To be honest, I think that '*Take me now*' would be ambitious given that you're going to the museum," said Nerys, "unless you think he's going to ravish you amongst the Flemish Masters."

Jayne looked at herself critically in the fireplace mirror.

"You look great," Nerys assured her. "Very demure, very apologetic."

"Are you sure?"

"Oh, just go. You're going to miss your minibus."

As they went downstairs, they found Michael and Clovenhoof on the landing. Clovenhoof was wearing an appalling pair of shorts, while Michael was immaculate in white linen trousers.

"Jeremy, what are those things all over your shorts?" Nerys asked.

"Badges. Proper cub badges," Clovenhoof announced with some pride.

"Did you earn them?" she asked.

"Not in the normal way. I passed a special initiative test to get these," he said.

"He means he stole the key to the badge store," said Michael wearily.

"Still, I'm impressed that you sewed them all on," said Jayne, peering down at them.

"Sewing? Nah. Staplers all the way. Much more practical."

Ben stepped out of his flat. He beamed at them all, and Clovenhoof gave a low whistle.

"A shirt!" exclaimed Clovenhoof. "With buttons and shit."

"You've seen me in a shirt before," said Ben. "I own several shirts."

"I think we've seen you naked more times than we've seen you in a shirt," said Nerys.

"You have not!"

Clovenhoof looked up in thought, apparently counting.

"She's right," he said. "Even counting today. More cocks than collars."

"Technically that's a polo shirt," said Nerys, "not a proper shirt, but you look very nice, Ben. Demure almost."

She nudged Jayne in the ribs and watched her cheeks redden.

NERYS WALKED with them up to St Michael's church, where the minibus was already filled with cubs, its windows smeared with the spray of fizzy drinks and unidentifiable flotsam. The only clean parts of the windows were the penis drawings that were being busily applied from inside and which Clovenhoof was enthusiastically appraising, giving a special thumbs up to any that had been given the extra detail of hair or dotted wee lines.

The St Michael's vicar, Zack, was there to see them off. Michael brandished a clipboard and, peering into the chaos within the minibus, ticked off the names.

Nerys whispered into Jayne's ear.

"Well, I don't think you need to worry about snogging Ben during any unguarded moments. You'll do well to make it back alive by the looks of this lot."

"I'm sure it's going to be loads of fun," said Jayne stiffly, and climbed aboard the minibus, followed by Ben, Michael and Clovenhoof.

The doors slammed shut, and everyone took their seats.

Nerys waved at the departing minibus.

"When are you expecting the regular cub leader to return?" she asked Reverend Zack.

"We're not at all sure," he replied, stroking his chin. "Angela's run into a spot of bother on her holiday."

"Oh. Lost her luggage?"

"Kidnapped by rebels, I believe. It can happen in some countries."

"It's been known to happen to day trippers to Wales," she replied as her phone began to ring.

"I'm sure it will sort itself out," said Reverend Zack with brittle hopefulness.

"Excuse me," she said as she answered the phone. "It's the solicitor. I'm expecting some good news."

THE MINIBUS REACHED the city centre without running a single light, forcing another vehicle off the road, engaging in a high speed pursuit with the police or stopping to pick up a single prostitute. All this, despite Clovenhoof offering to 'pop a cop in the ass' and pointing out several women who he suspected might be hookers.

Much to Michael's relief, Darren pulled up in Edmund Street behind the Birmingham Museum and Art Gallery safely and in one piece.

"We'll unload here and you can go and find somewhere to park," Michael told Darren.

Michael hopped out onto the pavement, clipboard at the ready.

"Cubs will form an orderly line, so that we don't get lost or separated. I will be at the head of the line and Kaa will be at the rear."

"Never a pitchfork to hand when you want one," said Clovenhoof, ambling into position.

The cubs poured off the minibus, excited to be somewhere new, but were eventually persuaded to form a line by Michael's refusal to move on until they did.

"Baghera Ben, will you give each of the cubs a worksheet please?" asked Michael. "These worksheets have a list of questions that you need to answer to get your hobbies badge, so make sure you read through them carefully before you get inside."

"What did you do for your hobbies badge, Kaa?" asked PJ, looking at Clovenhoof's shorts.

"He's too old to get cubs badges," said Spartacus. "He just gets to take them because he's a grown-up and they can break rules whenever they want.

"That's a vicious accusation and I resent it," said Clovenhoof. "I break rules because I'm good at it. Most grown-ups have no idea. If you do as I say, I might give you a few tips."

They walked across a large square, Michael glancing backwards to be sure that everyone kept in line.

"Nuddy woman, nuddy woman!" yelled Kenzie, pointing at the giant statue of a woman reclining in water.

Michael held up the line so that he could address the group.

"It's a work called 'The River'. It represents the life force, apparently. I'm not sure it isn't a little bit pagan."

"It's not called that!" Spartacus scoffed. "Everyone knows it's called 'The Floozie in the Jacuzzi'."

"It's not the official name of the -" Michael began, but Spartacus had the attention of the other cubs.

"She's not as big as Akela's mom though. His mom's so big that when the doctors diagnosed she had a flesh-wasting disease, she was given twenty years to live."

The cubs all laughed. Michael pursed his lips and walked on.

He steered the crocodile into the museum, and ensured that everyone was present when they reached the top of the stairs. He breathed a sigh of relief and addressed the cubs.

"We'll go at a steady pace as we move through the galleries. You should have plenty of time to look at the paintings and work through your worksheets."

He walked forward, head held high with pride at the beautifully disciplined convoy of boys. He'd been certain that with a firm hand and a carefully structured day, he could turn the rabble into something much easier to handle. The first room they entered was round, high and lined with huge paintings with a domed glass ceiling arching high above a large, striking statue of Lucifer.

Michael closed his eyes and paused for a moment, knowing that Clovenhoof would have something to say about it.

"Well it's in the right place, of course," said Clovenhoof, appearing at his side and gazing up at the bronze statue critically, "the first thing you see when you come in. It's all about making an impression."

Michael rolled his eyes.

"The thing is, it just doesn't really look like me, does it? I mean, I know I have the physique of a racing snake, but look how skinny it is," Clovenhoof walked around the base, looking up, "and what on earth is it doing with its hands? I can't tell if it's supposed to be dancing or making bread."

"Lucifer is warding off the fires of perdition," Michael told him.

"Warming his hands, you mean. But it's a bit girly, isn't it?"

"Oh for Heavens' sake! Only you would complain about such a thing," said Michael. "Anyway, you do know Epstein also created that depiction of our final battle that decorates Coventry Cathedral?"

"What, the one that makes you look like a football hooligan mugging an old lady?" Clovenhoof asked, grinning. "Well then, I guess that makes us even. At least I've got a decent-sized cock on this one."

Michael looked round to be sure that the cubs hadn't overheard Clovenhoof's remark.

"Er, where have the cubs gone?" he asked, swivelling urgently.

"Just there in the corner," said Clovenhoof, absently waving a hand behind him as he gazed up at the statue and thrust forward his own groin to compare.

"This is a round room. There are no corners, you buffoon," said Michael. "They've gone. All of them. Come on, quickly, we need to find them, let's split up."

JAYNE GAZED up at the copper tresses of another pre-Raphaelite heroine.

"So many beautiful paintings Ben," she said. "I bet there aren't this many in Paris, even."

"Well, I think there might be-" started Ben.

"This woman's in loads of them," said Jayne. "She's even more beautiful than my sister, Catherine."

"Elizabeth Siddal," said Ben.

"Who?"

"She was married to Rossetti, which is why she was painted a lot by him and his friends."

"How lovely that you knew that. He must have really loved her," Jayne said, gazing at the picture with a wistful sigh.

"Oh yes. They all loved her. They had her do things like pose for days on end in a bath of cold water. She died quite young and Rossetti slipped a book of poems into the coffin in his grief. It was only years later that he wished he still had them to sell."

"Oh how sad, and by then it was too late."

"No, not really," said Ben. "He had her exhumed so he could get them."

"No! You're pulling my leg, surely?"

"Nope. Gotta watch those romantic types when they run out of money or opium or whatever."

CLOVENHOOF FOUND an interactive area for children and pocketed a fat felt tip pen. He was pleased that the museum encouraged visitors to display their own creativity and thought he might go back there in a little while with the cubs so that they could share their penis drawings with the world. Some of them were rather good, after all. In the meantime, he ambled through the galleries, looking out for pictures that were violent, obscene, or preferably both.

He found the pre-Raphaelite collection rather boring. Pictures of soppy women who looked faintly miserable, as if they realised they'd run out of crispy pancakes and fancied a snack. Inspired by this thought, he used the felt tip to draw a giant speech bubble onto the wall.

'Bring me a crispy pancake and a glass of Lambrini!'

He stepped back and nodded at his handiwork. Now he'd found a way to improve the museum he felt a new sense of purpose. He looked at another picture, which featured a woman whose eyes were closed in anguish. It was a mystery why she looked like that, as there were no clues, apart from the dense text at the side, but who could be bothered to read that? The seated position indicated one obvious cause, so he stepped forward with his felt tip and made a new speech bubble.

'Put the loo roll in the fridge, that curry's a real ring-burner!'

He was on fire. A blind woman with an inquisitive youngster twisting around on her lap got a speech bubble saying 'Mom, I can see the pub from here!'

"Hey, you! You need to stop doing that!"

The voice made him turn around, and he saw a middle-aged woman in a floral dress.

He walked over to her.

"Who put you in charge?" he asked. "I'm just expressing my creativity."

"You're behaving like a common lout. A vandal," she replied. "I'm fetching someone from the staff."

"Hang on," said Clovenhoof. "Before you do, there's something on your face."

She looked momentarily puzzled, and as she paused, Clovenhoof dabbed the felt tip onto the end of her nose, turning it an inky black.

"Well there is now!" he yelled over his shoulder as he ran off, cackling to himself.

JAYNE AND BEN walked through the modern art display area. A large hall was dominated by a massive metal construction. Jayne wondered what it was supposed to be. It resembled the skeleton of a huge dinosaur rendered in steel. The most notable feature was the swarm of small boys wearing green uniforms climbing all over it. Jeremy Clovenhoof was on the floor, trying to convince them to come down.

"There's a place in here where they want penis drawings," he called up to them. "Who else is going to show these people what real art is? Imagine how cross Akela Michael will be if you make a load of cock pictures and we can say that the museum made you do it!"

Spartacus called out from the highest point.

"If they want a picture of a cock, you could use your smart phone to take a selfie."

The cubs laughed and continued to climb. Clovenhoof shifted in impotent annoyance and, Jayne was certain, had completely failed to notice the large tour group file in behind him. Cameras clicked as the Japanese visitors admired the athletic daring of the boys who were balanced twenty feet above the ground.

Clovenhoof assumed his most assertive scoutmaster's stance and bellowed at the cubs.

"Get down from there this minute, you little shits!"

He turned and noticed the tourists for the first time. He didn't miss a beat. He swept a demonstrative arm across the hall.

"...is the name of this installation, which examines the rebellion of youth. Notice the sinuous lines of the structure which is in direct counterpoint to the stumpy ugliness of the little boys who seek to defile it."

Jayne felt a hand on her arm.

"Did I mention that the tea room here is second to none?" whispered Ben.

"Shouldn't we stay to help Jeremy?"

"They have excellent cake."

"I like cake."

MICHAEL FOUND himself back at a painting that he'd passed several times already. Not only had the cubs lost him but also the geography of this place constantly turned him around, folding in on itself like an Escher picture.

Telling himself that he was simply stopping to gather his wits, Michael sat on a bench, wondering why he found this one canvas very compelling. It showed a vigorous young man, perhaps some Greek hero or god, driving a chariot pulled by lions. The lions looked as though they were protesting at being used in this way, but the man prevailed. His assertive muscular stance and radiant charisma had worked on the lions, but Michael realised that it had captivated him as well. The painting glowed with vitality and energy. Something about the taut muscles reminded Michael of that fellow, Andy, from the gym. He wondered who had scrawled the speech bubble at the side of the painting, and added 'good kitties, if you go faster I'll get you a nice gazelle'. He had a good idea who it might have been.

"Stunning, isn't it?"

Michael turned to the side to see who had spoken.

"Andy!"

"Hi. Michael, isn't it?"

"How strange to see you here when I was just..." Michael coughed. "...admiring this painting."

"It's one of my favourites," said Andy. "Apollo, the sun god. He glows, don't you think?"

Michael nodded as they both stared in appreciation.

"You haven't seen a group of cubs, have you?" Michael asked.

"Lion cubs? No those are all fully-"

"No, I mean the miniature boy scout kind."

Andy shook his head.

"Are they with you?"

"Yes," said Michael. "I've been helping out with the cubs, but it's not going all that well to be honest."

"In what way?"

Michael gave it some thought before answering

"Even though I'll never have children of my own, I had

the idea I might influence and develop this group. I have so much to share. Trouble is they're a complete mystery to me."

"Can't really help you there Michael, no experience of kids, and I certainly won't be having any."

"No?"

"No. All you can do is make the best of things in the here and now."

"That reminds me," said Michael, pulling out his phone. "My prediction app said to me *When I was a child, I spoke like a child, I thought like a child, I reasoned like a child. When I became a man, I gave up childish ways.* What do you suppose it meant?"

"Wow, your phone really said that to you?"

"It's just this app I wrote."

Michael took out his phone and opened the G-sez app.

"Impressive," said Andy. "Did you ask it about children?"

"No, it doesn't work that way, you just get a daily prediction," Michael said.

"Hang on," said Andy, taking out his own phone and bringing up the app store. "So it sort of collates all the horoscopes about you in one place."

"Not just horoscopes. It uses any relevant fortune-telling data."

"Just downloading it now," said Andy, fiddling with his own phone.

"It does have an accuracy of ninety eight point seven per cent though."

"You mean it actually tells you your fortune?"

"I guess."

"Wait. Look. You're not charging for it."

"Should I? It's just a little app."

"Oh, you really should, you know. You don't need to ask for a lot, but you should get something back to cover maintenance and so on. People will get disappointed if you don't keep it up to date."

"I suppose you're right," said Michael slowly. "Maybe that would be a good idea. By the way, what was your G-Sez?"

Andy looked at his screen.

"*See, I am sending an angel ahead of you to guard you along the way and to bring you to the place I have prepared.* What does that mean?"

Michael blushed.

"I have absolutely no idea. Must be a glitch."

Michael eventually found Clovenhoof and the cubs. Paramedics were carrying stretchers out of the large gallery room and several Japanese people were sitting on chairs being treated for cuts and grazes. Museum staff were hastily erecting a barrier around a large iron exhibit that was oddly buckled in the centre.

"What on earth has happened here?" Michael asked.

"It seems as though a tour group got confused," said Clovenhoof. "They thought that this exhibit was for audience participation. It broke when they were all climbing on that top bit, right up there."

"Strange that they should think that even though there's a sign there saying that people shouldn't touch it?"

"Yeah? Maybe someone was standing in front of it or something," Clovenhoof offered.

"Did the cubs see this happen?" asked Michael.

"Yes, but I think they're all right. Not too traumatised," said Clovenhoof.

Michael looked over to the group of boys who seemed to be gleefully comparing mobile phone footage of the collapse.

"Maybe it's time we got them back to Boldmere. Tell me Jeremy, as someone who's older than everything in this museum, at what age do you think you'll give up childish things?"

Clovenhoof gave him a grin.

"There's only one childish thing that's worth giving up, Mickey."

"Oh, really? What's that?"

"Celibacy," said Clovenhoof giving an enthusiastic pelvic thrust by way of demonstration. "Have you worked out all the stuff your *thing* can do yet?"

NERYS POURED Jayne a glass of wine as soon as she sat down in the flat.

"How was the date?" asked Nerys.

"It wasn't a date but I'm exhausted," said Jayne.

"By what? Ben didn't really ravish you among the Flemish Masters, did he?"

"Cubs," said Jayne. "I know I didn't have to look after the cubs, but they make you tired just watching them."

She sipped wine and leaned back, eyes closed, happy to be away from the restless green menaces that had accompanied them back in the minibus.

"I think they learned a lot from the museum. Not sure how, but they've picked up some Japanese. They were practising it on the way home."

"Well, as long as you brought back the same number of cubs as you started with then I'd consider it a win," said Nerys. "Particularly when Jeremy's involved."

Nerys smoothed a snowy white cloth over the table and got out Molly's best cutlery.

"But, yes, I think it went well," said Jayne. "Ben and I spent the longest time in the tea room. What a nice chap he is."

"Don't ever tell him that."

"What?"

"'You're a nice chap' sounds like the most awful back-handed insult."

"Well, he is a nice chap. We might pop out for tea and cake again someday."

"As long as you're not too full of cake to turn down a delicious home-made meal," Nerys said.

She set down a pair of steaming plates on the table.

"I've made Hunter's chicken with sauté potatoes and a side salad," she said.

"Nerys," said Jayne, surprised. "This looks really tasty. You've gone to a lot of trouble."

She sat down and inhaled appreciatively. She started to eat and then noticed that Nerys was looking at her.

"What?" she asked.

"What?" said Nerys.

"You're looking at me."

"Am I?"

"What's going on?"

"Nothing." Nerys topped up Jayne's wine glass. "I just thought you might like to relax after an afternoon with that lot."

Jayne took a sip.

"There was one thing," Nerys said carefully.

"Oh, so there is something."

"The solicitors called today about the flat."

"What did they say?" Jayne asked, putting down her cutlery.

"They have the original will. Apparently the one that I've got is only a copy, so theirs is the legal one."

"And?"

"It says that the flat goes to me. My name's on it."

Jayne stared at her plate for a long moment, processing this new information.

"Oh. I see," she said.

It was strange. Jayne had not consciously imagined that the will would say anything different but it was clear from her own reaction that some hidden part of her mind had been clinging to some fantasy that the will would provide for her too and give her an escape route from the grimness of life in her mother's shadow. She knew in her heart that the flat wasn't hers, but it had seemed as though while there was a shred of doubt, then anything might be possible. She looked up to see Nerys smiling at her.

"You think this is funny!" she said.

"What? No, of course not," said Nerys.

"Why are you grinning like a Cheshire cat then?"

"Can't you see I'm trying to be comforting."

"I don't believe it!" yelled Jayne, standing up and slapping the table. "You're actually enjoying this!"

She was suddenly furious and all the more furious because she knew that she had little right to be angry at all.

"Calm down Jayne. You're being a bit silly," said Nerys.

"Silly! You're calling me silly? I'll tell you what's silly. Silly is lording it over the rest of your family just because you've inherited a stupid tatty flat in the arse end of Birmingham. I mean look at this place, it looks more like a rest home with its old lady furniture, its knitted cushions-"

Jayne took a breath and cast around for fresh inspiration, but Nerys advanced on her, eyes alight with fury.

"Oh no you don't. Don't you dare bring Aunt Molly into this. There's a very good reason it looks like an old lady's place, and that's because it *was*, or had you forgotten her already?"

"No."

"Oh? You make me sick coming up here with some half-baked plan for pinching this place from under my nose so that you can get away from mom."

"That's not true!"

"You want to start acting like a sulky child when you can't get your own way? Fine. Just remember though that your best chance of getting out of there is Glyn Pettigrew, and that's a measure of just how desperate your life has become."

"That's really uncalled for!"

"My life looks pretty damn good when you compare it to yours, don't you think?"

∾

CLOVENHOOF RELAXED ON HIS SOFA, swigging Lambrini from the bottle. He had a handful of voicemail messages to respond to after leaving his phone off for a few hours. The messages might have been intended for Molly but Clovenhoof was only too happy to phone back and relay those important messages he was sure Molly wanted to send.

"Averill? Yes, love it's me, just ringing back. You wanted to know about bingo? They have sessions here in Heaven, three times a week."

Clovenhoof listened for a moment.

"Oh, yes, they have the pens you like, not those crappy dabbers. It's Heaven, isn't it? Must go, Richard Burton's popping round for a game of Twister."

He thumbed some more buttons and waited.

"Mavis? Hello, dearie. Now, I definitely wouldn't worry about vomiting on your daughter-in-law's carpet, Heaven understands the delicate nature of your constitution. Anyway, it's well-known up here that she's a terrible cook. In fact, you might want to tell her that. She'll be grateful in the long run."

He took a long slurp from the bottle as Mavis spoke.

"Attagirl. You're right, he definitely could have done better. Ciao Mavis."

One more. He burped happily as the call rang out.

"Cybil? It's me. Now that was an interesting voicemail that you left. Did you really say that you'd been ravished on the allotment? Tell me all about it."

Clovenhoof listened very carefully for the sordid details.

"Radishes?" he said. "Radishes! Oh for crying out loud woman, call back when you've got some real news, will you?"

He shook his head.

The last message was from G-Sez. Michael had told him that his phone was too old to run an application, but he'd set up Clovenhoof's details so that the server would push out his predictions as daily text messages. He opened it up to see what it had to say.

We are happy when we are growing.

"Hippy poetry quotes?" said Clovenhoof aloud. "Arsehole. Why would I be interested in growth? Apart from the expansion of my giant, throbbing member, obviously."

He stalked up and down, thrusting his groin in time to an invisible beat. Then he stopped, realisation dawning.

"Is this about radishes?" he yelled at the floor. "Are you taking the piss? How have you made the computer mock me, you feathery twat?"

He spent some time jumping off the sofa onto the floor, in the hope that he might dislodge some pieces of plaster in Michael's ceiling.

BEN ANSWERED the door to the insistent battering sound and found Jayne on the threshold. Her face was tracked with tears.

"Hi," he said.

Jayne sniffed loudly.

Ben knew that this was one of those moments when he should really have a clean linen handkerchief to offer. He patted his pockets, even though he knew he didn't have one.

"Er, come in. I'll go and get you a piece of kitchen roll," he said.

"Thank you."

He passed her some tissue paper. She looked at it and then noisily blew her nose.

"It's Post Traumatic Stress Disorder," said Ben.

"Sorry?" she said.

"I had a little weep after my first experience with the cubs."

She smiled despite her tear. "I need to get out of here."

"If I knew you were coming over I'd have hoovered, I swear."

"Any chance you'd come out for a drink with me?"

Ben didn't get offers like that very often and he was momentarily torn.

"That would be a bit tricky to be honest."

"Just down to the Boldmere Oak."

"I'm sort of in the middle of something."

Ben indicated the half-painted array of miniature lead soldiers on the table as he ripped off some tissue for Jayne.

She blew her nose again and sat down to take a look.

"What are they?"

"Seleucidian miniatures."

"Who?"

"The Seleucid Empire was created when Alexander the Great died and his empire was carved up. The Seleucids were one of the last strongholds of Greek culture before their ultimate colonisation by the Romans."

"I did not know that," said Jayne.

"I order these miniatures bare like this from the supplier

and then paint them up in the way I want them to be."

Jayne peered through the large magnifying glass that was clamped to the edge of the table. Ben looked over her shoulder. Any moment now, she'd tell him to get a life and come to the pub. Some of his wargaming friends had been known to snag a woman from time to time. It was a well-known fact that their hobby would take a back seat when they did. It was always a slow process, insidious and subtle, like some invasive cancer. Women simply didn't appreciate the hobby and it was for reasons that were a mystery to them all.

"Lovely detail," she said, as she studied the work in progress.

"Thank you."

"It reminds me of when I was a girl," she said. "My dad's always had hobbies. He likes to be busy doing something and I'd always sit with him. It was usually in his shed, back in the days before he permanently moved in there. He's an ancient history and mythology nut."

"Sounds like a nice guy."

Jayne nodded.

"Even if he was absorbed in what he was doing I'd sit in the room and read my book. It was lovely and relaxing just being there while he worked. Ben, can I sit here while you do your painting?"

"Er, yeah, sure."

"Maybe you can tell me about what you do with them?"

"Yes, okay," said Ben and then stopped. "Hang on. Just to clarify. You really want to hear about wargaming miniatures?"

"Yes, if it's okay."

"It's okay. It's just unusual. I don't think that's ever happened before."

One hour later, Jayne's tears had long dried, and Ben found he couldn't keep the smile off his face. A chance to talk to someone who seemed interested in his hobby was almost unheard of. He made them both a cup of tea and sat beside Jayne on the settee.

"Feeling better?" he said.

She nodded and made a noise like a happy cat.

"All I've done is talked about soldiers," he said.

She shrugged.

"Admittedly," he said, "it's quite nice that someone's here to listen to me just for once."

"It's not just that," said Jayne. "You talk with such passion. I can tell this is something that you really love."

"I suppose I do."

"And it's wonderful to see you come alive when you're talking."

"Come alive?"

"Oh yes. You should let that side of your nature show more often," said Jayne.

"What side?"

"The passionate side. The romantic side."

She caught his eye and his heart raced as her gaze dropped slightly. As if propelled by an unseen hand, he found himself leaning in to kiss her. His mind screamed at his impulsiveness. What if she pulled away? What if she slapped him?

Ben's racing mind was pulled up short as she not only

kissed him back but her hand came up to caress the back of his head.

"Now, what were your words the other day?" she said as they broke. "'Sort of nice'?"

"More than nice," said Ben.

"You'd better believe it," she said and he kissed her again.

She ran her hands across his shoulder.

"I'm a terrible person," she said.

"No, you're not," he said.

"You've no idea what I'm thinking right now."

"No..."

"Have you got an iron and an ironing board," she said.

"What?" Ben said in a hushed squeak, his mind full of incoherent images of sadistic sexual practices involving hot irons.

Jayne brushed her hand over his T-shirt.

"Let me get the creases out of this for you."

"MAKE A BLOG ENTRY LITTLE G," said Michael.

"Yes, Michael," said the computer.

"I have learned some interesting lessons today. Children cannot be relied upon to stay still or behave in a predictable way, much in the same way as the Adversary. It is a huge challenge to instil education and positive values within them, and yet I find myself still striving to do so.

"The museum was a fascinating place. It was filled with pictures that inspire or challenge me in ways that I don't fully understand. Admiring the physical form of humans as the pinnacle of God's creation is a wholesome and fulfilling pastime, but one that appears to provoke anger and confusion unless it is called art.

"I feel that somehow this is intertwined with the complexity of human sexuality. I find the subject impenetrable, and few humans are able or willing to speak with clarity on the subject.

"I believe that my G-sez prediction is suggesting that I should explore the difference between child and man. Does this refer to carnal love? I am really not sure how to do this, but I will maintain an open mind and continue to learn what I can from my stay here on earth."

Michael paused to review the text that had appeared on the screen. Was it a little confused? Well that was to be expected.

"Little G, can you tell me the status of G-Sez, since we made it chargeable? Are people still downloading it?"

"Yes Michael," the computer replied. "There have been two thousand and fifty downloads today."

Michael stared in surprise at the screen.

"Interesting phenomenon," he said. "It must be the cute picture. I'm sure it won't last. Good night Little G."

He turned off the monitor and gave the teddy bear an affectionate squeeze on the way to bedroom. Michael climbed under the covers and closed his eyes but sleep would not come. It had been a strange day, filled with incidents, but one image kept returning to his mind. Well, two blurred and overlapping images: that painting of the Greek charioteer with the divine body and the equally sublime musculature of the young fellow, Andy.

He could not shake those gorgeous images from his mind, nor did he want to. There was so little genuine beauty in this base and inglorious world it was only right to dwell on what beauty there was...

Michael came fully awake, aware that something was profoundly different and utterly wrong. He flung back his sheets and stared in stunned horror at his crotch. His thing was transformed. It was larger, fatter, inexplicably standing proud, engorged with feeling and, worst of all... it was looking at him.

"What's going on?" he whimpered.

His thing twitched, its waving eyeless gaze fixed on him.

Several wild theories crowded at the forefront of his mind. Was it angry with him for some reason? Maybe it didn't like the Soyuz space toilet? Was it going to unleash a bladderful of urine on him in revenge? Was it about to speak, to demand equal rights as a symbiotic entity? Or had he killed it and this was rigor mortis?

"What do you want?" he whispered.

His thing said nothing although its monocular gaze seemed to become more reproachful.

"What to do?" said Michael and then, fuelled by sheer desperation, leapt up, wrapped a dressing gown around him and went up to consult the Adversary in Flat 2a.

Clovenhoof took an intolerable age to answer the door.

"What?" he snapped.

Without a word, Michael pushed his way inside, undid his dressing robe and gestured frantically at his erect penis.

"Look!"

Clovenhoof looked.

Well, 'we are happy when we're growing,' aren't we?" he said.

"What's happened to me?" pleaded Michael. "Is this normal?"

"I can say with absolute honesty that I've never been in this situation before."

"Lord, help me," said Michael. "What's happened to it? Is it dead? Broken? It just happened. I didn't even touch it."

"Are you sure?" said Clovenhoof. "'Cos this kind of thing happens with excess touching."

"I swear," said Michael. "I hardly ever touch it. I was even contemplating getting some tongs to do the necessary toilet business."

Clovenhoof stroked his chin thoughtfully like a mechanic contemplating a dodgy motor.

"Maybe you've not been touching it enough."

"Not touching it enough? Is there a safe minimum? How often should I be touching myself?"

"Daily. Sometimes twice, I'd say. Come over here. Doctor Clovenhoof will sort you out."

He directed Michael to stand in front of his desktop computer. Clovenhoof sat down and turned on the webcam.

"So, tell me, what were you thinking about when this happened?"

"Nothing really," said Michael. "I was thinking about the cub trip to the museum."

Clovenhoof gave Michael and his thing a startled look.

"And Andy," said Michael.

"Andy?"

"He's a chap I met at the gym. I bumped into him at the museum."

"Oh?" said Clovenhoof, his momentary shock giving way to curiosity. "Tell me about Andy."

"He's really into his anaerobic exercise. His body's a work of art. Great musculature. Abs to die for. You know, the kind you just want to reach out and..."

"Right," said Clovenhoof. "And this walking torso. Does he have a face?"

"What?"

"Perhaps a job? Personal interests? A rich and complex personal history?"

"I'm sure he does," said Michael.

"But all you're interested in is his body."

"No, that's not true. Is it? I've shown interest in his-"

"Cock," said Clovenhoof.

"No," said Michael.

"No," explained Clovenhoof. "Your cock. This way."

He gestured for Michael to rotate towards the computer. Clovenhoof clicked his mouse.

"Did you just take a picture?"

"For scientific study," said Clovenhoof. "So we can get to the bottom of this medical mystery."

"But what do I do now?"

Clovenhoof shrugged.

"Go home. Try not to think about it. Use it as a hat stand."

Michael, churning with worry, reluctantly did up his gown and retreated to the landing.

"Don't worry," said Clovenhoof cheerfully. "We'll have you sorted in no time."

ST CADFAN'S

"Oficial history tells us little of St Senacus and St Veracius," said Abbot Ambrose, gazing at the tapestry.

"I did what research I could," said Brother Manfred. "Senacus's tombstone offers us only a few details and, although I read everything we have about them in this very library, all I found was..."

"Legends and wild speculation?" said the abbot.

"That is quite so," said Manfred.

"And yet they did exist. It was they who came here in the fifth century and set up the first religious community on this island. Tell me what we have in this tapestry."

Manfred got up from his stool and took a step back from his handiwork, winding up a loose spool of thread as he did so.

"And so we have here a scene depicting the arrival of the two founding saints on the island. This is the eastern side of the island, looking up towards the peak. I found the perfect shade of slate grey for the shale on the slopes."

"I noticed that," said the abbot. "It's very good. So this is St Veracius and St Senacus?"

"Yes. I couldn't work out whether Senacus was meant to be bald or had a tonsure but Veracius has a full head of hair so I assumed Senacus was just naturally bald. It's a fine look. In fact, he has your noble bearing, don't you think, Father Abbot?"

"I don't see it myself."

"No, very much alike I thought. Anyway, Veracius has this in his hand. I thought it was a staff but it seems to go all funny at the top."

The abbot gestured towards the corner.

"And these?"

Manfred nodded.

"These I think are the people who've come to welcome them to the island or maybe the first pilgrims. There was quite a bit of water damage in that corner."

"Because you've been quite inventive here, haven't you?"

Manfred grimaced slightly.

"I had no reference pictures to go on but I looked at these raised arms here and I thought to myself, 'these people are really pleased to see the two saints.' They are jumping for joy and there is a sense of celebration which I've tried to capture."

"Is that why they are dressed like circus performers?"

"I was going for a carnival stroke Mardi Gras feel."

"Pink feathers?"

"Nothing says excitement like pink feathers."

"You've actually sewn sequins onto the tapestry."

"Too much?" suggested Manfred.

"And as for this woman... she's seems to be wearing very little. Do you think it would have been either moral or practical to wear such skimpy frivolities on a damp fifth century hillside?"

Manfred seemed to contemplate this at length.

"It's Kylie Minogue, Father Abbot."

"Of course it is."

Abbot Ambrose turned away and made to leave.

"Do you want me to continue?" asked Brother Manfred hopefully.

The abbot gave him an offhand wave as he went and let Manfred interpret that has he wished.

He walked through the cloisters and into the orangery. The prior sat in his bath-chair beneath the healthy boughs of the apple tree.

"You would not be able to guess in a thousand years what that German buffoon has done with the tapestry of the arrival on the island," said the abbot as he unlocked a cabinet near the base of the tree.

The prior made no effort to guess.

The abbot removed a small watering can and inspected the contents. There was maybe an inch or two of blood in the base of the can and it had thickened, almost completely clotted.

"Still," said the abbot, "he probably captured the moment as well as anyone could. Happy times, eh?"

The abbot went to the base of the tree and emptied the

watering can around its roots. The blood seeped quickly into the soil.

"Do you know who Kylie Minogue is?" he asked the prior.

The prior said nothing.

"No, me neither, brother," said the abbot.

He looked at the empty watering can.

"Time for your treatment again, Arthur," said the abbot, leaned forward and placed a kiss on the prior's forehead.

5

IN WHICH A FLAT GOES UP FOR SALE
AND MICHAEL GETS IN TOUCH WITH
HIS INNER OWL

Two days later, Nerys pulled into the car park at Sutton Coldfield train station.

"This is a disabled space," called Ben from the back seat.

"It's okay," said Nerys, "I know loads of people who are disabled. We can just mention your allergies, if anyone asks."

"Allergies?"

But Nerys was already out of the car, and opening the boot so that Jayne could get her bags.

"Oh Nerys!" exclaimed Jayne, holding Nerys's hands in hers. "I've had such a lovely time. Who had any idea that Birmingham was such a wonderful place!"

Nerys looked around at the stained concrete of the car park and sniffed loudly.

"No, not here, silly," said Jayne, "but to come here and see all the busy, exciting things that a city has to offer after being stuck in Wales for so long, you've simply no idea!"

She caught the look that Nerys gave her and her smile fell slightly.

"Oh. Yes. Of course you do. Thank you for having me. And putting up with me."

Ben lifted the bags from the boot. Jayne beamed at him.

"And now I have another reason for wanting to come back here!"

Ben and Jayne gazed at each other.

"Right, I'll wait in the car while you two say goodbye," said Nerys.

"Wait Nerys, I wanted to ask you if you'd all come to visit? Ben wants to see the place, and it's ages since you came back."

"I've never been to Wales!" said Ben.

"Don't look so excited Ben," said Nerys. "Try to imagine Sutton Park with sheep and Methodist chapels everywhere. Oh, I don't know, Jayne. I don't much enjoy going back, these days."

"Oh please Nerys, just for a short visit?"

"Yeah, can we? It'd be brilliant!"

Nerys looked at their solemn, pleading faces, and hissed quietly through her teeth.

"Right. Yes. In the New Year. I'll bring *my* boyfriend to meet everyone as well."

She got back into the car and slammed the door.

She watched in the wing mirror as Ben and Jayne mashed their faces together with a thoroughness that reminded her of Ben's method of eating curry. He'd mentioned once that he mentally divided his plate into a clock face and ate around it, so that he could be sure he missed nothing. Was he applying the same technique to snogging her sister?

Ben got back into the car a few moments later, cheeks flushed.

"I didn't know you had a boyfriend," he said.

"I haven't," she said. "I just can't go back there and have them all sneering at me for being a sad loser."

"They're your family! Why would they do that?"

"Oh Ben, you have no idea what you're getting into. You've met Jayne, and she's okay. You know me, and obviously I'm great, but my sisters en-masse are a terrifying force. If you add my mother to the picture, it's like one of those mythical creatures with lots of heads."

"A gorgon?"

"No, you're thinking of the stone faces that look like Jeremy, but anyway, my family's worse than any of those things. Why do you think my dad left?"

"Where did he go?"

"He lives in a shed at the bottom of the garden."

"Seriously?" said Ben. Nerys looked up at him, quizzically. "Anyway," he hurried on, "they wouldn't be so callous when you've not been back for ages, surely?"

"No, you're right," said Nerys. "They might feel sorry for me, which would be much, much worse."

Nerys crunched the car into gear and backed out of the space with a grim smile.

"Nope. There's no other option. I need to find a boyfriend to take with me."

∼

MICHAEL ROLLED over in bed as he heard a small buzz from his phone. He scrolled through his emails, which told him that the last week's sales of G-sez had made him eight thousand and forty three pounds. He was pleased that it was working for other people. He consulted his prediction for the day.

KINDNESS IN WORDS CREATES CONFIDENCE. Kindness in thinking creates profoundness. Kindness in giving creates love.

IT WAS from the Tao Te Ching. Michael reflected for a few minutes on what it might mean.

"I'm to be kind?" he asked aloud, as he dressed himself. "I will, of course. It comes naturally for an angel. I haven't forgotten all of that just because I'm stuck in this imperfect body and surrounded by people who neglect their spirituality. Sometimes Little G, I wish we had the data to make the predictions more obvious."

He thought some more as he ate his muesli and yoghurt.

"Is it a particular act of kindness?" he asked. "Oh, I do wish I knew what I was supposed to do, but if there's a way to reach out to God through kindness, then you can be sure I won't miss it. I like to be thorough."

He regarded the dream-catchers that the hippy street vendor had pressed upon him, insisting that they would help him in his spiritual search.

"But *he* saw me coming. Definitely saw me coming."

· · ·

MICHAEL WALKED up Chester Road on his way to church. His thoughts were so wrapped up in the potential meaning of his G-Sez message that he did not notice the sheet pasted on the first lamppost he passed, nor the second, nor the third. Eventually, his conscious brain caught up with what his eyes had noticed some time ago.

Michael stopped and looked at the poster stuck to the next lamppost.

It was a computer-printed photograph of a man's member, erect and seemingly gazing directly into the camera lens. Above it, in a jaunty font, were the words, 'Have you seen this cock?' Michael recognised the dressing gown that framed the picture and the baleful look that his thing was giving to the camera.

Michael rotated slowly and saw that identical posters had been plastered onto every lamppost on the street, and a few garden gates besides.

"Jeremy!" he hissed in embarrassment and fury.

It was still relatively early and there was hardly anyone out. He could simply walk on and ignore the pictures – for who was to know that this thing was his – but he couldn't bear the idea of his own thing staring at him from all these posters, like some wanted criminal.

Michael spent five minutes running up and down the road, tearing down posters, screwing them up and thrusting the incriminating pieces into his pocket.

Later than expected, he arrived at church, flustered, angry, and too distracted to pay attention to the old ladies wittering on about their hip pains, problem grandchildren and their missing cats.

He smiled and told them all that God would provide the help they needed if they kept their faith. He didn't even hear the snort from Gladys, the woman with the missing cat as he walked to a pew.

It was the third Sunday before Christmas and Michael had been hoping for a stirring sermon at that most important time of the year. As it was, the sermon was themed around advent as a journey. Reverend Zack spoke about a journey of faith and increased understanding, which could be focussed upon this build-up to the most holy of Christian celebrations.

Michael shuffled slightly, frustrated by the half-baked nods that everyone was giving to the sermon. He had a strong suspicion that the congregation were taking away the message that eating advent calendar chocolates every day was bringing them closer to Heaven. A far cry from the good old days of *proper* journeys, *proper* pilgrimages.

He sat up straighter as Reverend Zack began a reading from Luke. Angels! Now this was more like it! He smiled and gave a small sigh of pleasure.

God sent the angel Gabriel to Nazareth, a town in Galilee.

He ignored the misguided favouritism that Gabriel always got because of his Christmas gig and settled in to enjoy the reflected glory of an angel doing important work for God on earth. He wondered what his own mission could be. What act of kindness was he supposed to perform today?

As the collection plate came round, he realised that he could start straightaway, in a practical gesture for the church that bore his name. He looked down at what was already there. A couple of buttons and a rusty washer sat amongst a mean collection of coins. He riffled through the notes in his wallet, shrugged and put them all onto the collection plate. There was less than a thousand, as he hadn't been to the bank in a few days. He closed his eyes and savoured the feeling of a kind act that was sure to be noticed.

IT WAS NOTICED.

As he took another biscuit from the fourth elderly lady who insisted that she'd saved him the *best,* Michael noticed that Reverend Zack kept glancing over towards him.

"Michael, I noticed your rather generous contribution to the collection plate today," he said, when Michael finally stood alone. "I just wanted to make sure that everything's all right with you."

"Of course, everything's all right."

"I just sometimes find that if people do something out of character, it can mean that they're trying to attract attention."

His gaze searched Michael's face.

"Is that the case Michael? Is there something you want to talk about?"

This wasn't how it was supposed to be! Michael had pictured a scene where his contribution made possible some essential project. He hadn't expected to be questioned or doubted for an act of unprovoked kindness.

"Don't you want the money?"

Zack made a small, waving motion with his hand.

"We're very grateful, of course we are."

"Good."

"I'm thinking only of your well-being."

"You think I'm trying to attract attention?" said Michael, raising his voice. "Of course I am. I want nothing more than for God to notice me."

"God sees everything, Michael. We don't need grand gestures to attract the attention of God."

"Yes we do when he's not talking! He hasn't spoken to me for weeks."

Zack put a hand on Michael's arm.

"When we're anxious, we sometimes think that God has abandoned us. I'm sensing a lot of anxiety from you at the moment, Michael."

Michael shook away his hand angrily.

"You have no idea what you're talking about," he yelled. "I'm trying to do the right thing. I ALWAYS do the right thing, and you're treating me like an idiot! How can you even call this a church when everyone's more worried about tea and biscuits than they are about the meaning of the holy scriptures?"

The word *biscuit* caused a wave of blue-rinsed ladies to swivel as one and head towards Michael in a solid wall of proffered plates.

"No more biscuits!" he shrieked. "Don't you understand that nobody even likes them! Especially the ones that say *Nice* on them. They should say *Nasty* to at least be accurate!"

Blue rinses bobbed and wobbled nervously as Michael glared around at everyone.

"I'm really, really disappointed in you all. I came here because you're Christians. I thought that would mean that you'd at least spend time in your lives thinking about God.

Who here has really thought about him, really spoken to him? Who?"

He rounded on Gladys who rallied after a moment. "Well I did ask him to find my cat for me."

"And did he?"

"No."

"You see?"

Michael shook his head and stormed towards the door. A bulky figure, dressed in a sweater embroidered with a large silver cross stepped in front of him.

"Erm, you will still be coming to cubs, won't you?" asked Darren.

Michael turned to face him.

"Cubs! Those dreadful beasts are the worst of the lot. If I could see even the slightest glimmer of goodness in any of them I wouldn't mind, but they're wretched little demons, all of them. I know you can't see that, but then *you* look in the mirror every morning and think you're fit to face the world when you dress like that, so frankly, your views can't be trusted."

Darren looked down at his mother's handiwork, no doubt wondering what Michael could be talking about. The door slammed shut, rattling the teacups and leaving ladies with plates of biscuits adrift with nowhere to go.

Nerys made herself her first cup of tea of the day and sat down in Molly's armchair. Even after moving the furniture around and clearing out the last of Molly's things, it was still

Molly's chair. It struck her, not for the first time, how her mundane routine must be an echo of Molly's in the years before she'd come to live with her. Get up, have a cup of tea. Go to work on a week day and go shopping if it was the weekend.

Was she destined to do this until she dropped dead, or smelled of wee and didn't care anymore? The same places, the same things, the same people, and for what? Her job paid the bills, but she wasn't going to pretend that she found it even slightly interesting, let alone fulfilling. She lived in a dull suburb, where nothing ever happened and she had no real friends to speak of. She had her flatmates, who were really more like drinking buddies than actual friends, but what did they *really* mean to her?

She drifted over to the window, sipping her tea. Clovenhoof was outside, crouching over something with intense concentration. He moved slightly and she saw that there was a dead fox at his feet. Hadn't she seen that in the gutter up the road yesterday? What was he doing with it? He worked a knife for a few moments and came away with the brushy tail, which he tucked proudly into his waistband and gave a couple of experimental twirls, cackling with laughter as it swished around his hips. She turned away from the window in disgust.

Moments later, she was through to the estate agents.

"Yes, I've got a property I'd like to sell."

MICHAEL POUNDED THE TREADMILL, his face set in a stony grimace. His induction, weeks ago had stressed the importance of doing everything as smoothly as possible, so that he didn't cause injury to himself or the equipment but he ignored that advice today. He worked his arms to the accompaniment of crashing weights. He moved on to stomach crunches, indulging in the brutal grunts that he'd always frowned upon in others. It felt good to express his frustration in physical ways, but the anger still simmered inside him.

"Hey, Michael."

Andy walked over from the changing room, a towel rolled neatly under his arm.

Michael smiled, but knew that his face wasn't up to it.

"You're not looking yourself today," said Andy. "What's up?"

"Oh, you have no idea," with more emotion than he intended. "I don't think I have the words to explain."

Andy sat down beside him.

"Let me get you a coffee and you can try to find the words."

They went through to the gym's cafeteria where Andy ordered skinny lattes for the pair of them.

Michael sat down with his coffee and sighed.

"Most people I've come across wouldn't understand. I've been searching for a direction, for a *meaning* ever since I got here."

"Here? Birmingham?"

"No, well, yes. Here. The people that I meet aren't

interested in spirituality. Everyone's too wrapped up in their selfish, materialistic lives."

"Too true," Andy nodded in sympathy.

"I've found nothing, nothing at all that works for me," Michael continued. "Do you know the worst thing?"

"What?"

"The one place that I thought for sure I'd at least fit into was the church, up at St Michael's."

"It's even got your name on it."

"Well, *absolutely*. Anyway, it seems to be more like a place where confused people go to gorge on tea and sympathy."

"The church is a hypocrisy, Michael."

"They treated me badly there, and it's made me unutterably sad."

He looked away as he felt again the pang of rage that he'd felt when his gift to the church was questioned.

Andy placed a hand over Michael's.

"You know, the church has a long history of being unkind to people like us," he said.

Michael's brow creased with confusion.

"People like *us*?"

"Exactly. I get your frustration, I really do. I've experimented with all sorts of things, looking for spiritual meaning in my life."

"Really?"

Andy drew back, a mock hurt look on his face.

"Don't I strike you as a spiritual guy?"

Michael shrugged.

"I just thought you were..."

He waved his hand vaguely at Andy's chest, toned and hairless and now concealed beneath a white T shirt.

"A gym bunny?" said Andy. "I do have the abs of an Adonis–"

"They're amazing," said Michael honestly and then remembered his conversation with Clovenhoof. "I mean, you're not just a walking torso," he said quickly.

"What?"

"I mean, you're a well-rounded human being with interests and a face, a really nice face, and a rich personal history."

"A really nice face?" said Andy, arching an eyebrow.

"That's just my opinion," said Michael.

"Thank you, Michael. I was going to say that I do have the abs of an Adonis but I'm a spiritual creature too."

"Exactly. That's my point. Spiritual how?"

"I spent three months at a retreat in Thailand, and I was privileged to stay in a Lamasery in Tibet a couple of years ago."

"Tibet?"

"You know, the place with the yaks. Those things brought me great peace, they really did, but if you need something here and now, and it sounds as though you do..."

"I do. I'm lost."

Andy stood up.

"I might know just the thing. A spirit guru, here in the West Midlands."

"A spirit guru?"

"Someone to guide you, to teach you. If you want inner

growth and spiritual healing, they can help you to achieve that."

"Sounds interesting," said Michael, sitting up straight, only half aware of the ball of paper falling out of his pocket as he did. "How do I meet him?"

"I'm due to see him tomorrow. I can call and check it's all right to..." Andy beamed at him. "To bring a friend."

He bent and picked up the screwed up paper. As he unfolded it, Michael saw that it was one of Clovenhoof's offensive posters. He reached across the table for it but Andy already had it open.

"'Have you seen this cock?'" he read and nodded thoughtfully. "I'm sure I would have remembered. But a man sees so many..."

Michael agreed.

"I once spent a night looking at so many, I thought I'd go blind."

Andy laughed.

"You are a strange one, Michael," he said, but, coming out of Andy's mouth, it didn't sound at all bad.

Nerys came home from work to find Michael carrying a large box towards the front door. She moved in front so that she could open the door.

"Looks exciting!" she said.

"It's a new coffee machine," said Michael. "I need cheering up and I decided to treat myself."

"I never knew you drank coffee," said Nerys.

"Well, I don't, but some of my friends do," smiled Michael. "Besides it's *una macchinetta con i contro-coglioni*, and I couldn't resist."

"Well, I'm very happy to be a guinea pig, if you want to try it out," she said.

In Michael's kitchen, she helped him unpack and unwrap the monstrous device.

"Do you know any more phrases like that in Italian?" Nerys asked, taking the tissue from a measuring jug.

Michael shrugged.

"How about *non mi rompere le palle, la mia giornata è già brutta abbastanza?*"

Nerys shuddered with pleasure. The Italian words brought to mind a hazy view in her mind's eye of a dark-eyed man gazing down at her from the prow of a gondola. If she sold the flat, maybe she could go travelling? Balmy weather, surrounded by handsome Italian men, talking in that most seductive of languages...

"Italian is such a beautiful language, isn't it?" said Nerys. "Can you teach me a couple of phrases?"

"Yes, of course. It's really pretty simple."

"If you say so."

Michael plugged in the machine and consulted the manual.

"Do you have any appreciation of Latin at all?" he asked.

"Not all of us went to a public school, Michael," she scowled.

Michael shrugged and filled the reservoir with water at the back of the coffee machine.

"Let's start with something simple. *'A quale santo è dedicata questa chiesa?'*"

"Lovely!" said Nerys, "what does that mean?"

"Which saint is this church dedicated to?" said Michael.

"Hmmm," said Nerys. "I can't honestly see me saying something like that."

"Really?"

"How about a useful phrase like 'Which way to George Clooney's villa?'"

"So that would be *'da che parte è la villa di George Clooney?'*"

Nerys muttered the phrase over to herself, committing it to memory. Michael kindly corrected her pronunciation whilst measuring out coffee grounds.

"Oh," she said, as a thought occurred to her. "I'd love to know what something means. The most handsome Italian waiter once said this to me. I was certain that there was a chemistry between us, and he whispered this to me. I've never forgotten it. *'Non sei brufolosa come la maggior parte di queste sciacquette inglesi palide, ma smetti di fissarmi, mi fai venire la nausea '*"

"Er, it's not really polite," said Michael.

"Oh *good!* Tell me, please!"

"It means 'You're not as spotty as most of these pasty English tarts, but stop staring, you're making me queasy,'"

"Oh, poo," said Nerys. "Come on then, let's have some of this posh coffee."

It was good coffee.

Nerys's mind raced as she sipped the frothy cappuccino. Here was an almost perfect male specimen: cultured, well-mannered, with an appreciation of the fine things in life. He would have been an ideal boyfriend if he had shown the least bit of interest in her (and she harboured certain suspicions about why that was). Mom and dad would have no reason to gripe if she turned up with him on her arm. If only he was hers, or at least appeared to be hers...

"You know, I think we might be able to help each other," she said. "I get the idea that you feel a bit awkward in certain social situations."

"Well, that is the case sometimes, certainly," replied Michael.

"My people skills are second to none. How about I help you out with that, in exchange for the language lessons? Spend a bit of time with each other, helping each other out?"

"Of course, that would be very pleasant."

"Fantastic! Let's start tomorrow. I was planning to do some Christmas shopping, and I bet you've been agonising over what to get us all!"

ON WEDNESDAY NIGHT, the cubs gleefully exploited the shortage of adult supervision. In Michael's absence, Clovenhoof had to break out his most demonic bellow.

"Right, cubs!" he roared. "Tonight's session will be supervised by me. Baloo will be assisting. We have an exciting new topic to look at today."

He frowned at a group in the corner.

"Baloo, are we practising first aid skills tonight?"

"Er, no."

"Well, Kenzie over there has gone a funny shade of blue,

so we might want to re-think that. I imagine that the first aid he needs most of all is for Spartacus to take the rope from round his neck."

Darren lumbered over to free the unfortunate boy as Clovenhoof continued.

"Tonight, we're going to do some geocaching."

"What happened to Akela Michael?" asked scabby-faced Jefri.

"He's had a nervous breakdown," said Clovenhoof cheerily.

"When's Akela Angela coming back?" asked another.

"When we've raised enough to pay her kidnappers. Enough. Who here has heard of geocaching?" he asked.

A few shoulders were shrugged.

"It will mean sweets for everyone who gets it right," said Clovenhoof. There was a small murmur of approval, and more faces turned towards him. Spartacus was absorbed in knotting the rope. He'd proven most proficient at snares and traps so he was rarely without a rope in his hands. At least he'd stopped throttling the smaller boys.

"It's like a hi-tech version of a treasure hunt. I will hide the sweets in some special containers, and then give you the co-ordinates. All you have to do is to find the containers and you can take one of the sweets. That's *one* of the sweets."

He glared round at them.

"The cool part is that you get to use one of these to find your way."

He held up a GPS unit.

"Or you could use a smartphone, like yours!"

There was a tittering from behind and he swivelled to see

who was mocking his phone. Spartacus, it had to be! But no, he was still knotting his rope, seemingly oblivious to the subject.

"We'll try it inside the hall tonight, and then we'll do it for real, outside, on the day after Boxing Day. Right! Let's split into groups. Half will go with Baloo... where is Baloo?"

He turned around again to see that Darren was hanging by his foot from a snare that hung from a light fixture, over by the windows.

"Oh, really. Well I hope the people that caught Baloo in their snare know what they're going to do with him now they've got him. How did you get him to walk into it by the way?"

Darren held out a hand with a half-eaten Twix, clearly chomping on the other piece as he hung from the snare.

Clovenhoof sighed.

"Cut him down carefully, boys," he said. "Just make sure he lands on his head."

MICHAEL TURNED off the A road and down a small, rural lane, where the nearly leafless trees met overhead to form a tunnel.

"I didn't know you had a Merc," said Andy, running his hands over the white leather.

"I didn't," Michael replied. "Not until yesterday."

"You've been splashing the cash about?"

"Don't I deserve some luxuries?" grinned the archangel. "What did you drive before?"

"I didn't drive before."

Andy gave him a startled look. Michael realised that his skills did not tally with what he had just said.

"I mean, I can drive but I never had to drive myself."

"You had a chauffeur, huh?"

"Something like that," said Michael doubtfully.

"Wow. Down here."

He steered into a courtyard outside a large, low house. It had the look of a Mediterranean villa, all whitewashed walls and red tiled roofs, albeit in wintry north Warwickshire.

A tall, spindle-legged man appeared at the door as Michael locked the car. The man wore a tie-dyed shalwar kameez and an air of absolute self-assurance.

"Michael, this is Elk Davis," said Andy.

Elk clapped Michael on the shoulder and shook his hand.

"This is a fine place you have here," said Michael.

"Appearances are meaningless and geography more so," drawled Elk, in an accent that Michael couldn't place. "But you've come to the right place, brother. You're looking for answers and I'm the man to help you find them."

Michael was equally impressed by the house's interior.

Styled with simplicity and serenity at its heart, there were few furnishings and distractions. Those that were there had been chosen for their significance. Backlit niches showed off a row of prayer wheels, some aboriginal totems and small carved idols. He realised that the dreamcatchers and hanging crystals that he'd used in his own flat were ridiculous trinkets compared to the startling collection belonging to Elk. He ran his fingers over a set of stylised antlers, carved from some highly polished wood.

"I take my name from my spirit totem," said Elk. "It empowers me with its strength and nobility. Come."

Michael followed Elk into a room with no chairs.

"Let us relax on my textured surface," said Elk, indicating a huge rug with a pile so deep that Michael's feet disappeared.

Elk sat down and arranged his legs into a lotus position. Andy did the same. Michael worked out how to do it and sat opposite, trailing his hands through the rug.

"Hands on knees, Michael. Neutral position. I want your focus on me now," said Elk.

Michael obeyed.

For a long time, Elk stared at Michael with an intensity that was unsettling.

"I see in you a shining purity, Michael."

"Thank you."

"You've trodden many paths in your quest for enlightenment."

"I have."

"Many paths, but they have always been strict and pure. Tell me, Michael, are you at all familiar with the writing of William Blake?"

Michael cast around in his mind.

"Didn't he write Jerusalem?"

"Well, yes, but I was thinking of his more revolutionary, philosophical works. Blake put forward some really interesting ideas. Let me see if any of these resonate with you."

"The road of excess leads to the palace of wisdom," he intoned. "You never know what is enough unless you know what is more than enough."

Michael frowned.

"That doesn't sound right," he said.

"Perfect!" boomed Elk. "Well done. I believe we've found the right direction for you."

"Have we?" asked Michael.

"I believe you're suffering from a fear of life's experiences."

"Are you sure?"

"Undeniably, brother. Your inhibitions are holding you back. You are like a jungle beast, wild and virile, but you are trapped in a cage of your own devising."

"Am I?"

"You pace back and forth in anger, not knowing how to break free. Did you ever stop to think why you resist doing certain things?"

"I don't." He looked to Andy for help at this point, but Andy was practising some silent meditation with his eyes closed. "Do I?"

"You wear man's clothes because society tells you to. You guard your thoughts and your words and do not say what you truly think. Society has conditioned us all to accept certain behaviour as normal or right. We no longer trust ourselves to make our own judgements. How do you know how much to eat every day? Do you read the government guidelines, or do you eat until you're no longer hungry?"

Michael was about to reply that he did both, but Elk pressed on.

"We trust our bodies and our minds to know what's best. One time we overeat, and we understand why it's a bad idea. Do you begin to see? We gain knowledge and enlightenment by allowing ourselves the full range of experiences. Have you heard of Cain and Abel?"

"The sons of Adam and Eve."

"Ancient Gnostics believed that by murdering Abel, Cain had done a good thing. He showed us all what murder was so that we might see it was wrong. Excess brings wisdom."

Michael nodded slowly.

"You want me to kill someone then?"

Elk clapped his great hands together.

"Ha! No need to go that far, brother, but I'm delighted that you're prepared to be open-minded," he said. "We can accelerate your programme so that you can work with Andy if you'd like?"

Michael nodded at Andy who grinned back at him.

"Now, let's think," said Elk. "I run a spiritual retreat once a month but – oh."

"What?"

"I had one planned for this weekend. Andy was going to come. A stag party from Cheshire had taken most of the bookings, but they've cancelled. I'm afraid we'll need to reschedule."

"Wait," said Michael. "That sounds like it would be great. Why can't you run it with just us?"

Elk sucked his teeth.

"I'd do it of course - it'd be expensive mind you - but the thing is, you need at least four people to generate the manifest chi that we need to work with.

"What's manifest chi?"

"Spiritual energy that we can all tap into. We make lots of use of it when we do the retreat, it gets really intense."

"Anyone can make manifest chi? I mean, really *anyone*?" asked Michael.

"Oh yes, the potential lies within each and every one of us."

"Well, in that case, I can sort out another couple of people, and the money shouldn't be a problem. Let's go ahead, I really want to do this as soon as possible."

Elk nodded.

"I'll work out a price for you, and we'll treat you and your friends to a weekend they won't forget."

MICHAEL PULLED up outside the flats, drawing in slowly at the kerbside to give Ben and Clovenhoof, who standing on the pavement, plenty of time to see him in his beautiful white car. However, the two of them were too busy examining a sign in the front garden of the flats.

He locked up and went over to them.

"Ben, Jeremy, I have the most exciting news. I'm taking you away on a-"

"Flat three's up for sale," said Ben.

Michael looked at the estate agent sign.

"It's Nerys's," said Ben, his face creased with confusion. "What does it mean?"

"It means she's decided to leave," said Clovenhoof.

"Anyway," said Michael, "my news-"

Clovenhoof clicked his fingers in inspiration.

"We should check to see if someone's holding her hostage."

"Hostage?"

"That's the only reasonable explanation for this."

Ben and Clovenhoof bundled through the door and up the stairs. Michael followed slowly in their wake.

After a barrage of knocks on her door, Nerys answered.

"Why are you selling your flat?" Clovenhoof asked loudly. "Wink your right eye if you're speaking under duress," he added in a whisper, tilting his head toward the interior of her flat.

Nerys rolled her eyes.

"I want to get away from here, Jeremy."

"Really?"

"I want to see something of the world outside of Boldmere."

"Why?" said Ben.

"Why?" said Nerys.

Michael watched her flounder momentarily.

"Are you on drugs?" said Clovenhoof. "Did the drugs make you do this?"

"No, I am not on drugs. Drugs would at least be exciting. I'm leaving this place. I need to see the world before it's too late."

"I don't think Armageddon is due for a while yet," said Clovenhoof. "I would have seen the memo."

"Too late for *me*," said Nerys.

"What about us?" Ben asked in a small voice.

"What about you? Why does it have to be about you?"

Nerys replied impatiently. "It's about me. I need to move on. Michael, are you ready to go?"

Michael shrugged agreeably.

"Good!" she said in exasperation, slammed the door and shooed him downstairs and out onto the street before Ben and Clovenhoof could make another comment.

"Oh, is that your car?" she asked.

Finally, one of them had noticed. Michael opened the door for her by way of an answer.

Nerys smiled broadly.

"Just the sort of car that a successful boyfriend ought to have."

"Boyfriend?"

"I'll explain later."

THEY HEADED into the city centre and Nerys hustled Michael through the Birmingham Bull Ring shopping centre from shop to shop.

"So you see," she told him, "the art of buying a perfect Christmas present is to get the person the thing they really need, but they just don't realise it. For instance. Ben needs more colour in his wardrobe, so I've chosen this pink t-shirt for him. It'll bring out his eyes. Jeremy needs to be more organised, so this memo board can go on his fridge and it'll help him to organise those little things. Like when it's his round."

She looked up from rummaging in her bags.

"So, now I need to go and get one last, essential gift."

"Oh? what's that?" asked Michael.

"A gift to me from my loving 'boyfriend,'" she said, heading into a shop that was filled with dummies dressed in female underwear of the briefest kind. Michael hesitated at the door.

"Do not degrade your daughter by making her a prostitute," he quoted automatically and then shook his head. "No," he whispered to himself. "Through excess comes wisdom."

He stepped inside.

Nerys flicked through racks as she talked.

"Everyone loves undies as a present, don't they? It's like a gift that keeps on giving, if you know what I mean!"

"Er, not sure I do," said Michael, gingerly fingering a pair of red lacy panties.

"For a special person, it's the most intimate thing you can do," said Nerys, "and they're going to *love* you for it."

"Okay," said Michael and took several pairs from the rack and Nerys hummed to herself and she selected a couple of skimpy sets.

Nerys was feeling very pleased with herself. She had bought nearly all her Christmas presents, she was in fine company and she was miles away from her depressing flat and two selfish, whimpering flatmates.

"How about some ice cream?" she asked Michael. "There's a place across the way."

"Or *gelato* as the Italians call it," Michael replied.

"Oh, really? Well we must go in there and have one, and you can teach me some more Italian!"

. . .

NERYS WORKED her way through a tall Knickerbocker Glory. The ice creams had been Michael's treat. It had been a long time since any man had treated her to anything.

"Mmmm, this is good stuff. Right, let me see if I've got that right. *Questa è la sua Ferrari? Credo di avere preso una storta alla caviglia, potrebbe darmi un passaggio per favore?"*

Michael nodded in approval.

"Remember to trill those 'r's."

"Ah yes, the Italian 'r's" she laughed. *"Può per favore farmi una foto che mi fa risaltare il culo?"*

"Perfect," Michael said.

"This *is* perfect," she said, indicating the two of them with her spoon. "It's as if we click, don't you think? If we were to pretend we're boyfriend and girlfriend, my family would definitely be convinced."

"I expect so," said Michael, looking sideways at her. "Do you really need to lie to your own family though?"

"Truth has no place in a Thomas family gathering," Nerys said. "You have to understand what they're like, we've been brought up on a diet of attention-seeking and scheming."

"You have only sisters?" Michael asked. "How many?"

"Three," nodded Nerys. "Jayne, who you know. Then there's me, then Catherine and then Lydia, the baby."

"Do they all still live in Wales?"

"No, Catherine bagged herself a footballer. Lives in Cheshire," said Nerys with a small scowl.

"Why are footballers so valued?" asked Michael. "It seems to me that their talents are rather limited."

"Oh, you have no idea! When my mom found out about Catherine, she was over the moon. Footballers have so much money! They live in these huge swanky houses and their wives swan around in the latest fashions. Lydia was so desperate to follow in Catherine's footsteps that she took up divining."

"Divining? The technique for finding water with rods?"

"Yes, but Lydia tried to use it to find men."

"How, exactly?"

"A copy of *Hello* magazine. She dangled the rod over each page until she got a twitch."

"I see," said Michael, not seeing at all. "I expect that your mother would stop such silly behaviour, though?"

"You're joking! Lydia told me that mom tried to get her to go all through *Who's Who* and find a millionaire, mom's age. Lydia lied, and said she couldn't do it without pictures."

"Your mother wants a new man?" said Michael "Oh. Your parents aren't together then?"

"Well, they've been divorced for years, but dad lives in the greenhouse."

"In the garden?"

"Yes. It's a big greenhouse," said Nerys. "With a shed attached. He's happy in there with his books and his maps."

"Isn't that strange and barbaric?" asked Michael. "Living in the garden, so close to his former marital home?"

"I thought it was cruel at first, but we told mom that there were frogs in the greenhouse so she doesn't go out there anymore. He's much happier now."

"Er, right."

"So, let's sort out some basics, then," said Nerys.

"Basics?"

"We should agree a story about how we met. Something that will stand up to interrogation."

"Oh, I see. Internet dating?"

"No," said Nerys. "Too desperate. I'm going to say that you slipped on the ice while you were jogging down by the canal, and you fell in."

"Okay."

"I jumped in and rescued you. We had to huddle together for bodily warmth when we were back on the bank, and the rest is history."

"It's not very traditional," said Michael. "I mean, I sound like a bit of an idiot."

"Thomas women always have to have the upper hand," said Nerys. "They'll lap it up. Now, I need to know more about your background. Where did you live before you came to Boldmere?"

"I was in a different city," said Michael. "They won't need to know those details, surely?"

"I need to know them," said Nerys, "or they'll smell the deception. Now, which city?"

"The celestial - oh. Ah..."

"Chester?"

"Yes, Chester," said Michael.

"Why did you leave?" asked Nerys.

"Oh, the usual reasons," Michael muttered.

Nerys looked at him questioningly so he went on.

"Urban decay, poverty, encroaching industrialisation. That sort of thing."

"In *Chester*?" Nerys frowned. "The cathedral city? Roman walls? Wall to wall fashion boutiques?"

"It's changed, Nerys," said Michael awkwardly.

"So, is that where you met Jeremy? I know you two go way back."

"In Chester? No. Jeremy doesn't belong in Chester. Not now, not ever."

Nerys scraped the last of her ice cream.

"I will need to write up some notes about our past," she said. "And yours. I think you need a more convincing back story."

BEN HEARD a banging noise outside his flat. He opened the door to see what was going on. Clovenhoof also appeared at his door. Nerys was wielding a feather duster on the upper surfaces of the landing.

"Got my first viewing in twenty minutes," she said, as she moved down the stairs. "Got to have the place looking spic and span."

Ben looked up and met Clovenhoof's eyes. They knew *exactly* what they had to do. They had spent considerable time planning it.

Clovenhoof had requested some of Ben's model paints, and had gone off to do something with them. Ben spent the time wiring up some extra speakers to his stereo. He was ready by the time he heard voices on the stairs. He riffled through his selection of vinyl and settled on seventies gothic rockers, *Bauhaus*, as being loud, sinister, and not all that appealing to most people he'd ever asked. He cranked the volume up and the walls shuddered to the bass notes.

Clovenhoof burst in through the door.

"Here, sit down while I sort out your face," he said.

Ben closed his eyes as Clovenhoof painted circles round his eyes.

"I'm not sure these paints are safe for skin, you know," said Ben.

"Well that's even better. We won't have to work so hard when she has her next viewing. We'll already look diseased, or drugged-up," said Clovenhoof.

They moved onto the landing, so that Clovenhoof could work on the walls with the paint.

Nerys came storming down the stairs.

"Will you turn off that horrible noise, Ben! Don't you know I've got potential buyers with me?"

She stopped and stared in horror. Two women appeared behind her on the stairs, peering around her.

"What's wrong with your faces? Have you both gone completely mad?"

Ben and Clovenhoof groaned and staggered around in time to *Bela Lugosi's Dead*, ignoring Nerys's protestations. Clovenhoof managed to point out the colourful outbreak of mould that he'd just painted on the wall as he lurched past. Nerys's face turned a deep, dangerous shade of red and she went back up the stairs, apologising to the two women whose frightened eyes kept glancing backwards.

CLOVENHOOF FOUND the drive down to Michael 'spiritual retreat' long and dull. He attempted to enliven the journey with some games, although no one seemed to be interested in armpit fart karaoke.

At least, he sighed to himself, the weekend away put some distance between them and Nerys, who had not seen their flat-viewing sabotage as the community service it genuinely was.

They arrived at the Wyre Forest campsite in darkness but Michael's 'guru' Elk had already set up the camp.

"The teepee is our living quarters for the weekend," Elk explained. "There's a woodstove in there, so we can be sure it's good and cosy. We'll take your bags in there and you'll see that you've got beds made up already."

"This isn't camping," said Clovenhoof, who had flicked through a scout manual, mainly looking for pictures of big knives.

"No, this is luxury, one-of-a-kind accommodation in the middle of the wilderness. This is why your friend had to pay such a handsome price for this weekend. I hope you enjoy it, and find it spiritually uplifting," said Elk.

"How do you suppose he got all this stuff out here?" Ben whispered to Clovenhoof.

"I saw a quad bike at the back of the teepee. Might have a go later," Clovenhoof winked.

"That's a heavy bag, Ben," said Andy, hauling their luggage inside. "What have you got in here?"

"Ah, just spare undies, and essentials," said Ben.

"Essentials like what?" said Clovenhoof, leaping out to take a look.

He unzipped the bag and rootled through.

"You must have enough underwear for a week!" he said.

"And why have you got all these books? One, two, three, FOUR books about military history! Whoppers, all of them."

"Just a little night time reading."

"Or spare toilet paper if we run out."

"NEXT WE COME to the sweat lodge," Elk explained on his tour of the camp. "You'll see that the door faces the sacred fire, which will be ready in a short while."

Clovenhoof peered inside the earthy-looking sweat lodge as Elk led the group on.

"Good. I'll christen it now if you don't mind."

He pulled apart the animal skins and stepped inside.

"It's not a toilet!" hissed Ben.

"Too late. I'll be out in a moment."

"The sweat lodge will form a central part of our ceremonies this weekend," continued Elk, in the distance. "We sit on the benches and the firekeeper will pour water over hot stones in that hole there. You will find it a very memorable experience, I promise."

"I don't doubt that," said Ben, as Clovenhoof swaggered out, zipping his trousers.

AFTER DINNER, Elk had the four of them change into loose, comfortable clothing and sat them down on rugs around the open camp fire. He gave them each a small drum.

"You will find your natural rhythm with the drum. I will

lead, but make your own way. We'll spend some time using this method to ease ourselves into a more relaxed frame of mind. Remember, the key phrase for this weekend is to do whatever feels right for *you*."

Elk began to slap his drum and made a nasal droning sound with his eyes closed. Michael and Andy followed a similar rhythm and murmured softly. Ben made a fast, rattling sound on his drum and started to emit a *wah wah* noise that sounded like a distant siren. Clovenhoof decided that he would re-create every drum solo he'd ever heard from an over-indulgent rock group. He improvised cymbal *tish* sounds and then roared his own rapturous applause after a few minutes.

Elk opened his eyes and addressed the group.

"I hope you're beginning to feel your inhibitions peel away."

"Some of us a bit too much," muttered Michael, shooting dagger glances at Clovenhoof.

"We're here in the wilderness, with only our trusted companions to bear witness," said Elk. "Show me that you're ready to go on a spiritual journey. I'd like you all to shout your name to the sky. Tell us who you are, and make sure you tell us with real meaning. We'll drum to the same rhythm now, to really accentuate what we're doing. Feel your name as you shout it, really feel the sort of person that sits behind the name. Let's move round the circle."

They started to drum in a single, simple rhythm.

Elk raised his face to the sky and bellowed out, "Elk! I am the mighty elk! Majestic, noble beast!"

The drumming continued. Elk turned to Andy.

"In your own time, Andy. If you feel you know your beast, your inner beast then shout it out. We each have a spirit totem."

Andy concentrated for a moment and then shouted up at the sky, "Andy! I'm Andy the eagle! I want to soar high above everything and be at peace!"

"Good work, Andy," said Elk. "Now you, Michael."

Michael shouted out, "I am Michael! Fearless warrior!"

"Do you identify with a beast, Michael?" asked Elk.

Michael looked around the group.

"Pigeon?" suggested Clovenhoof.

"Let's move on," said Elk. "Ben, let's hear from you."

Ben shuffled forward on his buttocks, enjoying the fire.

"I am Ben!"

"Good, good," said Elk.

Ben took a deep breath.

"I think I might be a squirrel," he said.

He looked around at the others' faces.

"What? I like nuts."

"Well done Ben," said Elk. "Now you, Jeremy."

Clovenhoof whooped at the sky with animalistic fervour.

"I am Clovenhoof, known by many names, and I identify with many beasts! Today, Elk, I'd like to be a Dragon!"

"Very uninhibited, Jeremy, that's excellent. Are we all ready to do the sweat lodge?"

There were nods all round.

They moved into the small, hut-like structure, where Elk had already placed hot stones from the fire into the pit.

"Now, it's going to get very steamy, but it's important that you all stay safe," said Elk. "You can take off your clothing, if it helps, we're all guys together here. If you need to step outside to cool off then that's fine. The forest is to your left and the lake is to your right. If you want to take a plunge in the lake, just remember that it's December. Don't do that on your own. We're all here to support each other, so take a buddy with you."

Andy thumped Michael's shoulder.

"Plunge buddies, eh?"

Michael grinned back.

Ben looked at Clovenhoof uneasily.

"If you fall in the lake and start drowning..." he began.

"It's my own stupid fault," said Clovenhoof.

"Damn straight," said Ben.

They settled onto the benches, and Elk started to pour water onto the stones. It hissed loudly and steam soon filled the space. Elk stripped to the waist and sat for a while, inhaling deeply. After a short while, everyone else was starting to peel off their clothes, and they lounged on the benches, puffing into the steam as they started to sweat. Ben tried to ignore the fact that Andy next to him had the musculature of an athlete. He was sure that, side by side, they looked like the before and after pictures for a protein drink advert.

"Can you feel it?" said Elk. "We can start to enter a more enlightened state. I shall now add some mystical herbs to the steam, to advance our journey."

He took out a pouch and crumbled something leafy into the steaming pit.

"Mystical herbs, my arse," whispered Andy in Ben's ear.

Elk ignored him, breathing deeply and encouraging the

others to do the same. Ben breathed in the smoky air and immediately began coughing. As he gasped, he dragged in further lungfuls and coughed further until he had a full blown hacking fit. When he finally brought himself under control, his head was swimming. There was a sweet tang in his nostrils and a pleasurable buzzing in his head.

All that could now be heard was the crackling of the fire, the hissing of the steam, and the steady breathing of the five men.

The silence was punctuated by a loud fart, and Clovenhoof giggled.

"Oh, really!" said Michael.

Clovenhoof continued to laugh.

"It's not that funny," said Ben, trying to hide his smile.

"I'm not laughing at that," said Clovenhoof. "I was just thinking."

"What were you thinking, brother?" asked Elk.

"Ben," giggled Clovenhoof. "Ben the squirrel."

He started to slide off the bench with his increased mirth. Ben did his best to look reproachful, but then Andy was sniggering too.

"You're nuts, Jeremy."

"They're not my nuts," snorted Jeremy. "They're Ben's."

Ben found himself pointing at his groin.

"And what lovely nuts they are too!" he grinned.

"And we all know where you'd like to store your nuts this winter," smirked Michael.

"Oh, Jayne!" simpered Clovenhoof, reaching for an imaginary woman and falling off the bench.

The howls of laughter that followed rolled around Ben's

skull like ball-bearings in a drum, round and round for hours in the thoughtless void of his expanded mind. The herbal smoke no longer irritated his lungs but flowed through him, in and out, air shared communally with these men, his friends, his brothers. Somewhere far off, a small Ben-ish voice kept asking him when he'd taken off the rest of his clothes, but he knew with no doubt at all that he was with his best friends, so it was fine that they were all naked.

A chunk of thought fell into Ben, like a jigsaw piece locking into place, and Ben opened his eyes. Ben and Clovenhoof were both lying beside the campsite, spreadeagled in the grass, staring up at the winter sky.

"I think someone's nicked our tent," said Clovenhoof.

"Nerys," said Ben.

"Yeah," said Clovenhoof. "She'd do that."

"No," said Ben, irritated. He was finding speech hard enough without Clovenhoof misunderstanding him. "*Nerys.*"

"What about her?"

"We can't let her move out. We just can't."

"We won't, don't worry."

"She's like the over-sexed cousin I never had," said Ben. "I think I really love her, you know?"

"You do?"

"In the way you'd love an over-sexed cousin."

"Oh yeah. I'd love one of those."

"Me too."

"I've got plans," said Clovenhoof.

"Yeah?"

"You see, we've been teaching the cubs about geocaching

and I thought our coal bunker would make an excellent geocache..."

Ben let Clovenhoof's insane plots carry him back into the world of sleep and unsettling dreams in which a gaggle of Welsh women and a pack of cub scouts were trying to take his nuts from him.

MICHAEL STOOD, cold and naked in the dark forest.

The world was silent and dark. The sound and fury of the city was miles away.

Michael wondered if he was closer to God here. God was everywhere but maybe even more so in these quiet places.

"I'm here!" he shouted at the sky. "You can talk to me now!"

There was no sound. His voice didn't even echo back to him.

"There's nobody around to hear us, Lord!"

Silence.

"Won't you please give me a sign?" he sniffed.

An owl flapped down from a branch overhead and skimmed softly away. White wings, fading between the lean trees. Michael's breath stopped.

"Is that your sign?" he shouted.

But what did it mean? The wings were significant. Soft, silent, but hiding a deadly purpose. Just like him. The owl was surely his inner beast.

"Owl! I'm an owl!" he yelled to the sky. "I am your owl, Lord!"

But no, there must be more. He racked his brain for the message he was supposed to take from the owl encounter.

He heard a twig snap and looked across the clearing. It was Andy.

"Couldn't sleep," said Andy. "Too spaced out."

"Oh Andy, I've had a rapturous encounter," gushed Michael. "It was beautiful."

"What was it?"

Michael shook his head.

"But I just don't know what it means."

Andy took Michael's hand in his own.

"Things don't always have to mean something."

Michael turned to face Andy. The intermittent, faint moonlight made Andy's skin pale and ghostly, white like the wings of an owl.

Michael opened his mouth to speak.

The silence of the clearing was abruptly shattered by the roar of an approaching quad bike. They both dived apart as Clovenhoof burst out from the undergrowth, whooping and revving the engine.

"I am the Great Dragon!" he bellowed, as he span donuts in the clearing. "Hear me roar!"

He over-revved the engine and then was gone again, crashing and hollering through the undergrowth.

Michael got to his feet, brushing leaf mould and dirt from his naked body.

"That cock," said Andy.

"Quite," said Michael and then realised he wasn't talking about Clovenhoof.

"I *have* seen that cock before," said Andy.

CLOVENHOOF WAS AMUSED, yet startled, that Michael had made 'mystical herbs' part of his daily routine. A week after the spiritual retreat, Clovenhoof stepped over the angel as he sat on the landing, smoking a roll up.

"How's it hanging, gorgeous?" he asked.

Michael was not his usual pristine self, wearing a baggy kaftan instead of an uptight Italian suit.

"I'm trying to summon my spirit totem again," said Michael.

"Of course."

"I really felt I was close to something until you trampled all over my karma."

"I'm sure you'll get results if you try hard enough," said Clovenhoof and knocked on Ben's door.

He went inside and emptied a bag onto Ben's table. Ben got out his clipboard and checked off the contents.

"Mushrooms for the skirting boards, did you get those?"

Clovenhoof thumped a tin down in front of him.

"Couldn't you get fresh ones?" Ben said.

"No. These will be fine, they've got that semi-putrid look already."

"Okay. Ooh, crime scene tape, I like that. Where did you get it from?"

Clovenhoof looked hard at Ben.

"Clue's in the name, knucklehead."

"What? Oh. Yeah. Forget I asked." Ben cleared his throat. "Right, well I've been in touch with that firm we found on the internet. They sent me samples of the aerosol cans that they use in haunted houses in theme parks. This one's called *Rotting Corpse*."

Ben gave a little squirt and Clovenhoof inhaled with relish.

"Mm!"

"And this one's *Hellish Sulphur*."

Ben gave another little squirt, in the style of a perfume assistant.

Clovenhoof inhaled deeply and froze. It was like being back in the Old Place, an olfactory slap in the face.

"Jiminy fuck monkey!" he exclaimed.

"No good?"

Clovenhoof wiped the beginning of a tear from his eye and grabbed the aerosol from Ben.

"We'll go with *Rotting Corpse* for Operation Scare-Them-Away. I'm keeping this one."

"Er, okay. Are you all right?"

"Yes."

"Are you sure? You look as though you've got something in your eye, it's gone all watery."

"Oh shut up," snapped Clovenhoof. "Have you got enough red paint to make the blood stains?"

"I'm on it. What time are the next batch coming round?"

"Ten minutes. It's going to look great. I've sorted the blood. Michael's toking on the biggest joint you ever saw in your life, so the place will reek of weed."

"Perfect."

"Now, you go up and distract her, so that I can make sure I intercept them when they get here. I've got to get changed."

Clovenhoof ran to his flat, dealt with his clothing and

then galloped downstairs and got himself into lounging position, slumped against the front door frame, just as the visitors walked up the path.

"Oh, do mind the blood stains," he called out, causing them to swerve in a big arc.

"Blood stains," said one of the men.

"That poor wee boy," he said, shaking his head.

One of the men stared back at the bloodstain, his eyes wide.

"Why are you naked?" asked the older one.

"Oh, we call it Hang Free Friday," said Clovenhoof. "It's not compulsory for everyone in the flats to join in, but if you want to fit in..."

He showed them up the stairs. They went past Ben's flat, with the scene of crime tape across the door. They climbed over Michael, whose face was slack and glazed, joint smouldering at his side. He sent them up the last staircase on their own.

"Just up there," he called, and saw them off with a friendly wave.

He then backtracked, collecting up the mushrooms, tape and Michael and stowed them in Ben's flat. Finally, he rolled up the bloodstain, confident that nobody who was in a tearing hurry to leave would notice its absence.

"HONESTLY, THE NERVE OF THE WOMAN!" said Nerys, stomping past Ben on her way downstairs to answer the door. "She made it sound as though there was something the matter, that flats in this location didn't *normally* take such an effort to move."

"It's a tricky time for selling a property," said Ben.

"I blame their marketing entirely."

"I should take it as a sign if I were you."

Nerys gave him a shrewd look.

"Well, she's bringing some people round today. My last chance before the new year. Apparently, they don't do viewings over Christmas."

With a final tut, huff and wave of the arms, Nerys opened the door.

She looked at the young and incredibly clean cut man on the doorstep. Dark hair, soulful eyes, a healthy tan and the scent of delicate cologne. This was her dream gondolier. She could picture him, a striped vest stretched taut over those proud pectorals, his strong hands gripping his pole...

"*Può aiutarmi? Devo trovare subito qualcuno con un motoscafo!*" she said automatically.

"I'm sorry," said the man.

Nerys smiled sweetly.

"Have you come for the viewing?" she asked. "You are a little early. Although, you could come up for a coffee. Is it too early for wine?"

"Actually, I was looking for Michael."

"Andy!" called out Michael from behind her. "What a lovely surprise! Do come in."

Nerys saw the smiles that passed between the two and then re-evaluated her opinion of the young man.

Of course, she thought dolefully. Even Michael gets a handsome man before I do.

ANDY SAT DOWN and ran his hand across the back of the sofa.

"What a beautiful flat you have, Michael, it really is."

"Thank you, I try."

"And the kaftan. Very... spiritual?"

"Mmmm. Perhaps a spiritual step too far. I think I can be spiritual and still wear Armani. Coffee."

"Sure. Listen," Andy said hurriedly, jiggling the carrier bag he had brought with him. "I wanted to say thank you for the Christmas present."

"Have you opened it already? Two days early. Naughty. Did you like it?"

"Well, the thing is, erm..."

"Wrong size?" said Michael.

"You do know that it's ladies' underwear, don't you?"

"Oh. Nerys didn't say. Well, I thought anyone could wear it."

"Wait, do you wear this stuff?" asked Andy.

Michael felt a sudden panic.

"What would be the right answer in this situation?"

"Take a wild guess," said Andy.

"Er, no."

"Exactly."

Michael nodded.

"Although the lace gives a certain pleasing frisson around the groin."

Andy laughed.

"Michael, you're unbelievable! You really are. But to be clear, no, I don't wear stuff like this."

"Oh,"

"It's just not me. Sorry."

"No problem. Hope I didn't embarrass you."

"God no. Not at all." He offered the carrier bag to Michael. "Do you want it back?"

"I think," said Michael slowly, "that we should invent a new game to use it."

"Not sure I'm quite ready for kinky stuff."

Michael opened the window.

See that gatepost at the end of the garden?"

"Yeah."

"Well the first one to get a pair of knickers on it from the sofa wins," said Michael.

"All right!" said Andy, sighting across his outstretched thumbs. "Let the pinging begin!"

CLOVENHOOF WAS at the door ahead of Nerys to greet the prospective buyers.

The estate agent was with the old couple who had come to look round, seemingly determined that this viewing would not go unsupervised. Maybe she wanted to see for herself why the flat was proving so difficult to sell. Clovenhoof was happy to demonstrate why it was more trouble than it was worth.

"Lovely to see that you've been able to find some more potential clients," he exclaimed, open armed. "Especially after the murder!"

"Murder?" said the elderly woman.

"That's quite enough of that," said the estate agent, "This man is-"

She was cut off as two pairs of ladies panties struck her in the face. The elderly couple recoiled in horror.

The estate agent hurriedly brushed the lingerie away, trying to pretend nothing had happened, and swept the viewers through the door and up the stairs.

Nerys met them at the door to her flat and welcomed them in. She forcibly stopped Clovenhoof following them, shutting the door firmly in his face. He stamped his hoof and listened in at the door.

"You'll see that the windows let in plenty of light, even during these darker days," said the estate agent.

"Oh, yes," said the old woman. "Whose child is that?"

"There are no children here," said Nerys.

"Look, down there. In the coal bunker."

There was a pause. Clovenhoof could picture them crowding round the window.

"Was it a child that was murdered?" the woman asked in a trembling voice.

"What? No. No children, no murder," said Nerys, annoyed.

There was a small shriek. Clovenhoof grinned.

"There! There!" shrilled the woman. "A small boy! I heard a ghoulish voice this time as well!"

"What did it say?" asked her husband.

"It wasn't that clear, but it sounded something like *'I said only one sweet you little scumbag or I'm telling Kaa.'*"

There was suddenly a large number of voices but it was clear the viewers had already seen enough.

The doorbell rang. Clovenhoof tap-danced downstairs to answer it.

"She's not selling," he began. "Oh, Reverend Zack."

The rector smiled earnestly at Clovenhoof.

"Hello, Jeremy. I've come round to see Michael."

"I think he's got company."

"I just wanted to see if he was feeling any better. We've not seen him for a while."

"He's an owl now apparently."

"He's...? I just felt that, if we spoke, Michael might think about coming back to the church and j-"

"Oh, is this the God-botherer who gave you crap?"

Andy had come out into the hallway. Michael stood behind him, a pair of knickers clutched in his hand.

"Michael," said Zack.

"Back off, black shirt," said Andy angrily.

Michael's gaze dropped to the floor. Clovenhoof took a step back to get a better view of the show. He sensed he would be needing some popcorn.

"You lot make me sick," said Andy, sticking a finger in Reverend Zack's chest.

"My lot?" said Zack.

"You have no idea how much pain you cause to simple, straightforward folk who just want to live their lives!" he shouted.

"I just wanted to –"

"Don't give me your Old Testament bigotry. We are what we are. Get used to it!"

"You mean you're...?"

"You're bloody right we are. What will it take to make you

leave us alone? Are we supposed to top ourselves, just to make the place a bit tidier for you?"

"I'm not sure that-"

"You make me sick! You really do!"

The elderly couple came down the stairs, uncertain and apprehensive. Clovenhoof waved them on. He gave a stage whisper,

"It's just another exorcism. None of the others have worked, but the good reverend does keep trying."

He solemnly indicated the vicar Zack and the shouting, gesticulating Andy, who now had flecks of spittle around his mouth as he really hit his stride.

The elderly couple ran out of the front door, and the estate agent scuttled after them.

"You'll see that the path features some original patterned tiles," she gasped, through force of habit as she ran to catch up, "and access to the rear of the property is round there."

As she indicated to the right, a small boy in a grubby cub uniform sprinted past them, closely followed by a second shouting, "Only one, scumbag! You're dead, you are."

The elderly woman fainted away into her husband's arms.

ST CADFAN'S

"We're going to get into trouble for this," said Novice Stephen as he peeled another apple.

"So you've said five times," said Brother Sebastian who was chopping apples and putting them in the huge pot.

"It's six," said Brother Manfred. "But we've stopped counting."

Manfred cleaned the kitchen surfaces, laid out the foodstuffs for the evening meal and kept a watchful eye on the door.

"Way I see it," said Sebastian, "is that we may be lying to the abbot -"

"Directly disobeying his orders," said Stephen.

"*But* we're doing this for the good of the monastery. Lesser of two evils and all that. We sell this preserve at the market in Aberdaron next week. If it's a commercial failure we pretend it never happened. If it turns a decent profit, we'll add that to the coffers and consider what to do next."

"And if the abbot finds out? Vengeance seven times over he said."

"That's what he always says. Anyway, I'll remind him it was your idea," grinned Sebastian and nudged the novice's shoulder to show he was joking.

Sebastian cut up the last of Stephen's apples, dropped them in the sugary pot and put the lid on.

"And now we let it stew."

"Come," said Manfred, "I have something to show you."

He beckoned them to leave the kitchen but Stephen hesitated.

"Shouldn't we stay here to watch the pots?"

"It is what they say, a watched pot never cooks properly," said Manfred.

"I meant in case the abbot comes."

Sebastian gave him an honest stare.

"So, if the abbot accidentally comes across our jam-making operation, you want us to be stood next to it?"

Stephen considered this.

"Good point. Let's go."

Stephen and Sebastian followed Manfred through the monastery to the almonry, taking a slightly circuitous route to avoid the dangerously sagging stonework in one corridor. The almonry had, once upon time, been the place where the monks offered food and money to the local poor but was now a general utility space and home to some of the equipment and supplies that had no other home.

"I see you've been at work on the tapestries," said

Stephen, indicating the scene of Christ's final day in Jerusalem on one wall.

"A labour of love," said Manfred. "Rather like this."

He shifted a heavy toolbox aside and opened a grimy cupboard.

Stephen and Sebastian looked in. On the floor was a convoluted piece of apparatus. Two bell jars, several funnels, a length of garden hose and a wire coathanger had been bound together with duct tape. Sebastian looked at the pale liquid condensing and dripping inside.

"Is that...?"

"It is," said Manfred with a smile.

"Apple schnapps?"

Manfred made a see-saw gesture with his hand.

"Apple schnapps or apple brandy. Let us see what it turns into before we give it a name."

Sebastian slapped the refectorian on the shoulder.

"You are a marvel, Manfred."

"I expect you to put that on my tombstone."

Manfred locked the cupboard and shifted the toolbox back in front of it.

"We are in so much trouble," said Stephen.

"You worry too much," said Sebastian and then stopped, his gaze on the wall-mounted tapestry. "You've been busy on this, brother. I don't think I've ever seen it so vibrant."

"Thank you," said Manfred. "It's a challenge to add new shape or colour without overpowering what is already there."

"You've clearly had to invent some detail."

"A little. The buildings up by Golgotha were indecipherably faded."

"And this street scene," said Sebastian. "Jesus being taken up the Via Dolorosa. Who is this figure here?"

Manfred nodded.

"I am glad that you have noticed that. I feel he is the central figure of this tapestry. It is the *Ewige Jude*. You would call him the Wandering Jew. The man who offended Christ and was cursed to walk the earth for the rest of time. I had to recreate him purely from his outline so I had to follow my instincts in his recreation."

"And your instincts told you..."

"That he was a man who could never settle. Always travelling, always surviving despite the odds. He is rugged, a lost pilgrim, a man who carried the weight of the world on his shoulders but would never let it show."

"And that's why you turned him into Clint Eastwood?"

"Yes," he said. "That's exactly what I did."

"With spurs and a gun at his belt."

"And a cigarillo in the corner of his mouth," said Stephen peering closer.

Manfred was unfazed.

"All art of this period has some anachronisms. I wanted to convey the very essence of the man."

They all looked at the tapestry in the company of their own thoughts.

"Nice poncho," said Stephen eventually.

6

IN WHICH MICHAEL DISCOVERS POT NOODLES AND THE LAST RESTING PLACE OF JOSEPH OF ARIMATHEA

I n Sutton Coldfield, Christmas came and went. Vast quantities of food and alcohol were consumed, there was a rowdy visit to Midnight Mass at St Michael's (during which *someone* shouted obscenities every time the Archangel Gabriel was mentioned) and there was the obligatory exchanging of presents, specifically a toasting fork, a lurid pink T-shirt, a coffee maker, a wickedly sharp hunting knife, a wet-dry vacuum cleaner, some belly button fluff and three books (*Teach Yourself Welsh*, *Italian Cooking Made Easy* and *Dr Faustus*).

New Year came and went soon after. Vast quantities of food and alcohol were consumed, there was a rowdy rendition of Auld Lang Syne and the obligatory exchanging of unwanted presents for cash or store credit. Ben subtly gave the hideous pink T-shirt to charity, Michael publicly flushed Clovenhoof's belly button fluff down his Soyuz space toilet and Clovenhoof used the wet-dry vacuum cleaner to wash

Twinkle and then attempted to ride it to the corner shop but only got as far as the pavement before the power cable reached its limit.

Two weeks into the new year, Clovenhoof was sitting in the back of Nerys's car, idly poking holes in the ceiling fabric with his horns and cleaning under his fingernails with the tip of the twelve-inch 'bushcraft' knife Ben had given him. The motorway had seemingly disappeared just as they had crossed the England-Wales border and he had rapidly become bored. No one had been interested in a game of 'belch that tune' or 'guess where I found this' and the Welsh countryside, contrary to Nerys's descriptions, was not filled with picturesque valleys populated by wandering shepherds with a song on their lips. In fact, he mused critically, Wales appeared to be exactly the same as England: cold and grey with the occasional dash of soggy greenery. It was a total con.

So when Michael declared that he really needed to stop somewhere "to visit the gents", Clovenhoof gave his hearty support. Anything was better than another ten hours in that bloody car.

"It hasn't been ten hours," said Nerys as they stepped into the roadside café cum gift shop outside Llangedwyn. "It's been ninety minutes tops."

"Time clearly runs slowly in Wales," said Clovenhoof.

"Actually, thinking about my childhood, you're probably right."

"Hey," called out the woman at the till shrilly, waving a

hand to stop Michael in his tracks. "Toilets are for customers only."

"That woman sounds like you when you're drunk," Clovenhoof said to Nerys.

"She's Welsh," said Nerys and then, to the woman, "It's okay. We're going to get something."

"Be sure you do."

Nerys ushered Ben and Clovenhoof towards the gift shop. With the woman's hostile gaze redirected to them, Michael slipped into the toilets.

"If you're Welsh, is it compulsory to be a miserable sod?" asked Clovenhoof.

Nerys nodded.

"Yup, just as it's compulsory for the English to be arrogant xenophobic wankers," she said happily.

Clovenhoof, whose nationality was a mystery even to himself, didn't disagree.

"And yet," said Ben, casually perusing a display of dolls in traditional Welsh dress, "this woman has elected to work in the hospitality industry."

"Don't touch something unless you intend to buy it," snapped the woman.

"Ha!" laughed Clovenhoof. He loved the idea of British hospitality in terms of the fact that it didn't exist. That huge numbers of people worked in the 'hospitality industry' without any social skills or a caring bone in their body was utterly delicious. It was like having a health service staffed entirely by abattoir workers. If he ever got back to the Old Place, he would install a Fiery Pit of Hospitality and get the British to run it.

"I see you Welsh struggle with baking skills too," said Clovenhoof, poking his finger at the glass-fronted food cabinet. "Those scones look like an elephant sat on them."

"They're welshcakes. They're a local, er, delicacy."

"And these?" said Ben, pointing to a row of intricately carved wooden objects, all plaits and hoops and hearts.

"Lovespoons," said Nerys.

"Oh, I've heard of them," said Clovenhoof. "You can order them from specialist magazines."

"Can you?"

"I thought you had one in your bedroom. Aren't they the ones that you turn on and the woman sticks up her-"

"Whoa!" said Nerys loudly. "*That's* something else entirely."

"Are you sure?"

"I am sure."

"It sounds like that kind of thing," said Clovenhoof reasonably. "*Love*spoon. It's clearly a euphemism of some sort. 'Hey, baby, want to sup some porridge from my lovespoon?'"

"No! No! No! For the love of fuck, no!"

"You need to read the label on these things."

A deep growled brewed in the depths of Nerys's throat.

"Shut up, you ignorant twat. Listen, we Welsh have precious little culture as it is. The bloody English annexed Wales then subjugated Wales and then spent the next seven hundred years trying to crush and belittle Wales. Most of the world hasn't even heard of Wales and those who have think Wales is somewhere *in* England rather than a country in its own right. Not that the Welsh get a seat in the UN or any sort of independence. We can't even be trusted to have our own regional parliament! No, we have an 'assembly'. What are we? Primary school kids, all sat on the floor, waiting for Tufty Squirrel to come in and tell us about road safety?"

"Er, you've lost me there…" said Clovenhoof, who had no idea who this Tufty character was, but Nerys was in a fifth gear rant and not stopping. Her furious gaze and accusing finger swung between Clovenhoof and Ben.

"And you're still bloody invading us. Half the people living here are English and they own all the good houses! *Your* Prime Minister, Maggie bloody Thatcher, killed off our mining industry."

"I was two at the time," said Ben timidly.

"I had nothing to do with it," said Clovenhoof who did know who Margaret Thatcher was and had even implemented some of her bolder policies in the Old Place.

"No wonder the average Welsh kid is a council estate chav with no job prospects and no dreams but to get out of Wales as soon as possible!" snarled Nerys. "And, yes, why is it that any Welsh person who achieves any modicum of success suddenly stops being referred to as Welsh and becomes *British*? Shirley Bassey, Anthony Hopkins, Richard Burton. You've taken or trampled any culture of ours that was ever worth a damn. Our national dish is cheese on toast, for fuck's sake. So, do not mock the welshcakes and don't defile our bloody lovespoons with your tasteless jokes. They are hand-carved decorative gifts a suitor offers to his betrothed! They are not dildos! And they are not a euphemism for your pitiful teaspoon-sized manhood from which not even the most desperate woman would lick your cock porridge! Do you understand?"

She stopped, gasping for breath, her face flushed with fury and exertion.

"We understand," said Ben in a tiny voice.

The woman at the counter had a concerned look on her face.

"Are you all right, pet?" she asked.

Nerys turned to her, still red in the face.

"Pobl Saesneg yn ffycin dwp."

"Amen to that," said the woman.

THE ARCHANGEL MICHAEL washed his hands for a second time and inspected them critically. He had a bottle of antiseptic handwash in his suitcase and felt the urge to get it. He dried his hand on one of the needlessly coarse paper towels and went out into the shop.

Clovenhoof was at the till buying several items. The place was otherwise empty.

"Where are Ben and Nerys?"

"Ben's gone looking for wood. Nerys has gone to scream at the hills or something."

Michael left the Angel of the Bottomless Pit to his purchases and went out into the car park. Ben was rooting around in some thick nettles at the edge of the road. Nerys leant against the car, her back to Michael and the café. Without even seeing her face, he could feel the fury radiating off her.

"Ah-ha!" declared Ben, holding aloft a short and splintered length of two-by-four wood.

"What's that for?" said Michael.

"A lovespoon. I need to carve one for Jayne."

"I see," said Michael, who didn't see at all. "And Nerys?"

"She hates the English."

"I can hear you," called Nerys, turning round. "It's not that." She kicked her way across the car park. "I don't hate the English. Actually, I do, but I hate the Welsh too." She sighed heavily. "Going home, it's not easy for me. And it's not made any easier by some people behaving like tits in the first Welsh shop we come to."

"Some people?" said Michael.

The café door swung open. Clovenhoof strode forth. He had swapped his Hawaiian shirt for a white T-shirt emblazoned with the Red Dragon of Wales. On his head, he wore a baseball cap with an embroidered Welsh flag.

"Look at me. Like a native. I'll just blend in."

"Oh, God," muttered Nerys.

Clovenhoof pointed out the emblem on his chest to Michael.

"Look, I am now the Great *Red* Dragon."

Nerys got in the car.

Clovenhoof, seemingly sensing that no one was overly impressed, said, "Well, we had to buy something so you could use the toilet."

Michael shuddered and hoped that the standards of plumbing and cleaning in the roadside café's toilets were not the Welsh norm.

"However much you spent-" he said.

"Thirty-two pounds," said Clovenhoof proudly.

"Definitely not worth it," said Michael.

CLOVENHOOF LOANED Ben his hunting knife and watched the young fellow attempt to whittle the lump of scrap wood into a lovespoon for his girlfriend. It was certainly a welcome distraction from the monotony of the journey. A man with more hobbies than pants, whose misspent youth was spent making scale models of ancient battlefields, Ben was a natural craftsman and worked the blade more skilfully than Clovenhoof ever could. However, Ben's tools and material were imperfect and, as he showered the back seat with woodchip and shavings, there was the occasional slip of the knife and delightful squeal of pain.

In the driving seat, Nerys kept up a constant narration, indicating 'points of interest' along the route. Here was Llyn Trawsfynydd with its defunct power station. Over there was Portmeirion which was supposedly very pretty and some weird sixties TV programme had been filmed there. They almost saw a steam train at Porthmadog, but only the steam was visible over a high wall.

Dressed in his spiffingly patriotic T-shirt and baseball cap, Clovenhoof tried to muster some enthusiasm for what he saw but it was difficult. As a former Prince of Hell, Clovenhoof had a fine grasp of all the tongues of men, so even the Welsh place names and road signs that amused Ben so much did little for him.

Maybe he was just too used to Birmingham, with its crowded streets and constant noise. He had not left the place in over a year, apart from their camping weekend before Christmas and even that had seemed like a mere dip into the quiet country. This countryside here, Wales, it was so...

"Where are all the people?" said Michael, echoing his thoughts. "It's as though Wales has shut up early for the day and gone home."

"That's Wales," agreed Nerys. "It's charms are sometimes hard to see. But, you know, there's a lot to like about my home town, Aberdaron."

"Oh, yes?" said Michael.

"Mmmm." Nerys thought for a while. "There's, um, Y Gegin Fawr."

"The Big Kitchen?" said Clovenhoof.

"Yes. I didn't know you spoke Welsh, Jeremy," she said, surprised.

"Lucky guess."

"Y Gegin Fawr was built in the thirteen hundreds. It's a tea shop now. It was where the pilgrims used to stop for a meal before the crossing."

"Pilgrims?" said Michael.

"To Bardsey. The Island of Twenty Thousand Saints. It's just off the tip of the peninsula. There's a monastery. The church used to say that three pilgrimages to Bardsey was as worthy as one pilgrimage to Rome."

"Three Bardseys equals one Rome," mused Clovenhoof. "Interesting exchange rate. What do these pilgrimages get you, eh?"

"Salvation," said Michael. "Forgiveness." He suddenly sat up straight. "Pilgrims can seek forgiveness," he said, clearly intrigued by the idea.

Clovenhoof punched the back of Michael's seat.

"It's going to take more than a day-trip to a damp Welsh rock for you to be forgiven, Michael."

"God moves in mysterious ways."

"Shifty, you mean."

Nerys reached over and patted Michael's shoulder.

"My lovely fake boyfriend doesn't need forgiveness. He's perfect."

"A perfect arse," muttered Clovenhoof.

"Ow," squealed Ben as the hunting knife made a nick in his thumb. Clovenhoof wished he had a camera in case Ben accidentally slit open an artery.

BEN HAD BEEN QUITE PERHAPS TOO intent on his whittling but, even so, Aberdaron appeared to be a blink-and-you'll-miss-it sort of place. It was mid-afternoon and the winter skies were already darkening. The lanes were narrow and high-banked with prickly gorse. Ben wondered what happened when you met another car but, remarkably, they didn't. Beyond the town, Nerys turned from a small winding road, onto an even smaller and more winding road and into the driveway of a large detached house.

"Okay," said Nerys, taking a nervous breath. "This is it. Everyone on their best behaviour. Remember, Michael is my boyfriend and we're very much in love. Michael, just smile and nod. Ben, behave yourself. Don't do anything geeky and weird." She glanced in the rear view mirror. "Why aren't you wearing that lovely shirt I bought you for Christmas?"

"It's in the packing somewhere," lied Ben.

"I've no idea what my sister sees in you but if you're going to screw it up and get dumped, save it until we've gone home. And Jeremy."

"Yes," said Jeremy.

"Why did we bring you? I forget."

Clovenhoof scratched his chin in thought.

"You said I couldn't be trusted to be alone in the flats while you were away."

"Oh, that's right."

"I am a grown man. It's not like I'm going to set fire to the place. Again. I mean, a third time."

Nerys pulled up outside the front of the house.

"You. I'd be more worried that you'd try to sell my underwear to Japanese businessmen or sub-let my flat to a suicide cult. Right, best smiles, gang."

They got out. Ben, brushed the wood shavings from his lap, sucked at the most recent of his fingertip injuries and regarded his workmanship. His lovespoon, his gift for his beloved was far from finished, but he was pleasantly surprised to see how spoon-like it was. It still needed some work and, for want of a better place, tucked it into the waistband of his trousers.

The Thomas house was a sprawling thing. The original house appeared to have been a fairly square farmhouse structure but had since been buried beneath extensions, a porch, a brick-built garage, a conservatory and the surface addition of white uPVC double-glazing, skylights and fascia boards.

The front door opened as they approached.

"Give me that," hissed Nerys and snatched two bags from Ben, filling her arms.

The woman in the doorway, gave them an appraising look. Ben attempted a smile as he approached but it crumbled under her gaze.

He had not met Nerys's mom before but the family resemblance was clear. In a not unkindly way, Ben had always regarded Nerys as striking rather than beautiful. Nerys's mother was not merely striking but downright stunning, at least for a woman of her age. Her nose was longer, sharper, her eyes more piercing, her arched brows more expressive. In fact, he concluded, she was just like Nerys, only sort of... *stretched*. Taller, slimmer and less curvaceous than her daughter, Mrs Thomas looked like Nerys after a lengthy session on the rack.

No wonder Nerys did everything she could to show off her cleavage. At least that was one thing she had that her mom didn't.

"Having a bad shoe day, dear?" said Mrs Thomas, looking at Nerys's pumps.

"These are for driving," said Nerys.

"Of course, dear."

Mrs Thomas made to kiss Nerys but Nerys's bags got in the way. The older woman had to make do with kissing air. She looked her daughter up and down once more.

"Nice to see someone isn't afraid of indulging too much over the festive season."

"Are you saying I've got a fat bum?" said Nerys.

"I hadn't even noticed *that*," she said and made a point of looking.

She then looked at the three men loitering behind Nerys. Ben felt her penetrating gaze on him once more.

"Hmm, and you would be Ben?" she said, pointing a manicured finger at Michael.

"Er, no," said Michael, with a self-deprecating smile.

"Oh," said Mrs Thomas, clearly disappointed. "You then?" she said, pointing at Ben.

"That's me," said Ben, not sure if he should be insulted at being her second choice or relieved at not being her third.

"Interesting," said Mrs Thomas thoughtfully and Ben didn't care to imagine what that meant.

"I'm Michael," said Michael.

"*My* boyfriend," said Nerys and leaned heavily against him.

Mrs Thomas smiled, like a vet about to put down a kitten.

"Punching above your weight again, dear?" she said and gave Michael an openly saucy look.

"Michael is lucky to have a woman like me," Nerys retorted.

"Absolutely," said Michael emphatically and unconvincingly. "I can't believe my luck sometimes."

"So who's this?" said Mrs Thomas, peering down her nose at Clovenhoof. "Are you Ben's dad?"

Ben laughed.

"No, this is our... friend, Jeremy."

Clovenhoof stepped forward and placed an enthusiastic continental kiss on Mrs Thomas's cheeks.

"Tasty. No, Mrs Thomas, I am their friend and neighbour. I suppose, to young Ben and Nerys, I'm like the father they never had."

"Nerys has a father," said Mrs Thomas sharply.

"So do I," chipped in Ben.

"Yes, but you've never had one like me," said Clovenhoof.

"Ben!"

Ben almost leapt at his squealed name. Jayne pushed past her mother, clasped his arms and grinned at him, teeth bright in the grey afternoon.

"You're here," she said.

Ben shrugged.

"Astonishing, isn't it?"

"Considering the way Nerys drives," said Clovenhoof but Jayne wasn't listening.

She tugged at Ben's hand and pulled him into the house, leaving Mrs Thomas tutting on the doorstep.

It appeared that the interior of the Thomas house had been decorated to replicate the pictures in a furniture store catalogue: colour co-ordinated furnishings and tasteful but meaningless ornaments perfectly arranged in spotlessly clean rooms.

But Jayne did not give Ben a chance to pause and nor did he care. She dragged him through the open plan lounge, along a short hallway and into a large hexagonal conservatory before physically spinning him round and planting a kiss on his lips that almost pulled out his fillings.

"You missed me, huh?" he gasped when Jayne was done.

"You know what they say about absence," she replied. "I get to spend a scant few weeks in Birmingham, with you, and then I have to return to this."

Ben looked about himself, at the fine wicker furniture in

the conservatory, at the well-tended pot plants, at the sweeping lawn beyond the window.

"Oh, this definitely looks like Hell," he said. "Hey, that's the sea."

"Very observant."

The back garden sloped downwards, between low hedges, past a large shed and greenhouse and then fell away to reveal the Irish Sea and, some miles off, a long hump-backed island.

"What's that place?" he asked.

"Bardsey Island. There's a big bird sanctuary there."

"That's some view," he said. "Dramatic."

"Lydia likes to stand at the end of the garden like some doomed gothic heroine about to throw herself to her death. But only when she knows someone's watching. I'm sure you'll meet her soon enough."

Ben shook his head.

"There's only one Thomas girl I'm interested in."

Jayne groaned.

"That is so corny."

Ben felt a quiver of inferiority and embarrassment take the colour from his face.

"But very sweet," said Jayne and kissed him again.

This time the kiss was less like an attack from an industrial hoover and Ben was able to respond without the fear of his kidneys being sucked out.

Jayne paused without breaking contact.

"What *is* that thing poking into me?" she said.

"Oh, it's my lovespoon," said Ben.

Her lips smiled against his.

"Whatever."

MICHAEL STOOD in the living room with Clovenhoof and Nerys while Mrs Thomas went to the kitchen to prepare what she had described as a 'light supper'. In his stomach he felt one of those nameless emotions that he had never suffered as one of the angelic host. He didn't want to stay standing up because he felt he was in the way, too obvious. He didn't want to sit down either because that would suggest a sense of comfortableness that he simply didn't feel.

Mrs Thomas's gaze (and hands) had lingered on him too long as she greeted him at the door. The woman had the eyes of a raptor and less feminine modesty than her daughter who, even now when her mother was in a completely different room, clung to him like a lovesick teenager. He knew it was all an act on Nerys's part but did she have to make it so... immersive?

He couldn't now remember why he agreed to come with her to Wales, into this well-furnished Venus flytrap. He could just close his eyes and imagine himself somewhere else: back home, lounging on the sofa and watching trash TV with Andy, or down at the gym, doing reps on the weights with Andy, or up at the Moo Moo Club, throwing some dance floor moves. With Andy.

"Take a look at this," said Nerys, wheeling him round to face the fireplace and the mass of photos arrange on the mantelpiece and the wall above it.

"Very nice," said Michael automatically.

"No, take a look," said Nerys firmly.

Michael sighed internally and regarded the photographs. The largest was a wedding picture of a stubbly jug-eared man with a woman who looked superficially like Nerys, assuming Nerys had been subjected to expensive quantities of fake tan, cosmetic surgery and eyebrow plucking. Michael surmised that this was Catherine with her footballer husband. Arranged around that were smaller images, of the Thomas sisters or Mrs Thomas herself. Many were from a decade or more ago: prize-giving ceremonies, a gymnastics event, school presentations and holiday snaps. There were other family members in certain shots and the occasional family pet. It took Michael a while to find Nerys and then saw her university graduation photo in a small oval frame next to a modest-sized picture of Mrs Thomas and Nerys's Aunt Molly that must have been twenty years old or more.

"Yes, very nice," said Michael.

"You're not seeing it, are you?" said Nerys.

"That's because he's a doofus," said Clovenhoof, who was experimentally sniffing a houseplant he had picked up.

"Really?" said Michael. "What have I missed?"

"It's a graph," said Clovenhoof.

"My mother's love-o-meter," said Nerys coldly. "The bigger the picture, the higher up, the more she loves you."

"I'm sure that's not true," said Michael generously. "And it's not as if you're the lowest or the smallest. Look there's one of..." He peered closer. "...Twinkle."

"Great! I'm one rung higher on the ladder than someone else's – oh, crap!"

She dropped Michael's arm and dashed from the room. Michael frowned at Clovenhoof.

"She's left the dog in the car," said Clovenhoof, nibbled at the houseplant and immediately spat it out.

"Why are you eating a plant?" said a young woman, entering the room.

"Wondered what it tastes like," said Clovenhoof.

"I should imagine it tastes like shit," she replied.

"I don't know. What does shit taste like?"

The woman wore a sweeping evening gown that, to Michael, seemed wholly incongruous in the domestic setting.

"You'd be Lydia," he said, making an educated guess. "The youngest of the Thomas sisters."

"And the prettiest," she said matter-of-factly.

"I'm Michael," he said and shook her hand.

"Very nice," she said and then looked at Clovenhoof.

"What are you meant to be?"

Clovenhoof considered himself.

"I'm meant to be the Morning Star, the most exalted of all of His creations but, hey, best laid plans of gods and men..."

To Michael's relief and amusement, Lydia stared at Clovenhoof as though he was some disgusting and impossible thing on the bottom of her shoe.

"And that's a *really* tasteful T-shirt and baseball combo you're wearing there," she said with dripping sarcasm.

"I know," said Clovenhoof happily. "Just blending in. I'm like a ninja of the valleys, *hyfryd*."

Lydia's expression of disdain deepened in a way that Michael hadn't considered physically possible and the woman was about to say something further when Nerys walked in, a wire dog carrier in her hands.

"Where's Ben?" she said.

On a square cushion in the bottom of the carrier, Twinkle lay snoozing, oblivious to the fact that he was buried under a fine layer of wood shavings.

NERYS'S MOTHER'S 'LIGHT SUPPER' turned out to be a monstrous buffet of pastry parcels, things on skewers and tiny piles of unidentifiable things on circles of bread. The seven of them sat either side of the long table in the dining room and watched each other carefully.

Nerys found the scene strangely familiar, no different to those times in her childhood when she had brought friends home for tea. Sure, more than a decade had passed since her school days but the Thomas family hadn't changed. Lydia was twenty-five, going on fifteen. Jayne was still the spineless goody-two-shoes of the family. And Nerys herself, under her mother's wilting gaze, felt very much the child again. With Ben, Michael and Jeremy as her visiting chums, it was just a case of waiting to see what happened first; whether her friends did something to trip up and incur her mother's wrath or her mom embarrassed her by saying something pompously stupid, arrogant and parochial.

Clovenhoof was, of course, the number one candidate for screwing things up. She made sure he sat at her side and she poked him with a fork every time it appeared he was going to do something. He scowled at her, hissed that he was behaving and tucked the edge of the tablecloth into his collar as a napkin. Nerys rolled her eyes. At least it covered up the hideous red dragon T-shirt he wore.

It appeared Clovenhoof had done something to annoy Lydia who sat directly across from him, staring at him furiously. Lydia sat with her hands under the table, occasionally fiddling with something. Was she texting under the table?

"I don't see why you still keep that thing?" said her mother, gesturing at Twinkle as he sniffed his way along the skirting board of the room.

"Because he's lovely," said Nerys.

"I mean, I understand why you would tolerate him while Molly was still with us but you can drop the act now."

"He's good company," said Nerys, ignoring Ben's frankly disbelieving stare. "And, yes, he reminds me of Aunt Molly."

"You could have him stuffed," her mother suggested.

"Stuffed?"

Twinkle looked up. Nerys's mother's eyes sparkled.

"Got it. Have him made into a stole."

"What?"

"Or a nice fur wrap. Then there'd be a practical use for him and he'd be a lovely reminder of Molly."

Nerys nibbled for a moment on a cheese and asparagus blini.

"I'm not having him stuffed," she said.

"Your loss. Horrible creatures really. Untrustworthy."

"Untrustworthy? Dogs?"

"Shifty. What about next door's collie?"

Jayne nodded in vague agreement. Nerys looked at her.

"Mom thinks it reads our mail," said Jayne.

Nerys's mouth froze around the opening 'w' of 'What the fucking hell are you talking about, you mad cow?'

"Very intelligent eyes," said her mother with a shrewd and knowing look. "It might have been a member of the KGB in a past life."

Jayne looked at Ben.

"Do you think we knew each other in a past life?" said Jayne to Ben, so openly that Nerys wanted to vomit.

"I always imagined that I had been a great military general in some former existence," said Ben with a casual shrug.

"Maybe I was Cleopatra to your Antony," said Jayne and popped a prawn pastry into Ben's mouth.

Nerys hid her grimace and snuggled up to Michael.

"I'm sure we were star-crossed lovers in a previous life, eh, darling?"

Michael's weak smile was not reassuring.

"We have only one life on earth, darling. Belief in reincarnation is heretical."

Nerys tried to make up for his lack of romance by feeding him a morsel from her plate. He looked at the offering critically.

"It's a blini," she said.

"Yes," he replied, "but you've touched it."

"So, Jeremy," said Lydia mordantly, "is there someone special in your life?"

"Of course," he grinned, flecks of chicken Satay between his teeth. "Me."

This actually raised a smile from Lydia but she quickly suppressed it and continued fiddling under the table.

"I meant a woman," she said. "Or a man. Or a goat."

"Who told you about the goat? There have been some ladies. I knew Lilith, back in the day, but she wasn't the monogamous type. I was busy with work for a long time after that. But since landing here, I've just been unlucky in love. There was the mail order one..."

"Like a Thai bride, you mean?"

"No, she came from a sex toy factory in Stockholm. That sort of fell through when Ben stole her, threw her out of the window and caused a police incident."

Jayne leaned back and through the secret language of frantically darting eyes, bombarded Ben with a number of very specific questions.

"I can explain," said Ben and then didn't.

"And then there was Blenda. Really lovely lady. But she split up with me when I fed her blood sausage made from dead pensioner."

"That was a memorable night," said Michael.

"That was when you and I really hit it off, wasn't it?" said Nerys.

"Er, yes," agreed Michael.

Nerys gave his hand a loving squeeze.

"So, mom," she said, "what are the sleeping arrangements?"

"Well, I've turned your old bedroom into a solarium but you can have the guest room at the back of the house."

"And the boys?"

"Oh, I've asked your father to put them up in the annexe."

Nerys and Jayne simultaneously indicated their boyfriends (one real, one fake).

"I thought-" said Nerys just as Jayne said, "Ben and I –"

"What would the neighbours think if we had unmarried men staying in the house?" said their mother with a humourless smile.

"What's the annexe?" asked Ben.

"The shed," said Jayne gloomily.

Nerys harrumphed to herself and wishing to vent her frustration turned on Lydia.

"What are you doing under the table? I'm sure there's nothing in your crotch worth that much attention."

Lydia recoiled, stung, and then brought out her hands in which she held a bent wire coat-hanger.

"Divining for men still?" said Nerys and then realised. "What? Jeremy?"

Laughter burst from her. Yes, Lydia would. A man immune to her scathing remarks, one who her mother clearly didn't like.

"Shut up!" snapped Lydia. "I was just doing it... speculatively. My G-Sez told me I would make a startling connection today."

"Oh, you use G-Sez, do you?" said Michael.

Nerys stroked his arm.

"Michael wrote that app."

"You wrote one of those phone doo-hickey things?" asked her mom.

"He's a clever guy," said Nerys. "And rich."

"An entrepreneur," said her mom approvingly. "You know, I'm sure we can put an extra couple of pillows on the bed in the guest room for you two. As long as you don't mind snuggling up."

Michael swallowed.

"No, the shed sounds delightful," he said. "Thank you."

"Very well," she said. "Now let's get these things cleared so we can have dessert. And maybe another bottle of wine, perhaps?"

"I'll get the wine," said Clovenhoof.

He stood up and, with the cloth tucked into his collar, dragged the tablecloth and the table's contents onto the floor. Nerys glared at him.

"Table's cleared," he said.

BEN FOLLOWED Nerys down the darkened garden. The land, sea and sky were only distinguishable as slightly differing shades of dark grey. Ben could just make out the black mound of Bardsey Island, skulking like a moody whale. Nearer to, frosty starlight illuminated the outline of the garden shed and greenhouse.

"So your dad really lives in a shed," said Ben.

"Yes," said Nerys. "Be nice to him."

"I'm always nice."

"I was talking to Jeremy."

Clovenhoof made an admiring noise.

"I like sheds. We should get one."

"We got one," said Nerys. "You burned it down."

"I meant another one."

Nerys opened the sliding door of the greenhouse that

directly adjoined the shed and led the way through, Twinkle scurrying at her ankles. Ben followed, taking in the rich aroma of potting compost, liquid fertiliser and – yes, he noted, seeing the clothes line – the aroma of drying underwear. It was, he had to concede, the only greenhouse he'd ever been in that contained a twin-tub washing machine, an ironing board and what looked like a mad scientist's chemistry set but was probably some complicated home brewing set up.

Nerys knocked on the shed door and lifted the latch.

The short fellow with rolled up shirt sleeves got up from his swivel chair and looked at the clock on the wall.

"Is it Tuesday already?" he asked.

"It's Saturday, dad."

He grinned toothily and hugged Nerys fiercely.

"Hello, petal."

Nerys kissed his balding pate with a sincerity of emotion that Ben had never seen her express before.

"Hello, dad."

"Not back for good are you?"

"No."

"Good. Or we'd have to resurrect the escape committee." He looked round her at Ben, Michael and Clovenhoof. "Brought fresh inmates with you?"

"Guests," said Nerys.

"Just in time for a Pot Noodle then. I'm Ewan."

"They don't want a Pot Noodle," said Nerys.

"Says who?" said Clovenhoof.

"Ooh, it's been ages since I've had one," said Ben, putting down his luggage.

"I don't think I've ever had one," said Michael.

"You should," said Ewan. "Sit down."

He gestured to the four seats arranged in one corner of the shed. That the shed was big enough to contain four comfy seats, as well as a shower, desk, fridge, coffee table, bookcase and chest of drawers, was not as surprising as the fact that all four leather-effect seats were car seats.

"British Leyland?" suggested Ben.

"1974 Allegro," nodded Ewan enthusiastically. "Reckoned that my arse spent more time in this place than the car so I swapped these for the wooden kitchen chairs."

Ewan filled the kettle from the shower (which Ben now saw was a jury-rigged garden hose) and plugged it in.

"I'm not stopping," said Nerys.

"Make for the Swiss border," agreed her dad.

"I've got to give Twinkle a walk before putting him to bed."

"Excellent cover story," he said and kissed her once more before she left.

He softly closed the door behind her, took down four Pot Noodles from the shelf by the window and ripped off their lids.

"Now," he said, "are any of you gentlemen practising Muslims or recovering alcoholics?"

Ben joined the others in shaking their heads.

"Good," said Ewan, taking a brace of recorked wine bottles from under the desk. "Well, by morning you'll be the latter and wishing you were the former."

∼

MICHAEL SAT with a beef and tomato Pot Noodle clenched between his knees, a fork in one hand and a mug of Ewan Thomas's cowslip whiskey in the other. The combined culinary experience of the two went beyond the merely unique and ventured into the unrepeatable. Michael had never before felt the need to describe a food substance as 'rude' but the rehydrated noodles in gravy quite clearly fell into that category. The cowslip whiskey by comparison was not rude but downright offensive, and yet was certainly warming to the tongue, toes, and everything in between.

Ben was wolfing down the Pot Noodle with relish but taking the whiskey slowly. Clovenhoof had already devoured both, knocking back the Pot Noodle to drain the dregs and immediately following it with the yellow spirit. Helping himself to a second cupful, which Ewan positively encouraged him to fill to the brim, Clovenhoof gestured at the large map pinned to the wall above the desk.

"Is that Wales?" he asked.

"The Llyn Peninsula," nodded Ewan. "We're right there." He got up and stabbed the westernmost tip.

"And the marks all over it?"

"Well the red dots are work places. I work for the Food Standards Agency. Sometimes we have to use a bit of detective work, and a map comes in handy. Take my colleagues in the Midlands, over your way, like. They had a spate of poisonings a little while back. They mapped out all the occurrences, and traced it back to the butchery counter in a supermarket in Boldmere. They found incinerated fragments of human remains all over the place. Would you believe it? Anyway, these lines here on the map are a more personal interest. Ley lines. Or dragon lines as we call them in Wales."

"I see..." said Ben slowly.

"A sceptic, eh?" said Ewan.

"I have yet to be converted," said Ben diplomatically.

"I've never heard of them," said Michael.

Ewan blinked at him.

"First Pot noodles, then ley lines. It's an evening of education for you, isn't it?" Ewan spread his arms across the map like a theatre impresario before his stage. "What if I were to tell you that this island of ours is criss-crossed by a series of lines, hundreds of miles long, each of them straight as an arrow, all of them more ancient than any of us truly realise?"

Michael was none the wiser.

"Like roads?"

"No," said Ewan.

"No, you fool," said Clovenhoof. "He means like those yellow lines the traffic wardens paint on the side of the road."

"No, these are invisible lines," said Ewan. "Their presence is marked out by Neolithic landmarks. Stone circles, barrows, dykes and such."

"Some bloke from the 1920s thought they marked out ancient pathways," said Ben.

"But," said Ewan excitedly, "John Michell went beyond Watkins original ideas and theorised – correctly, I might add – that these lines are not mere pathways but resonating sources of spiritual energy."

Ben made a doubtful noise, not impolite as such but suggesting that Ewan's theories were as believable as the tooth fairy, the Easter bunny and the snot troll that Clovenhoof left weekly offerings for.

"Man mocks what he doesn't understand," said Ewan. "But how else do you explain the Michael line."

"Michael line?" said Michael.

"Didn't know you were famous, eh? It's actually named after St Michael. You know the one? One of the archangels, defeater of Satan in the War in Heaven?"

"Colossal prick," added Clovenhoof.

"There's a series of monuments and holy buildings dedicated to him across Europe. Going from Monte Sant'Angelo in southern Italy, through La Sacra di San Michele in northern Italy, onto Mont San Michel in Normandy and even onward to Skellig Michael off the coast of Ireland. A perfectly straight line!"

"Impressive," Michael nodded, flattered.

"How is this possible," said Ewan, "without some connecting force compelling medieval man to build along this line? I've traced many of these lines myself."

"Is that where Lydia's picked up the dowsing habit?" said Ben.

Ewan shrugged.

"I used to dowse. I've used metal detectors, theodolites and seismographs. But my greatest tool in uncovering the secrets of the earth..."

He crossed the shed door, leaned out and gave a piercing whistle. Almost immediately, there came a scampering sound on the paved greenhouse floor and a black and white border collie leapt into the room. She quickly sniffed her way round Ben, Michael and Clovenhoof, licked at Ben's discarded Pot Noodle, sneezed over Clovenhoof's hooves and then sat down and looked up at Ewan expectantly.

"This is Jessie," said Ewan. "I would say she's next door's dog but, in truth, she's no one's dog but her own."

"Ah, this is the secret letter-opener," said Ben.

"Agnes has been feeding you that guff, eh? Well, Jessie is probably smarter than any two men I know but I don't think she's yet gone in for postal espionage. Watch this. Jessie, where's the kettle?"

The dog bounded over to the desk and placed her nose against the kettle.

"Where are my wellies?" said Ewan.

Jessie rooted the boots out from behind a pile of washing.

"Clever," said Clovenhoof. "Hey, Jessie, where's the biggest arsehole in the room?"

Jessie sat at Clovenhoof's feet, her tongue wagging out of the side of her mouth.

"I like this dog," said Michael.

"She can sniff out a ley line and pinpoint buried treasure, I swear," said Ewan.

"Buried treasure?" said Ben.

"Well, I've got a fair collection of Roman coins, arrowheads, belt buckles and stuff."

"I'd be interested in seeing those," said Ben.

"No problem," said Ewan and began poking around in the pots and jars on one shelf. "It's true I've yet to dig up any Celtic gold but Jessie helped me locate the spot where Joseph of Arimathea is buried."

"I beg your pardon," said Michael.

"Joseph of Arimathea. His tomb is here in Aberdaron."

Michael shook his head.

"Joseph of Arimathea? Uncle to Our Lord, Jesus Christ? I don't think he ever came to Wales," he said, mentally adding that he was sure the blessed one would have mentioned it on those occasions when they had met each other in the Celestial City.

"Then you don't know your Grail lore," said Ewan firmly. "'And did those feet in ancient times,' yeah? Joseph came to Britain with the infant Christ and, in later years, brought the Holy Grail and the staff of the Glastonbury Thorn here. And I mean right here. This is the land where Arthur lived and died."

"He was an English king, wasn't he?" said Clovenhoof.

"I read he was a Roman soldier left here after the occupation ended," said Ben.

"Poppycock and arse-gravy," said Ewan. "Your evening of education needs to go post-grad. Listen up, boys."

Ewan spoke as he poured a fresh round of drinks.

"You see that red dragon on your chest, Jeremy? The symbol of Wales. That's no mere symbol. There was a red dragon in these parts, a great fearsome beast. And when a white dragon came across the border into its territory, such were the roars and screeches from their battle that the sound drove men mad and caused women to miscarry. The people called on King Llud to deal with the matter. You've heard of King Llud now?"

"Sorry," said Ben.

"Well, you should have. Your country's capital, *Llud Lhwn*, is named after him. Llud, king of the Britons came here to sort the two dragons out. Now, he couldn't fight them. He was only a man after all. But he was clever. He dug a massive pit, filled it with mead and the dragons, drawn by the brew, fell in."

"I'd fall for that," Clovenhoof agreed with a merry nod.

"Llud filled the pit in and buried the two of them. And so peace was restored, that was until the later king, Vortigern, attempted to build a castle on the spot as a defence against the Saxons. The rumblings and thrashings of the dragons deep in the ground destroyed the castle's foundations every time Vortigern tried to build them. Vortigern was too proud to build his castle elsewhere and consulted with the wise men who told him that he would be able to build his castle if he made a sacrifice of a boy with no natural parents. Vortigern found such a boy."

"A boy with no natural father?" said Michael.

"That's a whole other story. This boy pleaded with the king to let him live and told him that if his life was spared he would solve his problem for him. Vortigern spared the boy who told him to release the dragons from beneath the earth. Vortigern must have trusted the lad for he did just that. The red and white dragons burst forth and set about their battle anew. But this time, the red dragon won and sent the white dragon crashing down on the hillside. The boy told Vortigern that the victory of the red dragon was a symbol of the victory of Vortigern's people over the Saxons who would soon try to invade their lands. And it was so. The Saxon, the English, tried to invade Wales but never conquered it. The red dragon prevails."

"Wahey!" shouted Clovenhoof and drained his mug once more.

"Sorry, what has this got to do with Arthur and the Grail?" said Ben.

"The boy," said Ewan. "The boy was Merlin. The ruins of the castle Vortigern built at Dinas Emrys can be seen off to the west. Porth Cadlan, the site of the last battle in which Arthur died at the hands of his son, Mordred, is not three miles from here. You're in Arthur country, boys."

"An interesting story," said Michael neutrally.

Ewan opened another bottle. The cowslip whiskey had gone and they moved onto something that Michael suspected was onion beer or similar. Ewan even poured a saucer of the stuff for Jessie but the dog, perhaps wisest of them all, left it alone.

"You and Nerys?" said Ewan, giving Michael a shrewd stare.

"Yes?" said Michael.

"That's a load of bollocks, isn't it? A smokescreen."

Clovenhoof slapped his knee, laughed and waggled his mug for a top up.

"He's rumbled you."

"Oh, I won't let on," said Ewan. "Anything to keep the peace. It's just you're, I don't know, the kind of man that Nerys would want for a boyfriend but not the kind she needs. Whereas you, Ben... You and Jayne. That's the real deal?"

"Yes, sir," said Ben.

"And she's not pregnant or anything?"

"No," said Ben. "I mean, not by me certainly. I mean, I'm not saying that she would.... I mean, she could if she wanted because she's her own person, not that I'd imagine her ever... I mean... I'll stop talking now."

"Probably wisest," said Ewan. "But you love her and want to make her happy?"

"I think so. Yes."

"Can't ask for more than that, can I?"

Ewan got to his feet, stumbled momentarily and then drew aside a low curtain under his desk to retrieve what looked like a bundle of knotted ropes.

"What's that?" said Clovenhoof.

"Hammocks," said Ewan. "You're sleeping in style tonight, lads. Here, take this."

As Ben helped Ewan unwind the hammocks, Michael watched Clovenhoof help himself to yet another home-brewed beer.

"Did you dig him up?" asked Clovenhoof.

"Who?" said Ewan.

"Joseph of Arimathea."

"Couldn't. The tomb's in a difficult spot."

"Oh?"

"Underneath the car park in the centre of Aberdaron."

Michael caught Clovenhoof's expression.

"Don't suggest it," said Michael, his mind already filled with images of Clovenhoof with pneumatic drills and pick axes. "Don't even think it."

ST CADFAN'S

The kitchens at St Cadfan's were lit by a series of high windows. Though it was midwinter, the early morning light filled the room with a bright, cleansing light.

While Novice Stephen screwed the lids and wiped down the last of the jars of apple preserve, Brother Sebastian cut up the labels. Brother Manfred sat on a stool at one of the preparation benches and muttered to himself, pen between lips.

"What are you working on?" asked Stephen.

"A menu," said Manfred.

"You're planning something special for us tonight?"

"Not for you, dear brother. We have spent the winter months refurbishing rooms for guests but, if we do have a wedding booking, what will we feed them?"

"The usual?" suggested Stephen.

"The usual?" squeaked Manfred. "There is no 'usual' in

my kitchen. You should consider yourself very lucky, young man. I should think no other monastery in the world offers its brethren the variety of food ours does."

"That's true," said Sebastian. "Melon balls and bacon. That was a varied and surprising treat."

"I think it worked, no?" said Manfred.

"It went to work on my innards," agreed Sebastian.

"Squid curry," said Stephen. "That one sticks in the mind."

"Not just the mind," said Sebastian. "Are you putting sardines on the wedding breakfast menu?"

"No," said Manfred. "You think I should?"

"Maybe. It's just that there's this Portuguese trawlerman I know who can get us a job lot."

Manfred scowled and returned to his thoughts.

"Here," said Sebastian and passed the labels to Stephen. "I'll glue, you stick."

Stephen read the labels.

"'Bardsey apple preserve. Honest Food, Tastes Divine.' Really?"

"I think it has a nice ring to it," said Sebastian. "Let's get busy, Owen will be here with the boat in half an hour."

Twenty-nine minutes later, they had thirty jars labelled and boxed up and, along with the pamphlets, brochures and small items of monastery craftwork, headed out. Sebastian, as procurator and the head of finances, carried the small lock box of money they were taking to the mainland. Stephen was laden down with everything else.

"Watch your step," said Sebastian as they crossed the lawns. "There's a stone there."

"Thank you, brother," said Stephen as he stumbled blindly on, unable to see over the top of his boxes.

"Brothers!"

"Oh, hell," hissed Stephen as they turned at their abbot's voice.

"Good morning, Father Abbot," Sebastian called back to the abbot at the door to the monastery.

"You are off to the town with our produce?" said the abbot.

"Yes, Father Abbot."

The abbot nodded and made a gesture of benediction.

"God be with you. Come back rich."

Sebastian smiled.

"Thank you, Father Abbot."

"He knows about the apples," whispered Stephen. "He's going to kill us. Remember what he said. However we wrong him, he'll get his vengeance seven times over."

"He knows nothing," Sebastian replied smoothly. "He's older than Methuselah and is twice as senile."

"How old is he anyway?"

"I don't know. Seventy?"

"Well, who was the previous abbot?"

"Some of the older monks like Brother Gillespie or Brother Henry might know. I've only been here a few years, took up the habit shortly after the Credit Crunch."

"Did you lose your job in the recession?"

"Let's just say I had eggs in all the wrong baskets."

On the way down to the coast, a peacock hooted as they crossed its path. Others took up the call in reply.

Stephen looked across and saw Barry the peacock stood

still and proud by the monastery wall. He found himself gripped by the notion that even if the abbot didn't know about their enterprise, somehow the abbot's pet did.

"I think Manfred should put peacock on the menu," Stephen muttered.

"I'll second that one," said Sebastian. "Look, there's the boat."

IN WHICH A QUESTION IS POPPED AND CLOVENHOOF IS UTTERLY (WELL, MOSTLY) BLAMELESS

Michael woke with a headache and a dry mouth. He was nonetheless surprised to realise that he slept well in the hammock. Ewan had strung the four of them from the shed's supporting struts, two high, two low, like hanging bunk beds. Michael had been lulled to sleep by the gurgling alcohol in his belly and the soft sound of Ben next to him whittling his lovespoon, a soft sound broken only the once when Ben slipped and stabbed Clovenhoof in the hammock above him. Clovenhoof's pitiful yelp had brought a smile to Michael's face.

Now, Michael was awake, thirsty beyond measure and not particularly content to have Ewan's gently farting backside in his face. He silently rolled out of the hammock, still fully clothed from the night before and slipped out the shed door. The sun wasn't up but a grey half-light suffused the garden and the greenhouse. Michael found a standpipe in the greenhouse ran his hands under it and splashed his face with the cold water.

"Awake," he said and stepped out into the garden to find Jessie, the border collie, sitting on the lawn, eyes bright and tongue lolling.

"Morning," said Michael.

Jessie ducked her head and shifted her feet as though preparing to pounce. Michael took it as a greeting.

"Ewan says you're the brightest button in creation, Jessie. Bet you can't rustle me up a drink, can you?"

Jessie ran off and hurdled the low hedge between this garden and the next.

"Didn't think so," said Michael.

Michael took out his smartphone. No signal. He hadn't been able to get one all night. Maybe there was a text from Andy hanging around the ether. Michael experimentally waved his phone in the air but to no avail.

There was a small bark. Jessie sat in front of him, a square plastic milk bottle with teeth marks on the handle on the ground between them.

"A drink," said Michael and, not wishing to appear ungracious, picked it up and drank it. It was cold, invigorating, and empty before he knew it.

"Good girl, Jessie," he said and stroked her head. "Now, if you could find God for me, that would be really impressive."

Jessie ran up the side of the house and then paused to look back at Michael as though urging him to follow.

"Are you serious?" said Michael but followed anyway.

Round the front of the house, Jessie leapt up at the side of Nerys's car, placing her front paws on the door. Michael looked in. Twinkle sat on the back seat, looking back out at them.

"Yeah, that's a 'dog', Jessie. A touch of dyslexia there. I was looking for 'God'. G-O-D, yeah?"

Jessie span around and then ran off down the drive, stopping once again to wait for Michael.

"Fine," said Michael.

He let Twinkle out of the unlocked car, clipped his lead on and the pair of them followed Jessie into the cold Welsh morning.

Two hours later, Michael discovered a number of things. Firstly, Wales was not England. Here, in the fresh light of day, he could see a rolling, rugged freshness in the landscape that England could never offer, like England before the English had smoothed off all the edges and turned their own wilderness into a garden. Secondly, exercise was a mightily powerful cure for a hangover, even one inflicted by meadow flowers and root vegetables. Thirdly, Michael didn't personally have any idea where they were, apart from being on a hill somewhere along the coast. Fourthly, his phone signal had returned, there were several texts from Andy and his phone GPS told him that he was standing on a hill above Porth Cadlan, the scene of Arthur's final battle. Fifthly and finally, God was nowhere to be found, although Jessie had led him to an almost invisible set of ruined stone foundations that Michael suspected might have been a church or chapel in earlier times.

Michael sat on one of the old rocks while Jessie and Twinkle sniffed and frolicked among the stones. King Arthur, he read from an information link from his phone map, died here and was carried across the sea to Avalon. Michael looked out across the water. Near to was the small island, Maen Gwenonwy, named after King Arthur's sister. Out of sight, along the coast, lay Bardsey.

"Avalon, eh? Hey, Jessie, reckon you can find Excalibur for me?"

Jessie barked and then rolled over.

There was a ping from Michael's phone. His daily G-Sez message had arrived.

Surely, the tree of Zaqqum is the food of the sinful. Like dregs of oil it shall boil in their bodies, like the boiling of hot water.

Michael recognised the quote from the Noble Qur'an and put a hand to his still churning belly.

"I could have done with that advice last night."

Twinkle yipped.

"What have you found there?"

Twinkle, clearly not as bright as Jessie, was barking at a small outcropping of mushrooms, growing in the shadow of a stone.

"Those things can be poisonous, you daft thing."

Michael grabbed an image of the mushrooms and made an internet search.

"Not poisonous," he said eventually. "In fact, positively magical, you hairy dope-fiend."

Michael found a folded paper bag in his jacket pocket and began to harvest the fungi.

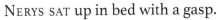

NERYS SAT up in bed with a gasp.

She looked around at the bedroom in her family home. It troubled her slightly. It was so familiar, yet at the same time, like a window to the past. A past where so much of her life seemed out of her control.

She'd been dreaming, but it had seemed so very real. She replayed the last few moments. The impression of remorse and despair was powerfully seared into her brain, but the details were already slipping away. She laid herself back and tried to recall as much as she could. It came easily, more like a memory than a dream.

She sits in a room that is unfamiliar. Jeremy Clovenhoof sits opposite. She holds in her hands two bared electrical wires and tears are running freely down her face.

"I'm rude to you and Ben," she says. "And my work colleagues. And I've driven away pretty much every friend I've ever had. I don't even love my own family. And I was never the niece Molly deserved to have. I'm a horrible person."

Jeremy addresses her.

"And do you wish you had been a better person?"

"Of course I do."

"Are you sorry for all those bad things you've done?"

She nods and Jeremy flicks a switch.

Nerys reached for more, but that was it. That was when she had woken up. The only other detail she could recall, strangest of all, was that the Jeremy in the dream was Satan. Definitely Satan, with the horns and everything. Dreams of

Jeremy as Satan. Why did that keep happening? She would need to look up what it signified.

She went downstairs to find Ben and Clovenhoof eating toast. Ben had marmalade spread thinly on his, but Clovenhoof was trying to find out how much Nutella he could fit onto one slice of toast. He seemed to be on course to manage the whole jar.

"The key is, to look as if you're official," Clovenhoof was saying to Ben. "Some hi-vis jackets and stripy tape to put around the hole, we can do what we want and people will think we're meant to be there."

"Yes, but how would you actually get through the tarmac?" asked Ben.

"Well, obviously, we find a real road crew and steal their tools," said Clovenhoof. "I quite want to try one of those big pneumatic drills."

"What are you two on about?" asked Nerys.

"How we'd dig up Joseph of Arimathea," said Ben, between mouthfuls of toast.

"Oh, that," said Nerys, starting on the toast herself. "Dad been filling your head with nonsense, huh? Well we've got more immediate fun on the cards today. It's the Farmer's Market in the town. The WI will have a bake sale there, so mom will want to make sure we all turn up and enthuse about cakes.

"I think I can manage that," said Ben.

"What's the WI?" asked Clovenhoof.

"The Women's Institute," said Nerys.

"Sounds like a madhouse for crazy bitches."

"Thank you. It's an organisation where women get together for meetings and to learn new skills."

"Oh yeah, I know," said Clovenhoof. "We used to call them 'covens' in the old days."

"There are quite a lot of young women in the WI," said Nerys.

"You're in it then, are you?"

"Well, no, but I could be," said Nerys. "It's very structured as well, not just a load of old biddies gossiping."

"More like the freemasons for women you mean?"

"No," said Nerys. "You shouldn't be so rude. Not in front of mom anyway. She's the chair."

"Oh. Interesting. Do they torture their enemies?"

"What?"

"That's quite popular with other underground organisations like the French Resistance. Or was I thinking of the Illuminati?"

Nerys squinted at Clovenhoof. She found that if she tried to imagine him with horns, it was easy. Very easy. She wondered what that meant.

"It's not underground. It's very respectable," said Ben, taking another slice of toast.

"Respectable women don't gather in covens to swap spells – why are you looking at me like that?" asked Clovenhoof.

"I had a dream about you," said Nerys.

"Women do."

"You were Satan. I was just picturing you with horns. I think they might, ah, suit you."

Ben joined Nerys in staring at Clovenhoof, his head cocked to one side.

Clovenhoof wriggled in his chair and scowled at them both.

"Where's Michael?" he asked. "He was gone when we woke up. Did your fake boyfriend pop up to your room for a fake shag?"

"Shhh!" said Nerys. "I haven't seen him. But Twinkle's out, so I think maybe he went for a walk."

At that moment, Twinkle scampered into the room, followed a few moments later by Michael.

"Ooh, Mickey! Loving the windswept look," said Clovenhoof. "Walking around in this countryside stuff is all very well, but your hair's going to look like a haystack all day now."

Nerys rolled her eyes.

"Hurry up and have a quick slice of toast then get cleaned up. We're going into town."

Her mother entered the room, wiping her hands on a towel.

"... darling," added Nerys, with an affectionate pat on Michael's shoulder.

"Nerys, you're going to have to come and pitch in with the baking," said her mother. "I know you've got guests, but I'm sure they can spare you for a while."

There were murmurs and nods from around the room.

"You can make the quiches for the WI meeting, can't you?"

"Quiches?"

"Lord save me from having to do *everything* myself."

Nerys nodded.

"What do you want in them?" she asked, but her mother was already making her way back towards the kitchen, berating Jayne for the icing on the cakes being the wrong shade of pink.

"Just find something," she called back. "Just remember there's vegetarians as well as normal people."

MICHAEL CLIMBED into Nerys's car with Clovenhoof and Ben. Jayne appeared.

"Can I come with you?" she asked.

"Sure. We haven't got room for Lydia and mom though."

"Lydia's not going, she'll be fine. Mom will ride her bike. Nobody needs to go in dad's car."

"What's so wrong with your dad's car?" asked Ben.

Ewan tooted as he drove past. They all looked across. As his car rounded the bend, the kitchen chair he was sitting on skated across the floor of the car, so he scooted it back over to where the pedals were and gave them a small wave.

Ben made wordless noises as he pointed, his eyes wide.

"At least he has a steering wheel to hang on to," said Jayne, with a sniff. "You should try being a passenger."

They drove the short distance into town and parked up.

PART of the car park had been annexed for the market. Michael wondered why it wasn't held in a market square, or perhaps indoors somewhere, but he quickly realised that the small cluster of buildings over the stone bridge was the entirety of Aberdaron's tiny town centre. Many of the buildings were freshly whitewashed, adding an uplifting purity to the scene. He inhaled deeply.

It was a chilly day for an open air market, but the sun was shining and the stall holders were wrapped up in a mixture of hi-tech all terrain clothing and things that looked like tea cosies and dog blankets.

The WI cake stall, two long tables of cupcakes, fruitcakes, icing, fondant and chocolate attracted a steady stream, but Michael with his mind still far away on a Welsh hillside, drifted away from his fake girlfriend to look at some local produce stalls. Clovenhoof was rootling through a charity table that was piled high with old clothing and bric a brac. As Michael looked across, he was already carrying armfuls of strange-looking goods.

He shook his head at his infantile neighbour-cum-adversary and walked towards a table covered in jars. He was less interested in the jam and honey than the two men who were selling them. They appeared to be monks. They wore the white robes, and seemed to be a world apart from the chattering crowds in their own small island of tranquillity.

They both smiled at him as he approached.

"Good morning," said Michael. "It's refreshing to meet men of religion in such an unexpected setting."

"Refreshing," said the younger one to the other with a wide smile. "That's better than 'weird,' isn't it?"

"So, your order does not forbid commerce and social fraternisation?" asked Michael.

"Not at all," said the older of the two monks with a small nod of greeting. "There are fewer hard and fast rules than people imagine. Each of us chooses when and how to maintain the silence that enables private prayer and contemplation."

Michael nodded with interest.

"As for commerce," the monk continued, "we must maintain the fabric of our splendid building, and meet the running costs. Even the modest life of a monk is touched by the economic climate. You might be surprised how much the cost of altar wine has increased. We are faced with making some repairs to the monastery this year, so we're all working very hard to try to raise some extra funds."

"So you're making jam," Michael said.

"Made by Novice Stephen's own fair hands," said the older monk. "Properly washed and everything. I'm Brother Sebastian."

"Michael. So, can you really sell enough jam to make a difference?"

"Jam is one of the many small efforts our community makes. Brother Manfred does excellent needlework," said Brother Sebastian and indicated some attractively embroidered cushions. "His work is much sought after. I have also produced these leaflets to promote the monastery for events and weddings. It's a new venture for us but I'm sure you'll agree it's a stunning location."

Michael took the leaflet and admired the pictures of the stone arches set against a spectacular sunset.

"St Cadfan," said Michael, closing his eyes for a second to remember. There were over ten thousand saints in the

Celestial City but he was fairly sure he had met every one of them.

"How funny, I can't remember him at all."

Michael looked up from the leaflet and realised that the young monk was no longer there. He looked in puzzlement at Sebastian.

"Where's Novice Trevor?" asked Michael.

"Stephen," hissed a voice from down low. "It's Novice *Stephen*."

Michael peered forward to see Stephen (Michael thought he looked much more like a Trevor) crouched behind the stall, his air of serenity in tatters.

"That woman there," said Stephen.

"What woman?"

"That one! I know her."

Michael followed his gaze and saw that he was staring at Nerys. Nerys was poking critically at a Victoria sponge and saying something.

"Don't let her near me!" pleaded Stephen.

Michael turned back to the monks and was about to say something but thought better of it. He picked up a jar of the jam and handed the money to Brother Sebastian before he moved off to look at the other stalls.

He noticed Clovenhoof, toting carrier bags stuffed with his motley purchases, loitering next to the WI cake stall. He appeared to be deeply absorbed in the list of ingredients attached to a ginger cake.

"What are you doing?" Michael asked him.

"Shhh! I want to hear what they're talking about," whispered Clovenhoof.

"Who?"

"The mad Illuminati women."

Michael paused for a moment.

"They're discussing what they're making for dinner," he said. "Come on."

He dragged Clovenhoof away by his elbow.

"I think it might be code," said Clovenhoof. "You know the sort of thing, *'do you put carrots in a shepherds pie?'* really means *'how many of us will it take to tie down the newcomers that arrived from Birmingham?'*"

"What are you talking about?" Michael asked.

"Matriarchal organisations like that can't really just exist to make cakes. They're like those tribes where they keep men in chains for their sexual pleasure and then kill them when they're of no further use."

"What tribes?"

"Those tribes you see on the television. Somewhere in the Lost World of Aphrodisia."

Michael looked hard at Clovenhoof.

"I'm fairly sure that's not real," he said eventually. "Let's assume that you've been watching bad films again, and these ladies really are just talking about food."

Ewan walked up to them.

"What did you buy, Michael?" he asked, nodding to the jar that Michael held.

"Jam from the monastery on Bardsey," said Michael.

"Hmmm, should be good," said Ewan, examining the label. "Bardsey's apples are famous, you know. The tree's ancient. An apple expert examined it a few years ago and said it was unique, a variety that doesn't exist anywhere else in the world."

"Well we've got some now," said Michael. "We can all try it for ourselves."

"Some people call it Merlin's apple," said Ewan. "Because he sleeps on the island, of course, in a glass casket."

"Does he?"

"Well, Avalon means *Island of Apples*. It all ties together."

He wandered off into the dwindling crowd.

"Avalon!" said Clovenhoof. "Even I know that's not real. It's a Roxy Music album, Ben's got it. That wine of his has pickled his brain. He ought to try a decent drink, like Lambrini."

Nerys walked over with Ben and Jayne.

"They're all packing away now," she said. "Mom's off with the WI for their meeting. Shall we head back?"

"We thought we'd go for a walk on the beach," Ben said. Jayne squeezed his hand and grinned at him.

Nerys looked questioningly at Michael, but he was ahead of her.

"I walked miles this morning, I think I'd rather get back," said Michael.

"Let's meet up later at the pub," said Nerys.

"Good idea," said Clovenhoof. "In the meantime, I have a mission."

"Mission?" said Michael, as Clovenhoof scampered off.

"Just walk away, Michael," said Nerys. "As long as we're nowhere near the blast radius, we can't be blamed."

CLOVENHOOF SLIPPED BEHIND the wall of the churchyard and emptied his carrier bags onto a handy gravestone. He shed his dragon t-shirt and trousers, and slipped into a gaudy floral dress that he'd bought from the market. He chuckled to himself as he pulled on the only wig that he'd been able to find. It had long blonde plaits falling down on each side. He found that his horns got in the way, so he gave it a sharp tug, and stuck them out of the top. He walked up and down, practising his best sashay, then he gathered up his other clothes and stuffed them into a capacious handbag.

He scuttled quickly into the toilets of The Ship Hotel across the way so that he could admire himself in the mirror. He was pleased with his reflection and tried out a pout, wishing he had some lipstick.

A man stepped away from the urinal and stopped with his fly half-zipped.

"What do you reckon?" asked Clovenhoof, indicating the dress. "Is it too flirtatious if I open the top buttons like this?"

The man fled without a word.

Clovenhoof went back to find the last of the market being packed away. The WI stall was stripped bare, and a pair of middle-aged women were folding the banner.

"Excuse me, ladies!" screeched Clovenhoof in an unconvincing falsetto.

They looked up in alarm.

"I was looking for the WI. I hear that a lady might learn valuable new skills at their meetings."

"Ah, yes," said one of the women, rubbing her ear as if it hurt. "We're going to a meeting very shortly. You can come with us if you like."

"Oh, that would be super!" exclaimed Clovenhoof, flicking his pigtails.

JAYNE REMOVED her shoes and pressed her toes into the cold sand, while Ben stopped every few feet to carefully empty his trainers.

They had come down to the beach through the town's curiously positioned beachside graveyard. Ben had pointed out that you could just ring the bell if you reached up for the chain that hung above the door of the church but then both had been distracted by a familiar figure in a dress darting among the tombs.

"So what's Jeremy up to, do you think?" asked Jayne.

"It wouldn't surprise me if he's sneaking into the WI meeting," said Ben.

"They don't let men into their meetings."

"Oh, that won't stop him. He has some funny ideas."

"Yes?"

"He used to insist that all women were men pretending."

"Interesting," said Jayne. "So if that was true, I'd be barely holding back the urge to pick my nose and scratch my balls?"

"Hey! That's a bit of a cliché."

"Is it?"

"When did you last see me doing those things?" protested Ben.

"This morning, when you thought I wasn't looking," said Jayne. "Just because something's a cliché, doesn't mean it isn't true."

Ben reddened slightly.

"Well there are loads of silly stereotypes that I could wheel out about women."

"Go for it."

"I could say, they're all devious, scheming and manipulative, but I'm better than that," said Ben, bent down to pick up a flat stone and skimmed it into the sea.

"And some might say men would rather do anything than have a *proper* conversation," said Jayne.

"I can't talk while I'm in the skimming zone," said Ben.

"No, men can't do more than one thing at once," Jayne replied, chucking a stone into the water.

"We're focussed individuals," said Ben.

"You have one-tracked minds."

"We think about the important stuff, matters both deep and lofty."

They stood in silence for a while, skimming stones into the bay. Ben did a victory dance when he managed a really satisfying distance.

"Some people would say that men can be insanely competitive," said Jayne linking arms with Ben. "But my lips are sealed."

Ben's attention focussed on Jayne's lips and he leaned in to kiss her.

"Score one for manipulative women," murmured Jayne, kissing him back.

∾

IN THE CHAPEL on the outskirts of Aberdaron, Clovenhoof listened to the WI meeting. He had learned very little so far, apart from the fact that Nerys's mom was called Agnes, and that these women were masters of self-control as they were able to say her name out loud without sniggering.

Fifteen minutes had been dedicated to refreshments and conversation. The conversation had mostly been lots of women telling Agnes how lovely the quiche was, although Clovenhoof thought that the sliced-up mushrooms looked a bit like slugs.

"Right everyone!" called Agnes from the front, and the chatter ceased. "Let's call the meeting to order. You should all have a copy of the newsletter with details of upcoming events."

Clovenhoof had read the newsletter twice, staggered by the tedium of it. There was no news here! Nothing scandalous was revealed, there were no lurid accounts of disasters. There weren't even any pictures.

Agnes drew everyone's attention to a skittles night, which needed more attendees. Clovenhoof puffed his cheeks and rolled his eyes. No wonder Nerys wasn't in the WI; an evening talking to Twinkle would be more fun. Suddenly he realised that the attention of the room was on him. Agnes was introducing him as a visitor.

"Ah, yes hello everybody!" he screeched.

"Could we ask your name for our records?" Agnes asked.

"It's, er, Geraldine. Oh yes, and the quiche was very nice." Clovenhoof smiled round at them all, knowing he'd cracked the code as they all smiled back at him.

"Now," said Agnes. "I'd like to introduce our speaker for

this evening. We have Susan Jenkins from Melin Morfa who will talk to us this evening about the history of the Welsh woollen industry."

There was a ripple of polite applause and a short woman wearing a tweed skirt took Agnes's place.

"Good evening everyone," said Susan. "I have some slides, samples and some small practical demonstrations to show you. We're going to be looking at the process that wool goes through, from sheep to shop. Here in Wales we have a long and proud history in producing fine woollen goods. We'll be looking in particular at the role of women in the industry, as production moved out of the small cottage workshops and into the mills."

Clovenhoof sagged. He must have come on the wrong day for arcane knowledge and secret rituals.

"I'm going to pass round the hand carders, so that you can all have a go at carding. You'll all remember that this is the process used to separate and straighten the fibres before spinning."

Clovenhoof took his turn at carding, which seemed to be a pair of dog brushes used to pull some wool into shape. He wondered vaguely if Twinkle's fur might be used for cloth.

"Does anyone have any idea what our ancestors used to use for carding?" asked Susan.

"Teasels!" shouted someone from the front. Clovenhoof resolved to kick them in the shins later for being a know-all.

Susan had moved on.

"The spinning wheel was so important for domestic industry in Wales that it has become a postcard cliché. A woman in traditional dress sits at the spinning wheel. Just stop to think for a moment what that really meant. For hundreds of years women formed the backbone of our national industry! Take a look at these slides. Women would raise the children, keep the house, cook all the meals, and fill any spare moment that they had with the work of carding, spinning and weaving. Let's take a look at some of the designs we have in our archive."

Susan clicked through the slides to show examples of old tweed patterns.

"You can see that these were produced on old domestic looms, with a narrow width-"

"Why's it moving like that?" called a woman from a middle row.

"Sorry?" asked Susan. "As I was saying, the narrow width-"

"Yes!" exclaimed another woman suddenly. "It moves!"

Clovenhoof couldn't see any movement in the dull fabric. Clearly two of the WI members were prone to flights of fancy.

"I think this one's got snakes," said a third woman. "It's moving like snakes."

Susan peered at the slide behind her.

"Er-"

A howl erupted from a woman by Clovenhoof.

"It's got teeth," sobbed another woman, her eyes wide and terrified. "Look at the TEETH!"

Clovenhoof frowned.

This was certainly more interesting but he had no idea what was going on.

"So," said Jayne, reflectively kicking a clod of wet sand into the air. "If women are calculating, manipulative, shallow and – what was that excellent word you used? Oh, that's right – *vacuous*, why on earth would you want to spend time with one?"

"I mean that's just the negative stuff. Women have many fine and... admirable qualities."

"Boobs, you mean."

"Them too. I think every man wants something different in a woman."

"Ah," said Jayne. "So what do *you* want in a woman?"

Ben gazed out to sea as the roll of the waves covered and uncovered the submerged rocks just offshore.

"I guess what I'd really like is to have someone to share my life with, give it some meaning. Sometimes I wonder who'd turn up to my funeral, and it's quite a short list." He frowned at himself. "Sorry, that sounds morbid, but that's how it is."

"You want a widow?"

"I want to mean something to someone. Come on, what about you? What do you want in a man?"

Jayne smiled broadly.

"Someone who really appreciates me for who I am. I've seen a lot of relationships based on superficial attraction, but that's not for me. If a man is only interested in a pretty face or a nice body then he's not what I'm looking for. I need someone I can be completely at ease with, you know, be myself."

"Yourself? Who is that then? Who is the *real* Jayne?"

"The *real* Jayne. Oh, really?"

"Really?"

"Jayne enjoys crafts and loves animals," she said, then she cast a sideways look at Ben and added, "but also someone who has been known to eat an entire packet of chocolate digestives for breakfast."

"Hah!" said Ben. "That's nothing. Sometimes I don't even get dressed for an entire day."

"I like European pop music."

"I like prog rock."

"Is that the ones with the twenty minute drum solos? I like Andy Williams."

"Iron Maiden."

"Val Doonican."

"Kate Bush."

"Cliff Richard."

Ben pulled a face.

"Well that is bad, I grant you, but you don't put me off that easily. I'll tell you something really shocking. The only reason that I ever thought about learning to drive was so that I could visit every motorway service station in Britain. I can't drive but I still want to do it."

"That's not shocking. What's shocking is when someone's so obsessed with soap operas that they read all the magazines."

"That's not so bad," said Ben.

"No? How about writing letters to fictional characters? Most of my Christmas card list is made up of people who aren't real."

Ben laughed.

"All right. You can't match this one. You know that bottle of sanitising gel that I keep in the bookshop?"

"Yes, I thought that was a nice idea for people who are worried about hygiene."

"The only reason it's there is for when my feet get sweaty in the summer. It cools them right down. Stops them smelling so bad as well."

Jayne looked at his sandy and soggy trainers.

"I'm not sure who's winning this argument."

CLOVENHOOF BACKED up against a wall and watched as the WI meeting descended into something altogether more interesting.

"Damn the spinning wheel!" yelled one, as she kicked over part of Susan's display. "Damn you and the centuries of oppression that you brought with you."

"Please don't," whimpered Susan.

"I hear the Virgin Mother speaking to me!" cried another, her ear against a wall carving. "She says we need to make a stand."

This raised a ragged cheer from the group.

"We need to be at one with all of our sisters, past and present!"

"She also wants the Spice Girls to re-form," yelled another.

Clovenhoof might have had no idea what was going on, but that wasn't going to stop him taking advantage of it. He strode to the front and addressed the room, which seemed to be buzzing with pent-up frustration and barely-contained violence.

"Sisters!" he screeched. "It's time for change. You've been denied your rights and your freedom for too long. Have you ever imagined what it would be like if things were different? If the tables were turned and women were in charge?"

Many voices muttered with approval.

"I'll tell you how things can be," said Clovenhoof, climbing up onto a table, careful that he didn't tear his dress. "There is a place I know that we can look to for inspiration. Let me tell you about the Lost World of Aphrodisia."

"DID you ever know a man called Stephen?" asked Michael as Nerys put a bowl of food for Twinkle onto the kitchen floor.

Nerys paused for a moment as she thought.

"Know? You mean in the Biblical sense?"

"Maybe."

"Stephen, or maybe it was Trevor. He was a bit confused. Didn't know what he wanted. Not even in bed! I tried to take him in hand but he seemed a bit, I don't know, *intimidated* by the fact that I'm a strong woman."

"I can imagine."

"Pity really, as I reckon I was just what he needed. I heard a scurrilous rumour he went off to be a monk."

Michael nodded in understanding, wondering if

Stephen's brief sighting of Nerys had renewed the trauma. His attention was drawn to a paper bag on the counter.

"Where are all the mushrooms that were in here?" he asked, looking into the almost-empty bag.

"I used them in the quiches for the WI," said Nerys. "Why do you ask?"

Michael turned to her.

"Would they have eaten them by now?" he asked.

"Yes, I think so," said Nerys. "What on earth's the matter?"

"They're magic mushrooms," said Michael.

"What?"

"Magic mushrooms."

"What? As in...?"

He nodded.

"*Hallucinogenic* mushrooms."

"No. No, I don't think so," said Nerys. "Not from the Co-op in Pwllheli. Mom gets everything from there."

"I picked them this morning, when I went for a walk," said Michael. "Twinkle sniffed them out. Try one for yourself if you don't believe me."

Nerys popped one into her mouth and rolled her eyes.

"There. Nothing. Just normal mushrooms. You have one as well."

Michael put one into his mouth and chewed it carefully. It tasted mushroomy, but not that unusual. Maybe he was mistaken...

～

"So you see, we don't need men. We can keep a few of them as curiosities, or sex-slaves," said Clovenhoof from his table. "Don't you want to end the years of oppression?"

There was a howl of approval from the group.

Agnes was the first to arm herself. She yanked at the curtains until she pulled the pole off the wall. Bracing it against the wall, she kicked it in half, kung fu style. Clovenhoof gave a small nod of admiration. Agnes handed half to another woman and supervised the removal of the rest of the poles.

"We have to make a stand against years of being downtrodden," she screamed. "Where are the men now? Where are they? Idling on sofas? Drinking in the pub? We need to show them that we won't put up with it any more. Show them we mean business!"

Several women bared their breasts with a shriek of defiance. Clovenhoof, who was not an ageist when it came to female nudity, thought this was a dramatic improvement. The women took up their curtain-pole cudgels and poured out into the night, a war anthem on their lips.

"And did those feet, in ancient times..."

Clovenhoof followed them out, grinning with delight.

Women started to clatter down the lane, singing *Jerusalem* at the tops of their voices, but Clovenhoof shouted above them.

"Wait, sisters. Halt! We will not walk into town, we will ride upon this mighty chariot!"

He indicated a tractor that was parked in a nearby gateway.

They followed him with whoops of enthusiasm punctuating the singing of their battle-hymn.

"I ALWAYS THOUGHT Twinkle's food looked good enough to eat," Nerys said, gazing at the dog bowl as she lolled against the kitchen counter.

"Jeremy says it's good," agreed Michael.

Nerys looked at him, her eyes darting between the dog bowl and his face.

"Are you saying that I just had a thought that Jeremy would have had?" she asked. "Oh *fuck*. These *are* magic mushrooms."

Michael nodded.

"Told you. I know everything, I do."

"Yes, well, hooray for you. What about the ladies of the WI? They won't have any idea what's hit them. Come on, let's go."

"No," said Michael. "I have to find Him, find Him now."

"Who?"

They stumbled from the house and ran towards the town.

"YOU KNOW," said Ben to Jayne as they walked towards the pub, "we've told each other the worst things we can think of about ourselves, and-"

He reached for the right words.

"And what?" Jayne asked with a smile.

"And it's... all right," he said.

"Is it?"

"We're both still here. We've summoned up our most horrible habits and our character flaws, and we seem able to accept them."

Jayne nodded.

"Yes?"

"We could be happy together, couldn't we?" Ben asked, turning to take both of Jayne's hands so that he could look at her face.

"I think we could."

Ben opened his mouth to speak, but at that moment a clattering of footsteps made them both turn to look up the road.

"Thank God I found you!" Nerys said. "You need to come now. The WI ate the quiches. They're just old ladies and it's not fair. I've lost Michael somewhere, but we can save the day." She stumbled forward a few feet. "I'm a first aider you know!"

Nerys swayed on her feet. Jayne and Ben took hold of her arms to steady her.

"Did you catch what she was on about?" Ben asked, as Nerys sighed and lurched forward, pulling them both behind.

"Not really. Something about quiches," Jayne said. "Can you hear something?"

"Yeah," said Ben, sitting Nerys onto a low wall. "It sounds like a heavy-metal version of *Jerusalem*."

～

MICHAEL HAD LOST Nerys somewhere between the house and the town. He'd also lost the road and, no matter how hard he stared, he also appeared to have lost his feet.

He had an idea they'd been replaced with wheels or hooves. He kept moving so that he wouldn't fall over, but maybe he already had.

He blinked at the blurry figures before him, two men, dressed in simple tunics. Where had they come from? One carried a rock and chased the other, holding it high in a way that seemed rather threatening.

"Stop," Michael called out but they didn't hear him. As they reached the edge of the forest, the man with the rock caught up, and the first man fell down. The one man bludgeoned the other repeatedly.

"Forest?" said Michael, or at least someone said it, except Michael realised it wasn't a forest. Before him was a tree, so huge that he couldn't see the top. As he watched, it bore fruit that swelled before his eyes.

"The fruit of the Zaqqum," he breathed in horror.

He turned away before it got him too. He started to run, or maybe freewheel. He wasn't sure. As he began to lose his balance, he held out his arms and realised that they'd been replaced by wings. These were not his heavenly angel wings nor the wings of his owl totem.

These gaudy colours and terrifying patterns made him gasp. They were peacock wings. He was a peacock. He tried to turn and see his tail, but it remained out of sight. He turned the other way, but it was no good, it whisked away, just on the edge of his vision. He looked around. He was in the most exquisite garden. A paradise.

Other peacocks milled around and cried out.

"Immortal! Immortal!" they sang.

Michael happily joined in.

"Immortal! Immortal!"

He smiled to himself. He knew without looking that his tail was the best of all the peacocks. He gave it a waggle to prove this point. It caught the wind, propelling him forward, which was a most uncomfortable feeling. He felt the wind and the water rushing over him, turning him over and over.

Water?

He was worried about his fine tail feathers and how they'd look, but he tumbled on and on. He had a vague thought that he might be drowning, and wondered if his feathers would lose their sheen if he died.

"But I can't die," he tried to say. "I'm immortal."

He frowned at the thought. He tumbled on. He had no idea how to stop himself.

As they reached the town, Clovenhoof heard a change in the pitch of the noise that the WI were making. They'd been bellowing *Jerusalem* as a battle-cry up to that point, but as they came to the outlying houses, the cries rose to a feral shriek. Agnes led the march and used her curtain pole as a club to smash windows, shouting to the men of the town to come and face them.

He did his bit by driving the tractor down the centre of the road, ploughing as he went. There was a deafening racket of abused metal warring against slabs of tarmac, which scattered and thumped behind them.

They drew level with the Ship Hotel and the noise reached a crescendo. Agnes and her entourage rushed into the public bar, and Clovenhoof parked the tractor on top of two cars that had been left outside.

"Don't forget to demand beer and bacon sandwiches for us all!" he yelled to Agnes, as he turned off the engine.

He entered the bar to find Agnes astride the counter.

"I declare this place to be the Welsh outpost of Aphrodisia!" she proclaimed. "I will be Queen of Aphrodisia and I claim this pub as my palace."

There was a muted snigger from a man at the bar, but Agnes silenced him with a sharp kick to the chin from her elevated position.

"I demand subservience from those who would mock or oppress me. Yes you, Dylan Davies!"

She rapped his knuckles with her curtain pole cudgel.

"Get down on your hands and knees."

His eyes widened with fear.

Agnes whispered instructions to one of the women who returned moments later with a bucket and scrubbing brush.

"Now let's see how *you* like a lifetime of fear and subservience!" Agnes said. "Come on, let's see you scrub!"

Dylan remained frozen in place, staring at the women who surrounded him. The other men in the bar squeezed back against the walls, but Agnes pointed her cudgel at them with the clear indication that they would be next.

A chant went up.

"Scrub, scrub, scrub..."

Clovenhoof took the opportunity to slide behind the bar and poured himself a much-needed pint. He felt he'd done a good night's work. He strolled outside, pint in hand and congratulated himself. How many men could say that they'd led a women's protest march? A slightly unexpected one, but most entertaining, and liberating in its own way.

"Scrub, scrub, scrub..."

The chanting continued behind him.

A woman who had declared herself to be Boudicca was outside the pub. Clovenhoof saw that she had cornered Ben, who was standing with Jayne and Nerys, rooted to the spot.

"You!" she bellowed at Ben. "I don't know who you are but I can tell you're as bad as the rest of them, come here and be punished for the years of oppression we've all suffered!"

Ben looked around and mimed a "me?" question back at Boudicca, pointing at his chest.

This seemed to enrage her further and she rushed towards him, her flame-coloured hair blazing backwards.

"Allow me!" screeched Clovenhoof, inserting himself in front of Ben. "I know exactly what to do with this sorry specimen."

"Good, good," said Boudicca, turning towards the pub. "Then come and join our sisters in the pub. We can reclaim it for womankind."

"I might very well do that," said Clovenhoof with feeling, and watched her drag her tablecloth robe behind her as she swept through the doorway.

"Jeremy?" said Ben, who was clearly shaken. "What just happened?"

"That was a WI meeting, apparently," said Clovenhoof.

"I told you," said Nerys, who swayed as she tried to hold onto the wall, "'Shrooms. They all must have eaten them. Off their tits."

She raised her head with a half-smile on her face, and looked at Clovenhoof. The smile froze in place.

"No!" she squealed. "The horns! My dream! Get away, get AWAY!" She fell backwards off the wall, scrambled to her feet and ran down the darkened road. Clovenhoof started after her.

"Hang on Nerys, wait a second-"

She looked over her shoulder and picked up speed.

"The horns! The HORNS!"

As NERYS and Clovenhoof disappeared from sight, Ben sighed and faced Jayne.

"It's at times like these you need someone else in your life to tell you that it's not you, it's the rest of the world that's gone mad."

Jayne nodded.

Ben prompted her with a cough.

"Oh, yes. I can officially confirm that the rest of the world has gone mad."

"Thought so," said Ben.

A woman ran by, flinging scones at fleeing men with uncanny accuracy.

Will you marry me?" said Ben.

"Yes," said Jayne. "Yes, I will."

"Good," said Ben.

They stood there, listening to the sounds of screams and smashing glass coming from within the pub.

"Do you think it's safe to go inside yet?" said Ben.

A dartboard exploded from one of the pub windows and rolled down the street.

"Let's give it five minutes," said Jayne.

MICHAEL WOKE with his face in a puddle.

He was so wet and so cold there was no room to feel anything else. He wasn't sure if he was able to move but managed to drag an arm towards his chest and raise his head to see where he was. He was outdoors, lying on a really uncomfortable rock. The sun was just rising over the horizon.

He sat up and then, after much concentration, wobbled to a standing position. A sharp *woof* from behind made him look around. Jessie the border collie stood on a rock above him. If he looked across the sea, he could see a long coastline.

"That's not right," he croaked.

Michael knew there were some islands off the Llyn peninsula, but none of them was that big. He looked backwards and saw a craggy headland behind him, rising sharply up to a large hill. The rough and rocky shoreline tapered away behind him in both directions.

The truth dawned on him. The coast he could see in the distance was the mainland. He was on Bardsey Island.

ST CADFAN'S

Novice Stephen was still at the breakfast table when Brother Manfred came round to collect the dishes. He didn't even notice Manfred, too lost in his own thoughts and intent on pushing cornflakes around his bowl, until the refectorian sat down opposite him.

"You know something?" said Manfred. "Every man is a treasure house of stories. I was once a zither player on the streets of Bad Königshofen. I took my unicycle on a tour of the music festivals of Europe. I was briefly personal assistant to Gianni Versace."

"Who?"

"The clothes designer. Briefly."

"Oh. That's impressive."

Manfred nodded.

"I am being given to understand that one of your stories came to the market in Aberdaron yesterday."

"You heard?" said Stephen.

"I heard you hid from a woman, cowering beneath the stall like a frightened child, but I am sure that this is not true."

"Oh, it's true," said Stephen. "Here."

He stood up and helped Manfred clear the pots and dishes. It was only while he was elbow deep in dishwashing suds that he managed to put his thoughts in order.

"The church has a history of misogyny," he said. "St Paul was a brilliant man but he said some stupid things. Women should be silent in church, they should worship at the feet of men, that sort of thing."

"He was a man of his time," said Manfred, drying and stacking plates.

"And then the image of women as nothing but tempters. Eve presenting Adam with the fruit, Lot's daughters, the idea that women are ravening succubi."

"Succubi? Succubuses?"

"Is it? Or is it succubae?"

"I don't know. I stay away from words with unusual plurals."

"Thing is," said Stephen, "my first... intimate encounter with a woman was like those worst stereotypes come to life."

"Ah, the woman in the market."

"Nerys."

While Stephen dried his hands, Manfred put the last of the dishes away in the kitchen cupboard.

"Dare I ask...?"

Stephen blew out his lips.

"She wasn't *un*kind to me. As company, she was pleasant enough, if more than a bit overbearing."

"Yes?"

"But in the bedroom... She treated me like a piece of meat."

"Some men would say that was a good thing."

Stephen shook his head.

"It was not a pleasant experience. It was like she was trying to suck my soul out through my... member."

Stephen could see Manfred trying to keep a straight face.

"I shouldn't have told you."

"No," said Manfred, breaking out an uncontainable smile. "Although if the monk business doesn't work out for you, I think you have one heck of a future in writing saucy top shelf novels for lonely ladies."

He clapped his hand on Stephen's shoulder and steered him out through the refectory and towards the cloisters.

"You had a bad experience with a woman. They are not all like that."

"How do I know that? I ran and I didn't stop running until I came here."

"And you are running still. Inside."

Stephen shrugged.

"I think you must face your fear," said Manfred. "What do we do when we fall off the horse?"

"We get back on the horse."

Manfred stopped, a slight frown on his face.

"Not the perfect metaphor in this instance. No getting back on the horse for you. Vows of celibacy and what have you. But you must not run from the horse. Go speak to the horse. Give it a sugar lump. Make friends."

"Easier said than done," said Stephen. His eye was caught by the tapestry on the corridor wall. "This is new."

Manfred looked and nodded.

"My restoration work goes on. A beautiful piece here. Joseph of Arimathea, Jesus' uncle, treading the hills and fields of England. Not much left of him when I started my work. Just the arm and the staff and a bit of his face."

"That's the Glastonbury Thorn. Legend says he planted his staff in the ground and that it immediately rooted itself and became a tree."

Manfred nodded.

"I had no reference materials for his body so I tried to produce something that seemed natural. A venerable man, staff in hand, robes about him as he strode across the green landscape."

"And the pointy hat?"

"It just seemed right."

Stephen nodded thoughtfully.

"It's Gandalf, isn't it?"

"It is, yes. From the films. I thought he would be a good model."

"No," agreed Stephen. "A good choice. He actually fits the role perfectly."

"Thank you."

"Not so sure about the four hobbits following him though."

8

IN WHICH BEN AND JAYNE MAKE A SPLASH

"N-novice Trevor!" whispered Michael hoarsely from cold-constricted lungs. He hurried stiffly across the garden towards the monk. Peacocks cried and fled before him.

The monk looked at Michael with horror. An understandable reaction perhaps at seeing a sodden man lurching at you across monastery lawns.

"Novice *Stephen*," the monk corrected him automatically. "Where...?"

Michael waved a frozen arm in the general direction of the beach which, as far as he could work out, was almost on the other side of the island.

"But how...?" said Stephen.

Michael pointed at the stout door in the wall.

"But..."

Michael indicated Jessie who was bounding about and

generally giving the peacocks as hard a time as they were giving her.

"Incredible," said Stephen.

"I know," agreed Michael.

"You look frozen," said Stephen.

"F-f-funny that," said Michael.

"Do you want to come inside?"

Michael looked at him.

"Of course you do," said Stephen, put an arm around Michael's shoulder and lead him towards the monastery proper.

The monastery, built from densely packed stones and ancient cement, was a grand building of pointed arches and narrow windows filled with stained glass. However, it was also a squat set of buildings, as though even this place was cowering from the cold sea winds.

Stephen guided him through a low doorway, along a stone corridor and into a square room with low benches and – Michael wilted with relief – a large open fire in full blaze.

"You need to get out of those clothes. I'll get you something to wear," said Stephen and left him there.

Not caring a jot for the prickling irritation of the heat against his chilled skin, Michael stripped directly in front of the fire. Jessie sniffed at his wet clothes and sat in the hearth. Naked, Michael left his clothes in a wet heap on the floor, drew a bench closer to the fire and sat down.

When he woke that morning, Michael had realised that he had never really suffered before in his entire existence. An angel didn't suffer. In constant service to the Lord, carried from moment to moment by the warm support of utter conviction and devotion, an angel felt nothing, was barely conscious at all. And, as a human (or something very much like one), Michael had previously suffered nothing worse than a congested bowel and a spot of emotional angst.

But being stranded on an island beach with the wind making stinging icicles of every pore of his face, had been intolerable pain. For the first time, Michael had wondered if an angel-turned-human could die and, long before Jessie had led him here, he understood why humans might pray for death.

"But I don't understand how we got here," Michael said to Jessie.

"Well quite," said Stephen, returning with an armful of white robes and another monk, this one with shoulder-length grey curls and a well-trimmed Van Dyke beard.

"A man arrives on the island without a boat," said the newcomer in a light German accent and a lightly amused tone. "This is not normal, no?" He gave Michael a raffish grin.

"Brother Manfred is our refectorian."

"The embroidery maker," said Michael, remembering the name from the market the day before.

"And clothier," said Manfred and whipped a habit from the pile in Stephen's hand and held it up against Michael. "Now let us see. You, young man, work out. You have the cheekbones of a young Rock Hudson. And the eyes!" He looked critically at the robes in his hands and cast them aside. "We need the right shade of white to bring out those brilliant blues."

"I think our new friend just wants to get, erm..."

Stephen waved at Michael's general nakedness and then,

immediately embarrassed, looked away, leaving his offending hand dangling unwanted in the air.

Michael frowned.

"Um. Shades of white? Surely, white is white. There aren't any, you know, shades."

Novice Stephen (it was Stephen, wasn't it, not Trevor?) gave the deep sigh of a man who had heard it all before, as a glittering mote of zeal came into Brother Manfred's eyes.

"That there is only one shade of white," began Manfred, "this is a common misconception..."

BEN STEPPED out of the shed into the greenhouse in his T-shirt and Y-fronts and groaned wearily. Two nights of sleeping in hammocks and drinking unusual brews had taken its toll on him. He stretched, standing on tiptoes and, as he did, saw that Jayne was standing outside the greenhouse door, two steaming mugs in her hands. Ben stopped stretching at once, checked that he was as decently dressed as a man in T-shirt and pants could be and opened the door.

"Tea?" she said.

"God, yes."

"I thought it would be better than some of dad's nettle tea."

"Actually, your dad went off early this morning. A call from work. What does your dad do, again?"

"He works for the Food Standards Agency."

"Yeah, he mentioned something about a poisoning outbreak."

"Oh, God. You don't think it's those quiches?"

"No. He said there had been incidents all over the peninsula. I wasn't particularly awake, mind."

He looked at the mugs.

"Which one's mine?"

"I didn't know if you took sugar so I made two," said Jayne.

"One sugar," said Ben and took the proffered cup.

He sipped it, relishing the hot drink on the cold morning. He paused thoughtfully.

"Did we...? Last night."

"What?"

"Did we agree to get married?"

"We did."

Ben frowned.

"Are we rushing into this thing?"

"Are we?"

"You don't know how many sugars I take. I'm sure there's tons of stuff I don't know about you."

Jayne shrugged.

"I don't know."

"Me neither."

"Should we call the engagement off?"

"No, no," said Ben hurriedly and put a hasty kiss on her lips. "I didn't mean that. No. I love you."

"Do you?"

Ben nodded deeply.

"Good," she smiled. "Let's not tell mom about our engagement for the time being. Her nerves are playing up since that nasty business yesterday. Let's keep it under wraps."

"Mum's the word."

"Exactly."

She raised the other mug.

"This one's for Michael," she said.

"Is he not up at the house?"

She shook her head.

"He never came back last night," said Ben. "Still, he's got to be around somewhere."

"I ASSUME you'll be wanting to get the boat back to the mainland," said Novice Stephen.

Michael shrugged genially.

"Are there any other ways?"

"You tell me," said Stephen with a wry smile.

Stephen was leading Michael across the monastery cloisters. Michael found it odd that the simple arches of the surrounding buildings though smaller and less physically impressive than St Michael's church in Boldmere had a noble and reverent aspect that he had not felt anywhere else since his banishment to earth. The habit Brother Manfred had fitted him with was very comfortable. It reminded him of the angelic robes the Almighty had him wear in the Celestial City but, more than that, it felt like he was walking around in a dressing gown: snug yet freeing.

"When is the next boat?" he asked.

Stephen stroked his chin solemnly.

"The next scheduled boat isn't until March."

"Hmmm, that might be longer than I would like to wait."

At another time, Michael might have leapt at the chance to spend a couple of months in this spiritual retreat but there were people who would be looking for him and a certain gymnastic young man who he was starting to miss quite keenly. Not for the first time, Michael patted pockets that weren't there for a phone that he knew was probably at the bottom of the Irish Sea.

Stephen elbowed him in the ribs and grinned.

"We can phone Owen the boatman at Porth Meudwy. He'll want paying, mind."

"I think I can sort that out."

Jessie barked and scrabbled frantically at the foot of a door. It was a short door with an unusual fan-like emblem carved into it that Michael felt he almost recognised. The door was dark with age and so scored and pitted that he feared Jessie might be damaging a priceless piece of history.

"No, Jessie. Away."

Jessie stopped at once and whined unhappily.

"I'm sorry," said Michael to Stephen. "I guess there must be something exciting on the other side of that door."

"No one is allowed through that door!" said a strident voice behind them in the corridor.

An older man with weathered brown skin, and such a full head of grey hair that it looked like a wig, strode towards them.

"Father Abbot," said Stephen with a respectful nod of the head. "This is Michael. He washed up on the beach this morning. Michael, this is the abbot of St Cadfan's, the Right Reverend Ambrose."

"Washed up?" said the old man with a confusion that bordered on disgust. "Was there a shipwreck?"

"No, Father Abbot. It appears that Michael swam here."

"I was drugged," said Michael. "I don't remember."

"A story both unbelievable and unsavoury," said the abbot with a sour twist of his mouth. "And your dog swam here too, I suppose?"

"Oh, Jessie's not my dog. She's the neighbours' dog. Well, not *my* neighbours..." Michael looked round and saw that Jessie had gone.

"Jessie?"

He span round on the spot and then, seeing a fleeting shadow on a corridor wall, set off after her with Novice Stephen and the abbot's protests following closely behind. Around a corner and through another door, Michael found himself with great surprise standing in a large glasshouse, full of sub-tropical greenery, humid air and a fruity vegetable aroma that was not so much strong as broad. It was a heavy scent that filled the nostrils and the lungs, a rich planty goodness he had not experienced since the Eden days.

Jessie was sniffing around on the red tiled floor by the wheels of a wicker bath chair. The monk in the bath chair, a thin and wrinkly man who seemed to be drowning in crocheted blankets, stared up at Michael with dulled eyes.

"Good morning, brother," said Michael. "I'm sorry about my dog. Well, it's not *my* dog..."

"You should not be in here," said the abbot, breathing

heavily as he entered the room. "The prior does not wish to be disturbed by you or your dog."

"Of course," said Michael. "I must say that this is a marvellous greenhouse."

"Orangery," said the abbot firmly.

"Orangery? You grow oranges?"

The abbot's gaze grew steely and cold.

"A greenhouse attached to a house is called an orangery, young man. My father always told me that if we are going to give things names then we should at least use them correctly. *This* is an orangery. *You* are a trespasser."

"My apologies, Father Abbot. Oh, but look!"

There was a narrow path through the crowding bougainvilleas and along it, fifteen feet from where he stood, Michael saw an apple tree. It was gnarled but vibrantly healthy-looking. Its curved canopy brushed the sloped ceiling panes of the orangery and hanging heavily from its boughs were...

"Apples," said Michael, walking towards it. "In winter! Oh, is this the Bardsey apple? It must be. I've heard it's a unique variety. Is this the only tree?"

"Not a step further!" commanded the abbot. "I'll not have your feet trampling the prior's precious plants."

Michael stopped at once and turned contritely. The prior gazed mutely at him. In those eyes, Michael could see an emotion, something plaintive, something urgent, but it was obscured by the lines on the prior's face and his sagging brow.

"I've not tasted any yet but I bet the preserve made from that fruit is delicious."

"Absolutely not!" said the abbot. "That fruit is *not* for human consumption."

"Oh, I thought that you had made-"

Michael was cut off by Novice Stephen bursting into a fit of violent and noisy coughing. Michael stared as the young monk waved his hands as he tried to clear his throat although it almost seemed as though the hand waving was aimed directly at Michael.

THERE WERE six at the breakfast table in the Thomas house once Jayne and Ben had returned from the garden. Nerys couldn't help but feel she was back in her childhood, six elbows bumping at the table with Clovenhoof doing an excellent impression of her dad in so much as he was a constant irritation to her mom, although Ben was a thankfully poor imitator of the absent WAG, Catherine. Jeremy's main weapon of irritation was the use of Nerys's mom's first name, which he had recently discovered and had decided to use like it was going out of fashion (which it had approximately forty years ago).

"Dear Agnes," he said, "would you be so good as to pass the fruit preserve."

Nerys's mom gave him a brittle smile as she passed him the already half-empty jar.

"It's very nice, isn't it?" she said.

"It certainly is, Agnes," said Clovenhoof, slathering the jam across three slices of toast and passing some to Ben and Jayne.

Nerys finished off her own slice, licked her lips and then drank her coffee.

"You know, mom," she said. "I never liked your coffee."

"I beg your pardon?" her mom replied.

"I never realised before how bitter and tepid you make it. I really don't –"

She stopped and made a credible attempt to stare at her own lips. The words had just popped right out of her mouth with no direct input from her brain. It wasn't that she had criticised her mother thoughtlessly; it was more than that. The opinion had formed clearly in her brain and had emerged directly from her mouth.

"I'm so sorry, mom," she said honestly. "I didn't mean to say that at all."

"I'm surprised that you'd have the guts to say such a thing," said her mom.

"It takes a lot of guts to stand up to a petty tyrant like you," Nerys heard herself say.

Clovenhoof tapped the table with both hands and stood up.

"Well, enough of this domestic bliss. I'm off into town to use that abandoned tractor and plough to dig up Joseph of Arimathea."

He frowned at himself as though he, like Nerys, hadn't actually meant to speak his mind.

"You truly are an unlikeable fellow," said Nerys's mom.

Clovenhoof bowed at the perceived compliment and left.

"He might be unlikeable," said Ben, "but that man is my best friend."

"Actually," said Nerys, whose mouth seemed to have

completely rebelled against her brain, "I secretly believe that Jeremy Clovenhoof might be Satan."

Nerys immediately slammed her hand over her lips to prevent any more slipping out. The house phone in the hallway was ringing. She pushed herself up from the table and out of the room.

BEN WATCHED Nerys go with her hand over her mouth as though she was about to vomit. However, she clearly wasn't that unwell as he then heard her answering the phone. He was helping himself to one of the final slices of toast when Nerys exclaimed loudly.

"You're where?! How the hell did you get there, Michael?"

Ben nodded.

"Ah, Michael's turned up, then?"

"Do you always state the obvious?" said Nerys's mom. "You know, I don't think you're ideal boyfriend material for my daughter."

Jayne gripped Ben's hand on top of the table.

"We're engaged to be married," she said.

Ben looked at his fiancée.

"I thought we weren't telling anyone yet," he said.

"So did I," said Jayne. "Do you know, it sort of just popped out of my mouth."

Lydia sighed loudly.

"Great. Now you're the centre of attention. What do I have to do to get people to notice me? I think I'm going to seduce Jeremy just to annoy mom. I bet he'd appreciate my Wonder Woman outfit."

Lydia's eyes widened in surprise at her own words.

"I'm not surprised," said Mrs Thomas. "Although, given the choice, I'd shag Michael. I would gladly have a handsome stud like that between my thighs."

She immediately gave a moan of shock at what she had just said.

"Well," Ben commented, "I am looking forward to marrying Jayne. That way I'll be able to have sex morning, noon and nigh- Oh, my God."

Ben leapt up from the table with horror to hear such a thoughtless (albeit honest) sentence slip from his lips. With a fleeting and apologetic glance at Jayne, he hurried from the room.

He went straight out the back door and down the garden.

"Stupid, stupid, stupid," he hissed at himself, punctuating each word with a slap on the forehead.

It wasn't easy to slam the sliding greenhouse door but at least he could give the shed door a satisfying bang as he stomped inside, and then threw himself into a hammock. The force of his leap almost pitched him out the other side but he managed to stay on board and lay there, arms crossed, staring furiously at the ceiling and silently berating himself for his idiocy.

The hammock was still swinging gently when the shed door opened. Ben looked round, frightened that it might be Jayne.

"Oh, it's you," he said to Nerys. "Just leave me alone, please."

"Ben, I need to talk to you."

Ben groaned.

"Did Jayne send you? Or your mom? They must both think I'm a sex-crazed pervert."

Nerys pulled a doubtful face.

"Ben. No one is ever in your entire life going to call you a sex-crazed pervert. You haven't got it in you."

Ben frowned.

"Should I be offended by that?"

"Probably."

"I don't want to talk about it."

"Neither do I," said Nerys. "I haven't come to talk about your potty mouth or animal urges. I need your help."

"Oh?"

"Michael called."

SAT in the back of Nerys's car on the way into Aberdaron, Jayne looked across the suddenly huge expanse of the back seat to her fiancé. Ben was sat firmly in the corner by the door, his hands at his side, his face turned to the window and the high banks of grass and gorse through which they drove.

He wasn't exactly refusing to talk to her. He was being stiffly polite and monosyllabic in his responses to her conversational gambits and that made it worse. He was angry and she wasn't sure if it was with her or not.

Jayne wanted to reach out to him but was worried how he might respond. She had slipped her hand across the surface of the seat to the middle seat where it sat, pathetic and untouched, hoping to meet his in that no man's land.

She sighed.

"There he is," said Ben flatly as they turned down the hill and into the town.

Jayne looked and saw Clovenhoof engaged in an animated conversation with another man in the riverside car park. It was hard to be certain but Jayne imagined it might have had something to do with the tractor in the river, its front wheels at the top of the bank, its fat rear wheels almost completely damming the River Daron.

Nerys swung into the car park and wound down the window.

"Get in," she said.

"It's all right," said Clovenhoof. "Gryff here is going to tow me out."

"Now."

"Fine," huffed Clovenhoof and got in the passenger side.

Nerys turned around and drove out through the town. All of the windows of The Ship Hotel were smashed and it looked as if there had been a small fire at some point in the night. There were also numerous discarded weapons and even some clothes in the town's one street but no one in the car was apparently up to making a comment.

"Where are we off to then?" asked Clovenhoof. "I fancy visiting a zoo. Does anyone else fancy going to a zoo?"

"We're going to collect Michael."

"Is he at the zoo?"

"No."

"Poo."

Clovenhoof grumbled and huffed all the way down to Porth Meudwy. A mile along the coast from Aberdaron, Porth Meudwy was a slipway launch for boats at the bottom of a deep gorge carved by glacial ice and millennia of Welsh rain. The twisted browns and greens of hardy vegetation hung on the towering banks on either side of the single track as Nerys's poor little car rattled down to the waterside.

Owen the boatman, who Jayne remembered had been in the year below her at school, was already winching his boat into the choppy waves. At the height of summer, it would be taking dozens of birdwatchers, hikers and day-trippers to Bardsey but today the thirty-seater boat was theirs alone.

"A boat trip?" said Clovenhoof. "Are we going fishing?"

"Not quite," said Jayne and thanked Owen as he helped her aboard.

She saw her sister give Owen an embarrassed smile and turn a little pink as he helped her too. His smile in reply was warmly amused.

Jayne whispered in Nerys's ear.

"I remember there were rumours about you and Owen and the school art cupboard."

"Let's not go there," said Nerys.

"That's what you should have said to him."

Nerys went and pointedly sat at the back of the boat, as far from the wheelhouse as possible. While Owen handed out the obligatory life-jackets, Jayne took a seat on the port side and patted the seat next to her for Ben to sit on. The expression he gave her in return was a grimace mixed with a deliberately silly waggling of eyebrows and rolling of eyes. But he sat with her nonetheless.

Owen pulled away from the shore and made towards Bardsey, all the while ignoring Clovenhoof's offers and pleas to help him 'steer the ship'. Once out from the sheltering harbour, the waves grew stronger, the wind picked up and the boat pitched and yawed like a see-saw.

Her hair whipping around her face, Jayne leant in towards Ben and shouted over the roar of the elements, "It's been years since I've been out to sea."

Ben paused in thought.

"Decades for me. Family holiday to the Isle of Wight when I was eight."

"I love being on the water."

"Perhaps when it's calmer."

Jayne nodded.

"I thought, for our honeymoon, we could travel up the Mekong River."

Ben frowned.

"Is that still in Vietnam?"

"Last time I looked."

"Not sure if I fancy Vietnam."

"Heard bad reports?"

"I've seen *Platoon*."

Jayne laughed and pulled her hair from her eyes.

"Listen," said Ben, "I'm sorry about what I said this morning. I don't know what came over me."

"Hey. I don't know what came over me this morning either. I didn't mean to break the news to mom. I just... I think I was overwhelmed by honesty. Besides..."

She took hold of his hand and he fiercely gripped hers in return.

"You were right," she said.

"I was?"

"Not the morning, noon and night bit. Otherwise, we'll *never* get out of bed. But we don't know each other well enough. I'm no religious prude and I do think we ought to get to know each other intimately before we tie the knot."

"You mean...?"

"Check that tab A fits in slot B."

"Go for a test drive before signing the contract."

"I think my metaphor was more tasteful."

"I'd beg to differ. Yours makes sex like sound like a flat pack wardrobe and I'm the one and a half inch screws."

"One and a half inch?"

"It was an analogy!"

"I think I'd better measure you up sooner rather than later."

"So while we're here in Wales."

Jayne thought for a while. Up in the wheelhouse, Clovenhoof, having given up being allowed to steer was blowing on his life-jacket's emergency whistle and attempting to dance a hornpipe.

"We can't do it at the house," she said to Ben. "Both mom and Lydia have ears like hawks."

"Hawks don't have ears."

"You know what I mean."

"Well, we can't do it in your dad's shed. I don't want to have sex in a hammock, with an audience, the first time I do it."

"The first time?"

"With *you*," he said hurriedly. "Why don't we book into the Ship Hotel or the Ty Newydd for a night?"

"Both run by friends of the family," said Jayne. "Don't worry, we'll think of something."

The boat bounced over a particularly jarring swell.

"Where there's a will, there's a way," said Ben and, to Jayne's ears, it sounded like there was twenty years or more of pent up 'will' behind that statement.

ON ONE OF the six computers in the locutory, Michael clicked the 'Send Friend Request' button.

"Excellent," said Brother Sebastian. "And now you'll be constantly up to date with the daily soap opera that is life at St Cadfan's."

"Super," said Michael.

"And don't forget to follow our Twitter feed."

"Of course."

He looked at the mass of cabling, router boxes and other unrecognisable items that filled the cabinets on the wall.

"I'm surprised that a remote monastery is so well-connected," he said.

"Global village," said Sebastian. "Our apostolic mission and commercial enterprises reach as far as the technology allows."

Stephen gave a grunt of amusement.

"When man colonises Mars, he'll find the word of Christ and a range of Bardsey products already waiting for him."

Sebastian nodded in sincere agreement. An image on one of several webcam feeds drew his eye.

"Here's Owen," he said, pointing. On screen, a boat had moored on the leeward side of the island and several figures were climbing ashore.

"Is Nerys with them?" asked Stephen, nervously.

Michael peered.

"Ben, Jayne, the Angel of the Bottomless Pit and... yes, Nerys."

"Right," said Stephen, rearranging his habit in preparation. "I'm off to hide then. If anyone's looking for me, I'll be in private prayer in the darkest corner of the cellar."

"Oh, come now," said Sebastian. "She can't be that bad."

"Brother, I was atheist before I met her," said Stephen firmly and left.

Brother Sebastian sighed the sigh of a man who has seen all life and has gladly left most of it behind.

"Shall we go and meet your friends then, Michael?"

THE AFTERNOON SUN was shining through the clouds as Michael, Sebastian and Jessie went to meet the landing party on the lawns but the winds were strong enough to send a chilly breeze up Michael's habit. He held onto his garment to avoid a Marilyn Monroe incident.

"I think you've got a lot of explaining to do," said Nerys, smiling despite her tone as she slapped Michael's wallet into his hand.

Clovenhoof looked Michael up and down.

"What's infinity add one?" he asked.

"What?" said Michael.

"Trying to work out your new 'looks like a twat' score."

"Hilarious," said Michael. "Thanks for coming. This is Brother Sebastian. These are my friends." He paused. "And Jeremy."

Sebastian shook hands with the three humans. Clovenhoof, having spotted a pair of peacocks had scampered off to harangue them.

"You owe the boatman eighty quid," said Nerys.

Michael opened his wallet. He turned to Sebastian.

"Surely, I must offer you something for the inconvenience."

Sebastian looked at the wallet and a venal glint passed across his otherwise serene expression.

"No, you must not. But don't forget to buy some of our lovely produce from our website or consider us for your next wedding or business conference."

"You do weddings?" said Jayne, looking up with admiration at the surrounding buildings.

"I was going to ask you about your produce," said Michael, as Ben and Jayne fell into quiet discussion. "Am I right in thinking the abbot doesn't know about your recent ventures in jam-making?"

"Ah," said Sebastian. "Mmmm. Yes."

"Do you have any availability for July or August?" asked Jayne.

"Sorry?" said Sebastian.

"For weddings."

"You're getting married?" said Michael.

Ben and Jayne, hand in hand, smiled at him.

"Announced it at breakfast," said Nerys.

"I can check our bookings," said Sebastian.

"I suppose congratulations are in order," said Michael.

Jessie barked at Clovenhoof's return.

"Did you know this?" said Michael.

"What?"

"These two. Getting married."

"Who to?" said Clovenhoof.

"Each other," said Michael.

"But that doesn't mean you can't enjoy a long engagement. A very long engagement," said Nerys.

"Strike while the iron's hot," said Jayne.

"And this place could be the ideal venue," said Ben.

"Bit hard for friends and family to get to," Nerys argued.

"The ideal venue," agreed Ben.

"It's probably best to book early," said Sebastian. "This place is proving increasingly popular."

Michael looked at the monk and imagined that what Sebastian meant was that potential bookings had recently leapt up from zero to one.

"Well, I think you'd better take a look around," said Clovenhoof.

"Absolutely," said Sebastian.

"Some of the stonework looks very unsteady."

"We're doing some repairs at the moment," said Sebastian.

"And some of the stained glass in the chapel is smashed."

Sebastian frowned.

"There's no damage to any of the stained glass," he said.

"How recently have you checked?" said Clovenhoof and conspicuously failed to meet anyone's eye.

Jessie growled at Clovenhoof's hooves.

On the boat back to the mainland, Michael sat down next to Clovenhoof.

Checking that no one else was close enough to hear, he said, "I've got a problem."

"I dunno," said Clovenhoof, gesturing to Jessie who was lying down at his feet. "You're popular with the bitches. Are you worried that your boyfriend will find out?"

Michael's mind ran through a quick succession of thoughts, starting with annoyance at Clovenhoof's lame humour, moving onto the desire to tell him that Andy wasn't his boyfriend just a special friend, the realisation that if both he and Clovenhoof knew that the boyfriend reference was about Andy then there must be some truth in it and the further realisation (coupled with further annoyance) that Clovenhoof had distracted him from his current concern.

"Shut up, I'm serious," he said.

"This from the man who wears dresses."

"That's the monastery of St Cadfan," said Michael pointing back across the sea.

"Uh-huh."

"Cadfan. Did he ever turn up in Hell?"

"Saints go up, not down, pigeon-wings. Part of the Other Guy's VIP club."

"Except that's it," said Michael. "I've been thinking about it. There is no St Cadfan in the Celestial City."

Clovenhoof shrugged.

"So maybe he's one of those made up saints. There are enough of them."

"Yes, but even they appear in the Celestial City if the faithful declare them to be real. 'As it is on Earth...'"

"'... so shall it be in Heaven.' Stupid rule, really."

"That's not the point. If St Cadfan isn't in Heaven and he isn't in Hell..."

"Purgatory?"

"I would know."

Clovenhoof gave a playful toot on his life jacket's emergency whistle. Michael instinctively knew that they would have a hard time getting Clovenhoof to part with it.

"You've got two possibilities," said Clovenhoof.

"Yes?" said Michael.

"One, a dip in the sea has addled your brains."

"Or?"

"He's still on Earth."

"What?"

"He's not dead."

Michael sighed and threw his hands up.

"You're no help. I wish I could explain. There was something really amiss in that monastery."

"Is that why you paid the deposit for the wedding?"

Michael nodded.

"We need to go back."

"And set fire to the place," agreed Clovenhoof.

"No! We need to investigate. The abbot was really

unwelcoming. The prior is a dribbling imbecile. He was just sitting there in the orangery."

"They grow oranges?"

"No, but they have an apple tree that flowers in winter and the abbot was very protective of the fruit. By the way, I bought some of the jam the monks made."

"We had it at breakfast," said Clovenhoof and then paused. "You know, something weird did happen this morning…"

NERYS DECIDED, long before they reached home, that her little car was not designed to carry five people, one hyperactive border collie and a bag of still-damp clothes. Jessie sat on Michael's knee and whined at every junction, like some inarticulate SatNav. In the back, squashed up to one side, Ben and Jayne whispered and giggled to each other like a pair of schoolchildren. And as for Jeremy… Nerys could no longer look at him without thinking of her incessant dreams and that magic mushroom incident in which he had so clearly and vividly transformed into a horned and red-skinned devil. Perhaps she needed her head examining.

It was a sheer relief and pleasure to pull up outside the Thomas house and have the menagerie of young lovers, would-be devils, night-swimmers and dogs out of the car.

"Your dad's car is here," Ben said the Jayne.

"Good," she replied. "I'll get the keys and get changed."

"Changed?"

"Into something more comfortable," she said archly.

Ben giggled.

"I'll go get some, you know, protection," he replied.

Nerys pulled a face. If they weren't acting like lovesick puppies, they were being sex-starved bonobos. It was sickening and, yes, she wasn't afraid to admit she was more than a little jealous.

She locked up the car, went inside and found her fake boyfriend chatting in the kitchen with her mom and dad. Her dad only ever came up to the house when he was seriously bothered about something or rainstorms had flooded him out, and there wasn't a drop of rain in the air.

"You all right, dad?" she said, kissing his bald head.

"Crazy day," he said, shaking his head. "There's been some kind of weird outbreak all over the peninsula."

"'Poisoning?"

He puffed his cheeks and shrugged.

"Who knows? No one's sure if it's food related. It's bizarre."

"Oh?"

His lined brow knitted with consternation.

"Aberdaron and the surrounding area appears to have suffered a mass outbreak of honesty."

He suddenly looked round at a rumbling sound.

"Is that my car?"

BEN BRACED himself against the glove box as the cut down kitchen chair that was his seat jumped around inside the British Leyland Allegro.

"Brilliant idea of yours," said Ben as the car bounced down the track.

"I don't think I invented sex," said Jayne.

"Ha ha," said Ben deadpan. "And you're sure no one else will be coming down."

"I've padlocked the gate. Owen's done for the day. It's not fishing season. We will be undisturbed."

The sun had not quite set but the Porth Meuwdy valley was so steep-sided that the sun had completely vanished from sight and darkness was already descending. Jayne parked at the top of the slipway to the sea, tucked in between a stone-built boathouse and a pile of stacked lobster pots.

Ben rubbed his buttocks as he got out.

"These chairs are impossible to sit on."

"Ah, but they're an integral part of the plan," said Jayne.

She opened the doors, removed the kitchen chairs and stacked them to one side. She climbed back in and rolled out the sleeping bags she had brought with her into the empty floor space.

"And our love nest is complete."

Ben got back in. It was surprising how spacious a car was without any seats.

"Clever," he said. "You don't think...?"

"What?" said Jayne.

"Is this romantic enough? Two sleeping bags on the floor of an Allegro?"

"With the sweet aroma of seaweed and the sight of old Peter's lobster pots for company? It's what we've got and, besides, it's not the surroundings I'm interested in."

Ben leant in and kissed her.

"It's cold," she said.

"Sleeping bags?"

"Sleeping bags."

Ben was half inside his sleeping bag when Jayne coughed pointedly.

"Unless you're a truly astonishing man," she said, "it's unlikely were going to be able to have sex whilst in separate sleeping bags."

"You want to squeeze in?" he said.

Jayne unzipped the side of his sleeping bag.

"We'll zip the two together and make one big bag."

"Wow. You're not just a pretty face."

"Wait until you see the rest of me."

EWAN THANKED LYDIA as she passed him a fresh mug of tea.

"Lydia," he said. "I've been meaning to ask you. Have you asked Jessie to find you a man? I found another one of those poor unfortunate fellows trapped up by the shed again yesterday. He'd been birdwatching off the road to Porth Oer and she'd herded him all the way up here."

"Well, really dad, that would *clearly* be a ridiculous thing to do," said Lydia, avoiding his gaze. "So, tell me about the outbreak that you're working on."

"The first cases were reported yesterday afternoon. Huw, the dodgy butcher in Capel Bryn told all his customers to avoid the pork and ham joints as he couldn't guarantee that they had actually come from pigs."

"You've had an eye on him for months," said Agnes.

Ewan nodded.

"He told everyone who came in the shop that at least half of his meats had come from Irish ponies."

"Overcome by guilt?" suggested Nerys.

Ewan shook his head.

"The traffic warden in Pwllheli wrote apology notes on every ticket she issued, most explaining that she would like to quit her job but she now depends on the income since her husband ran off with a librarian from Bangor."

"Embarrassing."

"This morning, a headteacher in Pwllheli loudly declared that her students were disgusting trolls, as ugly and as unemployable as their parents."

"She'll be in trouble when the parents find out," said Lydia.

"It was at a parent/teacher meeting," said Ewan.

IT MIGHT HAVE BEEN winter but the mere act of wriggling down inside a sleeping bag in their clothes had made Jayne all hot and bothered. She also realised that, even in a doubled up sleeping bag, there wasn't that much room for two people.

The number of elbows they had between them seemed to have multiplied tenfold. She had already poked Ben twice in the face whilst taking off her dress. Ben in return had given her a sharp jab in the boobs while undoing his own trousers.

But at least contact had been made.

She hadn't even bothered letting Ben struggle with her

bra and had slipped it off herself. She did her best to ignore the fleeting look of panic that appeared on Ben's face when her breasts were unleashed. It might have been her imagination but he seemed almost unwilling to touch them as though either he or they might explode if he did.

He also seemed to be having issues with her underwear, although she suspected that might be her fault. In a perhaps misguided effort to layer sexiness upon sexiness, she had put on a thong, and a pair of French knickers and a suspender belt. Already one of the suspender straps had pinged free like a mousetrap and snapped one of Ben's fingers. In his hasty desire to cover up the incident and gain access, he had managed to tie her underthings into a cat's cradle of lace and elastic.

"Here," she said and crouched down into the sleeping bag to resolve the Gordian knot of lingerie he had created.

She freed herself and then found herself wedged sideways with her head thrust against Ben's stomach.

"Bit stuck here," she said with some difficulty in the confined and increasingly hot space.

"Hang on," said Ben and tried to angle himself away from her.

She put her hand on his groin and he made a noise like someone going over the first big dip of a rollercoaster. He wriggled involuntarily and she slipped free.

"You've got a condom on already," she said, reporting back on her explorations. "You slipped that on without me noticing."

"I put it on back at the house."

She tried to straighten her tangled hair, hoping her face didn't look as flushed as it felt.

"Aren't you meant to put that on when you're... you know, standing to attention?"

"I did," he said.

"But since then, driving down, you must have..." She looked into his eyes. "Blimey, boy, how long have you had that stiffy?"

Ben looked up in thought.

"I'm going to go with nineteen ninety-eight," he said and kissed her.

And then finally he put his hands on her naked breast and neither he nor they exploded and nor did he attack them as if he was kneading a ball of dough. And then, very, very slowly one of his hands began to crawl south down her body, like a hyena approaching the corpse of a lion, hungry yet fearful that it might leap and...

"Oh, God," she sighed.

Ben kissed her more deeply. She rolled against him, reached down to take hold of him.

"Ow," he exclaimed.

"What did I do?" she said.

"There's something digging into me," said Ben, arching his back.

Ben pawed at the object through the sleeping bag material.

"Has your dad left some tools in the car?"

"Probably."

"Here it is," he said, grasping something.

There was a click and Jayne felt the earth move but definitely not in a good way.

"Handbrake!" yelled Ben as the car began to roll forward.

Jayne swore, raised herself up on her hands and looked out of the windscreen. Ben was scrabbling for the handbrake but Jayne already saw that it was too late. The car had crested the top of the short, steep slipway and was accelerating rapidly towards the waterline.

In the final moment of blind panic, Jayne recalled reading a Cosmopolitan magazine survey in which forty percent of men had declared that they would want to die in the throes of passion with a naked woman astride them. Sadly, Jayne had no time to explain to Ben how lucky he was to be in such a position. No time at all.

ONE MINUTE LATER, after a lot of splashing, shrieking and stumbling, Ben and Jayne staggered into the shallows, accompanied by the loud usage of more swear words than it was decent for any person to know. Something huge, translucent and rubbery drifted against Ben's thigh.

"Jellyfish!" he squealed.

Jayne pushed the water-filled condom aside and hauled her goose-pimpled fiancé onto the slipway.

"G-God, I'm sorry," he shivered.

Jayne looked at the sea. The roof of the orange Allegro stood just an inch above the waves, like a discarded lilo.

"Dad loved that car," she said.

"At least we've saved the s-seats," said Ben, pointing to the kitchen chairs up by the boathouse.

"We've got to get home before we freeze to death," said Jayne.

"We're naked," said Ben, pointing out the obvious.

"You're still wearing your socks," she replied.

Ben looked down at his sodden socks.

"This is the first and last time I'll forgive you for wearing your socks to bed," she said.

"Okay," said Ben.

Jayne couldn't help but reflect for a moment that the cold did weird things to the human body. A dip in the chilly sea appeared to have reduced Ben's wedding tackle to a tiny wrinkled ball of skin no bigger than an acorn. Whereas her nipples were now painfully proud and hard and probably would now explode if Ben so much as looked at them.

"We need to find clothes," said Ben.

"Where?" she said. "I'm not going back in for them and nor are you."

Ben cast about and then pointed.

"I've got an idea."

THE SHIP HOTEL was boarded up while repairs were being made to the WI-inflicted damage from the night before so Michael and Clovenhoof went to the Ty Newydd Hotel across the road. Michael bought Clovenhoof his customary Lambrini but, feeling that the ascetic spirituality of the monastery had rubbed off on him a little, Michael ordered only a mineral water for himself.

Despite the chill of the evening, they took their drinks onto the beachfront terrace where they could talk privately.

"We have a mystery on our hands," said Michael.

"How do they make Lambrini taste so bollock-bouncingly fantastic?" suggested Clovenhoof.

"No. The monastery."

Clovenhoof nodded.

"Indeed. Why would a bunch of dress-wearing men choose to live in a draughty castle with only other dress-wearing men for company?"

"You're not taking this seriously," said Michael with a harrumph.

"I don't take anything seriously," said Clovenhoof.

"You know, this could be the reason for my presence here."

"What?"

"On Earth. The Almighty sent me here for a purpose and perhaps this is it."

Clovenhoof gave a violently loud bark of laughter.

"You arrogant arse, Michael. You have been sent here as a punishment. You joined an attempted coup in the Celestial City."

"I didn't know that was what St Peter was doing!"

"Then you're a fool as well as a twat! Point is, you weren't sent *to* Earth, you were sent *away from* the Celestial City. There is no purpose to life on Earth and you have no mission."

Michael shook his head dismissively.

"And yet we have been presented with this mystery."

"What mystery?"

"One," said Michael, counting on his fingers, "I find myself on an island that, unless I'm a sleep-swimmer, I had no way of reaching. Two, there's a monastery dedicated to a saint who must exist yet is neither in Heaven or Hell. Three, there has been a sudden spate of unnaturally truthful utterances across the area, possibly sparked by a preserve from a winter-flowering fruit tree."

"The Jam of Truth!" declared Clovenhoof with theatrical pomposity. "Are you kidding me?"

"No, There's something going on." Michael paused in sipping his drinking. "And something else occurred to me. There are peacocks on Bardsey."

"So?"

"You know what peacocks symbolised to early Christians?"

"No, I don't know and I don't c- God's balls! Is that who I think it is?"

Clovenhoof was on his feet and pointing along the beach. Michael turned.

Two figures approached along the sands, scuttling around the rocks to stay as close as possible to the sheltering cliff. Both were wearing luminous orange life jackets. One seemed to be wearing some sort of short skirt fashioned from strands of kelp. The other carried a strategically positioned clump of gorse over his groin. Apart from that, they were naked.

"That's Ben," said Michael.

"And Jayne," said Clovenhoof.

"Not particularly dressed for the weather."

Clovenhoof nodded and then waved vigorously.

"Coo-ee!" he shouted.

Clovenhoof saw Ben look up and, although he was not a good lip-reader, particularly at a distance, Ben's unheard response to being spotted was perfectly clear.

"I think they're trying to hide from us," said Clovenhoof.

"You, perhaps," said Michael.

There was the sudden clatter of claws and Jessie rounded the corner onto the terrace, some form of clothing clamped into her mouth.

"She's brought them clothes," said Michael. "That dog really is a marvel."

Clovenhoof grabbed Jessie as she went past and dragged the underpants from her mouth. He stuffed them deep into his pocket and released her.

He vaulted the terrace railing to the beach twelve feet below and trotted over to the bedraggled pair. Ben, with the wide-eyed panic of a cornered animal, jiggled on the spot, unable to decide where to run and then, seeing there was no escape, stopped and stood still.

"Go on," he said. "Laugh. It's what you do."

Clovenhoof pointed at Jayne's life jacket.

"Owen said I couldn't keep mine."

"Well, we had to sort of... borrow these ones from his boat," she said.

"You stole them? Why?"

She gave him a blank stare.

"We were naked," she said.

"And afraid of catching our death of cold," added Ben.

Clovenhoof tutted.

"And, you know, if I had stolen one, I wouldn't have heard the end of it."

Jayne gave him a withering look.

"Well, you know what, you can have mine –"

"Thanks."

Clovenhoof reached forward and unzipped her jacket to take it from her.

"- when I've finished with it!" she shrieked.

ST CADFAN'S

Spring finally came to Bardsey, and the island acted as a handy stopover for multiple species of migratory birds who returned to Britain every year in the perpetual belief that the summer climate would suit them perfectly.

For the monks, they noticed mainly that both the temperature and the rainfall had gone up. However, there was only a light drizzle in the air as Brother Sebastian showed Abbot Ambrose some of the external repairs to the monastery stonework.

"What do you think?" said Sebastian with a dramatic flourish of his arms.

The abbot looked at the wall and the large shaped stones where a gaping hole had once been.

"When did you get this done?" he asked, incredulous.

"This weekend, Father Abbot. Owen brought the materials over on the boat."

"One weekend's work? But..."

The abbot was struck speechless. It was seamless, better than the original even.

"You like it, don't you?" said Sebastian.

The abbot nodded.

"You have worked something miraculous here, brother."

Sebastian grinned.

"Ready for the surprise?"

He stepped forward and rapped the repaired wall with his knuckle. It gave a hollow echo.

"It's fibre glass!" he said. "Brilliant, isn't it? Looks like the real thing. Costs next to nothing."

The abbot felt something sag and snap inside him.

"It's not real."

"Nope."

"And so, inside, there's still a hole."

"A covered hole."

"And the unsupported ceiling stones in the corridor?"

"Will still need propping up. But just until we raise enough money to make the proper repairs. But it's all secure. Perfectly safe."

Sebastian thumped the genuine stonework to make his point. A piece of stone fell from on high and landed on the abbot's open-sandaled foot. The abbot winced.

Sebastian was about to offer his apologies when a much larger stone detached itself from the wall above and slammed into his own foot. Sebastian hopped around, hissing and gasping and trying very hard not to swear. He thought he heard the abbot say something that sounded like, "vengeance seven times over" but he was so intent on rubbing his squashed foot that he couldn't be sure.

By the time he had soothed the pain away and was able to stand properly again, the abbot was simply stood, gazing sadly at Sebastian's fibre glass wall.

"You're not happy, Father Abbot?" said Sebastian.

"It's very clever, brother," the abbot said in a dead voice. "Ingenious."

He turned and walked away.

Suddenly, the abbot felt very old. He was very old, of course, but at this moment he felt ten thousand years old as though the weight of history was going to bear him down to the ground and crush him.

He struggled under that weight all the way to the orangery. The prior sat in his bath-chair and, for once, the abbot felt older and more frail than his brother.

"I think I've had enough," said the abbot, approaching the prior and sitting down on the wooden wall of one of the raised beds.

He looked at the prior and, in one of those rare moments, the prior looked back.

"No point asking you. You've had enough too."

The prior blinked slowly.

"Look at this," said the abbot, produced a glass jar from his pocket and placed it on the bed wall next to him. Congealed apple preserve clung to its insides.

"They turned it into a jam," said the abbot and almost laughed. "God alone knows what effect it had on them. There are rumours."

The abbot put the jar away.

"Rumours will spread. This place is falling down. One could almost give in. Lie down and die."

The prior made a slight noise although it could simply have been wind.

"Well, I don't have the option of giving in," said the abbot. "I have no way out."

He tapped the crown of his head beneath his thick wig of grey hair.

"The flood didn't touch me. No man will touch me. Death won't touch me."

He took a deep breath.

"Tell me again, brother. What is death like?"

The prior said nothing.

"You've been there and back. Does death hurt? What is *Sheol* like? Is it a world of cold and shadows? Would I find peace in death?"

The prior remained silent.

The abbot stood up.

"Well, I'm sorry, brother. If I cannot have peace, if death won't take me, it won't take you either."

He went and opened the cabinet near the base of the apple tree. He looked at the contents of the watering can. Much of the blood had congealed but it was still mostly liquid.

"This place has been good to us," he said, though whether this was directed to the prior or the tree he wasn't sure himself. "But it's probably time to move on."

The abbot poured the remaining blood into the soil at the base of the tree.

"All out. Time for your treatment again."

9

IN WHICH STAGS AND HENS CELEBRATE

Spring had also arrived in the Midlands.

Ben was quietly impressed. Less so with the weather, but more with the fact that seven blokes had been found to attend his stag do, which was an impressive feat considering that Ben would have struggled to say he had any real friends at all. The eight of them had all been picked up and driven in a minibus to a woodland location in Warwickshire, arriving in one piece and at the correct time.

This was *particularly* impressive given that Jeremy Clovenhoof had organised it all.

Ben was less impressed when he saw the sign on the gate as they drove through.

"Paintballing?" he said.

"Yup," said Clovenhoof, air drumming in excitement.

"Paintballing?" he said again, just in case he had misread the sign and misheard his best man.

"Yup."

"Super."

They drew up in a courtyard beside a farm shed on the edge of wood.

Ben glanced across at his friends Darren and Argyll from the wargaming club as they climbed down from the minibus. Argyll took breaths from his inhaler, alternately gasping and chattering about tree pollen. Darren pulled a battered Twix from his trouser pocket, and smiled as he unwrapped it. In terms of physical prowess, he and his friends might just rustle up the bits between the three of them to make one capable soldier.

He leaned across to Clovenhoof.

"What made you think that paintballing was the way to go?" he asked.

His best man beamed back at him.

"I mentioned to Manpreet that you were keen on wargaming. He says it's a very similar experience."

"Right," said Ben, "Manpreet's the guy that you work with?"

Clovenhoof nodded.

Manpreet was a big man, probably the same size and weight as Darren. However, whereas Darren had the physique of an overfilled water balloon, Manpreet was more like a tightly packed steel drum. Ben watched the powerfully-built man as he dug into his rucksacks and pulled out a paintball gun.

"He's got his own gun," Ben hissed.

"Yes. Nice, isn't it?"

"I thought we'd be given them by the organisers."

"He comes here all the time," said Clovenhoof.

"Apparently a lot of the expert players have their own weapons."

Ben sighed heavily.

"I think I hate you, Jeremy."

"Never mind him," said Clovenhoof. "The interesting stuff's going on with that little group."

He indicated towards Michael and Andy, stood a little distance from Reverend Zack who was gazing serenely at the trees and taking deep breaths of country air. Michael and Andy were in animated conversation, but kept glancing at Zack. The St Michael's vicar was apparently unaware of the attention.

"What do you mean, interesting?" asked Ben.

"I know you didn't have a ringside seat like I did, but Andy's the one who gave the good Reverend a fearsome telling-off for being a gay-hater when he came to the flats that time."

"Reverend Zack's homophobic?" said Ben.

"He's afraid to leave the house?"

"I mean is he prejudiced against gay people?"

"Oh. No, I don't think he is," said Clovenhoof. "He's not an Old Testament kind of preacher, really. But the entertaining thing is that Andy *thinks* he is."

"And you're going to put him straight on that?"

"Where's the fun in that? No, I'm going to stand back and watch. I expect one of them will have a bullet in the back by the end of the day."

∾

JAYNE PEERED at the stylised map on the back of the brochure as Nerys drove.

"If this map is to scale, then it's a few hundred yards after that motorway junction that we just went over."

Nerys glanced across.

"When has that kind of map *ever* been to scale?" she asked. "I think there's some special skill to drawing those. They try to make a place look easily accessible, even if it's in the middle of nowhere."

She looked at the SatNav.

"Which this place *is,* by the way. We keep going on this lane for another eight miles."

Jayne settled back and took the opportunity to scan the leaflet once more.

"We can walk away from these treatments with three inches off our waistlines," she quoted. "Three inches! Just think how much better my wedding dress will look."

"Your wedding dress is going to look sensational, whatever you do," said Nerys. "Ben's grateful to have a woman in his life at all, he doesn't need a supermodel. He's already seen you naked, so he's not going to recoil in horror, is he?"

Jayne shifted with the uncomfortable recollection of her unscheduled skinny-dipping experience several months before. In charitable moments, she hoped that Ben had seen her emergence from the Welsh waves as something akin to Botticelli's *Birth of Venus* but she had probably looked more like the *Creature from the Black Lagoon*. Of all the horrors that she'd experienced on that day, the knowledge that everyone had seen her stomach swinging like a sporran was the thing that haunted her more than the stinging cold and blistered feet.

"No, it's not just about pleasing men, Nerys. Wouldn't you like to lose a few inches and have a face that glows with health and well-being?"

"Of course. I wouldn't mind that at all, if they really can achieve it in one day."

"One Day Radical Detox," Jayne read aloud from the brochure. "It sounds like just the thing, and it's so much better for us than having the usual drunken hen party. We can relax and feel virtuous. It's a win-win situation."

They turned into the grounds of a country estate and drove along a tree-lined avenue. Signposts directed them away from a grand Georgian house and to a gravel car park within a quadrangle of low, modern buildings.

"So we don't actually get to stay in Applebower Hall?" said Jayne.

"Apparently not."

"Still," said Jayne brightly. "We're not here for a tourist experience. Radical detox, here we come."

Five minutes later, they were signing in at reception.

"Disclaimers?" said Jayne, scanning the small print.

"Against any reactions," said a small young woman appearing at their side. She had blonde hair, skin tanned a caramel brown and a broad Australian accent. "And any minor injuries."

"Injuries?" said Nerys.

"It's just standard stuff, ladies. You get this at any place."

"Really?" said Jayne, who had never had to sign a disclaimer against 'anaphylactic shock' before.

"I'm Opal," said the petite Australian over her shoulder as she marched them down a corridor. Her posture was as uncompromising as her pace. Jayne tried to stand a little straighter, but couldn't help feeling like a geriatric ox lumbering after Tinkerbell.

In a small ante-room, Opal turned to face them.

"We'll start in here. You get changed into these robes and drink these hydrating smoothies."

Jayne picked up the robe and looked around for a cubicle or curtained area.

"Oh no," said Opal. "No secrets today. I need to assess your body shape so that I can tailor the programme for you. You can get your kit off right here."

Jayne exchanged a glance with Nerys and they started to shrug off their layers, not wanting to look uptight and British, even though uptight and British was exactly how Jayne felt.

"Oh look, a couple of wobbly jellies!" said Opal, pointing at their exposed stomachs. "I once saw something like that wash up on Bondai Beach."

Jayne stared at her in mortified horror.

"It's fine, ladies," laughed Opal. "You'll soon get used to my sense of humour."

"Is that what it is?" muttered Nerys.

"I like to make these little jokes as we work on your well-being. I only do it with people I really like."

"So that makes it okay?"

"Exactly. We can soon sort those bellies out with some electric pulse therapy and you'll look back and laugh at this, I promise."

Jayne and Nerys wrapped their robes around them,

saying nothing. They sat down, grateful to be covered once again and picked up the hydrating smoothies.

"Looks nice," murmured Jayne and took a long swig. Nerys was a moment behind, but their reactions were perfectly synchronised. Retching and mewling they both put down the glasses and physically backed away from them, clawing at their throats in an attempt to eradicate the disgusting taste.

"Come on now ladies, don't act like babies. I don't know if you realise how good this is for you. Pinch your noses and think of something nice. It'll all be worth it, don't you worry. Down in one. Now."

Opal stood and stared firmly at both of them.

Reluctantly Jayne raised the glass and looked across at Nerys.

"Mine's a margarita," said Jayne.

"Screw that, mine's Sex on the Beach at the very least," said Nerys. They glugged the foul mixture down and both set their glasses on the table with a clink of triumph, screwing their whole faces closed until they could trust themselves not to vomit.

"Tastes of fish," said Jayne.

"No, sour milk," said Nerys.

"Probably both," said Opal brightly. "There's the ground krill, the blue-green algae and the fermented goats milk."

CHAD, the paintball instructor, had an interesting habit of punctuating his words with karate moves and grunts.

Michael wasn't sure if he was trying to be Chuck Norris or Vegas-era Elvis Presley.

"Welcome everyone to the toughest day out the Midlands has to offer. Hoo-ha! You've all got overalls and safety masks now, yeah?"

"Er, I can't do mine up," said Darren struggling with a zip that strained impossibly at the base of his stomach.

"Okay, go back and find a larger size," said Chad.

"This is the largest size you've got," said Darren.

"Right. Everybody do some star jumps to warm up while I see to this," said Chad.

He walked over to Darren, braced him up against the side of the storage hut and used his meaty forearm to hold back Darren's stomach while he yanked the zip up. Somehow, it closed.

"Good, right! Ha! How are those star jumps coming?"

Michael looked around as he jumped. Manpreet and Andy were star jumping enthusiastically, while Zack and the wargamers made half-hearted efforts. Clovenhoof was practising a quick draw with a stick.

"All right, you can rest now," said Chad. "I need to talk to you about safety. Hy-ah!"

Everyone relaxed. Everyone except Darren whose arms remained stuck out to the sides.

"No more star jumps now," Chad said to him.

"I can't get my arms down," said Darren. "Suit's too tight."

"Right. Safety," said Chad as he wrestled Darren's arms across his chest. There was a brief ripping sound, and Chad resumed his pose in the centre of the group.

"Face masks. Hoo!" He punched the air, holding his mask

aloft. "They're the difference between you staying in the game and coming out. It's *that* serious," he stared at them all for emphasis. "If you take them off in a game our insurance won't cover you - Hnh! - and we have to take you out of play immediately. But seriously. Who wants to go home with their eyeballs in their pockets? Anyone? Show of hands?"

There were no takers.

"Thought so. Ha!"

"Next thing. The paintball." He pulled one from his pocket and held it up between his thumb and forefinger. "Looks pretty harmless, doesn't it? Just you wait until it's coming at you at three hundred feet per second. Hoo-ha! You're going to get bruises today. Anyone who can't face that possibility might want to drop out now."

Andy shuffled slightly and eyed Michael sideways. Michael pictured Andy's perfect physique sullied by ugly bruises and had a brief urge to grab his arm and leave. He pushed the urge away and reminded himself that he was a warrior angel and could not be seen to back away from conflict. Besides which, Clovenhoof would never let him live it down.

"Right, we'll split you into teams. You four over here, you're team Red, and the rest of you over there, you're team Blue. Hoozah!"

The two teams lined up. Ben, Darren, Argyll and Clovenhoof faced Andy, Zack, Manpreet and Michael.

"Go team Red!" shouted Clovenhoof and pulled a moonie at Michael. Michael rolled his eyes, but was distracted by an elbow in the ribs from Andy.

"Why do we have to be on a team with *him*?" Andy hissed.

"What?"

Andy nodded discreetly at Zack.

"I don't know why he's even here."

Chad thrust colour-coded arm bands into their hands, and they all pulled them on. Darren tugged his up his arm as far as he could, so he ended up with something like a narrow tourniquet that was probably already cutting off the blood supply to his hand.

"I think we might have had a big misunderstanding with Zack," Michael said, taking Andy aside. "I was upset and confused when I suddenly got all that money. I think he was just trying to help."

"Oh yeah? Well I bet he still believes all that stuff about it being an abomination to lie with another man."

"I think the church's position on such things is not straightforward."

"Really? Remember Sodom and Gomorrah? A city destroyed because some of the men were gay!"

"Now, you weren't there, Andy."

"And you were?"

"No," Michael lied, "but it really wasn't about sexuality."

"Point is, I don't trust the man."

With masks in place, Chad handed out the guns and lectured them at length about the best way to operate them safely. Michael was surprised to see that Clovenhoof was listening carefully. He thought this was most uncharacteristic, until he realised that Clovenhoof was considering the reverse of every instruction, in an effort to make things more violent and interesting. Michael examined the mechanism of the gun. It seemed straightforward, although he'd have felt a lot more comfortable with a flaming sword. He caught Clovenhoof's eye. He smiled and nodded towards his weapon.

Oh, yes, Michael remembered Sodom and Gomorrah. He remembered Jericho. He remembered the Canaanites, the Amalekites and the Midianites. He remembered the War in Heaven.

"Let's re-live old times," he mouthed, as they all trotted off towards the battlefield. "Boom!"

NERYS RECLINED on the treatment bed and smiled across at Jayne. This was more like it. They would soak up relaxing therapies and emerge looking dewy and revitalised.

"Right ladies," said Opal. "We're going to prepare your skin for the treatments we've got lined up. These mineral-rich wraps will draw out toxins and open up the pores. We'll paint the guano onto your body and then wrap you with the heat retaining membrane."

Nerys mused for a moment on what Opal had just said.

"Guano," she said slowly, "is that a trade name?"

"No," said Opal.

"So guano...?"

"Yes?"

"That wouldn't be the guano that's like poo, obviously. What is it exactly?"

Opal looked up from slathering the sticky brown substance over Nerys's thighs. Jayne was being coated by a small woman with powerful forearms who muttered occasional words in Spanish.

"This contains the droppings of the Japanese Bush Warbler. Japanese women have prized its cosmetic properties for centuries."

"Bird poo?" said Jayne, propping herself up, to the clear annoyance of the Spanish woman. "Did you just say it's bird poo?"

Opal continued to apply the paste, and replied with a rigid smile.

"It's perfectly hygienic. It's been treated with ultra violet light. As long as you don't have any open sores, you'll be fine. You've signed the disclaimer anyway, haven't you?"

Nerys lay back with a small groan. Why on earth had she asked?

As their bodies were coated with liberal quantities of brown goo, Opal and the Spanish woman wrapped them with the heat-retaining membrane, which looked a lot like cling-film.

"We need to leave you for forty minutes," said Opal when they were completely wrapped. "You'll find it completely relaxing as the toxins leach from your skin, so you won't look as huge and bloated as beached whales."

She flashed them an enormous but rather brief smile and left them alone.

"Has she gone?" Jayne asked, propping herself up.

"Yes, I think so," Nerys replied. "I wonder where they do their customer service training? That woman couldn't be more offensive if she was," she waved a hand as she cast around for inspiration, "I dunno - Jeremy."

"She's awful," said Jayne, "and these treatments are bizarre. I just really hope they work."

"I'm just glad that Aussie despot has left us in peace," said Nerys, settling onto her elbows. "So, assuming these miracle treatments work, will I get to try on the bridesmaid's dress tomorrow?"

"If it's come in to the shop," Jayne said. "I'm sure you'll love it."

Nerys gave her sister a sceptical look.

"You're *sure* I'll love it?"

"I am sure. I think."

"Why do you say that? Please tell me it's not peach?"

"It's not peach."

"Peach satin is my worst nightmare."

"Really?"

"I don't want to look like a satin sausage."

"What's wrong with satin? I thought it was velvet that you hated?"

"I can hate them both, can't I?" said Nerys. "It's just that the pictures from your wedding will be around for years. People will look at their mantelpieces and see me in a shiny sausage skin and that's how they'll picture me *for ever*."

"I'm the one they're meant to be looking at."

"Well, as long as you're not wearing a meringue, you'll be fine. But bridesmaids..."

"Shut up, Nerys," said Jayne kindly. "The pictures will be amazing. We've got the monastery, the sea and the beautiful views. We'll all look like movie stars."

"Yeah right," said Nerys. "Boris Karloff." She grinned to herself. "What's Ben wearing, anyway?"

"We haven't decided."

"Don't let him have any part in the decision-making process otherwise it will be a jeans and t-shirt wedding. Although that might be worth it, just to see mom's face!"

"He's going to look perfectly handsome in a suit," said Jayne. "I'm sure mom will be impressed."

"Impressed? She's never going to be impressed with Ben, I'm afraid. I'm surprised she hasn't offered you cash to call it off."

Jayne stared fixedly at the ceiling.

"Oh no!" said Nerys. "She did! I can't believe it! How much did she offer?"

"It wasn't enough, let's leave it there," said Jayne.

Nerys gave her a nudge.

"How much would be enough?" she asked.

"A pile of gold," said Jayne, with a sniff. "The biggest pile of gold you've ever seen. No, the wedding is going to be fantastic but, you know, it's the honeymoon I'm looking forward to."

"And is Ben looking forward to it too?"

"It's going to be so romantic. Ben will get loads of inspiration for his bookshop, I'm sure. The travel section will really come alive for him when he's been to a load of different places."

Nerys wrinkled her nose and caught an unfortunate whiff of her guano coating.

"Have you talked to him about this?" she said. "Ben's not really the globe-trotting type."

"I've got a plan."

"Uh-huh."

"It's brilliant. What I'll do is lure him in with the Alexander the Great trail. We'll visit all the places where he fought his famous battles. Ben won't be able to resist that. Then for the second stage, we'll expand it out to cover all the places that were part of the Seleucid empire."

"Aren't lots of those places modern-day warzones?" Nerys asked.

"Not *all* of them."

Nerys sighed.

"Well, I'm sure the two of you can sort it out."

She stretched her arms and felt the tightening of her skin as the mask started to dry.

"It's certainly nice to have a few minutes to chat. I wasn't sure this was the sort of place that would give us any time to-good grief what's that?"

They both turned in alarm to the source of the sound, which was a speaker mounted on the wall. Echoing booms and eerie moans were amplified to a terrifying level.

"Listen to the sounds of nature," came the gravelly and distorted tones of the narrator at a deafening volume. "These remarkable sounds have been recorded in the deepest oceans of the world. Let your conscious mind float away as the song of the whale speaks to your inner core."

Nerys felt something float away. She wasn't sure if it was her conscious mind, or the last reserves of her temper and sanity.

～

BEN STOOD with his red team mates looking out across the sun-speckled woodland. The vibrant springtime growth on the trees was dense all around them.

"It's beautiful," he said. He hadn't seen any squirrels, foxes or badgers in the woods but the moment was so lovely he *just knew* they were out there. "So quiet," he said.

"Almost too quiet," said Clovenhoof ominously.

Ben gave him a look.

"Jeremy," he said. "When the klaxon sounds, we're going to be pitched into battle against the blue team. This is serious stuff. You're not going to... arse about, are you?"

"Absolutely, I am."

"I got sort of turned around as we came over. Is the blue base over there or *there*?"

Clovenhoof shrugged gamely.

"Ask Argyll."

Argyll was trying to push a large white handkerchief inside his face mask to blow his nose and grumbling frequently about the pollen count.

"I don't think he can even see," said Ben.

"This is probably the type of terrain that would give the Picts the edge over the Romans, don't you think?" Darren asked.

"You're right," said Ben.

"Lots of ground cover, so your big, disciplined legion will get split up. It favours the smaller, fleet-footed warrior who knows bushcraft."

"Yeah," said Ben, with a curious glance at Darren's vast, lumbering bulk. Did Darren picture himself slipping unnoticed between the trees?

"Do you think you could strap all the guns together and pull the triggers with a stick?" Clovenhoof asked, examining the mechanism, and holding his gun up against Ben's.

"Maybe," Ben said. "How do you think that will help us?"

"Oh, it probably won't help us at all," said Clovenhoof. "I just thought it would be fun."

Ben sighed in exasperation.

"Come on team! What are we going to do when that klaxon goes?"

"How about using Darren as a human shield?" Clovenhoof suggested. "It's not as if he can really move around in those overalls anyway." He leaned across and whispered loudly into Darren's ear. "There's a Mars Bar in it for you."

"No, we can't do that, we need to work as a team," said Ben.

"Hang on," Darren said. "Let's not be too hasty. King size or standard?" he asked Clovenhoof, eyebrows raised.

The klaxon blared.

"Never mind all that," yelled Argyll through his hanky. "Molon Labe!"

He ran for the top of a nearby ridge.

Clovenhoof grabbed Ben and Darren.

"Did he just say 'Molon Labe'?" he asked.

Ben nodded.

"I haven't heard that since there were ancient Greeks around to actually say it," mused Clovenhoof. "Why would he come out with that?"

"It's what King Leonidas said when Xerxes demanded

that the Spartans surrender," said Darren, who was keen to earn the Mars Bar one way or another. "It means -"

"I know what it means," said Clovenhoof. "It means 'come and work us over, vastly superior enemy.' Or thereabouts."

Darren shrugged, unable to find fault with Clovenhoof's interpretation.

"Said shortly before Xerxes crushed and killed Leonidas and his army."

"I think in this case," suggested Ben, "Argyll might have been using it as a battle cry, intended to motivate his brothers-in-arms to make an ill-advised charge on the off-chance that it might surprise the enemy."

"Probably," said Darren.

"Oh," said Clovenhoof. "Should we follow him then?"

"Suppose so," said Ben.

They gathered themselves together and trotted off in pursuit of Argyll, who was some distance ahead up the slope but easy to locate by the sound of his loud, wheezing breath. They were just a few feet behind him as he crested the ridge. A sudden burst of gunfire erupted from the other side, and Argyll was cut down, paint covering his entire upper body.

Ben, Darren and Clovenhoof turned and ran, screaming into the surrounding trees.

ZACK, Michael and Andy threw themselves into a stand of bracken as Manpreet tracked the retreating Clovenhoof. Michael found his head next to a decomposing log that spilled woodlice everywhere, as he nudged it. He recoiled slightly, nostalgic for celestial battles where the glory of Heaven was at stake, and insects were not a significant factor.

"I heard something," said Zack.

"Yes, it was the enemy screaming like girls as they ran away," said Andy.

"No, over there." He pointed. "One of them is in that clearing there. Follow me!"

Zack rushed forward.

"He's not the boss of us!" hissed Andy, but he and Michael scrambled after him anyway.

"MOVE OVER! THERE'S NO ROOM," Darren grumbled at Ben.

They jostled for position behind an ash tree, Ben too polite to point out that the tree was much too thin to hide Darren.

"Someone's coming!" Darren whispered.

Ben watched as Darren tried to make himself as thin as possible. His body remained unaffected, but he sucked in his cheeks to a considerable degree.

The woods had become perfectly silent. It was now indeed *too* quiet. If there were squirrels and foxes and badgers out there, they had gone home to hide under their beds.

"I'm going to have a look," Ben whispered.

Darren gave a small nod, evidently not wanting to break the intense concentration needed to keep his cheeks sucked in.

Ben leaned forward to peer round the tree. Long moments passed, and he could see Darren in his peripheral vision, quivering with anxiety.

"Anything?" Darren eventually said in a small, tight voice.

Ben pulled back behind the tree, coming face to face with Darren as the paint dripped from his mask. Through the pink smear of dripping paint, Ben could see Darren's eyes widen with terror.

Ben watched, a bystander now, as Darren emerged to face Zack, Michael and Andy crossing the clearing. Zack was at the head of the group, grinning wildly.

"Hey, Reverend Zack, I'm so glad it's you," said Darren. "I know you'll show me some Christian mercy."

"Beat your swords into ploughshares first, buddy," snarled Zack.

"Sorry? What?"

"Drop your weapon."

Darren's eyes swivelled to Ben who gave him emboldening gestures of encouragement and then back to Zack.

"No, sorry," said Darren. "Er, I mean Molon Labe."

Zack fired a burst of paintballs at Darren's feet and Darren dropped his gun with a small yelp.

"All right! I'll come quietly," he squealed.

Zack blasted him squarely in the chest with several shots.

"Vengeance is mine, sayeth the Lord," he said, pointing his weapon skywards with a huge grin.

Ben watched in mild horror as Zack leaned over the gently groaning figure of Darren and ripped a long strip of fabric from the sleeve of his overall, which was almost completely detached by now. He tied it around his head, bandana-style and leapt to his feet, weapon at the ready, alerted by a snapping twig in the undergrowth. It seemed as though Reverend Zack was enjoying himself. Maybe he was enjoying himself a little too much.

Manpreet appeared, a finger to his lips.

"I got this one, brother," he said, pointing into the trees. He gave Zack a high five, and melted back into the undergrowth.

JAYNE SIGHED with relief when the whale sounds were turned off. Opal and her burly Spanish assistant entered the room.

"Right, ladies, it's time to remove the guano. Are you starting to feel your skin tighten and glow?"

"I'm feeling like a freshly wrapped turdsicle," said Nerys. "Does that count?"

Opal beamed at her.

"You know, your kind of grey, pasty complexion shows the benefits best of all. I bet you're pleased to hear that, aren't you?"

"Bloody ecstatic."

Off came the wrap, and then Opal led them through to a shower. Jayne found herself really looking forward to a delicious, long soak. Maybe a massage was next. Something with scented oils.

She and her sister screamed as the frigid water hit their bodies.

"There's something the matter!" squealed Nerys just as Jayne yelled, "The hot water isn't working!"

Opal rounded the corner of the walk-in shower, carrying an extension hose.

"No, this must be cold water. We're not just cleaning off the guano, we're stimulating the circulatory system. You'll feel terrific afterwards, I guarantee it. It might firm up some of that flab a little bit too."

She blasted them with the hose, which carried an extra-powerful jet of cold water.

"Look at those flabby thighs jiggle!" said Opal.

"Can't we come out now?" asked Nerys. "The guano's all gone."

"Not until your twenty minutes are up," said Opal. "That's when you really get the health benefits. Let me get those bingo wings for you," she added, raising the hose higher.

CLOVENHOOF TURNED to see Manpreet right behind him, weapon raised.

As he spun to face him, the paintballs hit him across his torso.

He scowled briefly in annoyance at losing, but then realised that he had some considerable experience at losing. It was one thing he knew how to do properly. Some Sam Peckinpah western movies and Bugs Bunny cartoons had given him some new ideas as well.

He clutched his chest and staggered back and forth for a few minutes, yelling as loudly as he could. This had the desired effect of increasing his audience. The rest of the red and blue teams soon appeared. He moved on to theatrical coughing, coupled with a slow spin towards the ground, arms trailing as he collapsed. It was hard to do a slow motion death scene in real life but he gave it his all.

But, even when he was on the ground, he wasn't done. He propped himself up and coughed lightly again, before finally falling backwards, splayed on the ground.

A brief ripple of applause broke out from the observers, and Clovenhoof grinned. If there was a trophy for best defeat, he'd aced it.

Nerys and Jayne were back on treatment beds, their skin still red from the extended hosing with cold water.

"You'll have heard of cupping," said Opal. "It's an ancient form of Chinese therapy. Very effective."

"Effective at what?" Nerys hissed to Jayne.

" Lie on your fronts for me, ladies," said Opal.

Nerys rolled onto her front, with just a brief glance across at Jayne. Jayne seemed to have regained her composure, so Nerys resolved to accept the rest of the treatments with good grace. A curious after-effect of the cold shower was that she felt as if she could now face anything.

"Can you smell burning?" Jayne asked.

"It's just the small flame that we need to create a vacuum in the cups," said Opal. Nerys felt a strange pressure on her back.

"We place these across your body, and the suction will stimulate blood flow."

Nerys opened her mouth to ask a question, but her words were cut off as she felt a gloved hand part her buttocks and insert something.

She settled for yelling instead.

"What the hell is that?"

"Colonic irrigation," said Opal in a voice that suggested it should be obvious. "Honestly, I don't know why you're acting surprised."

"Anytime someone goes up my jacksy without first giving me a bottle of wine, a bunch of flowers and twenty-four hours notice, I reserve the right to act fucking surprised."

You read the leaflet before you came, surely?" said Opal.

"No, I didn't."

Nerys glanced across at Jayne, whose face was trying to cope with the dual task of displaying the horror that her body was experiencing as well as some mild expressions of sisterly guilt.

"Do you want to see if we can swap over to the other experience day?" Jayne asked.

"What would that be?" Nerys asked. "Leech therapy?"

Opal piped up, "Oh, if you're interested in the leeches, we could-"

"No!" chorused Jayne and Nerys.

"It's called 'Vajazzle me Happy'" said Jayne, with a worried glance at Nerys.

Nerys groaned and buried her face in her forearms in defeat.

Clovenhoof looked at the teams assembled along the picnic benches for lunch. The red team was entirely covered with paint, while the blue team was completely untouched.

"Does it remind you of the old days?" Michael asked, smoothing the fabric of his overall on his knees. Clovenhoof wanted to punch his smarmy face, but knew that the most satisfying response would be found in the paintball arena.

"Hoo-ha! Hot dogs and burgers everyone!" yelled Chad. "I bet you guys feel as though you've earned it, right? Yah! There's nothing like the adrenaline rush of a pitched battle."

Clovenhoof grabbed a burger and wandered away from the rest of the group. The base camp was situated in a set of old farm buildings, and he made a careful examination of each one, to see what might come in handy. He had a list already in his mind. It wasn't a list of words or objects. It was a list of petty acts of revenge and he was on the lookout for anything that could help him fulfil them.

He found a tractor in a barn, and climbed up inside the cab. Sadly, the controls were ancient and unfathomable and the tractor didn't look as though it had moved in many years. He climbed down again, sulking slightly that he couldn't appropriate it to adapt as a tank. He moved on and found some buckets and rope.

"Possible potential," he mused.

Moments later, in a tumbledown greenhouse, he came across a pump-action weed sprayer, which he added to his haul. He scampered back into the woods and carefully hid his unusual collection in a thick clump of holly trees before returning to the picnic benches.

Ben was already talking tactics with Darren and Argyll.

"Okay, so the afternoon's game is a standard capture the flag," he said. "We all understand the rules, yes?"

"Either we get their flag or they get ours," said Darren.

"It's clear," said Ben, "that we're not going to win this by being better soldiers. We're going to need better tactics. Listen to me, I've been thinking about the all-time hardest arcade game from my childhood, and I think I've got a plan."

IN THE 'REVITALISE' dining rooms, Nerys poked at her plate. It was filled with chunks of dry, unappetising vegetable matter.

"They forgot to cook this, let's take it back."

Jayne peered mournfully across.

"No, I think it's what we're supposed to eat. It's called a Raw Food Power Lunch."

"You're kidding?"

"No," Jayne shook her head, "and it looks as though we've got another hydrating smoothie to go with it."

They both leaned back in their chairs, as far away from their plates as possible and glared at the food.

The dining room was small, and they were currently the only people in it. Nerys glanced around to see if there was any other viable food or drink that they could swap or steal. Nothing.

"I can't face another one of these smoothies," she hissed

at Jayne. "You create some kind of diversion, I'll nip to the ladies, and tip them away. I can get us each a glass of tap water while I'm there."

"God, that sounds great. Never thought I'd say that about tap water."

Jayne wandered across to the door that led to the kitchen.

"Excuse me," she called through the door. "I'm looking for a leaflet about the leeches, do you have any?"

Nerys grabbed the glasses of the hateful smoothie and made for the other door, back toward the treatment rooms. She elbowed the handle open and backed out, so that she didn't spill the drinks. She backed straight into Opal who was standing with her hands on her hips.

"Going somewhere?" she asked.

Out on the field of battle, Ben shepherded everyone into position.

"Everyone knows what they're doing? Right. Darren, roll in the mud. Yeah, that's looking good. Jeremy, you know you don't *have* to be naked, right?"

Clovenhoof shrugged.

"When they're confronted by my enormous manhood, they'll be awestruck for long enough for us to gain an edge," he said.

"Right. That might happen I suppose," said Ben, doubtfully. He didn't like to point out that another possibility was an incredibly painful injury to Clovenhoof's genitalia. "Into position and quiet now. Very quiet."

Michael was at the head of the blue group, while Manpreet scouted slightly around to the side, watching out for an ambush. Michael saw the flag, their target. It was unguarded in the centre of a clearing, next to a large round bush.

"Idiots," he said triumphantly. "They've left it unguarded."

He stepped forward. His foot snagged on something, and, as he looked down to see that it was a rope stretched across the path, he felt a torrent of viscous liquid on his neck.

He stumbled and wriggled, the paint dripping onto his forearms. He was out of the game.

"I know this is your doing, Jeremy!" he shouted out. "Don't think you've heard the end of this!"

And then the iron bucket fell loose from the rope above him and dropped onto his head with a loud clang.

The fish spa wasn't so bad if you didn't think about it, Nerys decided.

She tried hard not to think about small carnivorous fish eating the dead skin from her feet. The harder she tried not to think of small, cold-skinned creatures, sloughing the skin off her body with fangs that had been sharpened on previous clients, the more queasy she felt.

"Nice, isn't it?" said Jayne, reclining dreamily with her legs swinging gently in the water.

Nerys didn't answer. She sat tense and uncomfortable,

trying to empty her mind or distract herself somehow. She reached for the leaflet at Jayne's side, wondering what other treatments lay ahead.

"Oh, no!"

She realised that she'd knocked Jayne's ankle bracelet into the water. They both sat and watched it settle on the bottom of the pool, attracting the attention of a number of fish.

"I suppose I'd better get it out," said Nerys, peering into the water. "What is it, four, five feet deep?"

Jayne nodded.

"About that."

Nerys tipped her weight forward and considered the prospect. She was wearing a bikini, so she didn't need to worry about clothes. She'd slip over the edge, quickly bob under the water, and climb back out after no more than ten seconds. Ten seconds where fish would nudge and probe her entire body. Ten seconds where fish might nibble her ears and eyeballs.

"Maybe we could find a pole or something to fish it out?" she said finally.

"Oh, for goodness sake!" Jayne said, and slid into the water. Her head bobbed beneath the surface and Nerys could see her hands groping the bottom of the pool.

Opal came rushing in to investigate the splash.

"Oh, I wouldn't do that," she said. "You know that those fish have been known to swim up a person's urethra?"

"What?" said Nerys.

"Surgery's the only way to get them out."

"Jayne, get out!" Nerys squealed. "The fish are gonna swim up your fanny!"

"What?" said Jayne, surfacing.

"Get out! Grab her arm, for crying out loud you silly bint!" Nerys yelled at Opal.

Nerys sobbed with relief as Jayne climbed out, surprised but apparently unviolated.

CLOVENHOOF CROUCHED IN THE BRACKEN, listening to Manpreet approaching. They were to wait for Ben's signal.

He'd decided that Manpreet moved with surprising stealth for a man of his bulk. He'd also decided that he would be quite happy to pay Manpreet back for some of his bossier moments in the working environment.

Ben's signal came. It consisted of Ben popping up from his hiding place, shouting "Eep!" and dropping back down into his hiding place. He let off a rattle of aimless gunfire on the way, which sailed over the treetops. Manpreet returned fire but Ben was back under cover.

In turn, Clovenhoof and Argyll copied Ben's performance. Up, fire, down. Clovenhoof added some embellishments of his own, like a pelvic thrust and a raspberry.

Manpreet fired his gun, trying to keep up with the baffling display, but lagged behind, his shots way off target.

Up and down they bobbed, each to their own count. On his third appearance, Clovenhoof took a more careful aim and splattered Manpreet with paint.

"Yes!" yelled Argyll, leaping up from his hiding place. "They used similar tactics at Rorke's Drift, you know."

Ben shook his head.

"That was pure Whack-a-Mole. The most impossible game ever invented."

JAYNE SAT in the more comfortable chair of the manicure lounge and glanced across at Nerys. She'd persuaded her sister to stay for the manicure, although she could see her glaring at Opal with open hostility.

She submitted to the filing, picturing how nice her nails would look when they were shaped and painted. There followed a painful session of cuticle pushing.

"I'm not sure they're supposed to bleed," Jayne mentioned tentatively.

Opal snorted.

"You ladies have terribly thick cuticles. What can I say? It's hard to know how best to advise people with such coarse features. You probably need to have your natural nails removed. We can give you some acrylic ones that will look much better. Last for years, which is more than enough for older women like you."

Nerys slammed her fist down onto the table, making Opal and her assistant jump.

"I've had enough of you people! You have no idea how dreadful you are."

"Us?" said Opal, genuinely surprised.

"Yes. You. Your beauty treatments have left us

looking as though we've been in a street brawl. We've probably got cholera from the bird crap, we've *certainly* got bruises from the cupping and Jayne's lucky she hasn't got a fish stuck up her fannyhole and it's laid its eggs inside her."

"I didn't say anything about them laying eggs," Opal began.

"Course you bloody haven't. You've been too busy traumatising us with bird shit, humiliating us with snide comments and torturing us with water cannons. I know we signed a disclaimer, but I reckon you're contravening the Geneva Convention in this place."

She paused for a breath as Opal and her assistant backed up against the wall.

"Jayne and I will be leaving now. You will bring our clothes back to us and you will not attempt to stop us, or make us drink any more of your foul smoothies."

"Yeah!" declared Jayne to add her own little emphasis to Nerys's act of rebellion.

Despite the loss of Michael, Andy realised that he and Zack actually had a chance at taking the flag while Manpreet was off distracting the red team.

They started across the clearing, skirting the large bush.

"Look out for traps," said Andy.

"The Lord is my shepherd," said Zack, as though that actually meant something.

Andy reached out and was about to snatch their prize

when the bush swivelled to meet them. It was Darren, covered in mud and twigs, gun already raised.

It seemed to Andy that time, right then, slowed down to a crawl, everything in uninterruptable high-definition like a BBC natural history documentary. Darren's gun fired. Once. Twice. Andy swore he could even see the pellets coming straight at him.

And then he saw Zack dive across in front of him, taking the paint rounds in the chest, a cry of "Get thee behind me, Satan," on his lips. Andy caught Zack and they went crashing down together. Andy raised his gun and shot at the bush which then, despite not actually getting hit, staggered back, fell over and rolled around on the floor unable to right itself.

"You gave your life to save me," Andy said to Zack.

"Greater love hath no man," said the reverend, "than he who lays down his life for his friend."

Andy, despite the machismo moment and the over-riding stupidity of grown men running around the countryside with toy guns, felt a tear prick the corner of his eye.

"I'm getting that flag for you, brother," he said and got up.

At that moment, Clovenhoof erupted from the bushes, wielding a weed sprayer. He saw the spray turn towards him, so slowly that it was almost painful to watch. A fat stripe of pink paint coated his torso.

"What's that?" said Andy.

"It's my paint 'flamethrower,'" said Clovenhoof.

"Cool," said Andy and then ran around like a man on fire, rolled on the ground to put out the unquenchable flames and then died hideously next to Reverend Zack.

Ben ran into the clearing holding the blue flag, whooping

loudly. Everyone, dead or alive applauded Ben as he ran a victory lap. Even Darren whose suit prevented him from getting himself to his feet and had to be levered upright by Andy and Zack.

"That was fun," said Andy.

"The best," said Zack.

Two hours later, with the eight of them ensconced in a corner of the Boldmere Oak, Michael smiled at the camaraderie that surrounded him. The minibus ride home had been filled with blow-by-blow accounts of the day's action. Manpreet congratulated the wargamers on their inventive tactics, and they all laughed at Clovenhoof's butt-waggling performance in the undergrowth.

What surprised Michael most of all was the newfound warmth between Andy and Zack, after the final moments of the battle. Andy had been profoundly moved by Zack's actions, and now chatted to him, re-living the events.

"The power of the paint," said Clovenhoof, seemingly reading his thoughts.

"I guess," said Michael. "Do you think those two are being a bit too... pally?"

Clovenhoof stared at him blankly.

"Sorry? Am I hearing you right? You think the minister's getting a bit too friendly with your boyfriend? You think they're about to elope together?"

"No, of course not," said Michael but kept an eye on them all the same.

Clovenhoof steered him to the bar to buy a round. Michael was in such a buoyant mood he didn't mind, not even when Clovenhoof insisted on having a Lambrini and a Lambrini chaser.

"What's that you've got there, Jeremy?" Michael asked, gesturing at the carrier bag in Clovenhoof's hand.

"Just a little keepsake," said Clovenhoof casually. "It might come in handy."

Michael peered inside. Of course, it was a paintball gun and maybe a hundred pellets.

"I'm not cleaning up after you," said Michael.

"I promised Ben I wouldn't fire it in here."

"You know, I think Ben enjoyed his stag do," said Michael. "I can't remember ever seeing him looking so animated."

Clovenhoof glanced across at the group, who were recreating the paintball battle on the top of a table with beer glasses.

"You've done well today," said Michael. "There's some good in you, you know."

"Hey, don't ruin my evening with insults," said Clovenhoof. "Yes, well at least it's stopped Ben moping around about getting caught out stark-bollock naked in Wales."

"I've been thinking a lot about Wales," said Michael.

"You still going on about that?" Clovenhoof said.

"Yes, I am," said Michael and nudged Clovenhoof to an empty and secluded booth.

"You know, I think you might have hit the nail on the head about what's going on," he said.

"In Wales?"

"In Wales. Specifically, at St Cadfan's monastery."

"What? You're the one with the wild theories about a saint that isn't in Heaven -"

"That's what I mean!" said Michael. "You said before that if St Cadfan isn't in Heaven then he must still be on earth. What if you're right?"

"So there's a saint somewhere around on earth still?"

"No, not *somewhere* around," said Michael. "He must be on Bardsey Island. One of the people over there must be St Cadfan."

"A fourteen hundred year old monk? I mean, I know life expectancy is getting longer and they say that if you take cod liver oil and eat blueberries you can live into your nineties but, please!"

"Come on, Jeremy. You remember back in the old days when God gave out immortality all over the place like sweets?"

"Not immortality, Michael. Longevity, never immortality. Methuselah clocked up nine hundred and sixty-nine years."

"Adam lived for nine hundred and thirty years. His surviving son, Seth, lived for nine hundred and twelve."

"But all of them died. Hang on, what about Elijah? He didn't."

Michael shook his head.

"The Almighty took him up into Heaven, body and soul, once he reached three hundred and sixty-five years. Tells anyone who'll listen to him all about it. But maybe there's someone, someone that no one would kill, that not even death would touch."

Clovenhoof considered this for a moment, but didn't get very far because Nerys appeared in front of him.

"Where did you spring from?" he said.

"I've had enough of this crap!" she snapped.

"What?"

Hands on her hips, she glared from Clovenhoof to Michael and back again.

"You two are talking some seriously freaky stuff."

"Just pub chat," said Clovenhoof and concentrated on looking innocent. It was not a look that came readily to him.

"God. Immortality. Heaven. Hell."

"I thought you were at a spa for the day," said Michael.

"It was shit. Don't change the subject."

"I really don't know what you're on about," said Clovenhoof.

"You!" she said, pointing a finger at him. "You're Satan, aren't you? You are!"

"You've been drinking, Nerys," said Michael smoothly.

"Shut it, Michael. I've been going mad thinking about it but I remember. You killed me, didn't you?"

"Me?" said Clovenhoof.

"You electrocuted me. I can almost remember. It was in this grotty, horrible place. The smell…"

"I don't think Darren would like to hear you describe his bedroom like that."

"Sodding hell! It is true! I knew it! You killed me."

"It was the only way to get you into Heaven to stop St Peter's mad plan."

"I wouldn't go so far as to call it mad," said Michael.

"And you were there too!" said Nerys to the former

archangel. "So if Jeremy's Satan, who on earth are you? Too smart and uppity to be another devil. You must be an angel or something, I think. Are you the Angel Gabriel?"

"Unbelievable! Absolutely unbelievable," spat Michael. "Will there ever be an end to it? Gabriel does that one little gig with the infant Jesus and after that he's the only angel that ever leaps to anyone's mind."

She frowned at him furiously.

"Well, I don't know! Who are you? The Christmas Angel? Tinkerbell?"

"Nerys, the clue is in the name! I am Archangel Michael."

"Who?"

"The warrior angel."

"Can't say I've ever heard of you."

"The local church is named after me. That huge tapestry on the church wall is of me!"

"Oh. I thought that was Jesus."

Michael sighed theatrically into his drink.

"I've had it up to here with it. I hate Gabriel. The git."

Nerys stumbled backwards. She'd expected some denial from Jeremy. If not to protect himself, to protect her at least. She wasn't sure that she was equipped to deal with this.

She turned to the bar.

"Lennox, can I have something a bit stronger, please? I've just had a bit of a shock."

"No problem, Nerys. Coming right up."

Her mind was whirling out of control. If they were devil and angel then that meant the whole religious deal was true. Heaven, Hell, God. So there was a God and He was everywhere. Oh, the things He had seen her do!

Lennox put a drink down on the bar.

"You found out they're the devil and an angel, didn't you?" he said.

Nerys straightened up and stared at Lennox with wide eyes.

"How could you possibly know that?" she asked.

"I've always known," he said. "The horns and the halo give it away, don't they?"

She looked back at the men in the booth and nearly wept. How had she missed it? Yes, there was a nimbus of golden light around Michael's head which even now seemed to be a certain trick of the light but how the hell had she missed the fact that the man from downstairs was a red-skinned devil with goat-like horns and...

"He's got hooves!" she gasped.

"I keep my eye on them," said Lennox. "They seem pretty harmless, don't you think?"

Nerys looked across at Jeremy and Michael. Unmasked, they were staring at her like a couple of whipped puppies.

"I suppose," she said. "But..."

"Take it from me," said Lennox. "If they start pulling any of that Rosemary's Baby or Bruce Almighty shit, I'll bar them just as soon as look at them."

ST CADFAN'S

Ⓘt was surprising how heavy gold was.

The accumulated gold of centuries stored in the caves beneath Bardsey Island wasn't just heavy. It had an inertia that was not just physical, but psychological, even mystical.

Abbot Ambrose emerged from the dark, battered door in the cloisters with a satchel filled with Greek gold staters over his shoulder. It was night and there was neither moon nor stars in the cloudy sky above. The brothers had retired to bed and the abbot was very much alone.

The abbot made his way round to the prior's house, which he and the prior had shared for countless years. En route, he passed the latest of Brother Manfred's tapestry restorations. For once, the restoration work appeared to contain no film actors or celebrities. It was a depiction of King Arthur and Merlin, Arthur come to the isle of Avalon, grievously wounded by his final battle at Porth Cadlan, his sword Excalibur clutched at his breast, Merlin reaching his final resting place, in his glass casket beneath the island, his staff clutched in his hand.

The image amused the abbot. It was a kaleidoscope of the truth. The dying man, the immortal, the piece of wood, the sword, the house of glass. It was all true, just none of it in the right place or order.

Being Arthur and Merlin, the warrior and the wizard, had been an adventure although both of them had been glad to put it aside. The personas of Saints Veracius and Senacus, quieter and humbler figures, were more to their tastes and their life on Bardsey had been a variation on that ever since.

The abbot pressed on to the prior's house, silently let himself in and went up to the bedroom he shared with his brother. The prior, propped up against a mountain of pillows, appeared to be asleep. A single candle sputtered and flickered in the windowsill, casting a faint orange light.

There were several stout crates throughout the prior's house, steel-bracketed chests that had come to the island over the last few months and which the abbot had spent the recent weeks filling. The abbot opened the lid of one at the foot of the prior's bed and tipped in the night's haul, adding the Greek gold staters to the huge pile within.

The prior's eyes opened.

"I'm sorry, Arthur," said the abbot. "I didn't mean to wake you."

The prior said nothing. He hadn't spoken in decades but the abbot knew how to read his every expression.

"I'm nearly done," said the abbot. "Another month or so and we'll be ready to leave. I thought Africa. Or South

America. There are some charming, isolated communities in Peru and Chile."

The prior didn't offer an opinion.

"And I've been thinking. Maybe we really should approach one of those biotech companies. Have them analyse and synthesise the fruit's properties. Get you sorted once and for all."

The prior's brow twitched.

The abbot turned to the washstand and the blemish-dotted mirror above it. He reached up and removed the wig to reveal his bald head. He scratched at the large fan-shaped mark on his crown. It itched constantly. He didn't recall itching being specifically mentioned as part of the curse.

"We need to get you sorted," he said, turning back to the prior. "I cannot do this alone. I need you, brother."

He went to the bedside cabinet, put his wig in one drawer and removed a folded leather doctor's kit from another. Within it were several large syringes, dressings and a rubber tourniquet.

"If we got the science boffins to sort you permanently, we wouldn't have to go through this rigmarole, would we?"

The abbot pulled the prior's arm from beneath the covers and rolled up his nightshirt sleeve. The prior's arm was riddled with a trail of needle puncture marks, the most recent covered with small dressings, older ones marked out by red dots or tiny scars.

The abbot readied a syringe to draw blood.

"You'll feel a small sting," he said, as he always said, "but you've felt worse."

10

IN WHICH A WEDDING TAKES PLACE

Had she not known what she now knew, Nerys would have been able to take the time to enjoy the moment.

The rooms at the monastery, where the advanced wedding party had stayed the night before, were not the draughty medieval cells Nerys had feared, but cosy, well lit and styled with an elegant minimalism. The refectory, despite its name, was not some grotty canteen but a high-vaulted hall, laid out perfectly for the wedding breakfast and reception. And Bardsey Island itself, the summer sun peering at it through thin clouds, illuminating the rich greens and delicate greys of its landscape, was almost breathtakingly beautiful.

Stood on the beach on that glorious morning, waiting for Owen's boat and the other guests to arrive, Nerys should have been able to take the time to enjoy the moment. But she now knew things she could not now *un*know and they were at the front of her mind.

She leaned sideways to whisper in Michael's ear, so that the others couldn't hear.

"So, where is Heaven then?" she said.

"What?" said Michael, picking lint off his fascistically pressed suit.

"Where is it? It's not in the clouds and astronauts have been into space and they've not seen it."

"I don't think we can talk about Heaven's location in physical terms," he said.

"You mean it's not real?"

"It's real."

"Real like an idea is real? Is it that kind of thing?"

"No, it's really real."

A hundred yards out, Owen's boat rolled gently in the swells. There were more than a dozen passengers in the stern, several trying to stop their floppy wedding hats blowing away.

"What religion are you anyway?" asked Nerys, trying not to sound like she was asking a door-to-door salesman which company he represented.

"I don't have a religion," said Michael. "I serve – served - no, still serve – the Almighty. Faith and religion are human concepts."

"Yes, but you've been going to St Michael's church, so does that mean Christianity is the one true religion?"

"It's not that simple."

"Isn't it?"

"God's truth isn't written in words. It is written in archetypes and metaphysical absolutes."

"Nah, you're talking bollocks now."

"Look. It's like... it's like... you see the waves? The sunlight reflects off the water."

"It's very pretty."

"It is and it's always changing. The Almighty is the light and religion is the surface in which His reflection is seen. And, depending upon where you're stood, the light appears different, but it's the same light."

"Ah," said Nerys nodding. "Same but different. All religions are equally true. I get it."

"Ugh! No! All religions are not equally true!"

"But-"

"No," said Michael firmly. "Religion is not some New Age hypermarket pick 'n' mix. It's not a buffet where the Buddha, Vishnu and Jesus meet for wine and nibbles."

"Sorry. I just thought you said..."

"That's not what I'm saying at all. Don't make religion out to be a sickly sweet Land of Do-As-You-Please where whatever you believe *is* true. Humans don't decide what God is like. They don't get to pick where they go when they die. There is the unalterable truth which is the light and there is the water and there is you."

"Right?" said Nerys, hoping for more, but Michael was now clearly irked.

"Humans," he muttered. "Always fixated on the little details. God's glory is not about churches and words and symbols. It's not about... *stuff*. Do you think my name is really Michael? Do you think I really look like this? The real me?"

Nerys prodded him in the lapel, leaving a dent in the white material.

"Yes," she said.

Michael growled quietly and tried to smooth his lapel.

"Look, it's your sister's special day. Let's focus on her, shall we? Anyway, are we still meant to be fake boyfriend and girlfriend?"

"We're fooling no one with that, are we? You're quite clearly gay. Are angels allowed to be gay?"

"Oh, it's all but compulsory for angelic beings to maintain a happy and optimistic attitude."

"Not that kind of gay," said Nerys, but Michael wasn't listening.

Jayne and Ben stood at the tide line, a significant and calculated distance ahead of Michael, Nerys and Clovenhoof. Jayne had wanted to meet Ben's parents alone but, if she was going to meet them for the first time on her wedding day, then the meeting was going to be as intimate and personal as it could possibly be.

The wedding service, to be conducted by Abbot Ambrose in the monastery church, was not until the late afternoon and it would have been both unlucky, impractical and downright risky to come down to meet the boat in her bridal gown. However, Jayne had chosen her current outfit – stylish but modest, flattering but not flaunting – with enormous care. First impressions and all that. She had also already chosen her opening words of greeting to them and, now, as

Owen tied up and positioned the gangplank, she rehearsed them under her breath.

"Mr and Mrs Kitchen. Welcome. I am so glad you've been able to come and share our special day. It's an absolute pleasure to meet you."

"It'll be all right," said Ben quietly, giving her hand a gentle squeeze.

"You reckon?" she said. "Your parents have been crammed onto a boat with mine for the last half hour. Anything could have happened."

"I'm sure they've all been really nice and friendly. This is them."

First down the gangplank was a woman in a green dress the colour of toothpaste and a man who Jayne immediately saw was a thinner, more round-shouldered and crumpled version of Ben. Desiccated, thought Jayne automatically, like a salted and dried Ben, preserved for longevity.

Ben's mother was fussing over his dad with a tissue as they struggled up the stony beach.

Jayne held out her hands in greeting.

"Mr and Mrs Kitchen –"

Mrs Kitchen rolled her eyes at the pair of them.

"Your father and boats!" she sighed and gave Ben a perfunctory kiss on the cheek.

Jayne saw the smeary stain on Ben's dad's jacket and caught the acrid scent of vomit.

"It's the up-and-down-iness," said the older man with a foolish smile, as though his seasickness was an unavoidable and ultimately humorous mishap.

"Then just aim it over the side," said his wife. "Away from

the boat and that new suit. Away. I hope you know what kind of a man you're letting yourself in for."

It took Jayne a moment to realise that this last comment was aimed at her and then struggled to be certain if it was a reference to Ben or his dad or both of them.

"Um. I do. I think," she said. "It's a shame we couldn't meet before today, Mrs Kitchen."

"Pam."

"Jayne. I gather you've been on an extended holiday recently."

Pam gave her a drolly exasperated look.

"I wouldn't call it a holiday," she said. "Trawling up and down the East Anglia coast and looking at World War Two radar installations."

"Fascinating," said Jayne with a wry smile.

"Isn't it just," said Ben's dad. "I've brought photos if you'd like to take a look."

Ben opened his mouth to say something but, before he did, Pam slapped her husband's arm.

"You'll do nothing of the sort, Tony," she said. "This is meant to be a happy day. Jayne, you look absolutely divine. That dress. Stylish but modest."

"I was going for flattering, not flaunting."

"Perfectly achieved, my dear. Now, I'd best take this great galloon and see if we can't sponge that sick out. Up this way?"

Jayne nodded and gestured to the uneven path leading to the monastery.

Pam paused as she passed them and looked Ben up and down.

"You have got some proper clothes to wear for the service, haven't you?" she asked him.

"Yes, mom."

"Ironed?"

"Yes, mom."

"Good."

Ben's dad, Tony, gave his son a conspiratorial waggle of his eyebrows and then dutifully followed his wife up to the monastery.

"Your mom," said Jayne.

"Yes?" said Ben.

"I like her."

"Good," said Ben. "She's the only one I've got. Here's your mom."

"Yeah, I like her less," Jayne muttered.

Agnes, Ewan and Lydia crunched up the stony beach.

Ewan shook Ben's hand and kissed Jayne.

"It's years since I've been to Bardsey. I was just telling your mother."

"Repeatedly," said Agnes. "At least you didn't throw up on the boat like that other chap. Still, at least it stopped him talking about... I don't even know what he was talking about. I switched off."

"That's my father, Mrs Thomas," said Ben.

"Of course," she said. "That explains a lot."

She appraised the soon-to-be-weds critically.

"Hmmm. And this is it. Today."

Jayne could hear the unspoken words loud and clear. Not too late to back out. You're making a mistake.

"Still," said Agnes, "at least it brings the family together. On a damp rock. In the middle of the sea."

Jayne looked past her parents and Lydia, past the aunts and uncles who were coming off the boat.

"No Catherine?"

"Your sister sends her apologies," said Ewan.

"She's very busy," said Agnes. "Can't expect her to attend every social event offered to her."

"This is not a social event," said Jayne irritably. "This is her sister's wedding. But I see you've managed to bring the neighbour's dog."

Jessie, the border collie, was frolicking in the surf, running up and down the beach.

"*We* did not," said Agnes. "I didn't even see it on the boat. It's probably a bad omen. My God, what is that man wearing?"

She pointed at Clovenhoof and his unusual all-white outfit.

"I believe it's a wedding smoking jacket with Bermuda shorts," said Ben.

"Wedding smoking jacket?" said Agnes. "I've never heard of such a thing."

"No. He made it himself."

Agnes glared daggers.

"And he had to come, did he?"

"He's my best man," said Ben.

"Really? He's the best man you've got?"

Ben looked at his neighbour, who was currently flinging stones at passing seagulls.

"Without a doubt," he said.

Nerys had walked back to the monastery in a less sunny mood than she felt the day deserved. Her mother's customary greeting hadn't helped. A hand on the shoulder, a sympathetic smile and "I see the weight loss isn't coming along as quickly as you'd like it to."

Nerys shook her head. No, she was used to that. The thing that had made her really angry was Michael's vague and cagey answers to her questions. How dare he imagine that he'd throw her off the scent with a few long words and some metaphysical bullshit. What a pompous twat!

She froze. Did God see her thoughts? Was she committing a sin right now?

She had walked through the archway to the cloisters where there were some welcome drinks for the wedding guests. The others had all taken drinks and seated themselves on benches laid out in the inner quadrangle. She approached the young monk who was serving the drinks.

His face was familiar. She'd heard the others call him - what was it? Trevor.

Surely, a monk would have spent time researching and understanding the practicalities of his chosen religion.

She went up to him.

"It's Trevor, isn't it?"

"Stephen," said the monk coldly.

"Sorry. I thought it was Trevor."

"Still can't get it right, eh? I wondered when you'd finally speak to me."

Nerys frowned.

"There *are* some things bothering me. You're very perceptive."

"Things bothering *you*?" he said, with a small scoffing laugh.

"Yes, indeed. For instance, does God see my thoughts?" she asked him. "Does he know what's in my mind?"

"What? Oh, I do hope not," he replied. "For your sake."

What a strange thing to say. Still, he spoke with clarity and confidence, so Nerys pressed on.

"What kind of thought would be a sin, then?" she asked, taking a flute of champagne. "If I think of doing something bad, and then I don't do it, then surely that isn't a sin? It means I resisted the temptation, doesn't it?"

"Does that ever happen?" asked the monk.

"What?"

"You, resisting temptation."

Nerys considered the question for a moment as she sipped her champagne. A small part of her brain was wondering why this young monk was challenging her in such a cheeky (but undeniably accurate) way.

"I do. I sometimes shut my mouth when I'm tempted to tell my mother what I really think."

The monk nodded.

"There are other kinds of temptations - " he started.

"I have another question," said Nerys, leaning over the table. "About getting into Heaven. When you repent your sins, how sorry do you really have to be?"

He looked at her in surprise.

"You have to be truly, genuinely sorry of course."

"Yes, but what does that really *mean*?" she asked. "I'd be

genuinely sorry for my sins, if they meant I couldn't get into Heaven, obviously. But only sorry like I was for parking illegally *after I got a ticket.* It's not the same as that twisted feeling you get in your stomach when you really, really regret something, do you know what I mean?"

"I know exactly what you mean," said the monk. He stared at her, an earnest expression on his face. "In my experience, it can take a long time to get over things that -"

"How about blaspheming?" asked Nerys, cutting across him as a fresh worry surfaced. "Does God really care about that stuff? I mean, I know that monks don't do things like that but nearly everyone else does. Are we all barred from Heaven? Is it really worse to say 'Jesus Christ' than it is to say 'fuck' or 'bollocks'?"

Nerys watched in surprise as the young monk turned and walked away, shaking his head. She heard him mumble as he went. It sounded like "for God's sake," but she must have misheard.

Michael appeared at her side moments later.

"Have you scared off young Stephen, again?" he asked.

Nerys shrugged. She had no idea what had just happened.

"Listen," said Michael. "I want to take a better look around the place. Cover for me, will you? If anyone asks, I've gone for a lie-down with a headache."

"Sure," said Nerys, watching a second man abandon her in as many minutes.

"Oh, wait," she called, but it was too late as Michael disappeared. "What exactly do you mean, have I scared him off *again*?"

ONCE ALL THE various friends and family had been brought ashore, Ben and Jayne followed the wedding party up to the monastery at a leisurely pace.

"Hmmm," said Jayne, mimicking her mother. "And this is it. Today."

"Yep, on a damp rock in the middle of the sea. Us and all our family."

Jayne linked her arm with Ben's.

"Your parents are nice."

"Thank you."

"Did they really go on a holiday to look at radar installations?"

"Three weeks in a camper van with the kind of itinerary only a real geek could come up with."

"Because you're not a geek, are you?"

"I'm the very best kind of geek. I was thinking about our honeymoon holiday. I hadn't booked anything because my –"

"I have," said Jayne.

"You have?"

"I thought it would be a surprise. A nice one."

"Oh? I'm sure it will be," he said. "Where are we going?"

"In the footsteps of Alexander the Great."

Ben stopped on the track and looked at his fiancée.

"In the footsteps? As in we're going to go there?"

Jayne nodded.

"Along the route his armies took. Takes us right into the heart of what would have been the Seleucid Empire. I know you're such a fan."

"Of miniature table-top wargaming. I... You know I'm not a big fan of travel."

"And this is a way to give you the chance to catch the travel bug," said Jayne brightly.

"Well, I think we're likely to catch something," said Ben, feeling slightly queasy. "So, what? Greece? Turkey?"

Jayne nodded. "Egypt too."

"Israel?"

"Yes."

"Iran?"

"It's apparently quite safe for Western travellers, depending upon the mood of the government when we go."

"But not India, surely? Or Afghanistan?" said Ben, struggling to keep the fearful tremor out of his voice.

"India definitely," said Jayne. "Afghanistan we will need to play by ear."

"You think?" Ben squeaked.

Jayne's mouth settled into an uncomfortable and disappointed line.

"This is meant to be a good surprise, Ben. I thought this would make you happy."

Ben tried to give her a smile but it flickered and died almost instantly.

"Okay," he said, taking a deep breath. "I hate Greek food and Turkish food. For two countries that hate each other so much, their cuisine is virtually identical and equally stomach-churning. I once got a verruca in a Turkish bath and was severely frightened by a fat, naked guy with a big moustache."

"Right?"

"Egypt has the highest rate of road traffic accidents in the world. It's all camels and badly ventilated tombs. And crocodiles! They have crocodiles."

"No one's asking you to going swimming in the Nile, Ben."

"I won't even begin to talk about the quality of the plumbing in India."

"You've never been to India."

"I've watched *Slumdog Millionaire*. The rest of the itinerary is a roll call of every warzone, fiercely disputed territory and downright dangerous place a Brit could visit. And don't get me started on the fretwork doors."

"Fretwork doors?"

"All of those countries. What's the point of having doors you can see through? It won't be bad enough that we'll spend every minute either frantically looking for a toilet that doesn't look like a sewage overflow or hiding from men with guns and very fixed views on what God wants them to do. No, we'll be doing that with everyone being able to see us doing it through closed doors."

"I don't think that's true at all," said Jayne.

"I'm sorry, my love," he said. "I know you meant well but it's an awful idea."

"I thought..."

"What did you think?"

"I thought..." Jayne blinked rapidly and gazed for a moment away and out to sea. "I thought it would be a chance for you to be like those ancient heroes you admired so much."

Ben sighed, a horrible and heavy weight inside him. He took Jayne's hands in his.

"Jayne. Why do you think I admire them so much?"

She shrugged, teary-eyed.

"It's because I am not them," he said. "I'm nothing like them."

"Maybe you're more like them than you think."

"Not enough," said Ben.

CLOVENHOOF STOOD in front of the mirror in his room's en suite bathroom to practise his best man's speech.

"I wouldn't say Ben is a virgin. He spent three months in prison on remand for murder. Don't worry, he got off the charge. And I'm sure, surrounded by all those burly sex-starved men in prison, there was some getting off behind bars as well, if you know what I mean."

Clovenhoof paused for the imagined laughter to die down. It went on for a very long time but, then again, he was very funny.

"But I wouldn't say Ben's never had a female wriggling between his thighs. There was the time when he mistook a female tarantula for a bath sponge."

As Clovenhoof began to mime Ben giving himself an all over scrub with a giant spider (to much hilarity), he heard the door to his room open.

"You in?" called Ben.

"Just knocking them dead with my best man's speech," Clovenhoof replied.

Ben came into the bathroom and looked at Clovenhoof frozen mid-mime with his hand over his groin.

"It is going to be a clean speech, isn't it?" said Ben.

"It's going to be honest, affectionate and paint you in an entirely positive light."

"Really?"

"Totally. Now, am I okay to mention your dinner date with a sex doll?"

"No."

"The time we set the fire alarm off in the adult education centre and had to run out naked?"

"No."

"The fact that your pre-nuptial 'back, sack and crack' waxing went horribly wrong and that you're bald on one side, hairy on the other and Nerys had to do some blending in work on your balls with her make up kit?"

"Definitely not."

"You sure? This is some of my best material."

"I am sure, Jeremy."

"Okay. But I can mention the time you ate a bowlful of horse tranquilisers because you thought they were M&Ms?"

"Er, I don't think so."

Clovenhoof sighed.

"Well, what about the time I thought you were a zombie snowman of the apocalypse and I went round the neighbourhood on a mobility scooter with a box of fireworks, blowing up all the snowmen in a bid to save the world from certain destruction?"

Ben thought on this.

"Yes," he said eventually. "Mention that one."

"Excellent. I brought some Roman candles for the re-enactment."

Ben shook his head.

"Look, Jeremy, I came to ask you some advice. If I make Jayne cry on the day of her wedding is that a bad sign?"

Clovenhoof nodded sagely.

"This is a wedding night question, isn't it? You've come to the right person."

"I'm not sure it is."

"You see," said Clovenhoof, putting a fatherly hand on Ben's shoulder, "the thing to remember is that 'down there' women have two holes."

"No, that's not what I'm asking –"

"And if you go for the wrong one it's going to bring tears to her eyes."

"No! Jeremy, that's not it. Maybe I'm getting cold feet but I'm worried about rushing into this thing."

"Of course you are," said Clovenhoof. "You can't go rushing into it. She won't like that either. There's this thing called 'foreplay'. It's called that because you have to do it for at least four seconds before leaping on and riding the bedroom rodeo."

"Jeremy! I'm asking whether Jayne and I are really made for each other."

"Oh, I see."

"You do?"

"Yes. And, of course you are made for each other."

Ben almost wilted with relief.

"You think it's going to work out fine?"

"Of course it is, dear friend." He patted Ben on the

shoulder. "You see, Jayne has what we in the business call an 'inny' and you have an 'outy'. You put the 'outy' in the 'inny' and jiggle it about. It's almost as if the Other Guy made you so that's the only way he wanted you to do it. However, I find that with enough imagination, there's an almost infinite variety of ways you can –"

The door slammed as Ben left. Clovenhoof stared at the door for a second.

"Glad to be of help!" he shouted and returned to his speech.

THAT AFTERNOON, Nerys, as bridesmaid, had a perfect overview of the wedding ceremony and concluded that it was a perfect ceremony but for one small detail.

Ewan walked Jayne up the narrow aisle, while Nerys held her train. Clovenhoof, standing beside the groom, danced along to the wedding march but at least limited himself to a subtle hand jive and soft tap dance. How could no one else hear the click of his hideous goaty hooves on the flagstones? Clovenhoof's white smoking jacket – which looked like a costume out of low-budget sci-fi movie – did a marvellous job of distracting everyone's attention from Ben's suit which, despite being hugely expensive and freshly pressed, seemed to slouch over Ben's almost boneless frame, becoming no more formal or impressive than Ben's regular T-shirt and jeans.

It was all perfectly adequate and adequately perfect. If only the whole affair wasn't being unsubtly and relentlessly critiqued by one Agnes Thomas of Aberdaron. The commentary was ostensibly delivered to Lydia beside her but conducted in a stage whisper that the building's acoustics carried throughout the entire church.

"Who's playing that organ?" Nerys heard her say from halfway down the aisle. "Far too twiddly. Who does he think he is? Jean Michel Jarre? These hymn books are disgusting. Look. Tell me that some disgusting man in a habit hasn't spent every Sunday picking his nose and pressing them in there. I tell you, they're not going to make up for that with a few twiddles and knobs on the organ.

"Oh, look. Here she comes. Well, she's certainly no Kate Middleton, is she? I told her that she'd show a visible panty line in that dress. Was I wrong? No, I wasn't. It'll be sweat patches before the first dance too, mark my words. Yes, she looks happy but let's see how long that lasts. You know your father refused to buy a new suit. That one's lasted longer than the Berlin Wall. Come sit down. You're an embarrassment.

"Well, at least it's a serviceable suit. The boy's parents clearly buy all their clothes from a charity shop. I bet they're not short of money, no. They'll be those 'oh, look at us being so frugal and austere' middle class types. It'll be all couscous and mushrooms in their house. No, too shabby to even pass for shabby genteel.

"Oh, lummy. They've got old father time doing the ceremony. He'd better not give us that 'love, honour and *obey*' claptrap. This is the twentieth century not the – okay, twenty-first. Don't interrupt me. I didn't sign up to obey you forty years ago so I'm not going to start now, Ewan.

"That's a wig, isn't it? That's definitely a wig. Who says monks can't wear wigs? It's not in the Bible. Of course, he's looking at us. We're the audience. We're paying for this charade. Well, not us exactly. Nerys' supposed boyfriend paid the *money* but we're paying out with time and effort. I'm missing a WI trip to Aberystwyth for this. Hmmm. Something suspicious there. Why did he pay for it all? He's a poof too, you know. Lovely people but you can't help wondering what they're up to. I don't trust his motives. Where is he, anyway? Probably off somewhere, doing something... you know... poofy."

IN HIS GUEST ROOM, Michael looked at the time on his smartphone. The service would be in full swing and everyone in attendance including, he hoped, many of the monks.

He looked at his G-Sez message for the day. It was from the book of Job.

WHERE THEN IS MY HOPE – who can see any hope for me? Will it go down to the gates of death? Will we descend together into the dust?

"WHERE THEN IS MY HOPE?" he said to himself, opened the door and stepped out into the corridor to find Jessie the border collie sat outside.

"What are you doing here?"

Jessie whined, rolled over and then scampered down the corridor a little way.

"I'm not playing games," said Michael. "I've got things to do."

Jessie barked.

"Shush. I'm trying to keep a low profile here."

"Can I help you at all?" said a voice behind him.

With an inward groan, Michael turned.

"Novice Trevor – no, wait – It's Novice... Stephen, isn't it?"

The young monk was both pleased and impressed that he was remembered.

"Yes. Aren't you meant to be in the church?"

"Well, I wasn't feeling very well so I came back to my room for a few minutes."

"And I see you've got your dog with you again."

Michael smiled.

"She's still not my dog, brother. Somehow I don't think she belongs to anyone but herself."

"I see what you mean," said Stephen, pointing.

Michael turned. Jessie had vanished.

"Best get after her," he said, seeing an excuse to get away from prying eyes. "Even if she isn't mine."

With Stephen wishing him a speedy recovery from his ailment, Michael hurried off in search of the errant dog and some answers to the monastery's mysteries. He quickly found Jessie in the cloisters, apparently waiting for him. He looked at the door beside her.

"Here again?" he said, recognising it. "Is this where they keep the sausages or something? I'm going up to the prior's house to have a poke around. Maybe investigate that orangery again. I don't want to go in here."

Jessie, a dog with a remarkable range of facial expressions for a creature with no lip muscles, simply looked at Michael.

"What?" he said. "When have I ever said I wanted to go in here?"

He peered closely at the door and the fan-shaped carving in its ancient and weathered surface.

"Almost like a peacock's tail," he said. "You know, St Augustine said that peacock's flesh had antiseptic qualities. In ancient times, many people believed that peacock bodies did not rot after death. Within the Christian tradition they are a symbol of immortality. Eternal life. Interesting, isn't it?"

Jessie, who was possibly neither of a philosophical or theological bent, simply looked at him.

"Suit yourself," said Michael, lifted the latch and opened the door.

The interior was dark but Michael could just about make a set of stone steps going down. There was an alcove just inside the door and a small electric torch. Michael turned it on. It worked.

He looked down at Jessie.

"Will it go down to the gates of death?" he said. "Will we descend together into the dust?"

Jessie led the way and Michael took that as a yes.

11

IN WHICH DISCOVERIES ARE MADE AND MICHAEL FINDS SOME LOST PROPERTY

I n the refectory, monks bustled to and fro with platters, whisking away the veal flamenco and wheeling in the Black Forest gateau for the guests.

The words of Nerys's reading from the wedding ceremony kept echoing through Ben's mind. They accompanied him throughout the remainder of the service and back to the refectory where the wedding breakfast was now being held.

The reading had been from an A.A. Milne poem, *Us Two*. It was not a religious reading, which had apparently caused some consternation to the fusty abbot; it was a children's poem, which possibly raised some eyebrows, but it was one Jayne had remembered from her childhood and it was about friendship, solidarity and companionship.

However, *Us Two* put certain other thoughts in Ben's mind, because when he heard Nerys read out "Where I am, there's always Pooh. There's always Pooh and me," it wasn't the 'Pooh Bear' kind of 'Pooh' Ben was thinking of.

His wife – yes, she was his wife now – had told him that she had booked a holiday of the type that sent shudders of horror rippling through Ben's body and he had told exactly why he would not be going on it and then she had cried. Was it just a minor spat, a thing they could look back on and laugh about in years to come? Or was it a terrible omen of the gulf between each of their desires and expectations?

Ben looked at his bride, sat next to him at the high table. Jayne was listening intently to Ben's dad's recollection of the recent East Anglian holiday and, remarkably, enjoying it.

How much could you really know a person? Didn't everyone truly and honestly live alone in the confines of their own skull? How could he possibly know what was going on in her head?

Jayne nodded, smiled, laughed politely when it seemed appropriate and tried to avoid yawning.

Every word her father-in-law said cemented her belief that she had never met a man as dull and uninteresting as Tony Kitchen. It wasn't the fact that he was talking about World War Two radar stations or the Suffolk coast, both of which were dull enough in themselves. Tony Kitchen was able to take it a step further and describe them in such circumstantial and digressive detail that Jayne was left with the feeling that he was saying nothing at all.

"And do you know what the most interesting thing about the radar dishes at Dunwich Major is?"

"No?" she smiled.

"They're actually not... there... at all."

"Wow," said Jayne. "What?"

"That whole section fell into the sea in 1956."

"Did they?"

Perversely, Tony Kitchen was so boring that there was something intensely fascinating about it. He wasn't just a bit boring, as all people are, which would have been dull enough but he took it a step further by waving the prospect of intrigue in one's face and then whipping it away at the last moment.

"You can actually get a boat out in the area and then dive down and see the old army base and indeed the local village which also fell into the sea," said Tony.

"I've heard about those kinds of places," said Jayne. "They say that the houses and churches are still standing and you can even hear the church bells ringing in the depths."

"No idea," said Tony. "We didn't do it. We stood on the beach, I read a chapter from Fritkin's guide to dismantled Second World War installations and we then went and ate an adequate lunch in Bungay. I gave it a six out of ten."

"Bungay?"

"The lunch. I rate all my meals in my diary."

"Even your meals at home?"

Tony nodded.

"I can only compliment Pam's divine cooking if there's a benchmark to measure it against."

Pam, who seemed to be enjoying the fact that someone

else was entertaining her husband for a while, leaned in.

"I've told him that if he ever gives me below five, I'm leaving him."

Tony nodded gravely.

"I gave her a four once in 1982. She moved back to her mom's for a month."

Jayne wasn't sure what she could say to that so decided to ignore it completely.

"And did you enjoy seeing, I mean not seeing, the radar station in Dunwich Major?"

"Oh, I was all for getting the scuba gear and diving to the seabed," said Pam. "I mean it's not the Aegean or the Caribbean but you've got to grab these opportunities when you can."

"Well, quite," said Jayne firmly. "But you didn't?"

"Wasn't on the itinerary," said Pam.

"Certainly wasn't," said Tony.

NERYS DECIDED to give the rest of the best man's speech a miss.

As Clovenhoof launched into another anecdote, she sighed inwardly. Of course, he would want to make a best man's speech that would last for over half an hour. Of course, it would be crass, mortifyingly embarrassing for everyone concerned and almost entirely true. Those things were inevitable when you were dealing with Satan.

Why could nobody else see it, why? His skin was Ferrari red, and he'd already spent five minutes popping balloons with his horns after realising that there was an archway made of them.

What was she supposed to do? Nobody was helping her to deal with this. Her world had been severely shaken up and she had no idea how to react. Should she be reading the Bible? Was this all a test? She didn't even know how she was supposed to feel about Clovenhoof.

According to every horror film she had ever seen, it was her duty to kill him at the earliest opportunity. She really wasn't sure about that, after all he was her friend, wasn't he? Well, not quite friend, but something that to the casual observer would look like friendship. It wasn't as if he'd set out to deceive her. Well yes, of course he had, like the time he'd tried to sell her belongings on eBay, or cheated his way into a teaching job at her agency, but he'd never really lied about who he was. She was quite sure that he'd mentioned things on occasion, about the Old Place. She racked her brains to remember what they were. If she was to live her life based on her new-found knowledge that Heaven and Hell were real places, she could do with knowing what they were really like. Why go to the trouble of avoiding Hell if it turned out to be quite nice? Hadn't Clovenhoof mentioned a Lake of Fire? He spoke about it with fondness, as if it were a bracing outdoor lido. She really needed more information. Actual facts.

One thing was certain, her tolerance of Clovenhoof's attention-seeking nonsense was at an all-time low. She murmured across to Jayne that she was popping to the loo and made her escape.

She made her way up the corridor with no clear plan.

Surely, she could find answers to some of her questions in a monastery, but where to start? She slowed down to look at some tapestries. Like the stained glass in the chapel, these seemed to depict scenes from the Bible. They might be a handy aide-memoire for someone who hadn't looked at the Bible since the hated Sunday school days of her childhood, where the enduring memories that had stayed with her were more about the coldness of the church hall and the fact that woolly tights for children were seen as an indulgence by her mother.

The first tapestry she saw depicted Cain and Abel. It was lucky that there was a title emblazoned over the top otherwise Nerys might have imagined it was some sort of harvest festival scene. One of them held a lamb in his arms and the other offered a basket of vegetables toward the central figure who looked like - Nerys stepped forward to take a better look.

"Morgan Freeman?" she said. "Um."

How strange.

She tried to remember what happened with Cain and Abel. Did the lamb get lost? Or was there some dispute about the land that they both farmed? She stepped back again and realised that the face of Morgan Freeman must be a recent addition. It was beautifully worked, but the colours were brighter and the strands of thread were a little thicker. It was clearly a repair. The two main figures were original though, she was sure of that. The brother with the vegetables gazed at the other. It was an intense and malevolent expression that made Nerys rather uncomfortable for reasons that were hard to put her finger on.

She moved on and looked at the next tapestry.

This was interesting. It depicted Arthur and Merlin. She was not an expert on the Bible, of course, but she was pretty sure that they weren't in it. The tapestry showed Arthur in death. Merlin stood over him, staff in hand. Behind Merlin there was a cave of glass, a sort of natural greenhouse. Merlin's own waiting tomb. Nerys peered at the face of Merlin.

"Hang on."

Nerys walked back to the other tapestry.

There was a striking similarity with between the figure of Cain and that of Merlin, although the wizard had a more mellow expression. Cain was much angrier-looking and the expression here was definitely more familiar.

"I've seen you before," she whispered.

Where had she seen that face? There was a mark on his forehead which didn't look right. Perhaps if the hair was different? She tried to imagine him with a wig. A wig, of course!

"Bloody hell, mom. You were right."

But why? What did it mean?

Nerys hurried along to look at the other tapestries.

THE SILENCE that followed Clovenhoof's best man's speech was eventually broken by the applause of the stunned guests. It was the polite clapping of those who had been bludgeoned into a trance by Clovenhoof's unbelievably and incomprehensibly vulgar tirade and now, upon waking knew that they should clap because that's what people did.

Clovenhoof patted Ben heartily on the back as he sat down and then downed two flutes of champagne and shouted out for more.

Jayne squeezed her husband's hand.

"Well, that was an education," she said.

"Ng," said Ben.

"How much of it was true?"

"Mmmm. Yes. All of it."

Jayne frowned.

"Even the bit about you getting your knob stuck in a clay pot?"

"Mmmm. We had to go to A&E in the end."

"You're a bit of dark horse, aren't you?" said Ewan, from Ben's other side.

"A dirty pig more like," said Agnes.

Brother Sebastian, as Master of Ceremonies, tapped a wine glass to draw everyone's attention.

"And now, ladies and gentlemen, a few words from the father of the bride."

"Let's pray it's a short speech," said Agnes loudly.

Ben was praying that it would somehow whitewash over Clovenhoof's speech and wipe it from everyone's minds.

Ewan got to his feet with a smile for his ex-wife and then his daughter and then began by thanking everyone for coming out to this beautiful place on this beautiful day. He name-checked some of the older relatives who, if his inferences were to be believed, had risen from their deathbeds to be there.

Whereas Clovenhoof had addressed the guests with all the charm of a taxi driver putting the world to rights, Ewan spoke with a quiet warmth that had everyone's attention.

"You know," he said, "I never thought that Jayne would be the marrying type. Too much of a tomboy in her youth, too much of a free spirit. I remember that on her Christmas list, when she was ten years old, there were three things: a quad bike, a crossbow and a goat. That pretty much summed her up, I think. And those of you who remember will know that she did get one of those three and she was a very happy girl until it had an unfortunate encounter with Larry Pearce's rear end four doors over."

A ripple of laughter swept through the room and, from one corner, came a loud but unintelligible comment. Whether that was Larry Pearce himself or not, Ben couldn't tell.

"She didn't need material things to make her happy," continued Ewan. "That's what I've always loved about this little girl of mine. As a toddler she'd play with fresh air and, when she was older, she'd be up on the hill, running hither and thither, on her own make believe quest like the knights and heroes of old."

Jayne groaned good-naturedly and hid her face and embarrassment in Ben's shoulder.

"Yeah," whispered Ben. "Me going to prison on suspicion of murder doesn't seem so awful now, does it?"

"I remember asking her," said Ewan, "whether a make believe knight in shining armour ever came to save her, my princess, from the evil wicked dragon. And she looked at me like I was daft – yes, just like she's doing now – and said,

'Dad, what would I need one of them for when I can just rescue myself?"'

There was more laughter. Ewan took up his glass.

"But, you know, dragons come in all shapes and sizes."

Ben wasn't sure but Ewan seemed to give a sideways glance at Agnes as he said this.

"And so do knights in shining armour," said Ewan. "And that's what this young man here is."

Ben, red-cheeked, shook his head.

"No, it's true, you silly sod," said Ewan. "I couldn't ask for a better or finer son-in-law than Ben here. I can't imagine a more perfect couple. Ladies and gentlemen, if you would do me the honour. Join me in raising your glasses..."

JESSIE WAS a brave and wilful dog but as they descended further, and the steps became rougher and more uneven, and the monastic crypts gave way to damp tunnels, Jessie slowed her pace and kept closer to Michael's side. Even dogs didn't rush in where angels feared to tread.

Eventually, they reached the bottom and Michael stood in a vast, cool cavern. Jessie whined. Apart from the trickle of unseen water, it was the only sound to be heard.

At first, the place seemed empty, a hollow conclusion to their murky descent, but then Michael saw something glitter momentarily. He approached, stumbling over black rocks. At the bottom of a shallow pool lay something small, round and golden. Michael dipped his hand into the chill water and lifted it out.

He read the inscription stamped on the coin, knowing that maybe only a handful of humans today would be able to translate it and that none would have heard it in the original tongue.

"This is Sumerian," he said to Jessie. "Unbelievably old."

Jessie yapped from some distance away.

Michael turned with the torch. The white patches on Jessie's fur were just visible in the gloom.

"What are you doing over there?"

Michael picked his way over the ground. He now saw other coins - gold, silver and even obsidian – dotted about here and there. It was if there had been a mighty and ancient hoard here, which had then been hastily spirited away.

Jessie barked again.

"I'm coming," said Michael testily. "What is it?"

And then he saw the sword. It was resting on a table-sized rock, resting in a recess in the stone.

Untarnished, it shone like silver but Michael knew that it wasn't silver at all. Michael had not seen the sword for thousands of years but he recognised the workings around the hilt, the simple patterns on the guard and fuller. He was stunned.

"Jessie. That day on the headland. I said. I asked you. The sword in the stone." He shook his head. "But this isn't Excalibur."

Jessie barked in disagreement.

"It isn't Arthur's sword," he said and picked up the blade.

At once, yellow flames flared along its blade, filling the cave with a holy golden light. Jessie whined.

"This is *my* sword," said Michael with an incredulous grin on his face.

Tony had gone off to consult his diary so that he could give Jayne a more accurate account of the third week of their holiday. Pam reached past her husband's vacant seat and patted Jayne kindly.

"Men are closed books until you check them out of the library, my dear. It's only when you take them home that you find out what secrets lie between their pages."

"Not sure I agree," said Jayne, giving a certain look at Ben. "Surely, that's why we browse through the books before picking one."

Pam smiled kindly.

"Yes, but who knows what twists and turns the book's going to take? Marriage is about taking the rough with the smooth though."

"Of course, it's all give and take," Jayne agreed politely.

"But, you'll find there's more give than take. More rough than smooth."

Jayne frowned.

"I don't see why that should be so."

"That's because you're young."

"You mean not jaded?"

Pam shuffled into Tony's empty seat to be beside Jayne. She struggled for a moment, her heels caught on the chair leg, perhaps suffering the effects of one too many champagne toasts.

"When I married Tony I had my own ambitions. I wanted to work abroad. I wanted to open my own health food shop. But then life takes over and things take a different path. Tony's a lovely man but he has his own ideas about things. Foreign travel doesn't agree with him."

"Ah, that's where Ben gets it from then."

"And his own hobbies and interests were so very important to him."

"More important than yours?" said Jayne sceptically.

"I had Ben then. He was a demanding young man."

"Oh?"

"We had the entire Trojan war re-enacted in our back garden when he was eight."

"Doesn't sound too dissimilar to my childhood games then."

"Really? Did your mom build you a six-foot high replica of the Wooden Horse of Troy out of corrugated card and egg boxes?"

"Er, no."

"I tried to get Tony to try different things. We did a trip round all the pillboxes and Nazi fortifications on Jersey one year. That's as 'foreign' as it ever got. I'm not telling you how you should live your life. I'm not telling you how you should behave. I'm giving you the wisdom of experience. Marriage is compromise, dear. It's sacrifice. And, one day, you'll realise that your hopes and dreams were just that. Dreams."

"That's too bleak for me, Pam," said Jayne.

"It's not bleakness," said her mother-in-law. "I'm a very happy woman, Jayne. Happiness is not something you go out and find. Happiness is something that comes and finds you wherever you are. You just have to accept the form it comes in. Speaking of which."

"Got it!" said Tony, returning to the table, waving his diary at them. "And look what else I've got. Maps!"

"Oh, good," said Jayne and Pam in unison.

THE BROTHERS MANFRED and Sebastian had organised the post-dinner disco between them. Manfred had decorated the room with imaginative festoons of coloured lanterns. Fashioned from recycled catering jars of sauerkraut, the room held only the faintest aroma of pickled cabbage. Manfred was especially pleased with the dance floor, which he'd designed as a stained glass window, lit from beneath. He had tested it out with some secret Saturday Night Fever moves days before.

Sebastian was the disc jockey, and sat at the control desk with his laptop, lining up the MP3s for the audio system.

It was clear to everyone that the best man was unfamiliar with the concept of the married couple's first dance. As Jayne and Ben swayed gently in each other's arms to the sound of Celine Dion, Clovenhoof cavorted energetically around them, with a repertoire of swaggering, pelvic thrusting and air guitar. Sebastian decided to play some crowd-pleasers to get everyone else up and dancing.

"Welcome everybody, to this celebration of a beautiful union of souls," he crooned. "Here's one that'll get the blood pumping. From the year when a surplus of crude oil made petrol prices collapse, and Ben was pictured with his first Rubik's cube. It's The Jam, with *A Town Called Malice!*"

Several more people got up to dance. Agnes did a discreet and angular shuffle, striking poses that were designed to show her silhouette in the most flattering way. Ewan made a brief jiggle across the dance floor as a short cut to the bar, while Jayne flung herself across Clovenhoof's path with a vigour that startled him, briefly.

"God, I love The Jam!" she yelled. She gestured for Ben to join her, but Ben had followed Ewan to the bar, and he pretended not to see her.

Abbot Ambrose stood at the back of the room, mystified by the vulgar loudness that was apparently a necessary part of a modern wedding celebration. He saw the father of the bride standing with Ben, the groom, both of them holding pints of beer. He walked over and clapped Ewan on the shoulder.

"Well done with your speech, I thought it went very well."

He thought he detected a fleeting look of pain on Ben's face.

"Thank you, Abbot," said Ewan. "I must say we're all enjoying your splendid monastery and the hospitality."

He raised the pint glass in his hand.

"Is the beer brewed here in the monastery?" he asked.

"No, we buy it in from the mainland," said Abbot Ambrose. "Is that a professional interest? I understand you work for the Food Standards Agency."

"No, it's a fine pint, that's the main reason for my interest," smiled Ewan. "While we're on the subject of my work though, I do need to come and look around at some point. Did you hear about the unusual symptoms that people suffered last winter?"

"No, I'm not sure that I did," said Ambrose carefully.

"It was a curious, localised phenomenon," said Ewan. "People spent several hours speaking with a rather damaging level of honesty. I've been shocked to see some of the longer-term fallout from that. It's taken us some time to pinpoint the origin, but now we believe it was one of the Farmer's Markets in Aberdaron, so we're contacting all of the stall holders. I believe the monastery was one of them."

"Ah," said the abbot. "I think you'll find we sell only needlework at the Farmer's Market."

"No, that's not right," said Ben. The abbot had assumed that Ben wasn't paying attention, as he gazed absently at the dance floor.

"Sorry?" Ambrose asked.

"No, you sold jam. Michael bought some," said Ben. "Made from the famous Bardsey apple tree."

"Oh, yes," said Ewan, nodding. "I think I bumped into Michael after he'd bought it and we spoke briefly about the tree being of interest as it's a unique variety."

"Ah, yes, of course," said Ambrose quickly. "How could I forget the jam?"

"Maybe you could tell me a little more about your apple tree?" said Ewan. "Perhaps I could even take a brief look, if it's convenient? I realise the food preparation area will be busy at the moment, but I can come back another day for that."

Abbot Ambrose clasped his hands together.

"I will see what I can arrange, but it will definitely need to be another day, I'm afraid. I'm sure you can imagine how busy we all are today. Now, if you'll forgive me, I must go and attend to some other pressing matters."

He walked away, as briskly as he could. He didn't have a moment to waste.

BEN CROSSED the dance floor and slipped his arm around Jayne's waist.

"Hello," she smiled and placed a kiss on his cheek.

"I'm astonished," said Ben.

"I *am* astonishing," Jayne agreed.

"The entire day has gone really well. Everyone's got on. There have been no organisational disasters. Jeremy's managed to keep all his clothes on and has yet to burn the building down."

Jayne patted Ben's chest.

"It has been a good day, my love."

"Look, I'm also sorry about that little hiccup earlier."

"Hiccup?"

"The business about the holiday. The whole Alexander the Great thing. It was really thoughtful of you. I can see a lot of time and effort went into that."

"Thank you," said Jayne emphatically. "I knew you'd see that."

"And you weren't to realise that it's really not my thing and I can't possibly go to those kinds of places."

Jayne's smile vanished.

"Can't?" she said. "Or won't?"

"I don't like foreign travel."

"And what about me?"

Ben searched for the right words but he was too slow. Jayne didn't quite push him away but it was only a matter of perception. She quickly disentangled herself from him and strode out the room.

"Wait," Ben called, in quick pursuit.

He caught up with her in the quiet of the monastery gardens. It was late in the evening but the summer sun still stubbornly hung on the horizon.

"Please," said Ben, coming up behind her. "I didn't mean to upset you."

Jayne's chest heaved with pent-up rage.

"I've booked it," she bristled.

"I'm sure we can speak to the travel agent and –"

"I don't want to un-book it, Ben!"

"Then maybe you can find a friend who'd like to go –"

"What? With me? You want me to go on honeymoon without my husband?"

Ben stopped, shook his head.

"I'm sure this is not as big a deal as it seems. I'm sure there's a way round it."

Jayne seethed and fumed. Her arms worked and gesticulated while the words failed to emerge. It was like waiting for a volcano to erupt. An overwrought, slightly sweaty but still dazzlingly beautiful volcano, Ben told himself. He didn't want to hang around for the eruption but he knew there was no avoiding it.

"I do not," she yelled in a pyroclastic cloud of fury, "want to spend my life doing driving tours of wartime bunkers and radar stations, sticking to your anal itinerary and hoping that my cooking gets high scores in your daily assessments!"

Ben grinned with relief.

"Is that what you're worried about? I'm not like that."

"Are you sure?"

"Completely. I'm not into that kind of thing at all. The whole World War Two thing is so nerdy. If I picked a holiday, we'd do something far more interesting."

"Really?"

"Oh, my ideal driving tour would be very different. There are some fascinating earthworks in the West Country."

"Earthworks?"

"Ancient fortifications. Dykes and ditches and such. Okay, some of them are barely visible and you have to use your imagination a lot but I think-"

Jayne didn't scream. She bellowed, loudly and wordlessly.

"Oh, Jesus Christ! You *are* turning into your dad! And mine!"

Ben staggered back and, from nowhere, found his own nugget of anger.

"Well, at least it's better than turning into your mom!"

Jayne reeled as though struck.

"Don't say that," she said.

"Well!" said Ben. "Listen to yourself. Dictating what people should and shouldn't be doing. Passing judgement."

Jayne shook her head vigorously.

"That's a horrible thing to say about me," she said quietly. "That's my greatest fear. Turning into my mom."

Ben approached her cautiously, fearful that she might explode again.

"I'm sorry," he said, holding out his hand. "Can I tell you something? Something that's been bugging me?"

"What?"

He waggled his hand at her. Jayne reluctantly took it.

"Your dad's speech really bothered me."

"What? More than Jeremy's?"

"A different kind of bother. Your dad called me your knight in shining armour."

"Yeah, I can't quite see that one either."

"Ah, well, I think he's right," said Ben.

"Delusional, you mean."

"You needed rescuing. From the dragon."

Jayne looked at him shrewdly.

"You are aware that only I'm allowed to insult my mother? You have to agree with me when I do but no independent mom-bashing."

"You've been trying to escape her clutches for years. All you needed was the means and a decent enough excuse."

Jayne said nothing. Ben hoped that meant she agreed with him.

"I'm that excuse," he said. "I'm the means."

"Maybe," said Jayne.

Ben nodded.

"And that's the real problem."

"What?"

"You are rescued now. You are free. I don't think you need a knight in shining armour anymore."

Across the lawn, a peacock hooted and leapt into the boughs of a low-hanging tree. Jayne bit her bottom lip in thought.

"Would you walk with me, Ben?" she said.

"Gladly," he said and linked arms with her.

ABBOT AMBROSE PACKED the charts he'd need into a waterproof locker on the boat. He was nearly ready to make his escape from this island and the closing net of people who were taking an unhealthy interest in him.

He checked over the boat. It was a squat but powerful motorboat that he had surreptitiously bought three months earlier for this very eventuality. It wasn't an ocean-going vessel but it would be enough to get them down the coast and across the channel to the continent. It sat low in the water, with the weight of the hoard that was already on board.

The weather reports were good, his personal outlook fair to sunny.

He was worried about Arthur being exposed to the cool wind that came off the sea, but that couldn't be helped. He would need to bring extra blankets, along with the rest of the paraphernalia that was needed for Arthur's care. As long as he could keep him dry and warm then they could find a new home and things would be as they always were.

Ambrose fought a wave of sudden despair. The only

thing that was more upsetting than the prospect of destroying their old routine was the thought that they would have to begin it again somewhere else. This was how it had always been. One final trip down here with Arthur and they'd be ready to go.

"EVERYBODY LOVES DOING THE *MACARENA*, don't they?" said Sebastian, beaming at the small crowd on the dance floor, several of whom were staggering back to chairs to catch their breath, or rubbing sore knees. Clovenhoof was undaunted, and waited eagerly to see what the next song was.

"Now a real treat, retro-fans," said Sebastian. "From eighty seven, when the DOW Jones index lost over twenty two points off its value and Jayne tried to create her own *My Little Pony* by colouring-in a neighbour's kitten, here's Bon Jovi with *Living on a Prayer*."

Clovenhoof leapt with joy as he recognised the anthemic rock tune that would show off his unmissable air guitar talents at their best. He woo-a-woo-a-woo'd along with the opening lines and punched the air.

Nerys appeared at his side, grabbing his elbow.

"Come with me," she said.

"Not while Bon Jovi's playing," Clovenhoof whined. "I'll come in a minute."

"No, not in a minute, you need to come now, there's something you need to see," she said.

"He hasn't even played my request yet," said Clovenhoof with a pout.

"Did you ask for *Do Ya Think I'm Sexy*, by any chance?" asked Nerys.

"How did you guess?" asked Clovenhoof as she steered him towards the door.

"Just lucky," she said.

They passed down several corridors, so that Bon Jovi was just a murmur behind thick stone walls.

"Look at these," said Nerys, stopping in front of some tapestries. "Tell me what immediately strikes you."

"Well," said Clovenhoof. "It strikes me that if you coop up a bunch of men on an island for most of their adult lives they will revert to the time-wasting pastime of embroidery just before their heads explode due to the boredom of it all. Embroidery's even more useless and dull than Ben's dad."

Nerys shook her head.

"Would you *look* at them! Never mind that you don't approve of embroidery, look here. What do you see?"

Clovenhoof looked where Nerys pointed.

"It's Cain. Shifty bugger, wasn't he?"

"And here." Nerys pointed at the next tapestry.

"Oh. Merlin," said Clovenhoof and then glanced back at the first tapestry. "He looks a bit like Cain, doesn't he?"

"Looks a *lot* like Cain," said Nerys. "Come on, there's more."

They walked a few feet further down the corridor.

"Now, I have no idea who Saint Senacus and Saint Veracius were, but here they are again. The same pair, look! The one saint has his head slightly obscured by these weird pink feathers, but this one here is definitely Abel from the first tapestry."

"So the monk who did this had no imagination when it came to faces."

"No. Look."

Clovenhoof stared hard at the scene depicted.

"Well apart from the interesting repair work on the hillside, this looks like Bardsey to me. I wonder if this pair of saints are the ones who founded the monastery?"

"Come and look at the next one," said Nerys.

She showed him the crucifixion.

"Oh, come on. That's Clint Eastwood, even I know that!" said Clovenhoof. "This is the handiwork of some monk on the brink of madness, like I told you."

Nerys rolled her eyes.

"You can quite clearly see which bits have been repaired, the colours are brighter. Those are the parts that seem a little more...eccentric. I'm talking about the original detail. Look. The Clint Eastwood character is holding Merlin's staff. It's quite distinctive, with that bit there that looks like a peacock's tail."

AMBROSE WHEELED the bath chair carefully down the path. The sun was setting and there would just be time to get Arthur onto the boat in its dying rays as long as there were no disasters like a wheel coming loose. The bath chair had spent years being pushed across the smooth stone floors of the monastery, so Ambrose was fearful that the stony path to the shore would prove too much for the antique mechanics of the thing.

"When we find our new home, I think we might need to get you a new chair, Arthur," he said. "I believe there are some fine new models available. I know we don't like to touch our hoard but I need to make sure that I can care for you in the best way possible. That's what family do, eh?"

Ambrose was forced to a sudden stop as Barry the peacock ran across the path in front of them. He screeched up at them, flashing his tail feathers.

"Shoo! Go on, out of the way!" shouted Ambrose. "Sorry Arthur, didn't mean to make you jump."

Barry reluctantly moved off.

"You know," said Ambrose, "it hasn't been so very bad these last few hundred years, has it? Let's face it, things have never been better." He smiled at a recollection. "Was there anything worse than the Middle Ages? Is it me or was everything covered in six inches of mud back then? Crowds of people coming out here on pilgrimages with their filthy diseases. The Black Death was nasty. Killed trade right off. You got a cold, do you remember?"

Barry's screeches faded to the distance as they neared the shore.

"Rome wasn't much better. Oh, they liked to think they were so very civilised, but the animals they had all over the place! I trod in giraffe dung over by the Colosseum one time. It took weeks to get rid of the smell. Funny, I can still remember that."

The path narrowed on the final descent and Ambrose leaned backwards to take the weight off the wheels as the chair lurched and wobbled over the uneven surface.

"Nearly there brother, nearly there."

CLOVENHOOF'S BROW creased in thought as he strolled back and forth between the pictures. Nerys was right. When examined carefully, the tapestries showed some sort of chronology. The same pair of characters popping up throughout history, almost as if they were immortal...

"Did you spot who they are yet?" asked Nerys impatiently. "Imagine this guy with a bad wig, covering up the mark he has on his forehead."

She held her hand over Cain's head to demonstrate.

"Abbot Ambrose," said Clovenhoof. "Abbot Ambrose is Cain."

"You mean he actually is Cain?"

"Yep. And the prior is Abel."

"Who?"

"Michael mentioned him. Some codger in a wheelchair. This is starting to make sense."

"Is it?"

"Trust me. We need to go to the orangery."

"The what? I'm glad you think that makes sense because I don't even know what you're talking about."

"The orangery. There's a tree growing here that's at the centre of all this. Come on."

MICHAEL SWUNG the sword back and forth, revelling in the weight of the thing, in the guttering roar of the flames as it swept through the air. Banished from the Celestial City for almost a year, this was almost like a homecoming.

He tried a few over shoulder passes, feeling the fire caress his face as it passed. Jessie kept at a very wary distance.

Michael grinned.

"Don't worry, girl. This thing's perfectly safe in my hands." He ran his hand along its blade, and it passed untouched through the flames. "You know this is older than all creation? I had this at my side during the War in Heaven. Jeremy will remember this, no doubt."

Michael laughed at the thought of taking it upstairs and waving it in Clovenhoof's face. Sure, it wasn't the lance, with which Michael had pierced the Adversary's side and thrown him down, but it was the next best thing.

"Can't remember where I lost it though. I didn't have it at the destruction of Sodom and Gomorrah. The last time I remember having it was at the gates to Eden. You know about that one, Jessie?"

Jessie licked her nose.

"The Almighty had placed the seraphim there, flaming swords abounding. He had kicked the humans out of paradise for their disobedience. It was our job to prevent them coming back, to guard the way back to the Tree of..."

Michael stopped.

"Of course!" he shouted in sudden realisation. "*That's* where I've seen it before!"

Jessie shifted on her feet, sensing something was afoot.

Michael raised his sword high and waved Jessie on.

"Come on! To the orangery!"

ST CADFAN'S

S tephen lifted the edge of his habit so that he could kick a stone in fury. It didn't really make him feel any better. He hadn't been able to stop inside the monastery after his encounter with Nerys. He couldn't decide what made him angrier. Was it that she hadn't listened to a single word that he said, blathering on about her own selfish thoughts, or was it that she hadn't recognised him, not even slightly? He couldn't decide, but he knew that he needed to go back and speak to her. How could he lead a life of peace and solitude if a single encounter with a woman could unsettle him like this?

What would he say to her?

He tried out some lines.

"I know you don't remember me, but we've been to bed together. You had a sex manual under the sheets and you treated me like a piece of meat."

No, piece of meat wasn't right.

"You treated me with all the tenderness of someone practising CPR on a dummy. I'm a sensitive man. I want you to recognise that I have feelings. Do you know how much I was damaged by that experience?"

Stephen stopped as he heard stones rattling on the path ahead.

"Hello, who's there?"

He walked towards the shore. He could definitely see someone now, on the steep stony slope, moving very slowly.

He caught up with Abbot Ambrose, pushing the prior in his bath-chair.

"Good evening Father Abbot. Are you all right?"

"Yes, yes of course I'm all right. Just taking the prior for an evening stroll."

Stephen caught the impatient tone in the abbot's voice.

"Ah, right. It's unusual to see you out this late," he said, "and the prior's bath-chair doesn't look all that secure on that pathway. Are you sure this is a good idea?"

"It is a good idea if I say it is a good idea!" shouted Ambrose without turning round. "The prior especially wanted to see the sunset this evening from the shore. Surely you can understand that a man of such simple needs must be granted this wish?"

"Yes, yes, of course," said Stephen, his brow wrinkling with confusion. He had no idea how the prior might have expressed such a desire to the abbot or anyone else.

Something bobbed up and down on the shore.

"Father Abbot, Is that a boat over there? Whose is it?"

The abbot started to speak, but the sound was drowned out by the inhuman screeching of Barry the peacock who launched himself across Stephen's path with a flurry of wings and a sharp, aggressive jabbing of his beak.

"Oh," said Stephen as he pedalled backwards, losing his grip on the uneven surface. He stumbled backwards and landed with a thump. As Barry advanced, he scrambled to his feet and retreated back up the path.

"Just call if you need a hand, Abbot!" he yelled over his shoulder as he brushed down his habit and attempted to restore his dignity.

ABBOT AMBROSE HAD GOT the bath-chair stuck on a large rock that jutted out from the side of the path.

"Sorry Arthur," he said, as he tipped the chair over to the side to free it. The Prior shifted dangerously, and the three bags that Ambrose had placed on his lap toppled off to the side.

Once the chair was safely level again, Ambrose grappled one-handed to retrieve the bags. Why was this ancient contraption not fitted with an effective brake? He found the bags, and quickly hefted them back onto the Prior's lap.

There was no time to lose before the sun set, and navigation became more difficult. The bags contained a small portion of the hoard that the abbot considered might be used as currency to assist their flight and ultimately their resettlement. He had estimated that even one of the bags would be enough to buy a remote castle in most countries of the world. This was travelling money and he needed to keep it handy.

The boat was still safely tied up, and Ambrose wheeled the prior across the access ramp that he had put in place.

"There we are Arthur, off for a boat trip. It's been a while, eh? If only we could have enjoyed such things when we were boys."

He had to use all his ancient muscle to avoid tipping Arthur into the boat amongst the crates. "I tell you," he wheezed, "there's nobody else who could appreciate how it was for the two of us when we were children. You look at the world today, so many millions of souls. We had only each other. So little joy in our childhood. Our parents lived a life of guilt and blame, I see that now. Our father couldn't bear the crushing guilt of what he'd done. And yet I secretly think he also blamed mother for taking the fruit."

He wedged the chair into place and put the extra blankets around the Prior's thin frame.

"We did all right in our own way, didn't we? You always had a way with the animals. I was the one with green fingers."

He raised his face to Heaven and called out.

"It wasn't good enough, was it? It was never enough! That bounty of food grown with my back-breaking work. I tilled the soil, watered the plants, pinched off the insects, but a single dumb animal was worth more than all of that. Why? Plenty of people live as vegetarians today. I was ahead of my time!"

He lowered his head and placed a hand gently on the prior's shoulder.

"Sorry brother. So sorry for everything."

He turned, seized with a sudden thought. He checked in

the top of a bag that he'd placed by the Prior's bath chair. The bag held a store of apples, which would be essential for the coming months, but where were the carefully selected shoots that he had taken from the tree? As long as he found a new rootstock at their destination, he could graft on one of the precious shoots and the tree would once again provide them with its bounty. He checked the other bags, but the waxed paper wrap that contained the shoots was nowhere to be found.

He must have left them in the orangery.

"Arthur, I need to go back and fetch something. I'll be as fast as I can. Don't go anywhere, will you?"

12

IN WHICH IMMORTALS MEET, A FIRE IS STARTED AND AN APPLE IS EATEN

N erys and Clovenhoof gazed up at the apple tree.

"Oh yes, I remember this tree," said Clovenhoof.

"What, this actual tree?" asked Nerys.

"Well, not this exact one. At least I don't think so. One of its forebears I imagine. Same air of smugness about it."

"How can a tree have an air of smugness?" asked Nerys.

"Oh, it knew what it was there for," said Clovenhoof. "Sure, I was there, coiled in its branches, doing my best to talk the woman into the idea that she should taste the apples."

"That was you?"

Clovenhoof nodded.

"They don't call me Jeremy the Python purely on account of my massive todger."

"No one calls you Jeremy the Python."

"The ladies on the premium rate phone lines do, if I ask them. But don't you ever wonder what it was doing there?"

"What?"

"The tree. A forbidden fruit tree, right slap bang in the middle of a garden? That's bloody entrapment. Tempt the poor sods and then act all surprised and angry when they give in to it. Ridiculous. It's almost as if the Other Guy has a sense of humour a bit like mine sometimes."

"So this is the actual tree of, er, life?" asked Nerys.

"If you read the Bible, it says there were two trees in the Garden of Eden," said Clovenhoof. "The Tree of Life and the Tree of the Knowledge of Good and Evil. They were actually the same tree, and this is that tree."

"And that jam we all ate at my mom's..."

"Yep," said Clovenhoof. "The Jam of the Knowledge of Good and Evil. Mind you, we must have also been eating the Jam of Life, so you've probably extended your life expectancy by a year or two as well."

"Why is it here though?" asked Nerys. "How could it have been here for all this time and remained a secret?"

"Secrets are easy to keep if you limit the number of people who know about them," came a voice from behind.

Nerys and Clovenhoof turned to see Abbot Ambrose.

The old man walked over and picked up a small bundle from beneath the apple tree. Nerys's eyes were fixed on the blade that he held out before him. It was a pair of spring-loaded pruning shears with a wicked point at the end.

"I don't know who you are," said the abbot. "I don't care. But you know too much."

"Oh puh-lease!" scoffed Clovenhoof. "Are you seriously

threatening us with those overgrown nail scissors? I promise they'll do nothing more than dent your ego if you try them on me."

"Bravado? Do you hold other people's lives in equally low regard?" said the abbot, looking meaningfully at Nerys.

Nerys saw Clovenhoof glance her way and his smile faltered slightly.

"Whatever," said Clovenhoof casually. "I have a question."

"Only one?"

"Where did you get this tree from? It should be in Eden. I think I would have heard of someone breaking in."

"I tried."

"Wait up," said Nerys. "Eden is a real place."

"Used to be," said Clovenhoof. "Its original location is in what's now Iran. Or maybe Iraq. Geography's shifted a bit since then. No, the Other Guy sealed it up and put Michael's crew on guard duty."

"I almost slipped by them." said Ambrose. "Even managed to snaffle myself one of their swords."

"You stole a cherubim sword?" said Clovenhoof, impressed.

"Cherubim. Seraphim. I forget. But I couldn't get in, couldn't get to the tree."

"So where did this one come from?" said Clovenhoof.

"A seed," said Ambrose. "My parents ate the fruit. Seeds and all."

Nerys mentally joined the dots.

"It grew out of Adam and Eve's poo?"

"I was always good with plants," said Ambrose. "Until He cursed me."

"You wanted immortality and knowledge," said Clovenhoof.

"Not at all," said Ambrose. "I don't need it. No, but my brother does."

Clovenhoof nodded.

"So that *is* Abel in the bath chair. I thought you killed him, back in the day?"

"I did kill him. I never meant to, but God made me so angry. I always regretted it though. I planted the tree on his grave, and slowly, very slowly it brought him back to life."

"Like a zombie?" said Nerys, disgusted.

"Zombie?" said Ambrose, who clearly had never heard the word.

"You know, brought back from the dead, all rotting flesh, snot and sinew."

Ambrose tilted his head.

"At first. And he grew stronger. And for several thousand years he was his old self, my brother Abel. But the past ten, twelve centuries, it's not been so good. He's degenerated, like the will, the life has gone from him."

"The guy in the wheelchair. You've kept him like that for... how long?"

The abbot waved the blade at her in annoyance.

"More than six thousand years. I love my brother. I've done nothing but care for him. The tree can't survive without him and he can't survive without the tree. I was cursed so that I could never grow anything again. Only the blood of my brother would nourish the tree."

"Urgh," said Nerys, seeing the rusty stains around the top

of the watering can in a fresh and unpleasant light. She was filled with a powerful sense of dread and loathing.

"You kept him alive. An invalid. Bleeding him like a vampire because... what? You're lonely."

"He's my brother," snapped the abbot. "He's family. Don't I deserve a little comfort? A little companionship?"

"But you died," said Clovenhoof. "Your house fell on top of you."

"That didn't kill me," said Ambrose. "Nothing can kill me. I carry this mark, this curse."

He pulled off his wig to reveal the mark on his forehead in the shape of a peacock's tail. Nerys decided she preferred the tapestry version, as this one had an ugly, scaly texture to it.

"Immortality. If anyone does me harm then they will receive seven times that harm from the vengeance of God."

Clovenhoof conveyed, by performing a short childish mime how frightened he was of the vengeance of God.

"So those tapestries out there. That's the story of you and your brother. All of those people were really you?"

"Yes," said the abbot. "The Wandering Jew, that was me. Joseph of Arimathea didn't come to England. That was me as well. The legend of the magical thorn tree that flowered all year round was a garbled recollection by someone that saw the apple tree."

"Not the only legend that's down to you," Clovenhoof said.

"No," said Ambrose. "The whole Arthur and Merlin business got a bit out of hand, to be honest. I blame Geoffrey of Monmouth who spiced up a few rumours he heard from some rather excitable monks. King Arthur and Merlin Ambrosius. Arthur got around a little better in those days, but his health was failing all the time and we could see that we needed somewhere secluded to live. I found this island for us. We came here to our Avalon, this isle of apples and built a glass house for the tree, and for Arthur."

He looked around the orangery, and Nerys realised he was saying goodbye to a place that had been a part of their lives for countless years.

"We were taken for religious hermits, and that was the very best thing that could have happened. A monastery was the perfect place for us. Men of religion and humility have proven to be ideal companions. They accept our eccentric ways and provide us with practical support. I like to think that we've created a small community here."

MICHAEL RAN up every stair and burst out through the ancient door and into the cloisters. He was barely out of breath. Ten hours in the gym each week for the past six months might have mostly been an excuse to hang out with Andy, but it had not gone to waste.

He grinned in the blade's light.

Oh, yes. Here he was, an angel in his prime. He had a flaming sword in his hand and, within his reach, the answer to a holy mystery. If this wasn't going to please the Almighty, he had no idea what would.

Jessie barked.

"Let's go then," said Michael and they ran, along the wall,

round the corner and through the orangery door. The room was not unoccupied.

Clovenhoof and Nerys whirled as Michael barged in.

"Fuck me!" exclaimed Nerys, staggering back from the fiery sword.

Clovenhoof appeared annoyed more than anything else.

"Where did you find *that*?" he snapped peevishly.

"Remember it, do you?" Michael smiled.

"It's not yours," said Abbot Ambrose, standing beneath the twisted apple tree.

"I'd beg to differ," said Michael.

"It's on fire!" Nerys squeaked. "Hasn't anyone noticed?"

Michael swung his blade to point straight ahead.

"It's the Tree," he said. "The Tree of Knowledge of Good and Evil, the Tree of Life."

"We know," said Clovenhoof.

Michael's victorious grin faltered.

"What do you mean, you know?"

"We know. We worked it out. Well, Nerys did. Well, it was me mostly because I'm the clever one."

Michael's sword arm drooped. The sword clanged flatly against a planter box.

"You worked it out?"

"He's Cain," said Clovenhoof, indicating the abbot.

"Er, Michael?" said Nerys.

"Cadfan, Veracius, Merlin," said Clovenhoof. "He's all of them. He's even been mistaken for Joseph of Arimathea. He's had more name changes than I've had fresh underwear."

He counted them off on his fingers to check and nodded.

"Michael?" said Nerys.

"And the prior?" said Michael, looking around for the prior's bath-chair.

"He's Abel."

"Abel's dead."

"Magic, life-restoring tree," said Clovenhoof.

"Michael!" snapped Nerys.

"What?" said the archangel.

"Your sword."

Michael looked down. His sword had charred its way through the wooden planter box and now the thing was on fire.

"Oh, silly me," he said and lifted his sword away.

The fire had reached the bone-dry ferns in the planter box and they crackled as the fire leapt between them.

"Best put that out," said Michael and leant the sword against the curtains by the door so he could use both hands to heap soil on the fire. "Soon have this out," he said, as the curtain material burst into flame.

Clovenhoof nodded.

"Now, when I start a fire people usually scream."

"Do something!" said Nerys and propelled Clovenhoof forward.

"Right," said the Fallen One, grabbed the burning curtain and yanked it off the wall. It landed on another planter box where it burned merrily.

Michael had almost buried the original fire but it had raced out of his reach and was beginning to lick playfully at the flaky paintwork on the orangery's wooden window frames. Smoke was quickly filling the air.

"Here!" said Nerys and thrust a plant mister into Michael's hand.

Michael looked at it and then gave a little squeeze. The puff of water droplets evaporated before they even reached the flames.

"Little help over here!" called Clovenhoof.

Michael looked up and immediately saw two things. Firstly, inexplicably, Clovenhoof had managed to spread the curtain fire further. More than a dozen plants, three wooden chairs and a significant section of the orangery woodwork were aflame. The second thing...

"Where's the abbot?" shouted Michael. "Where's Cain?"

Nerys and Clovenhoof looked round but it was clear that the old man – the very, very old man – had gone.

BARDSEY WAS NOT A LARGE ISLAND. As they walked, Jayne could see that with an hour's walk they would circumnavigate the whole thing. She hoped that they wouldn't be walking quite that far. Her wedding shoes were less than perfect on the island's stony tracks and the hem of her wedding dress was probably picking up more than a little muck as they walked.

"So, is international travel the only thing we're going to argue about?" said Ben.

"Lord, no," said Jayne gently. "Married couples argue all the time."

"Really? I don't think I've ever heard my parents argue."

"I'm not sure that's necessarily a good thing," said Jayne

and then took a deep breath. "It's not about travel, really, is it? It's not about holidays."

"No?"

"It's about two viewpoints. It's about striking out on new adventures versus settling down."

"I... I think I've had enough adventures in my life," said Ben.

"Oh? So what's marriage? Isn't this a brand new adventure?"

"Interesting point." Ben kicked at a stone as they walked and watched it roll down the island's sloping side towards the sea. "Getting married is just one of those things that I thought I'd always do. Go to college, buy a house, get married, have kids. Tick, tick, tick, tick," he said, ticking them off on an imaginary clipboard.

"Tick?" said Jayne.

"You know... tick."

"Oh, I got the mime, Ben. Marcel Marceau couldn't have done better. I'm a bit perturbed that I'm something to be ticked off on a list."

"Not *you* per se..."

"You are such a trainspotter!"

"I don't think I've ever been a trainspotter. I went through a phase of writing down number plates but-"

"Is there no passion in you at all?" said Jayne.

Ben frowned.

"I think that's a bit, well, insulting. I can be passionate when the mood takes me."

Jayne pulled a face.

"I'm not talking about your animal urges, Ben. I mean passion, drive, spontaneity."

Ben nodded along with her until that last word.

"Spontaneity? No. I'm not a big fan of that. I'm not a fussy person, but I do like to know what's coming."

"I know," said Jayne. "Wife, tick. Kids, tick. Favourite park bench, tick. Mobility scooter, tick. Don't tell me, you've already picked out where you're going to be buried."

"No. Although I do have a favourite bench in Sutton Park. I've always thought that, when I'm old, I'd sit there and I'd –"

"Stop," said Jayne. "Stop there."

"What?"

"I don't want a life that's all planned out. You may have had enough adventures and incidents to last a lifetime but I haven't. I want surprises."

"No, I don't like surprises," said Ben.

Jayne's foot connected with something in the grass, something heavy and unyielding and she stumbled forwards. Ben caught her by the elbow and stopped her falling.

Jayne shook herself, smoothed out her dress and looked down at the object in the grass. It was a heavy cloth bag. She picked it up – it was surprisingly heavy – and opened it.

"What is it?"

Jayne did not reply. Her brain was still processing the possibilities. She reached in and touched one of the coins.

"What is it?" asked Ben again.

"Um," said Jayne. "It's gold. The biggest pile of gold I've ever seen."

"Well, of course," said Ben, "there are *good* surprises."

WHILE EUROPE'S *The Final Countdown* had the hardcore rockers on the dance floor, Michael ran into the refectory, sword in hand.

"Fire!" he yelled.

More than a few wedding guests pointed unnecessarily at the flaming sword. A couple screamed.

"Not this fire!" he yelled. "The monastery's on fire!"

Brother Sebastian stabbed at his laptop keyboard, killing the music.

Novice Stephen stood at a respectful distance from the man with the burning blade.

"Where?"

"The orangery. But it's kind of spreading."

Stephen looked round.

"Where's the abbot?"

"Gone."

NERYS RAN, panting, down a corridor that was thick with smoke. The fire had spread with astonishing ease, considering this was a stone building and a damp one at that.

She wasn't sure where Clovenhoof was, but with the visibility as poor as it was he could be right behind her and she'd never know. She had a vague idea that the air might be clearer near to the floor. Was she supposed to crawl along to avoid smoke inhalation?

As these thoughts were crowding her brain, she collided

with someone else in the corridor. She landed with a loud *oof*, and found herself on top of an astonished monk.

It was true. The air down here was a bit clearer. She looked across at his face, angled, as she was around his navel and had a strong sense of déjà vu.

"Trevor, have we met before?" she asked. "Because from this angle you look awfully familiar."

"It's Stephen," said the monk, clearly a little winded. "And, yes, we did meet."

"I'm trying to remember."

"There was a time when, for reasons that escape me, I found you attractive and we ended up in bed -"

"Oh my life! It was *true* about you going off to become a monk!" she cried. "I heard it but I didn't know whether to believe it."

"Yes, all true," said Stephen, dragging himself from under Nerys's body.

"I mean it's one of those things people say. I think I should be insulted. Was it because of me?" she demanded. "Was it?"

He looked at her for a long moment.

"You really want to talk about this right now? You want to know whether the trauma of you practising your sexual techniques upon me was enough to drive me to a life of celibacy? You want to risk your neck in a blazing building because your self-indulgent ego demands the answers NOW? You really are the most sickeningly selfish woman I have ever met. How can you live with yourself?"

Nerys crawled after him on her elbows, eyes watering, coughing as she went.

"I'm gonna take that as a yes," she said.

Michael waved the guests onward, through the kitchens. "This way!"

Even here, some distance from the origins of the fire, there was a faint haze of smoke in the air. There were coughs from some of the more elderly guests.

Michael realised there was a smile forming on his face and he quashed it quickly. This was an emergency situation. He had a purpose. He was doing good. This filled him with an inordinate sense of satisfaction, joy even, but it was hardly appropriate to let it show.

He led the guests on, down the steps to the larder and then out through the scullery and then out into the monastery gardens and the cool night air.

"Come on, come on," he called, patting people on the back as they piled out, monks and wedding guests alike.

Against, the not quite black sky, smoke billowed above the monastery. Sparks of orange fire danced above the roofing tiles.

Last out through the door was resident DJ and entrepreneur, Brother Sebastian.

"Is that everyone?"

Sebastian shook his head.

"The abbot and the prior can't be found. Novice Stephen has gone to look for them." He scanned the people milling on the lawn. "The brothers are all here. And four of the wedding party are missing but I think they were elsewhere in the grounds."

He pored over a sheet of paper attached to a clipboard, moving away from the tetchy guests.

"So glad to see that you are in control of things," said Manfred, approaching. "Is that a list of the people that we have here?"

"No," Sebastian said, reaching into a pocket and thrusting a crumpled sheet towards Manfred. "That's here. No, I'm doing some quick calculations on the cost of the damage. It's just possible that this fire could work to our advantage you know. I took out some extra insurance just recently."

Manfred shook his head incredulously.

"What about the priceless artwork? Those tapestries are irreplaceable, if it is just possible that I can rescue some of them -"

He made to re-enter the building but Sebastian moved to stop him.

"No brother. They were already damaged, they are worth more to us if they are destroyed."

Manfred made a noise like a sad kitten.

"This is so shocking, that we should stand by while such woeful destruction takes place. I had to do this once before you know. My grandparents' house was set ablaze and my grandfather's collection of wooden squirrels was sadly lost. Oh -"

He turned to Sebastian, distraught.

"There is a factor that we have overlooked, and I fear, my friend that it is a significant one."

Sebastian raised his eyebrows and waited for Manfred to fill in the blanks.

"You will remember that one of our many small efforts to create some wealth for our order was my apparatus for the distillation of apple brandy -" began Manfred.

"The still!" yelled Sebastian. "Oh, this could be disastrous!"

"Hold on," said Tony Kitchen, who'd been listening. "Let's just keep calm and think about a few things. See how dangerous it really is."

The two monks turned and looked at him, expectantly.

"Number one," said Tony. "Has your still been working at all within the last day?"

"Yes," chorused the two monks.

"Right, ok. Next question," said Tony. "Did you already create some alcohol, and are the bottles stored nearby?"

"Yes!" chorused the two monks again.

"Hmmm, in that case, I think I know what we need to do," said Tony, nudging Pam, who looked at him with a tired smile.

"Very good," said Manfred, with a relieved smile. "What is that, exactly?"

"We need to run, RUN! Far away. It's going to blow!" yelled Tony.

Brother Sebastian held his phone aloft.

"I will call the emergency services, let's get these people mustered down on the shore."

"I believe I can help you with that," said Michael, striding over.

"This way!" he yelled to the eighty-odd guests and monks. "To the beach!"

He held his sword aloft. Now, in the night air, the flaming sword was a torch, lighting the way.

The guests and monks obediently followed Michael down the beach path, a winding exodus in posh hats, morning suits and smoke-damaged habits. Some were less obedient.

"I don't know who put him in charge," said Agnes Thomas loudly.

"I think he's just being decisive, Agnes," said Pam Kitchen.

"And he has got a flaming sword," added Ewan Thomas.

"Clever that," said Tony Kitchen. "Reckon it's a special effect of some sort?"

"Or magic," said Ewan.

"Maybe it's for cutting the wedding cake," suggested Pam.

"It's flashy, that's what it is," said Agnes. "I told you he was up to something... poofy."

"I don't think fiery swords could ever be described as poofy, Agnes. We should form a human chain, see if we can't get some buckets of sea water onto that fire. It would be a tragedy to see a fine old building like that seriously damaged," said Ewan.

"Brilliant, just brilliant. I could add salt-water rot to smoke damage of all my clothes. Honestly Ewan, you can be so clueless," said Agnes. "These shoes are practically ruined already from walking around on stones and sand."

CLOVENHOOF MOVED along a corridor filled with swirls of smoke. Had the abbot left already? No, there he was, edging between scaffolding poles and the far wall. Clovenhoof sucked in his belly and edged after him. It was a tight squeeze.

He saw that Nerys was at the other end with the young monk who insisted on being called Stephen.

"Nerys, stop him! He's coming your way," Clovenhoof called out.

"What's going on?" asked Stephen, looking from Clovenhoof, to the abbot to Nerys.

"Let me explain," called Nerys, while Clovenhoof concentrated on manoeuvring through the scaffolding. "Right, listen up, Stephen. You need to know that your Abbot is ancient."

"What?"

"He was born before the time of Christ and he killed his brother. Then he resurrected him so that he could sustain the Tree of the Knowledge of Good and Evil with his blood. That's pretty much what he's been doing ever since."

"Nerys," said Stephen. "Are you high on smoke fumes? None of that made any sense at all. We have to get out of here." Stephen looked up at Brother Sebastian's dodgy scaffolding. "This place isn't safe."

"No, look, I know it sounds a little bit unlikely," said Nerys, "but if you'd seen some of the stuff I've seen in the last year, you wouldn't be fazed." She cast about for a convincing argument. "Right, tell you what, if you can think of any time you ever saw evidence that there was someone else in charge of this monastery *since it was built* then I'll shut up."

Stephen opened and closed his mouth a few times and then made a huffing sound.

"Oh, this is ridiculous. Father Abbot, tell them they're being silly. I have no idea what went on here in the past, but I only arrived here within the last year, so how would I?"

Abbot Ambrose remained silent, and continued his progress between the scaffolding.

The only sound that could be heard above the ominous crackling of the approaching flames was Clovenhoof's grunts as he tried to shimmy through as quickly as he could.

"Stephen," Clovenhoof called. "The abbot has been playing a dangerous game. What would happen if the world found out that Bardsey holds the key to defeating death? People out there might think they want immortality but it's not all it's cracked up to be, I can vouch for that."

"Don't you think I'd like to die?" hissed the abbot. "It's all I've dreamed of for centuries, but nobody will touch me. No one. Vengeance seven times over! The Deluge didn't drown me. Starvation won't touch me. I'm obliged to keep my secret to protect my brother and you won't stop me. I'll leave this place and start again somewhere else. It's what we've always done."

Stephen stood before him, wide-eyed as the abbot emerged from the scaffolding.

"No," he said, firmly. "I'm sorry Abbot, but it seems to me there are some definite problems with this situation, so I think you'll need to stay here until we can find someone in a position of authority to decide what's best."

"Fool!" yelled the abbot and pushed Stephen against the

wall, the wicked point of the pruning shears against his chest.

Nerys acted quickly and without thought. She delivered an enthusiastic kick to where she guessed his groin was under that habit. She tugged briskly on the back of his collar at the same time, to yank the shears away from Stephen. The abbot was lighter than she'd imagined, and she pulled him straight over as his knees buckled with the pain. She tripped over him and landed on top, realising too late that the pruning shears were pointing directly upwards.

FLAMES CREPT along the floorboards of the almonry and raced across the tapestry of the crucifixion. They encircled the sixteen wooden casks that Brother Manfred had stored by the cupboard door, each one filled with sweet, life-giving liquor.

THERE WAS distant boom and a hot wind swept through the corridor.

Nerys lay on the floor, a ragged hole in her dress, blood flowing rapidly across the stone floor. Stephen was already by her side.

Clovenhoof roared and rushed the abbot. Ambrose was crawling away back towards the scaffolding. Clovenhoof pulled out a length of timber that supported a wall-brace and repeatedly clubbed him with it. Blow after blow after blow.

"Don't. Hurt. My. Friend!"

The abbot went down, gasping in pain.

"Vengeance..." he croaked.

A rumbling sound cascaded through the stonework overhead and the scaffolding started to buckle where it was now unsupported.

Clovenhoof looked up, stepped out of the way and, with a foul grin, gave the stonework a helpful poke with the wall-brace. The masonry thundered dully as it came crashing down. When the dust cleared, the abbot was gone, buried under tonnes of fallen stone.

Clovenhoof dusted off his hands. Above him, the stonework groaned.

"Vengeance seven times over?" he muttered.

He looked straight up, through the thousand tonnes of unstable masonry, through the heavens and right into the heart of the Celestial City and the Throne of the Almighty.

"Really, mate?" he said, directly to the Other Guy. "Come and have a go if you think you're hard enough."

The stonework creaked and settled and then fell silent.

"Damn right," he said.

There was a gaping hole in the outside wall. Smoking was pouring out, fresh air wafting in.

Clovenhoof dashed to Nerys's side. Stephen was dabbing ineffectually at the blood that was rapidly pooling in her lap.

"Can't believe you've killed me again," she croaked.

"What?" said Clovenhoof. "You can't blame me for this!"

"Can," sighed Nerys, "and will."

"No!" yelled Clovenhoof. "Don't you die!"

"There's a lot of blood here," said Stephen. "I think these

are serious injuries. Nothing's going to save her other than a miracle."

"Either a miracle, or some cockeyed throwback to the days when fruit couldn't just be fruit," Clovenhoof exclaimed. "We need the apples!"

Clovenhoof looked back up the blocked corridor.

"The tree's completely incinerated and the orangery's burned down. Do you store them anywhere in the monastery?"

"No," said Stephen. "The abbot never let us eat them. No wonder he was mad when we made the jam. He used to feed them to Brother Arthur all the time though, I bet he's put some on the boat with him."

"Boat?"

"Yes, I saw him loading up a boat earlier. It seemed like a strange thing for him to be doing."

"Right. Wait here, both of you. Make sure you keep her talking, I'll be right back."

Clovenhoof leapt out through the hole in the wall and disappeared into the night.

THE GUESTS ASSEMBLED on the beach, huddled together.

It was not a cold night but there was a persistent breeze coming in off the sea and many of the women's dresses were thin and offered no warmth. More than a few wives had their husbands' suit jackets draped over their shoulders, leaving their husbands to feel all chivalrous and slightly chilly.

Michael stood down by the shore, watching the faint

pinpoints of lights of Aberdaron, wondering when help was going to come.

Ewan and Tony strolled down to join him.

"All right, son?" said Tony.

Michael nodded.

"You did a good job there," said Ewan. "Leading everyone out."

"Thanks."

Ewan nodded at Michael's still-blazing blade.

"Tony and I were wondering, well, debating more like. How does it work?"

"Work?"

"I proposed the blade is hollowed out and that gas is fed up through the blade via the hilt, perhaps from a cylinder concealed inside your suit," said Tony.

"Whereas," said Ewan, "I said that it was more likely that this was an ancient magical blade."

"*More* likely?" said Michael.

Ewan shrugged.

"Legends abound in these parts. Round here, you can throw a stone and, like as not, it'll land on the tomb of some prince or king. You're standing on Avalon after all."

"Isle of apples," said Michael, thinking about the orangery, now a fiery ruin, and the tree that had grown in it for centuries. "Merlin's house of glass."

"Of course," said Tony with a meaningful waggle of his eyebrow, "what with there being a fire in the monastery and you holding that thing, the authorities might have a few questions."

Michael looked at his sword and grimaced.

"Oh, dear."

"I'm sure it wasn't your fault, son," said Tony.

Michael sighed.

"Well, it was fun while it lasted. Stand back, gentleman."

"Why?" said Ewan but did as he was told.

Michael positioned his feet carefully, drew back his arm and threw the sword out to sea with all his strength. It pinwheeled through the night sky, end over end, an orange disc of fire, and then arced down into the dark sea with an audible hiss.

The three of them – two men and one angel – simply stared out to sea. Ewan eventually broke the silence.

"Now," he said, "If that had been Excalibur, Arthur's blade, the Lady of the Lake's hand would have come up out of the water to take back the sword."

Michael peered out over the waves.

"And did that happen?"

"I don't know, Michael. It's dark."

STEPHEN MADE another attempt to dab up Nerys's blood, and gave her a smile that he hoped was encouraging.

He was supposed to talk to her, stop her slipping away. He wracked his brain for something to say.

"Just us two, eh?" he said. "A bit of quality time together. Nice, isn't it?"

Nerys blinked at him. It seemed to be an effort.

"Nice? You did just tell me I'm dying, didn't you?" she whispered.

"Sorry."

"About before. I can see that I hurt you."

"It's okay. Don't worry about it."

"If I was... overbearing then I'm sorry."

"No, no." Stephen patted her hand. "Don't exert yourself. I can't blame you for being so enthusiastic about things. I admire your spirit. How could I not? You saved me from the abbot!"

Nerys coughed and her whole body shook with the pain.

"So, how's celibacy been treating you?" she asked. "Was I...?"

"What?"

"The last one...?"

"Yes you were," said Stephen. He seemed about to say something more, but there was a grinding sound as the stonework above them shifted.

"You should get out of here," said Nerys. "You could be killed."

"What and miss what you do next?" laughed Stephen. "Not a chance. Your crazy friend will save you and you'll do something spectacular and horrific, won't you? Won't you?"

He leaned over as her eyelids fluttered closed.

"Nerys? Come on. Nerys!"

CLOVENHOOF FOUND THE BOAT. He'd always wanted a boat of his own. He hadn't realised until that very moment but he saw now that he had always wanted a boat. Now probably wasn't the time to acquire one.

He hopped aboard but found his hooves tangled in some ropes. He flailed impatiently and threw them over the side when he had managed to untie them. It was beginning to get quite windy now, and the smoke from the monastery billowed down to the water's edge. He was able to pick out shapes on the boat, and he moved forward, looking for something that might be a stash of apples. The first thing he found was the prior in his bath-chair.

"Evening," he said.

It was too dark to see any hint of a facial expression but Clovenhoof felt the question in the air.

"Your brother? He's gone I'm afraid. His house fell on him."

He rummaged through the bags and chests. He could feel the prior's gaze boring into him. It might have contained a request perhaps, or a wish.

"No, I'm not about to do that," said Clovenhoof. "Yes, immortality is quite a drag, but I've got other things to be seeing to right now. Quite a cargo you've got here on this boat, brother. Where are the apples though?"

Clovenhoof pulled a bag out from the base of the bath chair with a triumphant flick.

"Aha! Here we are."

He stumbled and tipped them over the side into the waves.

"Bugger!"

Clovenhoof leapt into the water and grabbed an apple as it bobbed around energetically with several others. He waded back to shore, holding it aloft. He registered dimly that the boat was a little further out. The rope that was previously tied to a wooden post was now snaking out behind the boat as it drifted away from the shore.

"Sorry about that!" he yelled to the prior and ran back up the path as fast as his hooves could carry him.

BEN POINTED AGAIN, stabbing a finger out to sea.

"There!"

Jayne screwed up her eyes and tried to see what he was seeing.

"Nothing."

"It's a boat. I can still just about see it. Floating away on the waves. I saw something glitter and there was a man sat on board."

"Right," said Jayne. "And you can see him smiling at you and waving, no doubt."

"I didn't say he was waving," said Ben. "Smiling perhaps."

"Maybe this is his gold."

"Oh, no. Finders keepers, I say."

"Come on," she said.

She would have taken his hand as they walked back down towards the monastery but she wasn't sure where they now stood on hand-holding and, besides, the gold in her arms was very heavy.

"So, what do we tell everyone?" she said.

"I don't think we need to tell them about the gold. If someone notices, you can say that a wealthy aunt gave it to you as a wedding present."

"Not about the gold," she said. "About us."

Ben popped his lips as he thought.

"We're married. We love each other."

Jayne could sense the 'but'. It was a big fat 'but' and loitered like a mugger in an alley.

"But?" she said.

"But we're not ready for our lives to go in the same direction just yet. You've got adventures you need to have."

"Without you?"

"If that's how it has to be."

"And you'll wait for me?" she said.

Ben shrugged amiably.

"I'll be sat on my favourite bench, waiting," he said.

"For how long?"

He shrugged again. It was clearly his default response.

"Until your gold runs out," he said.

"*My* gold?"

"Absolutely."

Jayne blinked and then, surprising herself a little, planted a small but heartfelt kiss on his cheek.

"You are an astonishing man, Ben Kitchen."

"I *am* astonishing," he agreed. Suddenly his face fell. "Oh, no!"

Jayne followed his gaze and saw the orange glow and the pall of smoke.

"Is the monastery on fire?"

"Oh, Jeremy," said Ben with a mighty sigh.

"I've got the apples!" yelled Clovenhoof as he burst back through the hole in the wall.

The first thing that he noticed was that quite a lot more stonework had fallen down, and the smoke was getting thicker. The second thing he noticed was that Nerys was slumped in Stephen's arms, eyes closed.

"Nerys! Wake up!"

Stephen lifted his head, eyes rimmed with red.

"It might be too late," he said.

"Fucking magic apples," murmured Nerys faintly. "Kidding aren't you? Rather have a glass of wine to be honest."

"No, no, this will work!" Clovenhoof said. "You need to eat it now!"

"You're Satan, why would I believe a word you say?" she said.

"She's delirious," said Stephen but Clovenhoof ignored him.

"I know, I know. Look the fruit of eternal life wasn't my idea. I did say at the time that I thought the fruit of uncontrollable flatulence would be a lot more fun. Nowhere near enough fart jokes in the Old Testament, but He wasn't having it. Look, if I eat some first will you have some?"

Clovenhoof took a bite of the apple and chewed it enthusiastically.

"Now your turn, yum, yum!"

He broke some off and offered it to her. Nerys took the piece in her mouth and chewed feebly. As the juice was released, her jaw moved more freely and she was able to take another bite straight from the apple. Stephen smiled up at Clovenhoof.

"It works."

"Yes, yes," said Clovenhoof with a dismissive wave of the hand. "But saving lives is not *at all* what I do. I hope word doesn't get around. I only did it because I can't drive and I need her to give me lifts. Uh oh."

Clovenhoof realised what was happening and tried to put a hand across his mouth, but the urge to speak the truth overwhelmed him.

"Also, I know where you keep your booze," he said to Nerys, "which is handy when the shops are shut."

Nerys had started to regain some colour and she was able to sit up slightly. Stephen moved forward to help her, but she put a hand on his arm.

"Hold on, I might not get another opportunity like this," she said. "Right, Jeremy. Last Easter when you blamed Twinkle for eating the whole roast, was it you, really?"

"Yes," said Clovenhoof, unable to lie.

"Thought so. Is it you that keeps phoning up the job agency and asking if there are any vacancies for breast inspectors?"

"Yes."

"Hm. A couple of months ago, my underwear drawer was all messed up. What do you know about that? Were you selling used underwear to perverts on eBay?"

"No, but I might now you've given me the idea. I made catapults out of your bras. I wanted to see which would send an egg the farthest, wired or unwired."

"Which one did?" asked Nerys.

"Dunno, I accidentally broke them, so I had to mop up the mess with your knickers. I didn't think you'd notice."

Nerys looked hard at him.

"Did we really go to Heaven and meet Aunt Molly?" she whispered.

"Yes we did. Totally kicked ass as well," Clovenhoof replied.

"It really happened," said Nerys to herself. "Now, how about this apple? Eve ate some and she was cursed. Am I going to be cursed?"

"Well," said Clovenhoof. "Eve's curse was to have pain in childbirth and to be ruled over by men."

Stephen and Clovenhoof both stared at Nerys for a long moment.

"So," asked Stephen. "Do you feel as if you ought to do what we say?"

Nerys laughed so long and so hard that she almost failed to get up from the floor.

"Come on," she said, as she got to her feet. "Let's go. We've done enough damage here."

"HERE THEY ARE!" shouted Pam.

Ben and Jayne were hurrying down the path to the shore. Jayne seemed to be struggling with a small but obviously heavy bag in her arms. Agnes ran to hug her daughter, an act of affection that clearly caught Jayne by surprise.

"We were so worried," said Agnes.

"We were just taking a walk," said Jayne. "We didn't even realise what had happened until –"

"And look what you've done to that dress! Is the bridal hire shop going to accept that as reasonable wear and tear? They are not. You don't think, girl!"

Jayne smiled, clearly happy to see her mom's emotional compass swing back towards more familiar territory.

"Is everyone all right?" said Ben.

"Nearly all accounted for," said Ewan. "It's certainly been a memorable evening."

"And making memories is what the wedding day is all about," said Tony.

"I hope someone took some pictures then," said Ben. "Where's Jeremy anyway? I'm going to kill him. This is his fault no doubt."

"Not necessarily," said Michael, stepping forward.

"Well, what happened then?" said Ben.

Michael tried to think of a response that wouldn't involve immortal monks and holy trees and absolutely definitely did not involve a flaming sword of the seraphim.

"It's complicated," he said at last.

"You're just covering for him," said Ben. "This has his fingerprints all over it."

"Are my ears burning?" called Clovenhoof, trotting down the path towards them.

He was closely followed by Nerys and Novice Stephen who seemed to be enjoying each other's company more than Michael might have expected. Nerys's dress was in tatters and drenched in a dark liquid.

"And what have you done to yourself?" demanded Agnes

annoyed. "That was a perfectly lovely dress and – oh, my – is that blood?"

"Don't worry, mom," said Nerys with a smile. "It's only mine."

Agnes staggered.

"You're bleeding. Quick! Someone!"

"I'm fine," said Nerys. "All better now."

"How?"

"Shush, mom," said Nerys and kissed her mother.

With every one of the guests now fully accounted for and no sign of any rescue, the monks began to busily discuss the options for containing the fire.

"I have to say," said Clovenhoof, "this is easily the best wedding I've ever been to."

"It's been a disaster," said Ben.

"Oh, that's just a matter of perspective," Clovenhoof grinned.

MICHAEL WALKED DOWN to the surf, out of earshot of the rest of the guests. He looked up at the sky. The stars were tiny pinpricks of light against the black. He picked one at random.

"Lord, creator of all," he said. "My friends are safe and whole. Thank you."

The speck of light twinkled at Michael.

"Oh, I see your hand in all things, Lord. My faith in you is without measure."

The light seemed to grow slightly, prompting more from

Michael.

"And, Lord, I have listened and I have looked. I've sought your guidance and the opportunity to show my worth to you. I have accepted the trials you've placed at my feet. Human life is a mystery, a beautiful and insane mystery. But I have tried, haven't I? And I've done good. And some bad. But mostly good, wouldn't you say?"

The light continued to grow, white and actinic. It was no illusion.

Michael frowned.

"Really? So, have I done everything you wanted? Are you happy now?"

There was no reply but the light grew further and the wind became stronger.

"Do you want to take me back?" said Michael, not sure if it was something he himself wanted anymore. "Really?"

The light swelled to an enormous size, casting its illumination across the entire beach. The wind became a howl, like a holy choir of roaring beasts. Many guests pointed as the wind whipped up sand across the beach and threw dresses and hats into disarray.

"Er, Lord?"

The yellow RAF rescue helicopter swept overhead and then banked round to bring its search light to bear on the beach once more.

"Oh," said Michael.

Clovenhoof slapped Michael on the back with such force, his lungs rattled.

"God flies a helicopter, does he?" he grinned.

"I just thought..."

Clovenhoof laughed.

"You are a gullible twat."

Michael gave him a penetrating look.

"And I beat you. I threw you down in the war. If I'm a gullible twat, what does that make you?"

Clovenhoof sighed amiably.

"You can't keep living on past glories, pigeon-wings. That's just sad."

Michael's phone beeped. He took it out of his pocket.

There was his daily prediction from G-Sez on the screen and, shown in a corner icon, an incoming call from Andy.

Michael answered, putting his finger in his free ear to mute the sound of the rescue helicopter.

"Hi," he shouted. "Yes. Still at the wedding. No, that's a helicopter. A helicopter. Yes, it has been quite a spectacular wedding. But we should be back tomorrow." Michael smiled broadly as Andy spoke. "Yeah, me too. Seriously. No, it's not the wine talking."

A thought crossed Michael's mind. *When then is my hope? Will we descend together into the dust?* There were worse things for two people to do together. In fact, he couldn't think of anything he'd rather do.

"Well, how about dinner on Friday? My place. I'll cook. Yes, I can cook. I'm not just a pretty face, you know. Sure. Bye."

Michael hung up.

"Your boyfriend," said Clovenhoof, "is really very short. Have you noticed that he's really, really small?"

"Not where it counts," said Michael.

"Oh, you mean *spiritually*," said Clovenhoof in a silly, mocking voice.

"Nope," said Michael happily and dialled his home number.

"Hello, Michael," said the smooth computer voice.

"Little G," said the former archangel. "What's our food situation looking like?"

"The fridge and freezer are fully stocked for your return tomorrow. You will need fresh milk. Shall I order some?"

"Please. I've also got Andy coming over for dinner on Friday. I want to make something special."

"What shall I order?" asked Little G.

"Oh, you decide," said Michael. "I have total faith in you."

SEEING Stephen go off to chat to his fellow monks, Ben sidled up to Nerys.

"Do you know, a certain thought has only just occurred to me," he said.

"That you're going to have to spend your wedding night, once we get back, in a hammock in dad's shed?"

"No."

"That your wedding cake is now a smouldering cinder, the bride and groom reduced to puddles of wax?"

"No."

"What then?"

"We're related," said Ben with a broad smile.

Nerys considered him and his statement at length.

"What?" she said.

"You're my sister-in-law. I'm your brother-in-law."

Nerys pulled a face.

"Not blood relatives, Ben."

"What God has joined together, let no man strike asunder," he countered. "You and me, sis. We're family."

"Oh, goody," said Nerys faintly.

"And as your younger brother –"

"Younger?" she squeaked crossly.

"As your *only* brother it behoves me to ask the question: is it true that you shagged a monk?"

Nerys humphed.

"Because that's another category you can tick off in your book of 'Men I've Done It With,'" he said.

Nerys growled.

"Okay, bro, listen up. One, Stephen wasn't a monk when we were... intimate. Two, I do not have a book of 'Men I've Done It With.'"

"Yes, you have. Jeremy showed me."

"Fine. But 'monk' is not on my To Do list."

"Oh," said Ben, turning his head to gaze at the helicopter hovering above the monastery. "I bet RAF rescue pilot is."

"Well, of course it –" She stopped and looked at him suspiciously. "Is that some sort of challenge?"

He shrugged.

"Whatever makes you happy, sis."

STEPHEN SAW Brother Manfred holding an unhappy bundle in his arms. At first glance, it appeared to be an oven-ready turkey. On closer inspection it turned out be a sorrowful peacock, seemingly unharmed but for the savage charring of its once fine plumage. Stinking of smoke and apple schnapps, Barry the peacock tried to preen and rearrange feathers that were no longer there.

"There, there," said Brother Manfred kindly and stroked the bird's head. Barry did not resist the monk's gentle ministrations.

"I did it," said Stephen.

"Did what?" said Manfred.

"Spoke to the horse. Metaphorically speaking," said Stephen, gesturing to where Nerys stood. "Gave it a sugar lump. Made friends."

"And are you getting back on the horse?" asked Manfred, mild concern in his voice.

"No. My riding days are behind me. *This* is my life." And he turned to face the burning monastery, which a line of monks with buckets of water was singularly failing to save from the flames. "That's if there will be a St Cadfan's by tomorrow morning."

Manfred smiled, the singed edges of his moustache twitching, and patted Barry.

"Peacocks are hardy birds," he said. "You know that the early Christians thought their flesh was like that of the saints, incorruptible and free from rot."

"I did not."

"Barry will survive. Sure, he is a little toasty and fire-damaged but he will pull through. So will St Cadfan's."

"And with the money we will get from the insurers," said Sebastian, joining them, "we will be able to rebuild.

Bigger and better. Those tapestries were insured for millions."

"Maybe I can make some new tapestries," said Manfred, hopefully.

"Why not?" said Sebastian. "We'll hang them in the lobby of the St Cadfan's Day Spa and Conference Centre."

"The what?" said Stephen.

"Don't make your judgements until you've heard me out, boys," said Sebastian. "This will be an absolute money-spinner."

"Do you believe in Providence?" said Michael.

"What?" said Clovenhoof, casually flinging stones out into the dark sea. "God's invisible hand guiding us through life? Absolutely. He's a fucking meddler."

"I was just thinking, if you hadn't accidentally phoned Jayne on Molly's phone, she would never have come to Birmingham and met Ben, and we wouldn't have come to Wales. And if Nerys hadn't accidentally put those mushrooms in those quiches, I wouldn't have eaten one and swam out to this island."

"And what are the odds of you writing a phone app that could genuinely predict the future?" put in Clovenhoof.

"Exactly. I thought the Almighty had abandoned me but I was wrong. He's been with me every step of the way. Do you think this is what He wanted all along?"

"Cain was a batshit crazy arsehole. He needed stopping."

"Can you imagine what it must have been like for Abel to suffer him all these years?" said Michael.

"Gee," said Clovenhoof. "An immortal trapped on a hostile earth, with only his bitter rival, his nemesis, for company through the long dark centuries? I think I can imagine what that would be like."

"I'm not your nemesis," said Michael.

"You'll do until a decent one comes along." He spun another stone into the night. "You know, the Other Guy isn't going to take you back. We're stuck with each other."

"For eternity?"

"Or something that feels very much like it."

Michael shrugged.

"Fine. An eternity in which to redeem you."

"You mean an eternity in which to utterly corrupt *you*."

"Ha! As if."

"Want to bet?" said Clovenhoof.

Michael stuck out his hand and they shook.

"Bring it on."

BARDSEY – AUTHORS' NOTE

Although *Pigeonwings* is a work of fiction, Bardsey Island, 'the island of twenty thousand saints', or to give it its proper Welsh name, *Ynys Enlli*, is quite real. It lies only two miles off the Welsh coast although some days, as we discovered, those treacherous two miles might as well be twenty thousand.

St Cadfan founded a monastery on the island at some point in the sixth century. Having said that, there were also two saints, Veracius and Senacus, who seemed to have been loitering around on the island some time before St Cadfan got there, although they never got a mention in the St Cadfan story.

The island is home to the Bardsey Apple, which at the time of its discovery in 1998 only grew on one tree on the island, a tree curiously free from any signs of scab, canker or other common diseases. Even though new trees have now been grown from cuttings of the original tree, the Bardsey Apple remains the rarest breed of apple in the world.

The island is linked to the legends of King Arthur and Merlin. Varying sources say that Merlin is buried in a glass casket in a cave beneath the island, lives there still as a hermit or indeed waits there in a magical house of glass. Porth Cadlan, the site of Arthur's final battle against Mordred is just across the water on the Welsh mainland. Popular accounts of the Arthurian legend say that Arthur's final resting place is on the Isle of Avalon. Avalon, or *Afallon* in Welsh, literally means 'place of apples'.

There is so much about Bardsey that we couldn't even mention in this novel, partly because of space and partly because it would seem far too outlandish. Yes, of course, we invented stuff about Bardsey for the purpose of our story, but you'd be amazed at what we *didn't* make up...

AFTERWORD

Many thanks for reading book two in the Clovenhoof series. You can find the link to book three in the coming pages.

We're grateful to all of the readers who continue to support our work and help us to keep writing.

If you can find the time to share your thoughts in a review, it not only helps us, but it helps other readers too.

We're very busy writing new books, so if you want to keep up to date with our work, you could subscribe to our newsletter. Sign up at www.pigeonparkpress.com

Heide and Iain

ACKNOWLEDGEMENTS AND THANKS

To our test-readers Helen Allen, Sarah Paddon, Simon Fairbanks, Danielle Green, Mat Joiner, Bernie Sorga-Millwood, Martin Sullivan and Rachel Wake who helped coax the plot into line, remove the unnecessary and spruce up the funny stuff.

To Mary Chitty, whose passionately researched two-part history, *The Monks on Ynys Enlli*, helped us answer many niggling questions.

To KLAUS REHR, not only the finest B&B owner on the Llyn Peninsula but also a one-man tourist board for the region.

AND, as always, to our significantly better halves, Simon and Amanda, for putting up with us and our ever-expanding cast of imaginary friends.

ABOUT THE AUTHORS

Heide and Iain are married, but not to each other.

Heide lives in North Warwickshire with her husband and children.

Iain lives in south Birmingham with his wife and two daughters.

ALSO BY HEIDE GOODY AND IAIN GRANT

Godsquad

The Team:

Joan of Arc, the armour-plated teen saint of Orleans.

Francis of Assisi, friend to all the animals whether they like it or not.

St Christopher, the patron saint of travel who by papal decree has never existed – no matter how much he argues otherwise.

The Mission: An impossible prayer has been received by Heaven and it's a prayer that only Mary, Mother of God, can answer. Unfortunately, Mary hasn't been seen in decades and is off wandering the Earth somewhere. This elite team of Heavenly saints are sent down to Earth to find Mary before Armageddon is unleashed on an unsuspecting world.

Godsquad:

A breathless comedy road trip from Heaven to France and all points in-between featuring murderous butchers, a coachload of Welsh women, flying portaloos, nuclear missiles, giant rubber dragons, an army of dogs, a very rude balloon and way too much French wine.

Godsquad

Oddjobs

Unstoppable horrors from beyond are poised to invade and literally create Hell on Earth.

It's the end of the world as we know it, but someone still needs to do the paperwork.

Morag Murray works for the secret government organisation responsible for making sure the apocalypse goes as smoothly and as quietly as possible.

Trouble is, Morag's got a temper problem and, after angering the wrong alien god, she's been sent to another city where she won't cause so much trouble.

But Morag's got her work cut out for her. She has to deal with a man-eating starfish, solve a supernatural murder and, if she's got time, prevent her own inevitable death.

If you like The Laundry Files, The Chronicles of St Mary's or Men in Black, you'll love the Oddjobs series.

"If Jodi Taylor wrote a Laundry Files novel set it in Birmingham... A hilarious dose of bleak existential despair. With added tentacles! And bureaucracy!" – Charles Stross, author of The Laundry Files series.

Oddjobs

Sealfinger

Meet Sam Applewhite, security consultant for DefCon4's east coast office. .

She's clever, inventive and adaptable. In her job she has to be.

Now, she's facing an impossible mystery.

A client has gone missing and no one else seems to care.

Who would want to kill an old and lonely woman whose only sins are having a sharp tongue and a belief in ghosts? Could her death be linked to the new building project out on the dunes?

Can Sam find out the truth, even if it puts her friends' and family's lives at risk?

Sealfinger

Printed in Great Britain
by Amazon